The Enigma

A Triquetra Chronicle

by Sarah Heximer

ISBN: 979-8-9990482-2-6

Any references to historical events, real people, or real places are used factiously. Names, characters, and places are products of the author's imagination.

This work is the original creation of the author. No generative artificial intelligence was used in the writing of this manuscript.

Front cover and book design by Sarah Heximer
Edited by: Rennie Dyball

www.sarahheximer.com

Prologue

As I came to, I felt like I was drifting, in something cold and liquid. When I finally opened my eyes and looked up, I realized I was not drifting...I was sinking. The inky blue water was becoming darker all around me as the little bursts of light from above grew dimmer.

In sudden horror, it struck. He had let go of me.

Why? He was supposed to be my protector. We were in this together. We had just been through hell and made it to relative safety for the time being, but now? I was sinking away from the water's surface, watching him watch me fall...further and further below.

I clutched myself in pure fear wanting to scream out, but I could not let the water invade my lungs. I tried to reach up and out to bring myself above the surface again, but my already heavy clothes were weighing me down, while the water around me was ice cold and restricting my ability to move.

I continued to sink, looking up to him, getting smaller and smaller, wondering...how had it come to this?

enig·ma / i- ‘nig-mƏ
noun

1. Something hard to understand or explain; 2. An inscrutable or mysterious person; 3. An obscure speech or writing; mystery; conundrum; mystification.

Chapter 1 – Sophia, June - Present Day

I woke with a gasp. It had only been a few months since spring and my realization that my previous recurring dream had resolved, but it was taking a bit for my body and my nervous system to catch up and reset.

I slowly sat up and slipped out of bed so as not to wake Bryce, who was clearly still floating in a tranquil sleep. I smiled. To look at him while he slept was like watching a small boy, all innocence and charm. His curly hair got even more tousled during the night and he always seemed to have a playful, impish grin on his chiseled face. I often wondered what was going on in that brain of his when I knew how powerful dreams could be.

I pulled on my light grey, ribbed long-sleeve shirt and went into the bathroom to get ready for the day, or at least my morning coffee. It may have been summer, but June in the Highlands still required an extra layer to keep the dewy chill at bay, and I had a ritual to perform that required me to go outside.

It had become my favorite whenever we stayed near Inverness. Bryce's work had brought us up here over the past few weeks on and off, and I truly loved the opportunity to explore further north than Kit and I had gone this past winter. We had stayed at a few local places in town, but this time we were scheduled to be here longer. So, we rented a waterfront farmhouse on the Caledonian Canal by Loch Ness, a seemingly fitting place of magic and lore for my equally magical friends. It was much larger than our typical purposes required, but since Maddy and Kit were both coming to stay, and bringing their respective families, we needed the room.

The property itself was seemingly out in the middle of nowhere by US standards, surrounded by abundant green landscapes and a canal on the front side of the house. The house was brick on the face and whitewashed around the back, with a covered hot tub, fire pit with log seating, and a back deck, complete with dining and conversation areas. Inside was a mysterious combination of old-world Scottish patterns and fireplaces mixed with new world appliances and modern bathroom finishes.

I loved it.

I wandered into the kitchen to brew my coffee, gathered up my journal, grabbed my recently acquired orange, blue, and forest green tartan wool blanket, and went out onto the deck to begin.

The view was heavenly. Though I had wished the back deck faced the tranquility of the canal, it did look upon the lush grounds and into a forest that set one's imagination alight. I sat my coffee mug down on a makeshift paper towel coaster on top of the circular glass-topped wicker table, and maneuvered the chairs so that I had a perfect angle out to the forest, while also putting my feet up on the chair opposite me for comfort. I cracked my journal to the last entry, but decided I needed some liquid gold first, so placed it facedown, trading it for my steaming cup of Highlander Grogg coffee. I closed my eyes and breathed in the unique butterscotch, caramel and vanilla aromas, and sighed. It was no Snickerdoodle, but had become the next best thing. I really could get used to this new normal, and yet I didn't know how I felt about that.

I had only planned on staying in Scotland until the end of March or beginning of April when Kit and I had made the original plans, which seemed like eons ago now.

I hadn't planned on Bryce.

Once we had our magical stay over the equinox, I knew I would be extending my trip, and up until now, I hadn't cared about how long. But reality had begun creeping in during the end of May in the form of Dean Smith and the harsh truth that the Spring semester was coming to an end, and decisions must be made. That, and I missed Violet intensely. I was certain she had all but given up on me, and I knew I needed to make a decision sooner rather than later for the sake of Kit's family; they had been adoptive parents to my fur-angel far too long to continue to be fair.

I opened my eyes and once again traded the objects in my hand so I could capture my thoughts in my trusty journal. It was a long-forgotten habit from childhood, as was writing in general, but I found the ritual helped me capture what I couldn't otherwise vocalize or express, and put words behind thoughts and intentions in a way that often eluded me otherwise. My hope was that by capturing everything running through my brain, I would come to some sort of conclusion about my present dilemma. I loved following Bryce around on his historical adventures, but I also didn't want to lose myself in the process. Hadn't that been the whole point in this journey to begin with? To find myself and not become diminished in my own world?

I let the words flow from my head through the tip of my pen and onto the page. It was interesting to see how my penmanship changed day by day based on my mood, time of day or how lost in thought I had gotten. This morning was no different and I had been so engaged with what I was doing, I hadn't noticed that Bryce had gotten up, prepared an entire breakfast and plated it to serve outside on the deck. It wasn't until I started writing "bacon" on the page that I realized my emersion had gone elsewhere.

I looked up to see him pushing a plate of bacon, eggs and toast my way, along with a fresh pot of coffee and some sweetener. "Guid mornin my bonnie lass," he said with a grin. Those sapphire-eyes positively sparkled in the morning glow and I couldn't help but grin back.

"Good morning, my Prince Charming." I smiled and set my journal aside. I had haphazardly referred to him as such during our first encounter back in January in Edinburgh, when his shoulder had bumped into mine and almost sent me flying down the steps on my way up to the castle on my first day there. Or at least, Kit had called him that when I told her the story. Little did we know how right she was.

"Did you sleep well, then?" he asked in his smooth Scottish lilt, as he buttered some toast with Irish butter and set to pouring milk into his coffee. We may have been in the land of the Scots, but I still insisted on having my Irish butter, one way or another.

"I did, in fact," I said, suddenly remembering how I had woken up with a start.

"Are you sure? You don't look too positive about that" he said, taking a bite of toast layered with scrambled eggs and bits of bacon.

"Yes, fine. Just my body adjusting to not having those dreams anymore," I said and continued making my bacon buttie. He smirked at what I was doing and shook his head.

"What?!" I asked, knowing full well he "dinnae" approve of my British approach to breakfast. He couldn't fathom how I would want to keep my eggs separate and just eat bacon on toast. It was constant breakfast banter that amused him.

"Nacht," he responded, mouth half full of his last bite. I smiled. He was too cute to be miffed at.

"Well then, what were you dreaming about last night?" I asked. "It must have been good since when I got up you were grinning from ear-to-ear like a little schoolboy. You must've been getting into some trouble!" I took a bite. There was nothing like the flavor and texture of perfectly cooked, thick, natural bacon on crisp toast.

"I do not know what you speak of," he said mischievously and left it at that.

We ate in silence for the next few minutes, appreciating the view of this great house, and the food in front of us. As he sipped on his coffee, he pushed his plate away and kicked his long legs up onto the rail of the deck overlooking the calm vista. He had his dark blue plush robe on over his boxers and white t-shirt, but his strong calves stuck out as the robe had to part to let him lift his legs up onto the ledge. I stared. I couldn't help it! It may have been three months of us traversing the country together, but I still couldn't get over how this beautiful man was all mine.

He didn't miss a beat and simply stared ahead, sipping his coffee asking, "like what you see, do ya?" then shot me a side-eye. I giggled. Caught.

"Nope. Just taking in the view," I said, to which he mock-pouted, but continued drinking his coffee.

A few more minutes passed and he set his cup down. "So, what are the plans for today then?" Caught in another reverie unto myself, it took me a moment to realize he had spoken.

"Well, remind me what day it is first?" I asked. I truly had lost track of time.

"Wednesday. June eleventh," he said matter-of-factly.

Holy cow, it was already the day of departure for my friends! Kit and family were leaving the States to come and spend some of their summer holiday here. Kit wanted to show off where we had been earlier in the year, and also explore more of the country, while Maddy was bringing Ryan over for a few days after that so we could all spend the Summer Solstice together. I practically jumped out of my chair, which jolted and surprised Bryce enough for him to almost tip over in his.

"Bloody he—!" he exclaimed as I moved. I stopped and couldn't help but laugh. He looked up at me stunned.

"I'm sorry…" I laughed through snorts, "it's just, when you told me what day it was, I realized everything I have to do to prep the house for Kit and everyone to be here. They arrive tomorrow! I wanted to get going. I'm sorry…" I said, trying to catch my breath from my hysterics. He didn't look as amused as I was, which only prolonged my fit.

"Oh, you think that is so funny. Just wait 'til I get my hands on ye" he teased and started towards me. I grabbed my journal and raised it as a shield in mock terror quickly making my way to the glass door back inside. I was almost able to get in and lock the door behind me, but my former Scots Guard was much too agile and beat me to it. Before I knew it, he had me slung over his shoulder, journal be damned, and was carrying me off to the bedroom.

"There's something we need to take care of first, my bonnie lass, before you start your 'preparations' and I lose ya to the masses," he roguishly grumbled.

I pretended to put up a fight but knew exactly where this was headed and was not about to complain.

Chapter 2 – Josephine, June – 1911

It had been a tumultuous year thus far. While I had been grateful that my parents had left me and my brother with such an esteemed family while they traveled abroad, they did not know the cruel streak of our new "mistress," and the underlying chaos within the household. Thankfully, there was a small break in the traditional mistreatment of the staff and their guests with the King's coronation next week.

Viscount Carlisle's family had been in the House of Lords for six generations. His grandfather had been the one to finally rise from Baron to Viscount due to his contributions in the Crimean War, and break the generations of fourth level peerage. While not a monumental step up, the family was proud of its elevation. As he was part of the hereditary peerage, his household were invited to attend the coronation, a seemingly once-in-a-lifetime event for most.

The Viscount, Victor, was pleasant enough. He had kind brown eyes and tended to keep to himself, which I appreciated given the way most of his family conducted themselves. He always seemed to be in a faraway place, never wanting to have taken over the duties of his title, but forced into it since his eldest brother had been killed in the line of duty during the Third Anglo-Burmese War, and his youngest had gone into the priesthood. He was relatively tall for a man of the time, standing at five foot ten inches. His medium sized frame and sandy blonde hair meant he was average looking and almost forgettable, especially when compared to the Viscountess, Lucille. She, was an entirely different story, and at the core of every heart ache, heart break and tenuous moment of my current existence.

It was well known that the Viscountess was thrust upon her husband strictly because his father wanted it that way. She was the daughter of the Earl of Falkland, not to be confused with the Falkland Islands. It was a small village in Fife at the foot of Lomond Hills; while her family was seemingly above the Viscount in status, being they were from Scotland, were not treated as such. The two fathers-in-law had hoped the match would result in elevation for both their families among their peers in the long run.

The Viscountess had a mean streak. She wanted all the wealth and power of their status she could possibly squeeze out. She reveled in all she had, yet was never quite satisfied. I found it hard to believe she was a mother at all, and even heard the staff make comical remarks about how they must have used a surrogate, "for how else could babes be born of one so selfish?" I honestly could not fathom where her wrath came from. It was not as if she were an uncomely figure. She stood at an appropriate five foot two inches, and had dark brunette hair that she always wore up in the latest fashion. She had countless custom-made silk dresses and accoutrement that flattered her tiny figure, and she made sure everyone noticed. It was her eyes that gave her away - grey, cold, and as desolate as stone. I was often reminded of the stones at Stonehenge, with the exception that even those stones seemed to buzz with energy and life, while her eyes were devoid of anything but the thirst for money and status. I had a sense there was a deeper story there, but knew better not to ask.

Ever since my brother and I had been dropped at their doorstep at the beginning of the year, I had done my best to avoid her. She did not scare me so much as repelled my very existence. I almost felt like Cinderella with an evil stepmother, had it not been for the fact I, thankfully, had not been placed into the role of maid and forced to serve her. Instead, I was simply a prisoner within these walls as she would not permit the staff to speak with me, nor would she offer to escort me anywhere that I would need a chaperone. No, I just needed to bide my time and stay out of her way until my parents returned, whenever that would be.

My brother did not mind the respite in the least. He was in his glory staying at their house in Belgravia; it was a far cry from our country estate near Bath. The grand Georgian-style stucco-fronted townhouse and access to the picturesque Belgrave Square was all the "garden" he ever wanted to see. Being in and amongst industrialists, politicians and members of the aristocracy kept him entertained for hours every day. He could remain relatively unseen by many, and a voyeur into the lifestyles we did not see on the regular in our historic town. It was all he needed in life at thirteen years old. Soon enough my gangly, mop-headed brother would be off to boarding school, a thought he did not relish, so he was absorbing all the freedom he could. I often referred to him as the "green-eyed monster," both for the intensity of the moss green in his eyes, as well as his tendency to be caught watching everyone, as if he was studying human nature itself.

Thankfully, because he kept to himself, and was a boy, the Viscountess paid him no mind. It was me with whom she found the most fault over these past few months, and it had grown in potency ever since the coronation invitation. At first, she had been thrilled at the prospect, and I think I had seen an actual genuine smile crack her otherwise marble-like face. However, one night I could not sleep and had gone down to the kitchen to make myself some tea, when I overheard her and the Viscount speaking in his study. She was furious over something, which would not have caught my attention as unusual, except I heard my name. I listened more closely and, sure enough, they had been discussing whether my brother and I should attend the event along with the family or not.

"I forbid it!" Lucille spat.

"But Lucille, why on earth would you forbid such a trivial thing. They are guests in this house, their father is a fellow member of the peerage, and they have every right to come with us" Victor responded.

"Victor. It is our chance to have both of our children recognized in a grand setting, I will not have them, especially Gertrude, upstaged by those two!" she practically bellowed.

I heard the Viscount sigh an exasperated exhale. I could not see him from my vantage point, but I could almost hear him hang his head and cover his eyes and forehead with his hand, massaging at his temples. He was likely seated in his oxblood chesterfield chair behind the dark mahogany desk near the fireplace, and I could hear her footsteps pacing back and forth.

"Lucille, sit down, you are giving me a headache," he said in his monotone voice, the one I had come to recognize as him trying to keep his natural calm. I then heard her skirts swish and she must have sat across from him because the pitter-pat of her satin slippers ceased.

A stand-off was clearly going on because there was silence for a long moment. I was about to walk away, completely dismayed at the prospect of my brother and I not being able to attend such an illustrious event, and then I heard him clear his throat.

"Lucille. This is not up for argument and I will not listen to your protest a moment longer. The Baron of Crowley is a longtime friend of mine—" to which she interjected…

"…but that is just it, they are not the same *status* as us!" she exclaimed. He clearly cut her off.

"I do not care! We promised to take in his children while they went abroad for business on behalf of Parliament. I will not besmudge their name or their family in the eyes of the aristocracy because you are too self-involved with your own plans. Bring our children to show them off if you must, but Josephine and Charles will be by our side! Period."

She said nothing to that; the final verdict had been given. However, she had a way of having the last word, even if it did not involve speaking. I heard the chair creak as she stood, and she must have slowly turned away from him, likely glaring with those stone-cold eyes, and began walking towards the door. As much as I wanted to hear how it ended, my instinct to not get caught was stronger. Tea forgotten, I quickly ran back up to my room and silently closed the door. I plopped down in the wing-backed chair near my own fireplace and contemplated what I just witnessed.

I had a dichotomy of emotions bubbling to the surface, as well as some long-awaited epiphanies. I was grateful to the Viscount for standing his ground, something I had not seen him do in front of anyone and realized he must reserve it for private conversation. I admired him for it. And I was also excited at the prospect of attending the coronation. However, the niggling suspicion that the Viscountess harbored some special animosity towards me had now been confirmed. I knew her to be a dislikeable creature, but still I sensed some specific disdain thrown my direction. The answer had been obvious and in front of my face the entire time, yet I had not considered it: Gertrude.

Gertrude and Oscar were the Viscount and Viscountess's only two children. I had heard my parents talk of it often, at their surprise there had only been two. "Not for a lack of trying," my father would often chuckle, because his friend the Viscount had wanted multiple.

Then my mother would retort, "I do not understand what Victor sees in that woman or why he would want to have children with her at all! And those names..." she would trail off.

"What the devil do you mean Cassandra?" my father would inquire.

"Well, first of all, she is clearly a woman who thinks too highly of herself and would never want to willingly share attention. Secondly, with those names, you can tell she did not want to have any children at all!"

She had been right. For all the pomp and circumstance the Viscountess was making about wanting the attention for "only" her children and not sharing it with us, I knew deep down it had nothing to do with them, and everything to do with her being seen as the doting wonderful mother society should think her to be. Poor Getrude did not stand a chance of being noticed unless there was a carbon arc searchlight thrown upon her. She was one year younger than me and, if I were being honest, quite homely looking with mousey-brown hair, thin stature and slate-colored eyes.

Her demeanor was one of a timid and shy mouse, always concerned the cat was around the corner waiting to capture her; which, considering who her mother was, was not far off. I felt bad for Gertrude. She probably could have blossomed under a more caring and kind-hearted touch, but she had lost in the game of mother roulette.

Oscar, on the other hand, was an enigma to me. He had eluded me over these six months in the same house. I saw glimmers of his presence here and there, but he was otherwise spending his days elsewhere. I often wondered where he went, and wished he would take me with him so I could get out of these walls accompanied; but as we had yet to utter ten words to each other, I thought it best to leave him be.

He was mysterious. Taller than his father at almost six feet tall, dark hair like his mother, though warmer somehow, like raven's feathers instead of a cold abyss, and what looked like blue eyes from afar, or at least how they were represented in the family portrait that hung in the main parlor. He had a quiet strength about him that overtook a room, if he was ever in it long enough. Surely, he would not be upstaged by my brother and my presence, if his parents could get him to stand in one spot long enough. He intrigued me. I could not imagine why worked so hard at staying away from the house, unless...I shook my head at the thought. There was no way his mother could have been as shrewd towards him as the first-born and a male as she was to me.

I realized my room had gone cold shortly thereafter and went to bed, if not with pure joy, at least some puzzle pieces were fitting into place.

That had been three weeks ago, the house abuzz ever since with the preparations, and the Viscountess's distaste for me growing more and more palpable by the moment.

Chapter 3 – Sophia, June – Present Day

Friday, the thirteenth. The date had always held intense mystery for me, and yet now with all I had begun to learn and uncover, it just held more depth.

Last night had been a whirlwind, I thought, as I lay in bed in the wee hours of the morning. Kit and family arrived with all the fanfare of modern-day royalty. The kids came running up the drive, barely letting the car settle into park. They ran into my arms as if they were my own and knocked me over to the ground. We were all giggling so much it took me a moment to realize a warm tongue was licking my face.

I looked up to see the tan and white face of my beautiful Violet staring back at me. I sat up with a "Eh?!", close to an exclamation my grandmother used to make when I would walk into her apartment, and confusion on my face. The kids rolled off of me and Violet jumped into my lap as I looked up at Kit and Erik. Kit had the goofiest grin on her face and tears in her eyes. "I told you we had her covered," she said with a smile, referencing my concern with where Violet was going to stay when they journeyed over.

"How in the world?" I began to ask.

"Easy" replied Erik and gave a knowing wink to Kit.

I wanted the full story, but was too enthralled with hugging that warm fur-baby to my body at the moment to ask more. It had been five months since I had seen my girl and I couldn't believe how much I had missed her. I felt tension leave both of our bodies as we snuggled there on the stone path. Bryce's voice behind me broke the bubble and I looked back. As soon as I had done so, Violet glanced up and behind me at where the new voice was coming from. I just looked at her and smiled, she sniffed my shoulder as if just now realizing there was a new scent on me, gazed back at him and took off running. Bryce knelt down at her approach and held his hand out for her to sniff. She barreled past it and directly into him nearly knocking him over too. The group of us just stood watching in awe and then laughter broke out across all.

I walked with the crew back to the car to help with luggage and Violet came trotting close behind me. "Hey girl, don't worry, you don't have to leave my side right now." I swear I heard her breathe a sigh of relief.

We all made our way into the house to let the travelers get settled in. I heard the kids running back and forth from their room with bunkbeds, to their parent's room next door. "Do we really get to stay here?" and "Can we stay here forever?" I heard Kit and Erik laugh and tell them to get washed up and change.

Meanwhile, I got some bowls down from the cabinet and filled one with fresh water and placed it on the floor by the island. Violet immediately went over and lapped up almost the whole thing. I wondered what it must have been like for her flying. I grabbed the bottle of sauvignon blanc I had chilling out of the fridge, pulled the cork and poured four glasses. Bryce got the Italian sodas out and found some short rocks glasses for the kids. "Are these okay for them?" he asked as he considered the glass.

I laughed. "Yes, of course, they're not toddlers!" I could tell he wasn't used to being around kids, but seemed excited at the prospect. It gave me a quick pitter-patter in my heart to think of him around children, but a thought I quickly released and turned my attention back to the matter at hand. I had just opened Spotify to play some music in the background when a husky familiar voice boomed from the stairwell.

"Okay, time for proper introductions and a fair amount of interrogation," Erik said as he walked into the kitchen. I looked behind him for Kit and he smirked. "She will be down in a minute, she needed a moment to freshen up."

"Oh-kay," I sighed, mockingly disappointed. "Erik, Bryce. Bryce, Erik. I refer to him as 'The Viking,'" I said, to which Erik raised an eyebrow at me and then shook Bryce's hand. I could see it would be a battle of wills between the two of these ex-military guys. "I'm going to leave you two to it while I go make sure the kiddos are settling in and Kit doesn't need anything," I announced, and promptly left the room. It was important our guys could bond as quickly as possible, otherwise it would be a long few weeks.

As I began climbing the stairs, I felt a familiar presence at my heels. I had almost forgotten in that moment that Vi was with me. I immediately knelt down on the stairs, cupped her head in my hands and massaged her ears as I always had. She became pure putty. "Alright girl, let's go see how the tiny humans are doing and show you around," I said and we ascended in lock step.

I entered the guest room adjacent to mine. It looked remarkably similar, the mirror image of mine with the same velvet purple armchair in the corner and a different quilt on the bed. Kit was already busy unpacking her things and Erik's, trying to get their room in order before she attempted to work with the twins. She seemed lost in thought with a perplexed expression on her face. She looked up as I entered and we both smiled and teared up a bit.

"I don't know why I'm crying, but it is so good to see you!" she said.

"I know! It feels like yesterday and forever all at once. And you bringing this little one..." I reached down and patted Violet's soft head as she nuzzled my palm, "what a treat!"

Kit looked around the room. "This almost reminds me of..." she started.

"Yup, me too." I said.

"With the plaid curtains," Kit continued.

"Yup, exactly." I finished. We laughed.

"We still got it!" we proclaimed in unison, causing us to completely break down in laughter and collapse on the bed. Violet thought this was amazing fun and jumped up with us to snuggle and get in on the vibe.

"So, how the heck are ya?" I asked.

"Well, it's funny you should ask. I..." she started, but then the approach of little feet and voices of children knowing they were missing out on adult fun came barreling into the room.

"Mommy! Have you seen the room that Miss Maddy is staying in? It's got a *princess* bed!" Thora announced with sheer excitement. Kit smiled at her.

"No, darling, I have not. Maybe you can show me when I'm done in here." Kit said with practiced patient grace as if she had not just been interrupted in telling me something of importance.

"...and the bathroom...has a window in the roof!" exclaimed Tate.

Kit and I looked at each other in confusion, and then I recalled seeing a skylight in the small bathroom. With it being a much older house, I assumed it was the best way to ventilate that particular room and thought nothing of it since.

"Skylight," I mouthed to her.

"Oh," she mouthed back. "That's cool!" she responded to Tate, who was nonplussed at our delayed reaction. He was too busy petting Violet and giving her a belly rub as she stretched and turned over.

I wasn't sure if Kit was going to shoo the children out so she could tell me what she had been about to say, or if the moment was lost and we would revisit it later. She must have read my mind.

"Alright kids, maybe we should go down and rescue Mr. Bryce from Daddy's interrogation before it's too late," she suggested.

"Oooooo, you're right!" they both squealed, and jumped off the bed, bounding downstairs without argument. We laughed.

"Should I be worried?" I looked at her, half-joking.

"Not unless you think he has something to hide," Kit said, arching her eyebrow.

I thought for a dramatic moment and then smiled at her. "I don't think I would mind if he did..." I blushed.

We linked arms and walked out into the hallway to go downstairs. Then we quickly remembered the staircases were not built for two-by-two travel and fell into single file. Violet joined us, not wanting to be left alone anywhere.

The kids were nowhere to be found as we entered the sitting area and saw our two guys, arm wrestling.

"What the heck is this?" I asked. Kit just guffawed. Neither of the guys would speak because they were so engrossed in their task. I was also amused by the song "Further Up" playing in the background, seemingly egging them on.

"Seriously guys, an arm wrestle? Erik, just because I called you a Viking didn't mean you had to live up to it," I admonished, eyeing them suspiciously.

Both of their faces were red and it looked like neither was going to win. With some sort of signal between the two of them, they released their hands at the same time and exhaled a deep breath.

"We are at an impasse, it seems," Bryce announced, a trickle of sweat running down the side of his face.

"I thought it was awfully quiet down here for an interrogation," Kit added, shooting a questioning look at Erik.

He grabbed his glass of wine and took a sip. "What?" he said back to her. "I was just doing what you asked, you wanted me to 'measure the strength of his character.' What better way to do that than the original method?" he smirked. Kit blushed and I held my hand up to her, knowing full well that this was all her husband's doing.

"Uh huh," I retorted and walked into the kitchen to prep some pre-dinner snacks and take a much-wanted sip of wine. Kit followed, grabbed her own glass, and we clinked. I realized it been a while since I had enjoyed a glass, and was happy to have Kit by my side. The playlist I had selected moved onto the next song in the background and I smiled at hearing the lilting upbeat melody of "Black Horse and a Cherry Tree" by KT Tungstall.

The rest of the night had been wonderful, picking on a simple meal of charcuterie, fresh veggies and fruit, and some Scottish shortbread for dessert. I knew they wouldn't want anything heavy after a long day of travel, and it would be a good way to keep dishes to a minimum.

Erik shared the saga of how he had been able to leverage his status with the VA to pull some strings for

Violet to join them on the flight, in cabin, so she wouldn't have to fly below in the cargo-hold for all those hours. They had drugged her a bit and she had been a gem the entire flight, making easy friends with the flight attendants and earning herself extra treats from all. I smiled. My girl knew how to make an impression when needed. She sat at my feet the entire evening.

The kids passed out on the couches inside, while the adults enjoyed the evening air and fire pit. Kit and I wrapped ourselves in blankets from the bedrooms and sat looking at the stars while the guys traded literal war stories into the wee hours of the night. When all that could have been said was exhausted, we retired to our respective bedrooms for the evening with full bellies and complete contentment on each of our faces. It had been a great day of reunion on many levels and we knew it was only just the beginning of our joint adventures for the next few weeks.

Smiling at the memory, I made a pot of coffee and started to ponder what would happen today. Kit and I had already mapped out an appropriate tourist schedule of some sites to see around the area that would both keep the children entertained as well as the boys engaged, or so we hoped. I was back together with my soul sister in this magical land, and had Bryce officially by my side. Still, I had an odd feeling about it being Friday the thirteenth. It was going to be an interesting day.

Chapter 4 – Josephine, June 1911

It was the week of the coronation; the past few weeks had been a frenzy of activity in preparations. Not surprisingly, the Viscountess had arranged for a series of dresses for herself and Gertrude to be made for all the festivities in which we would participate.

Also unsurprisingly, I was not accounted for in the planning. It was not until my parents sent word they would make their own arrangements for me that she had even taken notice or care with what I was going to wear. I assumed it was out of fear of not wanting to be upstaged, but knew she had no worry of that as her creations were...well, would not have suited me.

I knew I needed three gowns. I had hoped that if there were any more events we were invited to, I could use a different shawl or accessories to make each look altered enough no one should notice I did not have more. There was the gown for tonight's ball at Albert Hall, the dress I would need for the coronation at Westminster Abbey, and then last but certainly not least, the gown I would need for the dinner that evening at the Palace. I did not know by which fate the Viscount had secured a seat, let alone several, to attend the incredibly exclusive dinner, however I suspected it was at the "insistence" of his wife.

I was in absolute awe of what my parents had been able to obtain for me. The attendees of the ball were encouraged to dress as characters from Shakespeare's plays, seeing it was a fundraiser for the theatre. My mother had agreed that I needed only to dress according to theme, not a direct character, as the Viscountess had done for herself and her daughter. The Viscountess had aptly chosen Lady Macbeth for herself, and Bianca from *The Taming of the Shrew* for Gertrude. I had wondered about the choice for Gertrude since she felt to me more like an Imogen or Perdita. Once again, it seemed the Viscountess' ego was leading and she had hoped that her daughter would somehow miraculously personify the sweet and beautiful Bianca, a perfect bridal vision in white for the obvious namesake, sadly a bit of a stretch.

I opted for an Italian Renaissance cotta gown of scarlet damask that further accentuated my fair porcelain skin and warm chestnut hair. It had a tight bodice, high-waisted design with wide skirt, delicately trimmed in gold. The bustline was a bit lower than I was used to and showed off my smooth decolletage nicely, without being too buxom, drawing just enough attention to showcase the gold and ruby equilateral cross I had been gifted by my father for the occasion. The gown was simple but elegant, and I loved how it swished as I walked.

The second gown, and the one to be worn for the coronation, was a bit more regal, and thus constricting. Knowing I would not want to stand out in the crowd, my mother had recommended a soft lavender silk, empire-waisted, and decorated with lace at the bust, to be worn with a cascading string of pearls. Thankfully she did not expect me to do more with my hair for this occasion than wear it in a psyche knot with a matching embellished hat.

The last gown, for the dinner reception, had taken my breath away. It was slightly older in style, having been one of my mother's, but the seamstress was able to update it such that its age was hidden. A storm-blue layer of beaded silk cascaded over a matching, but lighter blue layer of delicate, almost transparent silk, with gorgeous gold beading and trim. The sleeves were delicate, and draped my arms, while the neckline fell into perfect ruching with cream satin in the middle, accenting the bodice most elegantly. This dress needed no further adornment than the simple diamond and sapphire chandelier earrings I had received from my Grandmother years ago, and a delicate string of crystals that would be woven into my hair.

I had never seen a dress such as this, and could not wait to wear it.

As I was looking at it in the mirror, I allowed myself a daydream, just for a moment, that Prince Charming would see me at this grand affair, and whisk me away from my exhausting situation under this roof. I beamed at my reflection and curtsied. While only two days away, the opportunity to wear this magnificent frock seemed so far away, and I could hardly wait.

Suddenly, I heard a knock at my door. I quickly set the dress aside on the burgundy chaise lounge at the foot of my bed and raced to see who was there. I opened it to see Charles. He was already dressed in his matching Italian Renaissance ensemble and pulling at his rather tight Shakespearean collar, clearly bewildered as to why he had to wear it, let alone attend this first event. He looked at me with those burrowing eyes.

"Are you not ready?" he exclaimed rather brusquely.

"No, it is not time," I said, but second guessed myself. How long had I been daydreaming in that mirror?

"It is! The Viscountess has already been in her rooms getting ready and most of the household is preparing for us to leave," he implored. I looked out the window again. With the longer days as we approached the middle of June, I had completely lost track of time.

"Alright, I will hurry. Thank you for interceding so *she* did not have to do it!" I said to him with a warm smile. For all his thirteen-year-old boy faults, he understood on some level that the living arrangements were not treating me well and wearing thin. I quickly closed the door and prepared to don the first of the three gowns.

Thankfully, once the dress was on and situated, I only had to place my hair into a delicately woven snood. I had elected for the hair piece rather than the other hairstyles popular at the time, since I knew there was no way the Viscountess would lend me a maid with which to create the effect of plaited ropes crisscrossing over my head. The snood itself was made with gold thread, and had small pearls at each cross section, the ornaments both matching the gold trim on my dress and nicely accenting my dark hair. I slipped on my matching scarlet-colored slippers, grabbed my cream-colored silk summer shawl, and walked out the door.

As I came bustling out of the room, I bumped into someone equally in a hurry. The collision made them grunt and fall off kilter. I managed to sway with them and grab their arm while leaning in the opposite direction, thus pulling both of us upright with the help of gravity. I started to mutter my apology and offer an excuse, but they were by me in a flash and down the stairs. I could not recognize who it was, so turned my attention to my own descent so I would not trip on the front of my gown. For all the comfort it provided in a looser fit, the skirt billowed awkwardly in front of me as I stepped down.

I was proud of myself getting ready so quickly, but was only rewarded with a scowl when the Viscountess saw me out of the corner of her eye. I looked into the ornate mirror at the front of the hallway to see if I had forgotten anything, but could not see what would have caused her reaction. The Viscount must have understood and came over to offer his arm.

"You look lovely, Miss Findley," he said, giving me an apologetic look. I began to say thank you, but was cut short.

"...as does your daughter, *Victor*" steamed the Viscountess, narrowing her already small eyes at him.

"Yes, I am sure she does, and I will tell her so when she joins us down here. Until then..." he said, but let his words trail off.

I was relieved that the group had not been waiting on me. I took a moment to absorb the scene. Charles was quietly leaning against the dark oak banister, still pulling at his collar. I tried not to laugh as I saw him in his costume. We had agreed he could match the theme I had chosen, but I had forgotten what that meant for the poor lad in the early days of summer. The Viscount, if only to match his wife and not be completely overshadowed, had donned a kilt in the tartan of her family, and vintage Scottish attire with matching tunic, cloak, and crown. Her 'ladyship' was wearing a magnificent shimmering green medieval gown, embellished with long open sleeves, gold trim, and a lavishly jeweled belt that wrapped around her tiny waist and hung down the middle of her skirts. Her hair was plaited, wrapped in gold, and hung down her back. She elected for a matching jeweled headpiece that wove into the crown of her hair, with a dark green emerald that hung in the middle of her forehead. I had to admit she was a rather remarkable sight.

"GERTRUDE CARLISLE!" she bellowed. The mirage faded.

"Honestly, Lucille. Must you?" the Viscount admonished.

Suddenly, we heard rustling and a door slam above. Gertrude appeared at the top of the stairs. I watched the Viscountess's expectant facial expression immediately sour. Gertrude was seemingly not living up to the expectation in her mind for the evening already, and the poor girl had not even come downstairs yet.

Gertrude must have noticed the expression as well and I could tell she was already deflated. The Viscount, meanwhile, turned and started to usher everyone out to the waiting carriages. I decided to wait for my fellow 'doormat' and walk out with her, if for no other reason to bolster her and pay her a much-needed compliment.

"You look beautiful, Gertrude," I said as she approached those of us remaining. And she truly did. I was rather impressed given what my own expectation had been. Her light cream gown was simple and conservative, with a high neckline and full coverage, however the jeweled hairnet accent and a modest pearl necklace offered an ethereal type of beauty that was wholly unexpected. We had not interacted all that much in my time there, so I was unsure if my attention would be welcome.

She shyly smiled and looked down at her feet as we moved toward the door. Her father, not wanting her to feel left out, came back to escort her to the carriage and allowed me to trail behind.

The ball was truly one for the ages. From the Italian-style Tudor garden décor, to the costumed characters in a sea of 4,000 attendees, the energy in the Albert Hall was positively vibrating and it felt like anything was possible. I watched longingly as couples graced the dance floor and whirled to the music. Charles was lost somewhere to the crowds with other teenage boys who had been forced to wear an assortment of costumes and join their families for the evening. I continued to survey the scene with a smile on my face and flush to my cheeks as the room continued to climb in temperature with bodies and activity.

I turned from the scene to go retrieve another punch. I was basking in my relative freedom for the evening as the Viscount and Viscountess engaged with the crowds, and while Gertrude was in tow, her ladyship wanted nothing to do with my presence that would otherwise spoil her introductions for her daughter. I smiled to myself as I walked away from them, but felt a momentary pang of guilt as I saw Gertrude's eyes follow me with what seemed like jealousy.

I slowly walked over to the line for refreshment, taking in all the sights, sounds, and smells. It was unlike any event I had yet been to in my almost nineteen years, and I was completely besotted.

I was quickly brought out of my reverie however, when I heard a voice say, "excuse me miss, but are you going to ever *move*?" It sounded quite rude, even if I had been distracted, and I turned to see who had made the remark.

"Honestly, you would think they would minimize the number of silly girls they let into an event like..." he continued, brusquely laughing with his friends in line, and then stopped when I turned my attention to him.

His face looked quite familiar, and as I gazed at his features trying to place where I had seen him, he stumbled over himself to make an introduction.

"I am sorry, my lady," he began, clearly making a smart reference to my attire. "Forgive my rude behavior. It was just that my friends and I are parched and in need of refreshment. The line was moving and you seemed not to notice."

I continued to look at him, searching his face for clues as to why he was so familiar and yet I did not know his name. His costume gave no obvious clue either, or his family or station, since he was dressed in a simple dark brown linen tunic and tights, clearly not wanting to assimilate to the festivities, but also needing to have some guise to enter.

My silence seemed to confuse and frustrate him further.

"Perhaps I shall introduce myself," he said, turning turned to his fellow companions to give them a side-eye, which caused them all to laugh; clearly, he lacked patience. "I am the Honourable Carlisle, son of Viscount Carlisle, at your service," he said and did a roguish bow.

Of course! I thought to myself. It finally dawned on me. His face was one I had been seeing for months, in several portraits around the house. Finally solving the mystery and forgetting myself completely I said, "Oscar?" then quickly covered my mouth realizing the faux pas I had just made.

This stopped him short and his group ceased their laughter. "Pardon me, miss?" he said with one eyebrow arched.

"My apologies, sir. I forget myself. I am The Honourable Josephine Findley, daughter of Baron Crowley," I said, and curtsied as best I could in my costume.

He considered me, and I could tell he was now trying to work out why the name bore familiarity. Not wanting to embarrass him in front of his friends by reminding him my brother and I were living in his house, but also not wanting to hold up the line further, I nodded and turned to approach the punch bowl.

I heard whisperings behind my back and when I went to leave, he was being pushed around by his friends amicably to approach me again. I watched him in that moment, as it was the longest I had held him in my gaze in person to date, regardless of the fact that we had shared the same roof for half of a year.

I already knew he was taller than his father, but what I had not noticed, or recalled from the portraits even, was what a chiseled strong jaw he had, a straight and angular nose, and those eyes. While I had noted they seemed to be blue in the paintings, they were unlike any color I had ever seen. His mother's were a stone grey, but his were a clear ice blue, the color of the winter sky...or perhaps ice, given his odd mix of charm and indifference. They were piercing, and yet somehow also soft as a cloud. I was mesmerized for a moment and then remembered myself and walked away, not wanting to be caught staring. Thankfully, I was able to melt into a crowd of passers-by.

I briefly peered over my shoulder to be sure I had gotten far enough to break off and find another vantage point to watch the dancers, and noticed him searching around himself.

Good, I thought. *Perhaps I can be as elusive as he has been all this time.*

The rest of the evening went by beautifully. I did not even mind that I did not dance. The floor space was limited, and as I was under the Viscount's charge, meant he would have to make any introductions, and I knew that opportunity would never surface since Gertrude needed to be his sole focus if he wanted a moment's peace from his wife. I was perfectly content to simply standby and observe, soaking up the music, enjoying the frisson that occurred across my skin with each new waltz, and revel in being outside of the house.

It was towards the end of the evening, as I was considering whether I should grab one last piece of petit fours, when I felt a tap on the back of my arm. I thought for sure it was Charles trying to get my attention to leave, and I almost decided to ignore him so I could stay there a bit longer, but thought the better of it and turned.

"Charles, it cannot be time yet. I think I see the Viscount and Countess out on the dancefloor," I began, but stopped quickly as I looked up into ice blue eyes.

"Hello, miss," said the velvety voice.

"Hello," I managed, and went to sip from my glass, my throat having gone suddenly dry, only to realize it was already empty.

"So why is it, Miss Findley, that you seem to know me, and I not you? And that you wished to say more earlier, but did not, as I assume you did not want to speak in front of my positively brutish mates?" He smiled, a playful grin knowing he was just as much of a "brute" as his friends, but trying to win me over nonetheless.

I allowed myself a small grin in return, which made him flash a smile of sincerity and warmth that instantly reminded me of his father.

"Well, sir. It was only that I did not wish to embarrass you in front of your comrades," I said. He gazed at me, confused.

"Do you really not know?" I asked.

Just then, we both heard a familiar, grating voice, "Oscar *darling*, come here, there is someone we'd like you to meet," said the Viscountess, at her most shrill and disingenuously happy.

"One moment, mother," he turned and called back. Not wanting to delay him any further, or give her reason to question me later, I turned and fled into another group of passers-by before he could turn back. Again, I watched him raise his head above the crowd looking around, but heard his mother call him over and he walked away.

That was close. I had a nagging disappointment in the middle of my chest that he truly had not recognized me at all. I had no reason for such disappointment, but there it was. *Oh well, I won't let it ruin my evening.* I almost felt bad for him and whoever he had to meet. If the Viscountess had that expectant note to her voice now, I could only imagine what it would turn into later.

Soon, Charles was coming to collect me for the carriage so we could return to the house. I retrieved my shawl and wrapped it around my shoulders before we hit the cool night air. Despite being the beginning of summer, the evenings in England were volatile to say the least, and with the bustline of this dress being a little lower than I was used to, did not want to catch a chill. I had hoped to see Oscar getting into the carriage with us for the drive back so I could see his face as realization struck. But just as he had gotten to the ball on his own earlier in the evening, he was apparently finding his own way home.

That night, once I had disrobed from gown number one, had tea by the fire, and settled in for the evening, I dreamt of twirling dancers, Shakespearean tragedies, and in the middle of it all, ice blue eyes.

Chapter 5 – Sophia, June – Present Day

The smell of coffee brewing seemed to wake everyone up, except for the children. While most of us were familiar with jetlag and managing through it, Thora and Tate were not. They had fallen asleep the night before quite early, woken up in the wee hours of the morning wide awake bustling about, and finally crashed again only shortly before I had gone downstairs.

Bryce set to cooking breakfast family style, while Kit and I grabbed our proffered blankets from the night before and went out onto the porch to enjoy the cool morning.

We sat amicably sipping our coffee and breathing in the warm steam. I wanted to give her time to wake up, but also wanted to hear all the goings-on. "So, what the news from home?" I ventured.

She was lost in thought and had not broken her focus on the horizon. I could see I was going to have to interrupt her reverie. "Earth to Kit...come in Kit..." I said.

"Hm? Oh, right sorry. Good, how did you sleep?" she took another sip.

"I slept fine thank you, but that was not my question. What's up with you, everything okay? You had that same far off look on your face yesterday when I came in to check on your unpacking." I said.

"Oh, fine. It's nothing. What did you ask me?" she brushed off my concern.

I knew from the past that Kit would not talk about anything until she was ready. Clearly there was something on her mind, but me pushing her to say anything was not the best strategy, so I acquiesced.

I stared at her and considered, while she stared back expectantly. "Okay, if you say so..." and she nodded her head. "I had asked what news from home."

She still had the far off look in her eyes, but she launched into tales of the twins' end-of-school sagas, activities, and timeline that led them to getting onto the plane.

"Wait, so they aren't technically done with school yet and you guys came anyway?" I interjected.

"Well, it was only by a few days, and they're still in elementary school, so Erik and I thought it couldn't hurt anything. The teachers were very understanding. And anyways, all Erik has to do is take one look at the teachers and they practically swoon so..." she was half-blushing, half-annoyed.

"That's not surprising. You do have one handsome Viking!" I said and winked. She dropped her head and took a sip of her coffee again, seemingly having remembered something. I sat quietly and waited. I reminded myself that it was Friday the thirteenth, but anything she had to say couldn't be that ominous, could it?

She looked up at me and opened her mouth to say something and, as if on cue, the glass door burst open, and the twins, Violet, and the guys came barreling out, all carrying something in their hands to set up the breakfast table outside. I shot her a look of apology and she chuckled. I guess whatever it was would have to wait yet again. But I was concerned with what it could be since Kit had never held back before…

"Mommy, Mommy, Mommy!" Tate shouted as he ran over to her.

"Yes, my darling" she said as she also brought her pointer finger in front of her lips to indicate he should quiet down.

"Sorry," he managed with a small pout, now wrapped in her arms. "It's just, we smelled the food and hoped it was okay for us to get up *now*," he said and looked over at his sister, who seemed not to care because she was already grabbing food for her plate.

"Thora!" Kit reprimanded, but Erik held his hand up in front of her.

"It's okay, I told her she could start." Kit gave him a side-eye glare but relinquished control. We all settled in.

"So, what's on the docket today ladies?" Erik asked between bites.

"How on earth should I know?" Kit teased.

"Because I know you, and there is no way that you and your comrade-in-arms don't have us planned down to the minute!" he retorted. Bryce grinned. He seemed happy having another male around that understood me and Kit.

"Yeah, Mom, what are we doing today?" Thora asked, mouth full.

"I'm going to let Auntie Sophie fill you guys in, I need more coffee." She rose from her seat. I looked after her as I was mid-bite, about to gesture if she could pour me more too, but she wordlessly grabbed my mug and walked inside. God, I've missed having her around. Not that Bryce didn't take care of me, but there was something about a soul sister knowing what was needed without a second thought that just warmed my spirit.

I swallowed. "Well, I thought today we would start in the city center." The kids looked at me expectantly, clearly not knowing what that meant. "Do you guys like...castles?" I asked.

"Yeah!" they shouted in unison.

"How about shopping?"

"Yeah!" they sang out again.

"What about gardens?"

This time only Thora beamed, knowing full well this was going to be her favorite spot since she'd become more and more fascinated with herbs and learning about old world medicine. Tate looked slightly deflated.

I elbowed him and whispered, "What if I told you they have carnivorous plants there..." and winked.

His eyes grew wide. "You mean like *Little Shop of Horrors*?" he shouted. I laughed. Of course Kit's child would know about that reference.

"Possibly. We'd have to check it out to know for sure though." I replied, ominously.

"OK! I'm in."

Kit came back outside with our coffee. "Well, what does everyone think?" she asked.

"Your kids are in…I'm not so sure about the guys." I responded, looking at them both since neither had spoken.

Bryce looked up from his plate. "What? Did you need us to respond as if we had a choice?" he smirked and looked over at Erik for support. He was getting a little cocky having a buddy around.

"Well, if that's how you feel, you do have a choice…you can come with us, or you can stay here!" I replied with mock agitation.

"Ooooo," the twins mumbled in unison.

"Alright, that's enough," Kit said and filled her plate.

"Actually, we did have something separate planned for the boys, but since neither of you seem too intrigued by our plans, I guess I can cancel it," I teased. Erik whipped his head over to look between Kit and I expectantly.

"Yes?" he asked with mild enthusiasm.

Kit and I traded looks to see how long we could play this out.

"Well, I thought that after we all go to the Castle and walk the city center shops, Kit and I can take the kids to the Botanical Gardens and you guys could go to…" but Bryce interrupted getting excited.

"Uilebheist?!" he hopefully questioned.

I nodded.

"Ulba-what?" Erik asked.

"Oh, mate, you're in for a treat. Just stick with me. Let the lasses take the wee ones and we will go have some fun," he explained with his brogue as thick as ever, and he tucked away the rest of his breakfast.

Erik seemed content with that answer and Kit and I both laughed. I had called in a favor on behalf of Bryce's reputation to get them a private tour and tasting at the well-known distillery and brewery. While it was a bit away from where we would be taking the kids, I figured we could take the car, leave them be, and go back and pick them up when it was time to head back to the house for dinner.

"But wait!" Tate suddenly shouted. We all stopped what we were doing.

"What?" Kit asked, concern creeping across her face.

"It's Friday the thirteenth. Do we need to worry about anything?" Tate sounded upset.

Thora rolled her eyes. Kit and I looked at each other and smiled and the guys chuckled.

"Well, it is..." he exhaled under his breath defensively.

"Are you telling me you don't know the origins of the date and the legend, sir Tate?" Bryce asked. Now it was my turn to roll my eyes. I could see he was going into full historian mode. Meanwhile, Tate's attention was now fully focused on the big Scot.

"Hey, before you launch into a full dissertation, professor, let's put a pin in it and come back to it in the car on our way. We've got to get a move on!" I said.

We all quickly cleared the table, got the dishes scraped and into the sink, and took turns getting ready for the day. I set up a special spot in the bedroom with one of my comfiest sweaters for Violet so she could snuggle away and not feel like I left her again. "We will be back girl, I promise. You behave yourself and try not to destroy anything in the house. I hadn't thought to check if they allowed pets here since I didn't know you were coming, but it can be our little secret because you are such a little angel." I cooed at her while massaging her ears again. She just looked up into my eyes.

"She is," I heard from the doorway. Bryce had taken to Violet quickly last night, and he let her up on the bed to snuggle between us. He was all mush and it was positively adorable.

I stood and Bryce pulled me in for a quick hug and kiss on the cheek. "Your friends are just as wonderful as you said they were, and I'm so happy we get to spend time with them," he said.

I hugged him back and then touched his nose gently with my pointer finger. "Well, you already had met Kit, but as a family unit...told you so."

"Come on, you two," I heard from downstairs. "No shenanigans, we have things to do and places to see!" Erik shouted.

"And I want to hear about Friday the thirteenth!" Tate called.

We were off. Bryce regaled everyone with the origin story of Friday the thirteenth and how it actually was not a day of bad luck as most presumed. Just as he was finishing up explaining how thirteen was actually a sacred feminine number.

The Inverness Castle experience had only just opened to the public. As Bryce explained, it had undergone a huge renovation and the government was involved in creating a new visitor attraction in the area. The "Castle" wasn't quite a castle at all, but the old local prison and courts. Now they had turned the grounds into a literal experience of Highland history, with each building showcasing what made the area so special: landscaped gardens, sensory experiences, an exhibition focused on music, and of course, a bistro. It was absolutely remarkable what had been accomplished, and Bryce took the time to seek out the curator to let him know his thoughts.

It was an advantage having a Scottish historian in our group who could tell us about everything we were seeing. If he was impressed, then we all knew what we were looking at was special. Of course, the tour ended in the with a small snack for the kids, and water and lemonades for us (and a shot of whiskey for the guys). I noticed that neither Kit nor I had the same taste for alcohol as we had only a few months ago. I knew mine was related to my epiphanies while journaling—the less I drank, the better my meditations. But I wondered what had shifted for her.

Once we finished, we left and toured the streets of city centre. In true European fashion, there were plenty of side paths with shopfronts and indoor markets. No one really purchased anything being that it was the first day. It was just a simple palate cleanser for our group between stops.

I could tell the kids were getting anxious to get to the botanic gardens, for different reasons of course, but ready all the same. I checked my watch, and while it would be a little early for the boys' tour, I figured they could entertain themselves there nonetheless. I smirked at Kit. She already knew what I was thinking and nodded her head.

"Okay, boys, this is where we part ways," I announced. Bryce and Erik looked at me as excitedly as the twins. "Bryce, when you get there, make sure you check in at the desk and give them your name," I instructed.

He cocked his head at me confused and then realization dawned on him. "You dinnae," he said.

I nodded my head. "I deid," I responded in my mock Scottish brogue.

"Oy, you're the best!" he said, pulling me into a hug. The kids thought that was pretty cute and smiled, while Erik looked on, perplexed.

"I need the keys," I said and held out my hand. Without another word, Bryce fished them out of his pocket, dropped them in my hand, gave me a peck on the cheek and turned around to sling his arm over Erik's shoulder.

"Nicely done," Kit remarked, shaking her head in approval.

"Thanks!" I said, corralling them all towards the car.

"Where is Daddy going?" asked Thora, somewhat dismayed. "I thought we were doing this trip all together as a family?"

"We are, dear," Kit cooed. "But now we get Auntie Sophie time, and the boys get to go do their thing for a bit. We will meet back up and return to the house all together, don't you worry."

"And I get to see a carv-na-vorate plant!" Tate shouted.

"Carnivorous" Kit corrected.

"Yeah, that" Tate said.

We all loaded into the rental, a sleek graphite Peugeot 5008 that sat seven, as Bryce's car could never handle the six of us, let alone with another two people joining in a few days. We drove to the Inverness Botanic Garden and Café, just over the River Ness.

Thora was practically bursting out of her seat by the time we arrived, and I wasn't sure if she was going to make it to the entrance. The parking lot was relatively empty for an afternoon on a Friday, but I presumed that we had beat the late afternoon rush before people got out of work and onto their weekend.

"Okay guys, since you have your GPS watches on, you can go ahead of us a little way to explore together if you want, but don't go too far out of sight please," Kit directed after we paid our admission and received our stickers. She knew full well she was not going to be able to contain them, and did not see the harm in loosening the lead a bit if they promised to stick together.

The gardens were beautiful. I always appreciated the space and the warmth they provided. We quietly strolled on through making our way among all the gorgeous vegetation. We found a beautiful staircase with palms overhead and a statue of some Greek Goddess that Kit stopped and stared at. The kids were just up ahead and our conversation had long since stalled as we took in the sights and fragrances.

"I've been having visions," she said, under her breath and almost inaudible. I looked to see where the kids were, to make sure they weren't within earshot.

"Visions?" I questioned patiently. I did not want to startle her and put her off the topic, especially if this is what had been on her mind.

"Well, not 'visions' like a seer or something, but dreams. They've been very hit or miss, and honestly, I can't even call them dreams because they are more like split second views or pictures of something that doesn't ever quite come into focus" she mused.

"Okay. Well, …" I started at a loss for words. "…how do they make you feel?", knowing the emotion tied to it would be telling, and a simpler place to start.

She seemed to consider that for a moment. I impressed myself with the question, especially for my Psychologist friend, the best in her field. "I don't know," she finally said.

"That's fair, especially if you can't even piece together what you're seeing, I just wasn't sure if they evoked an emotion for you," I said and she interrupted.

"Familiar?" she suggested.

"Okay, that's a start. Any reason they are throwing you off as much as they are versus other dreams you've had in the past? I mean, surely this is not your first time dreaming of random things, so why this? Why now?" I continued. Kit walked a fine line between the mystical and the logical, so I could see why she was a bit dysregulated.

She looked crestfallen. "I don't know" she admitted.

"Hey, that's okay!" I jumped in, not wanting to make her feel uneasy about what she was sharing. "We will figure this out," I reassured her.

"I guess it all started after the Spring Equinox. Do you remember that book I was reading on the train to Edinburgh? About anomalous cognition?"

I wasn't surprised. A LOT had happened leading up to the equinox and since then. At least for me, it seemed like my breakthrough had been completed, but it sounded like perhaps hers was just starting. We had each gotten further into our "awakening," as we had come to call it. It wasn't just ourselves waking up to the current reality, but our minds and spirits realizing what our eight-year-old versions had understood as gospel; that there really is more out there, and magic is real. Maybe not the kind in *Harry Potter*, but the old adages of "mind over matter," "spelling," and "manifestation" were all real energetic practices that worked, if you got out of your own way.

"I can't say I'm surprised, Kit. I mean, look at me. I had that crazy recurring dream all my life, we head off to Scotland on a relative whim, and, *voila*, I meet my soulmate. Then I come to realize the dream was recognition of a past life—one in which you and Maddy both shared—and once I found my <insert blue spark>, my dream reconciled itself. As if breaking a pattern, and I haven't had it since!" As I finished, I had a random chill pass me through me and I shivered.

Kit seemed to consider what I said.

"Yes..." she said slowly, "...but mine seems to have just started. Not to mention Thora and all that she has been experiencing." My eyes opened wide. Thora? How could she be linked to this? We had long suspected that Thora and Tate were actual fractals of Kit's past life persona we had experienced during the Shaman reading, coming forth from that time to help Kit's soul given its traumatic ending. But could they have memory imprinted on them as we had? I had learned enough in recent months to know that anything was possible.

"What has Thor..." I began, but quickly quieted myself as the kids came shuffling around the corner. They were paid rapt attention to whatever they had been admiring in this place. They approached Kit and she came to.

She mouthed "later" to me and I shook my head.

"Momma, you should SEE all the pretty flowers they have here, like the birds of paradise and orchids! There're even medicine plants like aloe vera, calendula, chamomile..." Thora trailed off as she saw the statue we had stopped in front of.

"I know dove," Kit said stroking Thora's head to remove some static that had built up on top from her shuffling. "We've seen them."

Meanwhile I watched Thora's eyes dance as she talked about the "medicine plants" and named things off that I had known of as being helpful, but not until I was an adult. Maybe there was something to what Kit had shared...

"...and a Venus Flytrap!" Tate enthused. He was clearly taken with it. I made a mental note to get him one as a gift back home.

Home. That word evoked so many emotions and questions lately, that I did not know what it stood for anymore. A deep thought for another day as the kids continued prattling on in the background, their excitement obvious. I mentally patted myself on the back for my choice of venue to occupy our time today.

I looked at my watch. The guys should be ending their tour right about now and I could tell blood sugar was running low for the kiddos. It seemed now was as good a time as any to depart the fix, grab the guys, and head back to the house for some well-earned vacation rest.

I said as much to the crew and we went towards the exit, all the while keeping an eye on Kit. The dreamy quality of her facial features from before when she was opening up was gone, and her resolute "mom" face was back in place, but what exactly was my friend going through? And what was that random chill? It must be 85 degrees in here, not to mention the humidity. Was it confirmation of my own experiences...or a warning shot of something to come? And, anomalous cognition? I remembered the book Kit spoke of, but since she had not chosen to educate me on the subject, it was a bit beyond my immediate grasp, though I could sense her own neurons were quickly making connections between the experiences.

This Friday the thirteenth was proving to be an interesting start to our trip, indeed...

Chapter 6 – Josephine, June 1911

"Miss…Miss Findley?" I heard my name being called through the mist, but could not quite make out from whence it came. "Miss Findley?" I heard again, and then some knocking noises. I slowly came back to myself and realized I was in bed. Opening my eyes, I looked around the room. It was still dark, but I noticed some soft grey light streaming in through the cracked drapes on the east side wall. Then the delicate knocking again. *Who on earth?* I reluctantly got out from under the lush covers and padded over to the door.

"Hello?" I called, opening the door as I wiped the sleep from my eyes.

"I am sorry to bother you, Miss Findley, but as it is almost 6:30 in the morning and no one had seen you about yet, I wanted to be sure you did not need help getting ready this morning?" said a small kitchen girl with a strong cockney accent. I looked at her confused. Neither she, nor any of the house staff, had said one word to me since I had been here, and I thought perhaps I was still dreaming. I looked back at my bed to make sure and then my feet planted on the floor. She must have realized my confusion.

"The Viscount had said I should check on you so as to be sure everyone is able to leave on time…and the

Viscountess should not know about it." This she added in an even more hushed tone and gave me a wink. I crinkled my forehead for a moment and then realization struck. My mouth flew open and I quickly covered it with my hand.

"Yes, miss," she affirmed, handing me a napkin full of buttered bread, and curtsied.

"Oh, thank you Miss…" I stalled, in not speaking with the staff, I had not learned any of their names.

"Alice, miss. But you need not worry about all that." Now that her errand was dispatched, she looked eager to get back to her chores.

"Well, thank you all the same, Miss Alice" I said, and nodded to her before closing the door.

Six-thirty. The Viscountess had given strict instructions that we were to leave the house no later than seven o'clock. Westminster Abbey, at most, was a fifteen-minute carriage ride from the house, and guests were not expected to be seated until 8:30, but she had made it abundantly clear that everyone who was attending must be in the carriage by seven or they would leave without them. This, I knew, was directed at me since I had a proclivity for sleeping in past whatever time she deemed proper; something I had only recently given into since my basic house arrest and wont of anywhere to go whilst also avoiding her.

I had twenty-five minutes with which to get myself ready and downstairs if I aimed to beat her original departure; and I had a sneaky suspicion she would have no qualms leaving earlier if everyone else made it in the carriage before the seven o'clock mark.

I took a quick bite of the proffered bread and butter, bless Alice's heart for thinking to bring me something, and quickly ran over to the wardrobe. I slid my nightgown to the floor, washed myself from the washstand adjacent to the wardrobe, and began the process of layering on my chemise, drawers, corset and petticoat to be worn under my lavender satin gown. The corset was always difficult to do by oneself, but in my months of having to dress on my own, I had gotten it down to a relative science.

I took the understated, yet gorgeous purple dress from the wardrobe, slipped it on over my head and proceeded to secure the buttons with the ivory button hook the best I could. I sat down to look in the mirror and pin my hair up into a loose psyche knot at the top of my crown. In so doing, I stopped to stare. I suppose it had been a while since I had paid any mind to my own reflection. Over the past months I had felt myself fading into the background of life. When I looked, really looked, what I saw was actually quite remarkable. What little "baby fat" I may have still had at the beginning of my stay seemingly melted away to reveal a set of high cheekbones and a thin but soft jawline. My nose, while never a distinguishing characteristic, had softened into a slight button, and while my skin was still fair, a sprinkle of freckles danced across my nose and over my upper cheeks. I blotted a bit of soft pink rouge on my cheeks, and put a bit of stain on my lips to make them the color of a ripe berry, completely appropriate for a daytime regal outing.

As I was finishing, I caught my own eyes. My naturally hazel irises somehow seemed brighter today, with a richness in color I had not noticed before. I realized I was smiling at myself. I was surprised at how much I had matured in only a few months, and I felt ashamed that I had let my surroundings almost diminish my own existence. I looked back into my reflection and make a solemn vow to not let that happen again.

I heard bustling downstairs which snapped me back. I got up, grabbed my matching hat from its box on the top shelf of the wardrobe, slipped on my grey satin shoes, and went for the door. I did not anticipate needing a reticule for the occasion and left it behind, sitting draped over the chaise from two nights ago.

Two nights ago. Oscar. My heart fluttered and my stomach did a flip. I suddenly lost my appetite in anticipation of seeing him today. Would he finally realize who I was?

I raced downstairs as elegantly as possible, stopping to place my hat on my head with its pin. I grabbed a white lace parasol from the front hall, and gracefully walked out into the now shining morning light. Much to the obvious chagrin of the Viscountess, I was not only early, but the first to arrive, other than herself, and ready to leave. I had impressed even myself, though I could not let her know that.

"Good morning, Viscountess Carlisle," I greeted her, with a slight head bow.

She looked me up and down, as if deciding whether I was worth the effort of a greeting. Just then, the Viscount emerged, causing her to play along.

"Good morning, Miss Findley," she said through gritted teeth. I smiled, knowing that was a small battle won for the day. Knowing full well I would not be riding in the family carriage, but the one trailing behind, I walked back and climbed in. I was surprised to find Charles already inside and asleep with his head jammed into the corner.

"Charles," I half-hissed, half-whispered, so as not to jolt him awake, but also get his attention. He did not budge. I tried again, a little louder this time. "Charles!" Still nothing. The carriage took off towards its destination. How he could sleep through the jostling on the streets, I never understood. At least now that we were moving I could be more obvious, I kicked him in the shin and nearly shouted, "Charles!" That did it.

He shocked awake and sat up at attention as if he was already at boarding school and caught sleeping in class. That made me giggle.

"Bloody hell, sister. You did not have to make all that ruckus," he said once he realized where he was and what was going on.

"And you...do not speak that way, dear boy, or do I have to let the Viscountess know you are using such language under her roof?" I asked raising an eyebrow. He just stared at me.

"Why do we have to be there so *early*?" he whined.

I stared right back at him. "Because her ladyship wants to be there in accordance with the timing the guests were advised, so as to procure her preferred seating for the family..." I offered, nose held high.

"And stick us in the back?" he finished.

I smiled. He knew all too well. He sat back in his seat and leaned his head against the side behind the window of the carriage once again. It was only a few more minutes until we would arrive, but I thought the better of chiding him and just let him close his eyes. I looked ahead to the carriage in front of us wondering who was in there. Well, just one person.

Why was I being affected this way? I shook my head to rid him from my mind. I did not even know why he was in my thoughts at all, until I remembered ice blue eyes from my dream.

Suddenly, we were there. The carriage stopped and the footman got down to help us both out. The family had already gone ahead and was merging with the crowd of the peerage flowing into Westminster Abbey. I guess no one was going to be caught late to this affair.

Charles and I found our seats towards the back of the Abbey and prepared for the long wait before the royal brigade arrived. It was said that the soon-to-be King and Queen would not leave Buckingham Palace until 10:30, and here it was only ten past seven.

Charles struggled to sit still, but eventually fell asleep again in his seat. He was not the only one, it seemed, so I let him. I took the opportunity to marvel at the beautiful interior of the Abbey. While I had been countless times before with my parents on our ventures into London, I had never allowed myself the indulgence of simply looking up and soaking it all in. I had always been in awe of how old this building was.

It was an eleventh century monastery that had been remodeled and added to over the centuries, having survived countless English monarchs, wars and other events. It was a beautiful testament to history. I wondered what the walls would say if they could speak. What pictures could it paint? The gothic architecture, though not my preferred aesthetic, was still fascinating to regard. How had they been able to craft such detail and build so high with the materials and tools with which they had available at the time? I could tell the mahogany of the choir stalls had been polished until they practically shone as the light of Christ himself, given the smell wafting all the way back to where we sat. So lost in my thoughts, I had not realized that the moment we had all been waiting for was upon us, until a flash of a person came dashing through the door, aiming at the open seat in front of me.

Who on earth would be so audacious as to enter the Abbey so close to the processionals coming? Someone sat down and settled themselves into their seat. Whoever it was, they were remarkably put together for being so rushed. Just then, there was a commotion outside, indicating the arrival of the royal procession, much to the delight of the onlookers from the streets. Everyone stood and turned to face the main doors. I kept my eyes trained on the gentleman in front of me, out of pure curiosity, and suddenly was looking onto ice blue eyes.

Realizing it was Oscar, and not wanting to be caught staring once again, I whirled myself around to face the entry. As I did I knocked Charles leg. He had still been asleep, but now rose to attention and gave me a quizzical look. If I was not mistaken in my haste, those ice blue eyes had caught mine at the last moment and a look of recognition crossed them, but I could not concern myself with that now.

The crowd gazed expectantly at the archway for the Windsors to appear behind the long procession of military, state officers, and members of the Royal Family. At last, as the guests of honor walked up to the front of the Abbey towards the St. Edward's Chair, a 615-year-old wooden throne commissioned by King Edward I for such occasions, the crowd each bowed and turned as they passed.

It truly was a miraculous ceremony to behold. For almost six thousand people in the Abbey and the hundreds of thousands who crowded the streets outside to be as quiet as they were was a miracle in and of itself. When the choir sang Handel's *Zadok the Priest*, it was as if angels had descended from heaven. Most found the smell of incense over-powering, but I found it comforting, and breathed in the smoky aroma as it wafted to the back. It was just the right essence to augment the senses during the event.

Bearing witness to the Archbishop of Canterbury presenting the king-to-be to the people, the king then taking the coronation oath and being anointed by holy oil, was inspiring. Witnessing the royal robes and regalia being placed on him, followed by the St. Edward's Crown, was spine-tingling. Listening to the peerage then pay homage to the newly crowned King George V, quickly followed by the shorter, though just as powerful ceremony to crown Queen Mary, I knew was something I would never forget, and felt sadness that my parents were unable to experience it.

I noted there was not a dry eye among us watching such an auspicious occasion. The feeling of British pride swelled in my breast as the procession exited the Abbey and commenced the journey back to the palace through the streets of London so everyone who wanted to could catch a glimpse of our new King and Queen, whether along the streets or upon their return to Buckingham on the Palace balcony.

I had hoped that as the crowds began exiting to the carriages, I would be able to finally speak with Oscar and set things right, but as quickly as he had appeared in the seat in front of me, he was gone again, out the door, before his family. I shook my head. Enigma had been the perfect word to describe this beautifully mysterious stranger.

Charles nudged me in the back to get moving before others passed us by and we missed our ride back to Belgravia. I shot him a look, but moved along nonetheless. Once back at the house, everyone took to their rooms for a much-needed respite. While the ceremony had concluded around quarter past two, by the time the Abbey cleared and the attendees could depart, it was well after three o'clock. Knowing there was still a long evening ahead in attending the coronation dinner, and the early hour at which we had all gotten ready that morning, a lie down was non-negotiable.

Dinner at the Palace was not to be served until half past eight. The Viscountess had determined we needed to arrive no later than quarter past seven, so as to give her ample time to see and be seen. I could almost hear the collective groan of the household at the prospect of preparing for this last event. If she had been strict in her timing and preparation before then, she would be positively militaristic in the execution of this affair now.

I slipped off my shoes and melted into my wingback chair. While we had just come from an event where we were seated or kneeling most of the time, the emotional and mental exhaustion of experiencing such a patriotic moment had me spent. I closed my eyes for a moment and replayed what I had just witnessed. It was positively delicious in every sense of my being, and I decided I must write and tell my parents of the grand adventure while it was still fresh in my mind.

As I finished my valediction and placed my pen back in the inkwell, I heard a soft knock at the door. I shuffled over to open it to find Alice there again. I smiled. "Why, hello Miss Alice. Twice in one day! I should think myself lucky." She smiled.

"Yes, miss. Very kind of you, miss. The Viscount sent me up again to be sure you had not forgotten the time and to see if you needed help?" I was surprised. I could not imagine that the Viscountess could spare anyone in her hour of preparation. Alice must have heard my thoughts.

"The Viscount asked me to do so discreetly, miss. He had assumed your last gown may need a bit more help than your previous and did not want you to have to ask anyone. He also sent this up." She produced a small silver tray of tea sandwiches with steaming pot of water and a delicate tea cup to the side.

My eyes lit up. "Well do come in, Miss Alice. I would not want you to get caught in the hallway with such contraband!" I let her into my room. We both stifled a laugh. She set the silver tray down on the side table by my chair, and set to retrieving my gown from the wardrobe so she could familiarize herself with the closures and details. As Alice prepared my dress, I got to work on the tidy tea sandwiches and practically gulped down the tea. It was only just then I realized I had not eaten anything since my one bite of bread and butter that morning and I was famished.

Alice watched with amusement as I consumed everything in sight. "Alright, miss. Let us get you ready to be the bell of the ball!" She smiled wickedly. It was nice to know, even if only for today, I had a sympathizer among the ranks in the house.

I wiped my mouth and fingers so as to be sure I would not get anything on my dress, and walked over to her. While I had previously loosened some buttons on my current dress when we returned this afternoon, I had not yet completely taken off my lavender silk. She helped me out of it the rest of the way and we swapped out my corset and chemise for a set that would work better under this next dress.

The dress. My dream dress. I could not believe it was time to put it on and found it hard to concentrate. I was grateful Alice was there as I wasn't sure I could have been successful without her. She seemed to hesitate at seeing how I had done my previous corset and I shrugged my shoulders apologetically at her in quiet acknowledgement that it was the best I could do with what I had access to. She shook her head and continued. Once the dress was on and the buttons were in their place, she sat me down at my vanity to work on my hair.

"Oh Alice, you do not have to..." I began, but she cut me off.

"Quiet, miss. If I am to be a renegade agent for the Viscount, we shall do it right. Agreed?" she asked, looking at me in the mirror. "Besides. Hair is sacred and must be honored as such, especially for a once-in-a-lifetime occasion such as this."

I simply nodded my head. She deftly took the psyche knot down and let my hair fall. Standing back, she seemed to be assessing something with her hand on her chin, tilting her head this way and that. I started to blush. It was more attention than I had been paid in a long time. She noticed a quizzical look on my face as she evaluated the situation. I thought I had better express my thought.

"Alice?" I started.

"Yes, miss?" She was still considering my hair in concert with my gown and the string of crystals set off to the side.

"You said 'hair is sacred,'" I began.

"Yes, miss," she answered matter-of-factly and then broke her concentration to look at my reflection looking back at her in the mirror. "Do you not know?!" she asked, accent heavy, clearly confounded at my confusion. I shook my head. "Well, I suppose someone of your upbringing probably would not..." she mused to herself. "Hair, is said to be our connection to the divine, or at least general spiritual energy, as me mum says," she continued, looking quite pleased with herself that she was able to share this knowledge and be in a position of authority. I must have still looked unconvinced because she went on.

"Hair can hold ancestral knowledge and wisdom. It is why women, among other reasons, let it grow long so we do not lose what came before us. And why cutting it off in the workhouses is such a punishment, because when not done so with intention as a ritual for change, can be seen as a ritual of cutting you off from one's past and purpose."

I considered this nugget of information. I had always assumed that hair was hair and women had it long because we were women and needed to fashion it. Like an accessory. This young kitchen girl's knowledge on the subject was extraordinary to say the least, and I wondered what else she might know.

Alice's gaze went back to my own locks, to which my eyes now followed and began to see them in a new light. She approached the back of my head again and before I knew it, she had arranged my hair into a loose chignon, the likes of which I had not seen, and had woven the ribbon of crystals throughout the style as if it was my own strand of hair, showcasing my inner ancestral soul for all to see. Without a curling iron, she had managed to make my waves work unto themselves and created quite the striking frame to my face. I felt...beautiful.

Pleased with her creation, she nodded her head in approval and moved toward the door. For someone relegated to the kitchen, she knew her way around as a ladies' maid better than most, with the added benefit of thoughtful conversation; I was impressed. Just as she reached the door, she must have remembered the tray and went over to retrieve it. I opened my mouth to thank her for her help, but she wordlessly slipped out the door, like the Ghost of Christmas Past having discharged their duty, or perhaps some version of a Fairy Godmother.

I turned and looked at my reflection. I was stunned. The slightly more mature version of myself I had noted from this morning had completely transformed into a woman now. I found the sapphire and diamond chandelier earrings, slipped them onto my ears and decided it was time to go. I grabbed my matching beaded reticule, dark blue satin slippers, opera-length gloves, and my cream satin shawl from the other evening. While not a perfect match, it did emphasize the color of the rouching in the middle of the dress and brightened the overall look so it was not too dark. I once again departed my room and took to descending the stairs to the waiting carriages. Charles was there at the bottom and when he turned to look at me, started a bit and let his mouth drop.

"Are you alright? What is it?" I asked, concerned, bringing my hand to my hair to make sure nothing had gone astray.

He stared. "It is just…you look almost like mother, and I had thought she was the one standing before me" he said in awe.

I kissed him on the cheek, a rare tender moment between us. "You are too kind my dear brother, you do me a great compliment in saying so."

My green-eyed-monster then raised his arm for me to take so he could escort me to the carriage. What a perfect little gentleman he was becoming.

When we got outside, I immediately draped the shawl over my shoulders. The evening had a bit of a chill to it, and I wondered how it was possible given it was June. I also noted that for once, I had beaten her ladyship outside and would be able to ascend into my carriage without her watchful eye scrutinizing my every inch and move. Charles helped me up and joined me inside.

Shortly after, I heard, rather than saw, the Viscountess making her way outside. I peeked out the window with pure curiosity. She was draped in a burgundy satin gown with black netting overlay, and a black brocade shawl so long that it almost created a cape-like effect. Her hair was up in a psyche knot, with an ornately jeweled comb at the top, almost as wide as a tiara with points sticking out, like the Statue of Liberty the French had gifted to the Americans only a couple decades ago. Gertrude was at her heels in a less ostentatious evening gown of pink chiffon, with flowers at the slight Edwardian train behind. Unfortunately, the effect of the color against her mousy brown hair only served to make her look younger than she was, rather than older, which was probably why the Viscountess was once again scowling.

The Viscount followed close behind in his coat and tails, placing his top hat on his head. I looked around for any other family member that might be joining, but there was none. The carriage ahead of us started and we followed. I caught Charles watching me out of the corner of his eye, evaluating me.

"Yes?" I asked, raising my chin up slightly.

He considered. "Nothing," he responded.

We drove on in silence. The air was thick with the summer breeze and something else. Anticipation?

As we arrived at the Palace gates, there was that chill again. I pulled my shawl ever tighter around my shoulders. Something was coming, I was just not sure what.

Chapter 7 – Sophia, June – Present Day

Once back at the house, the kids tore into the applesauce pouches and carrot spears that were immediately available in the fridge. Kit found the bottled water and split one between the two of them in the only plastic glasses we could find in the cupboards, knowing full well neither would finish a bottle on their own. The guys grabbed a couple of beers and went out to the patio to continue the conversation they had started at the brewery about Eric's work at the Veterans Association, or VA as we referred to it in America, and its impact.

Which left Kit and I in the main sitting room. Violet had moved from the upstairs to downstairs finding a cozy pillow on the floor by the empty fireplace with which to snuggle up and be amongst the energy. Wordlessly, I decided we needed some tea, and set to arranging the kettle, gathering the necessary accoutrement to bring in on the tray. Kit had encouraged the kids to head upstairs and have a lie down, even if it was just with a book, as their little bodies were still adjusting to the time difference.

Unsurprisingly, when I walked into the cozy room with its hodge-podge crocheted pillows on tartan cloth covered couches, Kit was staring off in the distance, again. I set the tray down on the brown chesterfield ottoman, prepared her a cup and placed the cup into her hands. She looked up.

"Alright, spill. Normally I would be into letting you come to at your own pace, but as we seemingly keep getting interrupted at every opportune moment, I am skipping the niceties. What's up with you?!" I asked, a little harsher than I intended, but I felt like I needed to jumpstart her.

She stared at me. I was about to interject again, but she spoke first.

"I don't know. I think I'm just losing it," she said and sipped her tea, realizing it was still very hot, she blew on it, cupping it in her hands in her lap.

"You and I both know that is not the case. Spill. You started to say something about visions in the gardens, and then brought up a book you were reading on the train," I offered.

"Yes. Anomalous Cognition," she replied, sounding sure of herself for the first time.

"Okay, start there. Explain." I urged.

"Oh Soph, come on, you would know this stuff. Its psychology based," she let out a big sigh.

"I get that by the word 'cognition' in the title, however I, am not a world class practitioner, so, explain." I was unrelenting.

She sighed and I could see I had her now. "The book I was reading was all about the studies that were conducted back in the 1930's. It showed, even back then, and before, that there was a niche group of psychologists that believed humans were or are capable of information transfer outside of known sensory channels or interactions; at least in the traditional sense."

Now it was my turn to stare. "And?" I asked, clearly not picking up what she was putting down.

"It's a fancy way of talking about ESP, remote viewing, and other parapsychological phenomena," she said, and sipped her now-cooled tea.

I waited, but she wasn't giving me more. "Okay...and why does this seem to have you in such a tizzy?" I asked. "And what does it have to do with your visions or dreams you alluded to?"

"I don't know. It's just...after your recurring dream experience and us having that Shaman experience, I feel like it's all tied together somehow. How else would you explain what we saw in that tiny little room that uncovered the entirety of a past life in which we didn't even know existed or was possible?" she asked, almost to herself, and clearly on a roll. "And how is 'seeing' a past life possible if something like remote viewing doesn't exist...which also led me to epigenetics, but I'm not ready to go there yet. And, if what happened to you is even possible—you did heal a past life experience which broke some sort of karmic or generational curse for your soul and Bryce's— you can't be the only one out there who has done so, which then leads me to trying to wrap my head around my own visions." She took a breath.

I had never, not once, seen my friend spiral in a conversation in the way she just had. It was actually quite remarkable and made me feel more human in a way that was inexplicable. I smiled and caught her eye.

"Kit, you okay?" I asked grinning. She realized how all of that just tumbled out of her and breathed a sigh of relief.

"I did not know how much I needed to get that off my chest!" she exclaimed, regaining some of her normal energy.

"Been holding onto that one for awhile have ya?" I questioned, sipping my tea. I only now realized that I made us blue lotus tea…whoops! I meant to save that for later when all three of us were together. Hopefully, she wouldn't ask and I wouldn't have to explain.

"I guess so," she smiled. "Though saying it out loud doesn't make me feel any better or shine a light on any answers."

"No, that jumble definitely wouldn't," I smirked, giving her a side-eye and trying to bring some levity to the situation. "However, speaking it out loud so you are not constantly internalizing it must help a bit. It's a start in unraveling what you have going on in there." I pointed, swirling my finger in the direction of her head.

"That's just it. The more I try to discern and make correlations, the more jumbled it gets. I feel like there are connection points I'm not seeing, just out of reach, and it's maddening," she whispered to herself.

"Well, professor, we are back together and have the magical energy of Scotland on our side. I have no doubt we will figure it out and have you right as rain by the time the trip is done," I responded, though I didn't actually know what the phrase meant. She looked at me and raised an eyebrow.

"Even with our dear skeptical Maddy in tow? Soph, Even I have my doubts with this. I can only imagine what she might do if the topic comes up!"

"Even with our dear skeptical Maddy in tow. She has progressed since we last saw her, and while she may not completely understand what happened to the three of us, she seems to be embracing her newfound outlook on life and all things spiritual since the Equinox, too," I tried to reassure her.

And I meant it. While neither of us had seen Maddy since our trip, she had stayed in touch more than ever; regaling us about her travel exploits with Ryan as he received even more photography work. She took full advantage of the fact that he was her employer's brother, and thus received more holiday time than most. As they traveled the world for his shoots, she endeavored to visit every religious sanctuary in the immediate area to learn and absorb all she could, now open to other thoughts and ideologies. Her turnaround was rather remarkable, thanks, in part, to her own Romeo she had found, who had given her the space to figure out all her messy bits that had kept her from finding a life of fulfillment or stability before.

"If you say so," she acquiesced and sipped her tea again. She looked contemplative as she stared down in the mug. I waited for the inevitable question. "What is this? I'm not familiar with the flavor profile and it smells floral. A bit different than our traditional brews."

I bit my lip. Damn, I was hoping she wouldn't go there. "Um, well...I had actually gotten it for the three of us to try over the Summer Solstice. I guess in my hurry to get something made, I neglected to look at the bag and grabbed the wrong one," I admitted.

She looked at me expectantly as I had yet to actually answer her question.

"It's blue lotus," I sighed, and cringed a bit, waiting for her response. She looked confused and then realization dawned on her.

"Blue lotus as in the tea that helps with lucid dreaming and shit?" she spat.

I nodded my head.

"Soph!" She stared down into her mug. I couldn't tell if she was excited or disappointed. We had talked about wanting to try it a month ago, and I thought it would be fun to have on the trip, but I didn't mean to introduce it so soon.

"I'm sorry. But, there's no harm in us trying it out before Maddy gets here." I quickly tried to assuage her doubts. "Who knows, it's probably bunk anyways..." I knew full well that it wasn't.

She sighed. "It's fine, it's just...Friday the thirteenth, and the dreams I've already been having, and 'all the things'...this should be interesting," she concluded as she took a large gulp.

"Yeah, about those. What do they have to do with the cognition theory stuff?" I asked.

She considered. "Nothing. Everything. I'm not sure yet," she said shrugging her shoulders.

"Say more." I pushed.

She smiled at that. It had become our own magical phrase in getting us to talk; similar to one I used to use with someone else, but instead we said "full disclosure" when we wanted the other to speak their mind.

"I guess...well...I'm trying to integrate your experience to validate and justify in my own mind how it could happen, while also starting to have one of my own. I guess when one starts to 'awaken', they don't get to choose how it happens," she mused.

"Ha. There's a complete understatement" I joked.

"I've only had flashes, really. And you asked me why they stand out versus other dreams I've experienced, and really, the only thing I can come up with is that they seem familiar." She looked out the window.

"Okay, but what are the dreams? You still haven't said," I prodded.

"I'm not sure," she admitted. "I get snippets. Furs, weapons, symbols. Nothing concrete and nothing that stays long enough to completely recognize what it is." She looked frustrated now. I quickly stepped in to stave off another bout of quiet introspection.

"It's okay! You're obviously processing a lot. I have every confidence you will figure this out. In the meantime, take it as it comes. I've started journaling everything. Even things that pop that don't seem to make sense. I've found, even over only a couple of months, something that I write down one day winds up resonating another, even when at the time I captured it, it didn't make sense. I'm positive you will sort this out, and we will do it together." I reached over and grasped the top of her right hand to show my solidarity. She looked down at it and back at me smiling.

"You always know how to make a girl feel less crazy," she said.

"I'm going to take that as a compliment." I grinned at her.

I'm glad I finally got her to open up, and wanted to leverage the time to inquire about what she meant by Thora and her experiences that she alluded to in the gardens, suspecting it had something to do with the other term she referred to...genetic something or other. But we heard the guys making their way in from outside and rifling through the kitchen, clearly on the hunt for snacks of their own. We looked at each other knowingly, and put a silent pin in the conversation. I wordlessly took the mug from Kit's hands while she grabbed the tea tray, and we left our little cozy sanctuary to go throw together a small snack for the household while we prepared dinner.

The guys were munching on a sleeve of crackers over the island while breaking off chunks of the leftover smoked Gubbeen cheese from the night before. Kit set the tray down by the sink and I went over to grab a package from the fridge. Luckily, there was a butcher nearby and I had been able to procure some beautiful grass-fed ribeyes with the perfect amount of marbling. We may have eaten light the night before to keep it easy for my friends' arrival, but tonight, after a day of sightseeing and everyone acclimating to the new environment, it was a time for a proper meal. Steaks on the grill, roasted root vegetables, mash for the kids, and a sticky toffee pudding for dessert.

Erik looked on in anticipation as I unwrapped the brown butcher paper and twine. He practically lunged at me when he saw the four rib-eyes and I thought he was about to go full caveman on me and gnaw on the raw the steak.

"Well, this is great, but what are you all going to eat?!" he joked. "I'm famished!"

"Easy there, killer" warned Kit, eyeing him from the opposite side of the island.

"Don't worry Viking, there will be more than this. I got us the rib-eyes and two filets for the kiddos. If they don't eat all of theirs, I will fight you for the remnants." I grinned at him. "Now, how do you prefer yours prepared, charcoal or mooing?"

"Mooing for me!" he responded enthusiastically. I looked to everyone else and they all concurred.

"Fabulous. I will get the grill started so as to stave off the Viking from trying to gnaw into any other flesh." I flashed Kit a broad smile. At the same time, Bryce grabbed the turnips, parsnips, and carrots from the counter, as well as the bag of potatoes and set to work. Thankfully, the potatoes were already pre-washed and he preferred to make his mash with the skin on, so the timing should work out perfectly. Not wanting to miss out on helping, Erik sorted through the drawers to find a peeler and grabbed the roots from Bryce's hands. I looked at Kit in awe.

"Well, I guess the menfolk have the rest of the cooking sorted." I smirked.

Kit laughed. "Indeed." And she smiled approvingly at her husband for jumping in.

"What about the kiddos? Should we get them downstairs?" I asked looking up to the stairs.

"If I know them, even if they drifted off for a bit, the sound of a bustling kitchen will have them down here tout suite!" she declared.

No sooner did she say that then we heard rustling from above, and we all broke out in a hearty laugh.

"Like clockwork," said Erik with pure joy on his face.

The kids came tumbling down the stairs in an unspoken race with each other. The sudden ruckus caused Violet to pop up to attention, only to realize it was her adopted siblings making the noise and she decided to get in on the fun. Trotting over to them, she started jumping around playing.

Tate suddenly stopped and looked up, remembering something. "Dad!"

Erik paused peeling for a moment and directed his gaze at his son. "Tate!"

"I did some more digging on Friday the thirteenth," he said.

Bryce and Erik exchanged a glance, Bryce looking apologetic and Erik smirking in an "I told you so" sort of way.

"And?" asked Erik.

Tate proceeded to launch into a veritable dissertation of everything he uncovered in a Google search about the subject. He covered off on the Christian vs. Norse mythology, historical references from Knights Templar and 20th century pop culture, the fear of the number itself, and finished with the pagan traditions seeing it as a number of divinity and femininity. Of course, doing so in nine-year-old speak, and almost completely regurgitating all that Bryce had shared just that morning. But it hit different because he had done the research himself.

I looked over at Bryce to see how he would react to this monologue that he obviously influenced. He seemed nonplussed by the fact his original conversation had been usurped, with a look of pride that he had a kindred spirit in history.

I then looked to Kit to see what she was making of all of this. I hadn't seen a child this excited about a topic since Thora had first gravitated toward her plant studies. It made me wonder: Just where was this natural affinity for the subject coming from? My friend seemed to have a similar thought and we looked at each other, putting a quiet pin in that too.

"Right you are, Sir Tate!" Bryce said, breaking the momentary silence. "Nicely done. You will make a fine historian someday."

Tate beamed at that.

Soon dinner was ready, and we all sat down at the kitchen table. We had enough of the outdoors for the day, and it looked like there might be rain. We all enjoyed the bounty in front of us, and Erik even got some extra steak since neither of the children could finish their filets. I almost fought him for it, but thought the better of it. As dessert wrapped up and we settled in for an evening in front of the TV to watch a movie, the boys deciding on *Indiana Jones and the Last Crusade*, I began to replay my conversation with Kit.

When the movie finished, the kids had long been asleep, and Kit was passed out on Erik's shoulder on the couch. I had stretched out across Bryce's lap on the loveseat with him rubbing my feet. Erik heaved Tate on his back like a monkey and then picked up Thora in a fireman's hold to carry them both up to bed in one trip. I watched Bryce observe the scene unfold with a sensitivity I had yet to experience in his already soft eyes. They seemed to smile at the sight of witnessing another wholly "manly-man" effortlessly fall into the role of dotting father.

Erik came back down shortly thereafter to wake Kit. He might have wanted to whisk her up to bed as well, but the narrow stairwell would not have cooperated. So instead, he lightly touched her cheek to wake her just enough to guide her up the stairs, half walking and half leaning on him. I wondered if she was already in the grips of a lucid dream thanks to the tea I had given her earlier, and I looked forward to our coffee talk in the morning.

Once our guests were upstairs, I shifted and nuzzled my head into my Scot's strong chest. He began stroking my hair and started humming one of the many Scottish tunes he liked to sing. The deep bass vibrated in his chest, massaging my head, and I felt like I was laying on top of a giant purring jungle cat. Almost asleep myself, on that fine line of awake and dreaming, I thought, "when was the last time you were this content?" I smiled, and then saw a flash of twenty-year-old me, laying in a similar position with my head on a strong chest, him stroking my hair, and a tear came to my eye.

I had not thought of him, or that seemingly forgotten moment, in a very long time.

Chapter 8 – Josephine, June 1911

I was completely beguiled. The Palace, while known to be beautifully appointed under Queen Victoria's care, was everything anyone ever dreamt of experiencing in their own royal fairytale. Not one opulent detail had been overlooked. Everything seemed to be gilded, with warm rich colors and textures everywhere.

Charles had left my side as soon as the Viscount and Countess had been announced, not wanting to be associated with them, nor missing out on any fun to be had with his cohorts. I managed to slip away myself and enter the ballroom, where I was handed a beautiful crystal glass filled with golden champagne. I found myself drawn to the musicians' gallery at the other end of the room so I could enjoy the music. Enraptured with the organ and background music being played, I forgot myself and began swaying where I stood. I could not help it, the frisson across my skin was back. Dressed in my most gorgeous gown in such a beautiful environment, without the Viscountess looming over my every move, I was in bliss; dreaming of ballrooms, dancing, and large skirted ballgowns swirling around the floor, instead of the latest fashion that was much more contemporary and restrictive.

"It is you," I heard somewhere off in the distance, though not yet ready to break with my daydream.

"Hmm?" I softly replied.

"How is it we keep meeting like this?" responded the voice, clearly amused with the situation and finding me in my own little world.

"I know not..." I realized I should turn and face the voice behind me, and was stunned to see Oscar. I quickly came back to myself. "I know not what you speak of, Son of Carlisle," I managed and took a quick sip of champagne as my throat has gone surprisingly dry again in his presence. He smirked.

"I am a daughter of the peerage. I thought a boy such as yourself would have figured it out by now." I emphasized the word boy, though for who's sake I was uncertain, and was proud of myself for gathering my wits about me.

"I, miss, am no boy, and find myself hurt by your accusation," he mused. "I am, however, intrigued at this little mystery and will dedicate myself fully to discovering its core," he continued, and then proceeded to stare at me, raising an eyebrow.

"Excuse me sir, but as a supposed gentleman, you should know that it is not polite to stare, especially at a lady who is also unchaperoned," I teased, thoroughly enjoying the attention he was paying me.

"I agree, Miss Findley, but if I am to unravel this case, I am afraid I must take in all aspects of the subject in question. I cannot help that the subject in question happens to be you." I tried to hide the smile that was about to spread across my lips, but was completely unsuccessful.

"And why is it that the lady is unchaperoned? You do not seem old enough to be a spinster. I would imagine whomever is responsible for you would be dismayed at finding you alone, and now in the company of a stranger," he said.

"I..." I paused to think of a witty reply, but with none forthcoming, I answered truthfully. "I managed to slip away from those that are responsible for me, and my brother, so as to enjoy a bit of respite and listen more closely to the music."

Sensing our repartee was over, he considered this new information. "So, you have a brother? Why would he not be required to stay with you for the evening if you are not betrothed to another?" he queried.

"Just as you have a sister that you are not required to entertain, my *younger* brother would hardly be the appropriate master of my chaperonage," I answered. Was I trying to give him clues on purpose, or was he truly that good at getting me to lay my thoughts to bare?

"Well, you clearly know more about me than you have let on. Pray tell, how is that?" he asked.

I was about to open my mouth and tell him everything, if for no other reason than to end this questioning, and have the satisfaction of showing him the riddle's so obvious answer, when a gentleman wearing a robe and seal came over to us.

"Oscar, my boy. How are you?" he asked, completely ignoring me.

"I am well, My Lord. And you?" Oscar responded in kind, and then looked to me as if he was willing me not to leave him alone.

"Splendid! Katerina was so happy to have met you the other night at the hall. She has not stopped talking about it since," continued the man, who I was beginning to recognize as being an Earl. Oscar must have noticed my curious look.

"As I was her, Earl" he confirmed, both for the Earl and his obvious jubilation over whatever meeting had taken place."

"And may I introduce the honorable Josephine Findley, daughter of Baron Crowley," he offered, including me in the conversation. I curtsied, and when I looked up, I saw this man evaluating my every feature, but not in the comforting way Oscar had just been moments ago.

The Earl was watching me like a hawk gauging if his prey was even worthy of the hunt. Oscar clearly had picked up on the slight and proceeded anyway.

"Miss Findley, may I introduce the Honorable Sir Waverley, Earl of Airth." He said it with a touch of disdain. I was beginning to get a clearer picture of Oscar and perhaps an understanding why he was always so "come and go" when it came to his family and the gentry at large. Though he also seemed resigned to play the game.

"A pleasure, I'm sure" mumbled the Earl. "Now, boy, I was hoping to speak with your parents. Where might I find them?" he asked while looking through the crowd.

"I believe you can find my mother anywhere there is a crowd of royalty, and my father should likewise be with his fellows from Parliament," Oscar half-joked, forgetting himself in present company. The Earl raised an eyebrow at him and then looked over at me as if I was to blame for this rupture in decorum.

"Perhaps you should take me to them young man," the Earl said with a bit more force than was necessary. Oscar realized then how he must have sounded and immediately straightened his stance.

With an apologetic look towards me, he responded "Yes, My Lord," and they were off.

I looked on with amusement at Oscar the playful "brute," and Oscar the Honorable Son. There was a depth behind those ice blue eyes that was beginning to unfold, and I found it warmed me to my core. Perhaps he was not so flippant in attitude in owing to his heritage, as much as it was in spite of it; and yet there was still something I could not quite put my finger on. Given the welcome, or unwelcome, receipt I had been given in his family home, it made me slightly more comfortable knowing there may be a fellow kindred spirit among the walls, even if I had yet to meet him there. I vowed I would not go another night without revealing our association. Perhaps, once he knew of it, he would finally take me with him on his daily adventures so I could be out from under the roof with his mother.

Glass empty, and music clearly changing to rally us to sit down for dinner, I found a server with whom I could leave my glass and decided to find Charles so we could sit and wait for the meal to commence. The Viscountess had actually taken charge of him this evening out of concern that he had not been trained in the proper protocols for such an esteemed event. She clearly did not want to be guilty by association with him should he misbehave during her "hour of glory." The look on his face said everything when I approached him.

"Where have you been?" he practically hissed. I had not heard that amount of fervor in his voice since he found out our parents were leaving for America.

"Enjoying the music," I replied. "Why, did you miss me terribly?" I smiled sweetly.

"Hardly. However, your company is a lot more palatable than Lady Macbeth over there, keeping a watch of me. I swear she does not approve of the way in which I breathe," he sighed.

It took everything in me not to tell him "welcome to my world," but I thought the better of it, simply shrugging my shoulders. "It seems her way when she wants something, does it not?" I replied.

"I suppose," he said, looking down at his shoes, clearly mulling something over. "Is this what you have been managing with all this time?" he sheepishly asked, realization dawning on him. I just nodded. "It is a miracle she still stands," he said with a small smirk on his face, knowing full well under normal circumstances I would never tolerate such treatment, but that out of an abundance of love and respect for our parents I had been unnaturally avoidant.

I considered him. "Thank you," I said and winked.

"For?" he asked, surprised.

"Seeing me," I responded. He seemed confused, but as compliments could be few and far between with us, he took the small win and nodded his head.

We watched the crowds shift and begin heading towards the table in the middle of the ballroom. "Shall we?" I asked, and wrapped my arm around his elbow so we could be the proper brother and sister escorting each other to dinner.

The table was spectacular. How the Palace servants had been able to pull together such a marvel so perfectly, fell short of words. Golden goblets. White china bearing the new mark of King George V and Queen Mary emblazoned on them, clearly showcasing their debut. Matching golden flatware; all beautifully arranged on a rich burgundy damask tablecloth lined with golden candelabras, ivory candles, and other similarly appointed accoutrement. The room seemed to be glowing from the inside out.

Once again, not wanting us to be a distraction from her own children, but also not wanting us to be out of sight, the Carlisles all sat on one side of the table: the Viscount, followed by the Viscountess, Gertrude, and finally Oscar, while Charles and I sat across from them. I noticed that Oscar had been placed near the Earl we had only just been speaking with, and in between them, a girl. Perhaps seventeen or eighteen years old, she looked younger than she probably ought to, given her fair hair and complexion and positively rosy cheeks. Whether from too much rouge or the effect Oscar's presence had next to her, I could not be certain. I watched, amused, as the Earl engaged Oscar in conversation so that the girl in between them could be silently included. This must be Katerina.

I turned my attention to my own place setting as the first course was served, consommé de tortue. I looked at Charles. He did not seem impressed as this was one of his least favorite foods, but I quietly admonished him with one look and he silently picked up his spoon and began eating with the rest of the table. It was clear it would be a relatively somber dinner for us as we did not know the parties to which sat astride us, nor were we worthy of attention since no one could clearly identify to whom we belonged. I was thankful for the anonymity so I could drink in the details of the evening in peace.

I also took full advantage of my view from my seat and observed my enigma in his "natural" habitat. It was the first time in which he was staying still long enough for me to truly appreciate him as a human, and not a thunderous flash of energy.

He sat with all the rigor and decorum of someone with his upbringing should, but there was something behind it all that still mystified me. A spark, or something, that caught my attention and drew me in closer. Perhaps it was the air about him, not quite as dense as it was with others. That he seemed to live and appreciate life on a different level than what I had seen in fellow cohorts or even others in general. Whatever it was, I felt like a moth to the flame.

I felt an elbow in my side. "Ouch!" I exclaimed and looked at Charles.

"You're staring," he whispered.

"I am not!" I quickly defended myself.

"Yes, you are, and besides, they're bringing the second course. Thought you would want to know," he whispered.

The salmon with mousseline and cucumber mayonnaise sauce was set before us with as much pomp and circumstance as the processional itself. I giggled at the thought, and looked around to see if anyone else had noticed. It appeared I wasn't the only one amused as I saw Oscar cover his mouth with his napkin. Our eyes met. He seemed appreciative that I too was caught enjoying the moment and then turned away as his mother reprimanded him for the gaffe and he set his fork to the dish. He also seemed relieved at the opportunity to eat rather than speak. It seemed Katerina was not much of a conversationalist and instead merely sat in his presence staring into his eyes as if they held the key to something. We had that in common.

I glanced over at the rest of the Carlisles, more to gauge how Gertrude and the Viscount were doing than the Viscountess, however she was the one who caught my attention. She was akin to a hunter watching its prey as she observed the interaction with Oscar and Katerina. She would then glance over at the Earl, sharing a conspiratorial look that confused me. *What on earth*...and then realization dawned.

The person she called Oscar away to meet with the other night at the Hall. The Earl seeking him out this evening to speak with him about his daughter. Them being seated next to each other at a formal event. The

Viscountess did not have plans for Gertrude, she had plans for her son!

Suddenly, I felt ill. I could not finish the salmon in front of me, nor could I stand the smell of the filet mignon and foie gras with truffle forthcoming. I needed to excuse myself, but how could I without making a scene? I decided discretion was my best option and waited for the flurry of the course change to make my escape. Charles looked at me confused as I wordlessly stood and pushed back my seat, leaving my napkin behind. I left with the servers and made my way outside to catch some air.

So, Oscar was to court Lady Airth. It was none of my business and I barely knew him, so why had the realization affected me so? Was it the fact that I now saw him as a kindred spirit and fellow caged bird by the Viscountess? Or perhaps that he seemed such a wandering soul and at first glance his potential betrothed had absolutely no spirit. That was unfair, I did not know her at all and only barely had gotten to know him through our limited missives and short engagements over the past few days. I should not care to whom his family was engaging him, I chided myself.

"But you do…" I heard myself say.

"You do what?" I heard someone ask. I whirled around. Oscar was standing before me in the doorway. He looked positively resplendent in his coat and tails, dark hair combed back, and ice blue eyes glinting in the moonlight. "Are you alright? I saw your face go stark white and the next moment I looked over, you were gone" he continued.

I was in disbelief that he would have noticed, let alone followed me.

I took a moment to gather myself. "I am quite alright, thank you. I think it is all the people in the room. I suddenly felt lightheaded and needed some fresh air," I said quickly. "Nothing for you to be concerned with, sir," I added.

He took another step in my direction and reached out his hand to me. "Are you sure?" he seemed unconvinced. I took a step towards him, hearing the phrase 'moth to a flame' in my mind again and smiled. He smiled in return and relaxed at my obvious calm. Little did he know it was his presence having that effect on me.

Suddenly, there was a figure standing behind him. "Oscar! What on earth are you doing out here?" she said. My stomach tensed at the mere sound of her voice. He turned to look at her.

"Mother? What are you doing out here, and leaving your royal audience behind?" he seemed to hiss in her direction. I had never seen them interact, but his words were dripping with disdain. Whether she noticed I could not tell, but she was clearly not happy with him.

"I saw you leave Katerina's side and she looked dismayed. I wanted to be sure you were alright and your father said he had seen Joseph...I mean, Miss Findley...leave just before, and sent me to check on her as she looked unwell" she said, glaring in my direction. I could hardly believe she would have come on her own accord. But it would have been unbecoming for the Viscount to check on me and there was no way she would have let Gertrude run the errand, leaving the eyes of everyone at the party. At least this way, if anyone asked, she could present herself as a concerned guardian.

"I saw Miss Findley turn white before she left and so...wait. How do you know Miss Findley?" he queried his mother.

I really wanted him to know who I was and our association, but I had not wanted him to find out in this manner. It was happening in slow motion, and I could do nothing to stop it.

"Oh, darling, Josephine and her brother Charles have been staying with us since January. I know you do not take notice of much in our household, but surely you would have noticed two additional people under our roof!" she said, amused.

He turned to look at me as if for the first time. 'Is this true?' his eyes asked. I hesitated, trying to find my words, and then simply nodded.

His hand, still midair reaching toward me, now fell to his side. I likewise stopped my advance in his direction. Seeming pleased with herself interrupting something, but not quite sure what, the Viscountess stepped in. "Oscar, be a dear and go back to the dinner. Katerina will be wondering where you went off to and if anyone else noticed Miss Findley left just before, well, we would not want a scandal." She peered down at me as if all of this was my intentional doing.

Oscar had not stopped looking at me as his mother spoke. He was trying to assess something in my features, or my soul, I did not know. But he turned to her when she finished, quietly acknowledged what she said, and walked away ever the obedient son, leaving me on the outside of the doorway with her. She watched him leave and then slowly pivoted to face me. The way in which her features changed from "mother" to "menace" were startling, and I backed away out of instinct.

"Now. I do not know what game you are trying to play with my son, but it ends here and now. As of the other evening, the Viscount and I are in discussions with the Earl of Airth. He is looking for a suitable husband for his daughter, and while he would prefer to wed her to a Duke, there are...complications preventing that from taking place. Regardless, all you need to know is that you will not go near my son." She seethed with such venom; I felt as if I had been physically struck. I placed my hand to my chest where I felt the ghost wound to keep myself protected.

Games? I thought to myself. How could she possibly think I had any intentions with him when I had not seen him in the entirety of my stay and only recently spoken to him. Aside from that, he had no clue who I even was until the moment before. I stared at her in sheer amazement of the accusation. She took that as silent agreement from me, turned on her heel, and left me to ponder my own existence.

For a night that was supposed to have been filled with wonder, I was now only filled with dread. Whatever had just transpired in the last few minutes had not only broken the connection I had started to feel with Oscar, but it had also put me squarely in the sights of the Viscountess, something I had been trying to avoid for the past six months.

I did not want to go back inside. I wished I could return to the house and crawl into the relative safety of my bed; however, I knew that was far from happening. There were still at least two, if not three courses left in the dinner, and for all the Viscountess's faults, I did not want to embarrass the Viscount after he so valiantly fought for my brother and I to be included in this week's festivities. I took a deep breath, adjusted my waist, and turned to walk back into the Palace that now felt more like a dungeon than a magnificent ballroom for celebration.

Chapter 9 – Kit, June - Present Day

Settling into bed after having fallen asleep during the movie, Kit tried to not lose the sense of drowsiness she still felt. She vaguely recalled the conversation she and Sophia were having in the front room around her latest dream experiences and musings on autonomous cognition, but the hazy veil of sleep fell around her again and she drifted off.

This time, instead of seeing flashes of things she couldn't quite recognize, Kit truly dreamt. She saw, from a first-person perspective, her hands coming out from under a heavy cloak. It was rabbit fur-lined and felt warm and secure on her shoulders. She looked down and noticed she was walking along a snowy path, and was in a village. There were clusters of turf-covered outbuildings that had wood frames, and smoke was billowing out of the roofs.

As she continued walking towards what looked like a main longhouse at the center of the village, she became aware of a small bag bouncing against her leg. She reached down to grab it and saw that it had been made out of deer hide, and fastened with a length of twine. As she opened it, she saw small dark stones inside. She took a few out and tumbled them in her hands. They were black and smooth, apart from the line markings across them, and noticed each one was different. As she turned them over in her hands, she felt a surge of energy run up her arm as if they were transferring something to her. The jolt almost made her drop them.

Suddenly, there was a large hand atop hers, forcing her fingers to wrap around the stones. It maneuvered such that the stones were being dropped back into the bag from which she had gotten them and quickly closed.

"Ekki her ast min," she heard a deep bass voice whisper in her ear and felt herself nod in understanding. *'Not here, my love'*. What language was that?

She looked around in confusion and tried to find where the voice had come from. The hands had disappeared and she was standing still, alone, on the path. She also realized that for all the smoke coming out of the tops of the structures, she felt like she was the only one in the village. Just then, the scene shifted and she was on a boat on the high seas. The wind was whipping ice cold sea water at her face and she huddled in a corner with others as she watched a group of men work to keep the ship afloat through the storm. She sensed they were all in grave danger.

As she looked on, she tried to discern any familiarity in the faces around her, but then a huge wave crashed in front of her and it all went dark. She bolted upright in bed.

Kit looked around her to gain a sense of her surroundings. She realized she had been sweating profusely and needed some water. It was 3:33 a.m. She hated when she woke up like this. It would take forever to fall back asleep, especially as she continued to adjust to the time zone shift. So as not to wake Erik, she thought it would be best to go downstairs to grab a glass of water and see if she could lull herself back into sleep. She grabbed her cotton robe, slipped on a pair of slippers and padded down to the kitchen. She grabbed a bottle of water from the fridge, reflecting on it being in a glass bottle and not plastic, and took a long, cool sip. She stopped a moment to listen. The house was silent. She couldn't even hear the typical nighttime breathing, which made her feel perilously alone...just as she had in the dream that woke her.

The dream. It was the first time that any of the flashes she had seen had come together. She considered the tea that Sophia had given her the afternoon before and wondered, *could blue lotus tea have done all that*?

She took the bottle of water over to the windows and stared outside. She really wanted to go out and get some fresh air, but would the glass door opening wake up Violet? She had learned over the past five months that the little one missed nothing. She decided to chance it given Violet was upstairs, likely snuggled between Sophia and Bryce and would not want to leave their side. She quietly unlatched the lock and smoothed the door open.

Once outside, she stood at the railing, set the water down on the ledge, placed her hands on the top and inhaled, deeply. Holding for four seconds and exhaling for eight, she turned her face up to the sky, staring at the moon.

"Alright girl, what do you have for me tonight?" she found herself asking as she looked up. Surprising herself with such whimsy, she snorted. *Talking to the moon now, Kit? Oh, you're really headed for the nuthouse.*

As if Goddess Diana herself was challenging her request, a thought popped in her head in response to her own question. What if what she had seen tonight was not a traditional dream metaphor for the dangers and perils in life. What if what she had seen, and been experiencing previously, was another past life trying to break through? Then another question dawned on her.

Could you have more than one past life? She had never considered it. It seemed a logical extension from what her and Sophia had experienced with the Shaman, but she really hadn't delved deeper into it. If you could have more than one past life, how many were there? How many times had she actually walked this earth? Who were the people with her? And what time period had she just witnessed?

As she mused on all of this, she allowed herself a glimpse back at what she had seen. The scene was cold, there was snow, and she was wrapped in a long winter cloak. She seemed to be herself and yet not. What were those stones she held in her hand? And who was that voice that had caused her to hide them? She didn't recognize the language that was spoken, but she could tell from the way the other hands had forced the stone back in the bag, she was not supposed to have marveled at them out in the open.

She sipped on her water a bit longer. When no other awareness or epiphanies seemed to come forth, she decided it was best to head back up to bed and try to fall asleep again. What had Sophia recommended? Journaling? That had never been her thing, but as she was brilliant at taking case notes, she made a mental list to be sure to record all of this in the morning. She would be hard-pressed to keep it from Sophia too long. That girl's intuition had sky-rocketed since the Spring, but she also wanted to honor whatever had come through and keep it sacred to herself until she could discern more, and have more answers than questions.

"Alright, Friday the thirteenth, I see you. But go easy on me, will you? Especially going into the Summer Solstice. I am not nearly as well versed as my friend in all of these things, and I need time to process," Kit said out loud to...who?

She shook her head at herself and returned upstairs to at least get some rest, if not sleep. She had a feeling that her request would not be heard since life always had a way of forcing things on you when you least suspect them, and as she had seen so far in their awakening, this would likely be no different.

Chapter 10 – Oscar, June 1911

He could not believe it. He walked slowly back to the ballroom as his mother had requested while pondering this new development. This girl. His muse from the past week that had kept him guessing, kept him up at night wondering who she was and if he would ever see her again…was the daughter of his father's friend who had been staying with them this entire time. How had he not noticed? He chided himself. No wonder she had wished not to embarrass him in front of his friends. Had they known how oblivious he was, he would have been forever ridiculed.

Oscar took his place back at the table, set his napkin on his lap, and proceeded to cut into the filet at his setting. He took a bite; the dish had gone cold and he had completely lost his appetite. The girl to his side took notice and actually attempted a conversation.

"Is the beef not to your liking, my Lord?" she asked in a small, unconvincing voice. How had his mother decided that this was who he should sit next to at this dinner? And why were they not seated next to their own guests? If he sat next to Josephine, at least he could have unraveled the mystery sooner, and probably on his own. Lost in thought, he barely remembered to answer.

"It is adequate," he managed, and took another bite, if for no other reason than to keep from having to speak with her.

"Well, you know I have grown up with the finest cook in our household. I hope to one day have one such as she in my own," she said, as if it had been overly rehearsed.

It took everything for him not to groan. He had to get out of here. This was the exact reason he always kept himself on the move—so he would not be in any one place long enough for any silly girl to notice him; that, and to keep his mother's influence at bay. It seemed no matter how hard he tried sometimes, she still managed to get her way, much to his chagrin, and he would always wind up despising himself for it. Suddenly, he could see right through her rouse and having him sit next to this...Earl's daughter. The looks that passed between his mother and Katerina's father also had not escaped him. The only one who seemed oblivious to the whole thing was his father. The thought of his father made him relax a bit; if anyone could take the situation by hand and navigate his mother away from whatever ends she had imagined, it would be him. He would speak to him when they returned home tonight. For now, he realized, there was nowhere for him to go. At the very, he least did not want to cause an embarrassment for his family by abruptly leaving.

He glanced over at the still empty chair across the table where the enchanting Josephine had been. Where was she? And come to think of it, where was his mother? Neither had returned yet. He looked to the young boy seated to the left of where Josephine had sat and realized this must be Charles, the brother she had spoken of. He clearly was her younger brother in every way, as he could not be more than thirteen or fourteen at most. The family resemblance was subtle, but there.

The boy had the greenest eyes he had ever seen, and he could swear he'd been watched by a similar set of eyes just recently. But if the young lad was staying under the same roof, that would make sense. He realized how unaware he had been since the beginning of the year. How could such a beautiful and mysterious creature have been living in the same house as he, and she'd gone completely unnoticed by him? She must either always be out, for which he would not blame her, or, another thought hit him, hard. Perhaps she stayed in her room all day in order to avoid his family. While regrettable, the latter seemed the more likely option and he finally understood their earlier exchange. Of course, she slinked away to listen to the music and have a moment of freedom. Her brother, young as he was, would not have been any concern to his mother, just as he had never been, but Josephine, for all her obvious beauty and upbringing, would have been seen as a challenge to her own daughter, his sister.

He sighed heavily. What could he do? Perhaps as the son of the chaperoning family, he would be permitted to take her with him on some adventures around the city, though he doubted she would have much interest in his exploits. But perhaps...

His mother reappeared at his side and sat down next to Gertrude with a satisfied grin on her face, like a cat who had caught a mouse. Josephine soon followed sitting down quietly, dabbing the napkin at her cheek as if she was swiping away a tear. What on earth had transpired?

Oscar tried to catch her eye to verify if she was alright, but she did not look up from her setting for the rest of the evening. When it came time to go, she and Charles silently slipped outside to the secondary family carriage and took off. He had hoped to ride along with them, if for no other reason than his was a bit crowded and he wished to avoid his mother, and any conversation of the evening's events. As soon as they were all tucked in, he looked at her and was about to ask what had happened, when she opened her already smiling mouth.

"Well, that was a successful evening, was it not?" the Viscountess beamed as she turned to her husband. Oscar's father looked out the window, not hearing her. He seemed to do that more and more lately. Clearly wanting a response sooner rather than later, and knowing full well Gertrude would not add to the conversation, she repeated herself, looking directly at the Viscount, boring her eyes into his side. Oscar tried to nudge his father's foot, discreetly getting his attention; he turned.

"Oh yes, quite" he said with about as much enthusiasm as a plant.

Not to be deterred, she continued. "Oscar, the Earl of Aith, had very complementary things to say about you. And..." she said with unnatural elongation of the vowel, "his daughter seems to be quite taken with you." Pleased with herself and the arrangement unfolding.

Oscar did not know how to respond, or if he should. He looked to the Viscount.

"Victor?" the Viscountess pushed, and she waited.

"Yes, dear. A successful evening indeed. The Earl did seem to be quite loquacious which is not his usual state, so I assume he was pleased," he said, knowing the only way out of this conversation was through.

Oscar smirked.

"Really, son, you could be a bit more grateful. Katerina will be a fine match for you; you should be down on your knees thanking me for finding you such an arrangement," she said with all the manipulative energy she could muster. He felt his sister flinch next to him as if it was she who had just been spoken to that way; as it usually was.

He stared at her. Match? He knew his mother had delusions of grandeur, but he had done his utmost to stay out of her way on such matters. He felt a little guilty about that, given it left his sister in the wake, but better she married soon and got out from under his mother's wrath. He was a man, and could much more easily maneuver himself away. In fact, if he had his way, he'd be off to university in a few short months and out from under her forever.

"Match, Mother?" he responded. "Why whatever do you mean?" he played aloof.

She seemed exasperated. "Oscar. You are far too old to not understand how this works. You should have been betrothed a long while ago with the level your father has reached. You need to start your own household."

He looked to his father again, seeking some support. He could tell none was coming. His father, for all his faults, knew when and how to pick an argument with his mother, and apparently now was not the time. He took his cue from the lack of response.

"I do know how this works, however…" he started, but saw his father raise an eyebrow from the corner of his eye and stopped what was about to be a seething diatribe from his lips. She looked at him to continue. Was that amusement on her face?

The carriage stopped. As they came to a halt, Oscar looked out the window and saw Charles helping Josephine down. He found himself jealous of the little brother being able to touch Josephine's hand and assist her alighting from the carriage. He flashed to a scene where he was the one entrusted with the job and a small smile came to his face at the thought, which surprised him in no small order. His mother took this as a different sign.

"Good, you will come to your senses eventually and will see that I am always right" she said with self-satisfaction, and proceeded to leave the carriage.

It had been a long evening. He needed time to assimilate all the information he had learned as it seemingly came at him from all fronts. He needed a plan. He decided, based on his wavering understanding of the current situation, as well as the bags under his father's eyes, his conversation on what he wanted for the future would have to wait.

He watched Josephine climb the stairs into their house, and he could swear she turned her head slightly to look toward their carriage. Was she looking for him? When she noticed it was his mother appearing from the carriage, her head softly snapped back around and she hustled inside, clearly to avoid the Viscountess. He did not blame her. He could only imagine what the past six months had been like for her and admonished himself for not having taken better notice. Yes, he was trying to stay out of his mother's way for the very reason she had spoken of tonight; to remain out of the cross-hairs of her aspirations to elevate her own position. He did not want to be another one of her pawns. But how could he have been so oblivious to two people moving into the same house?

He resolved to speak to Josephine in the morning and set the record straight. Maybe he'd even see if she had any interest in joining him the day after next when he had plans for a day trip to the countryside to celebrate Saint John's Day. Yes, that should lift both their spirits and perhaps they could become co-conspirators in his plan to evade his mother...whatever that may be.

He was getting ahead of himself. First, a nightcap, and then some sleep. When he got to his rooms, he called on Alice to bring him his nightly sherry. He had always liked the kitchen girl. While relegated to the kitchens, she was clearly smart and he knew his father relied on her to do other household tasks and fill in gaps when he did not want the Viscountess involved. Then a thought dawned on him: Perhaps she had gotten to know Josephine over the past few months and could tell him a bit more about her.

Chapter 11 – Sophia, June – Present Day

I had the first fitful night of sleep since spring.

I was back in my study abroad days. We were living in the heart of London but traveling every weekend: Spain, Netherlands, France, Germany. I was the travel planner and my roommate was the onsite coordinator. We had only just met in the program, but had become fast friends given our mutual love of movies and music. I would book the travel and she would determine our path of discovery when we got to our destination, based on what the groups interests were and what was available to us.

And him.

I had tucked him and all our memories away a long time ago. While it had only been about fifteen years, it also seemed like a lifetime.

We had met at orientation. I was the only one from my university in the program. Everyone else had come from other institutions across the country, all rallied by the same international opportunity, and the obvious chance to get away to be on our own for a semester. We were all seated in the first floor of a local pub, being given a warm meal of chili con carne, sitting amongst all of our backpacking bags and luggage. I had managed to get a spot at a table with two other girls who had friendly smiles, and there was an open seat next to me. He came strolling in, late but unbothered by his obvious tardiness. He dropped his bags, bowed his head in apology to our group leader, and grabbed the closest open place he could, which was the one to my right.

A wave of nostalgia and something approximate to familiarity washed over me at the time, though I had no clue why. He just seemed like someone I knew. He smelled like, home; not in the literal sense, but in a way one remembers the feeling of a home within your heart and far away. I resigned myself to him reminding me of a friend, though which friend I couldn't quite put my finger on.

Once the group leader was done running through all of the rules of the program, telling us how to avoid using the hospitals and reminding us that British pounds did not equate to US dollars, we turned to eat and introduce ourselves to our table mates. He immediately stuck his hand out and shook all of ours, saying his name was Paul, he was originally from West Virginia, and enjoyed all outdoor activities, reading, and chess. It felt perfunctory, so I mentally questioned how much of it was true, but I let it slide. The rest of us introduced ourselves in turn. There was Lillith from Tennessee, and Judy from New York City. They seemed to be in quiet awe of Paul and didn't say much else. He was a force. He turned and introduced himself to the next table over and I decided he must want to be the mayor of the program, the rate he was going with the glad-handing.

We all finished our meal, completed the obligatory icebreaker exercise of everyone going around and telling one 'surprising' fact about themselves, taking note that Paul only re-used the tidbit about chess he told our table. I remembered thinking to myself, 'Huh, what's with this guy?' As we all began gathering our bags to make our way to our respective assigned flats, I realized Paul's full stature. For someone who was seemingly larger than life when he came in the room, he wasn't as tall as I had expected him to be. We were almost the same height, him perhaps just a shade taller. As I bent down to heave my backpack on my back, we knocked heads. He laughed, and I was stunned. He apologized and then grabbed my suitcase as I was reaching for it.

"Let me help. It's the least I can do since I almost just knocked you out" he grinned. His smile was infectious and I just silently nodded my head. I heard Lillith and Judy snicker behind me and realized I must look out of it.

"Thanks" I managed, "but you don't have to. We probably aren't even in the same building."

"Oh yeah, where are you headed?" he asked. I looked down at my paper.

I read aloud: "202 Great Weymouth."

"Perfect! Same for me. Let me help," he said and walked away with my bag somehow connected to his own. I ran to follow.

The rest of the dream went into random flashes of the remaining study abroad experiences, like a movie being shown in fast forward. Over time, every slide increasingly more and more of him and I on our adventures. Day trips here, picnics there, planes, trains, cars...even without sound playing, you could tell our relationship had blossomed into something out of a fairytale. Then the movie in my head slowed to the end of the program, I felt the same sense of anticipation...and I woke up.

I opened my eyes and looked around the room. Pale streams of light were entering which told me it was early morning, far earlier than I was used to waking, but at least it was not the dead of night. I realized my face was wet and moved my hands up to my cheeks. I'd been crying. Then I remembered the content feeling of being on Bryce's chest and the tear that fell. The memory, long forgotten, of *him*. The dream that felt all too real, like I had jumped back in my own timeline and relived something in parallel, and all at once, emotional rollercoaster included. Where the hell had that even come from?

Blue lotus tea. Damn it.

I wondered if Kit felt it too? We were learning there wasn't much we didn't parallel path in our lives, so I was positive our morning coffee discussion would be...unique.

The feeling of loneliness and melancholy had attached to my bones and I realized I needed to do something to get rid of it. I reminded myself I was not alone. I had Bryce, sleeping soundly in bed next to me. All I would have to do is cuddle up next to him and like touching a Venus fly trap, he would curl around me and cocoon me in his embrace. It was one of my favorite things he did, and he didn't even know he did it.

But there was something about my dream, and the disturbing reality of it being an actual memory I thought I had buried a long time ago. It had me wondering if it would be appropriate to use Bryce and his embrace in that way. Instead, I decided I wouldn't be able to sleep anymore, and it was just as good of a time as any to get up and make the first pot of coffee.

I slid out of bed, threw on my grey shirt, and slipped downstairs, realizing Violet decided to stay curled up with Bryce instead of following me down. I grabbed my journal from the end table drawer near the glass door and went outside with my phone and a blanket. The sunrise was gorgeous, so I decided to throw on some meditation music and closed my eyes.

A stag appeared in my mind. Complete with a misty wooded scene in the background. I realized what was going on and immediately opened my notebook to a clean page, recording what I just saw. Then I closed my eyes again for the second image. Athame, but made out of some kind of crystal instead of metal...obsidian, perhaps? Then, tribal art in a cave, like a prehistoric Neanderthal vibe. Interesting.

I finished recording everything and picked up my phone to do a quick search on the spiritual meaning of those symbols. I let the meditation music keep playing, keeping me in whatever zone I'd entered. First, I typed in, "stag spiritual meaning." The search overview read:

Spiritually, a stag represents strength, wisdom, nobility, and renewal. It is often seen as a messenger between worlds, symbolizing a spiritual quest, and its ever-regenerating antlers represent abundance and spiritual growth.

Interesting...though I found myself wondering if it was referring to my "quest" I just recently finished, or if there was something on the horizon. I continued to the next part:

Key spiritual meanings of the stag:

- *Spiritual guidance: the stag acts as a guide, leading seekers on a spiritual journey or acting as a messenger between the physical and spiritual worlds. Its antlers can be seen as a connection to the divine, like a spiritual antennae."*

Huh. I continued skimming to see if anything else resonated, and saw phrases like, *"renewal and regeneration, rebirth, overcoming obstacles, royalty, nobility, heightened intuition..."*

Okay...next! *"Athame, spiritual meaning..."*

An athame is a ritual dagger symbolizing masculine energy, the element of fire, and the will to direct magical power; It represents duality, discernment and the cutting edge of truth; when paired with a chalice it performs the Great Rite, symbolizing divine union.

Now I was scratching my head. Was this meant to represent Bryce and I? He was one strong definition of "masculine energy," but it felt...off. Plus, it described it being black handled with a steel blade. What I saw was more stone-like. I raced my fingers over the keyboard: *"Obsidian spiritual meaning..."*

Spiritually, obsidian is a powerful volcanic glass known as the 'Stone of Truth', primarily used for deep protection, grounding, and spiritual cleansing, acting like a psychic vacuum to absorb negativity, reveal hidden truths, and facilitate profound transformation, self-discovery, and breaking old patterns by reflecting one's shadow self. It's associated with the Root Chakra.

Whoa. My pen couldn't write fast enough recording this information.

Finally, I looked up, *"tribal art spiritual meaning."*

Tribal art's spiritual meaning centers on deep connections to nature, ancestors, and community, serving as a conduit to the divine, not just decoration; core concepts: interconnectedness – art embodies the belief that humans, nature, and the spirit world are linked; honoring the divine & ancestors – creation is a sacred ritual to honor deities, ancestors and the natural world, reinforcing spiritual continuity; preserving lineage and history."

I read through everything again. There seemed to be a thread there that I wanted to pick at, but it was just out of reach. And why was it coming up in conjunction with the dream? Or was it?

I started sketching out the cave. As I was drawing, lost in my own thoughts, I didn't hear the door open. I suddenly sensed a presence at my shoulder and nearly jumped out of my seat. Turning to look back, I saw Kit, with an amused look on her face.

"What, can't get enough of our tattoo so you have to sketch it?" she asked.

I looked down at the page. On the wall, I'd been mindlessly drawing a triquetra. Weird. I set my pen down.

"No, not exactly," I replied and picked up my mug of coffee, unsure when I had actually gotten up to retrieve it after the pot was made. It'd gone cold and I made a face.

"Don't worry, I just made a fresh one. How long have you been up?" Kit asked, sitting down with her own blanket.

"Great, thanks. Too early I'm afraid. I needed to come out here and clear my head" I said, almost to myself.

"Ha, great minds. Me too." Kit replied with an odd tone. I looked down at my phone.

"It's only just 7:15, that's not too bad I'd wager," I offered, confused.

"Oh no, I've been up since 3:30-ish. Woke up with a start and couldn't get back to sleep. What's your excuse?" she asked, nodding her head in the direction of my journal.

"You first. I've never known you to not sleep soundly through the night like it was an Olympic sport. Spill," I said and closed my journal.

Kit proceeded to share her dream. I could tell by the way she was building the visual it was more than that, and was starting to sound like how I experienced my recurring dream; more like a memory. She finished and I looked up.

"It didn't happen to be 3:33 did it?" I smirked. Her mouth dropped open. "I only ask because that is the number of spiritual awakening, divine guidance, and creative manifestation," I continued. She looked dumbfounded. "Just sayin'..." I added and winked at her.

"And, you?" she inquired, wanting to move on. I pondered for a moment and knew this was not the time nor the place for my morning musings.

"Not time to switch gears yet. However, we do need that coffee you made," I proclaimed and grabbed both our mugs to go get refills.

When I walked back outside, I could see Kit staring at my journal.

"What do you keep in there?" she asked, not taking her eyes off of it and also gracefully taking a sip from her mug I just filled.

"Stuff," I said innocently and gave her a grin.

"Uh huh," she retorted, smiling back.

I made up my mind and said, "I want to try something," and ripped out a piece of paper from the back of the book. She looked at me horrified, as if I'd just defiled a precious artifact. I laughed. "It's okay, it was the second to last page, I promise." I handed over the page and my pen.

"Okay, what, are we doing a drawing class?" she quipped.

"Nope. Just humor me," I responded with as much patience as I could muster at this hour of the day. She sighed in resignation.

"Alright. But only because I love you." She winked.

"Think about what you just told me. In a moment, I'm going to have you close your eyes and I want you to breathe and give yourself a moment, then record whatever you see, hear, smell, etc. Then we will do that two more times. Okay?"

She looked at me dubiously, but nodded her head in agreement.

I softened my voice to sound more like my guided mediations. "Okay, close your eyes, take a breath, and let whatever comes to your mind reveal itself. Have it? Good, now open your eyes and record it." She did. "Great, now close your eyes again, and give yourself another moment to capture whatever comes. Good? Okay, open your eyes and record it." She did, and we executed it again for the third time.

Kit looked at her paper and then me, and then asked, "now what?"

"We look it up sassafras!" I exclaimed, not completely enjoying her reticence with the experiment. "What did you get?"

She looked at her page and considered. "Well, it's more nuanced than that, but..."

I sighed. "This isn't like Rorschach cards and you are revealing how crazy you are, Dr." I clarified.

She laughed. "Okay, okay. The first thing I saw was an eagle. Soaring in the sky at first, but then on the ground. The second thing was a large shield, painted blue, with some sort of line drawing or marking on it..." she stopped. I was riveted.

"And the third thing?" I asked.

She hesitated. "I didn't necessarily see something the third time, but I did smell something." She paused. I waited. "Fire. Smoke. I don't know, but it gave me the heebie jeebies in that moment." She sipped her coffee.

I nodded my head and pursed my lips. "Understandable." I typed in the search engine: "*Eagle spiritual meaning*." Then I read aloud: "Search overview says: the eagle spiritually symbolizes freedom, power, vision, and a strong connection to the divine, representing a bridge between the earthly and spiritual realms with its ability to soar high, signifying higher perspectives, divine messages, courage, and clarity, a guide for spiritual awakening."

I looked up at Kit to see how she was receiving the information, but also over to my journal. Hadn't I too just gotten a symbol for a divine messenger?

"Okay, next: shield. Survey says: 'Spiritually, a shield symbolizes divine protection, faith, and defense against negativity or evil, representing trust in God or a higher power.'" I looked at her again. "Well, that tracks."

She was obviously absorbing all of this. "Yes, but what about the blue color and the markings?" she asked.

"Hmm, let me see...*A blue shield spiritually symbolizes divine protection, peace, truth and heavenly connection,*'" I read, then I clicked over to images. "Ha! No, I don't think it is about health insurance," I laughed to myself, then updated the search bar. "Now this is interesting..." I trailed off.

"What?" Kit asked, staring at me intently.

"Could it have looked like this?" I asked, and I turned my phone to her. There were several images of a Viking-type shield, circular, blue paint with runic markings on them. Her face went blank. "What?" I asked, seeing her expression.

"It's just that...those markings. Now I know what was on the stones in my hands..." and we looked at each other in mutual realization.

"Runes!" we both cried in unison.

"Well, I'll be..." I retorted.

"You'll be what?" we heard, and both snapped our heads to the door. I smirked.

"Look Kit, a *Viking*!" I cried, placing extra emphasis on the last word. She started to nervously laugh like we had just gotten our hands caught in the cookie jar.

Clearly not getting the inside joke, but also not wanting to ask for an explanation, Erik walked over to Kit, planted a kiss on her head and took the seat next to her. "Mornin', darlin,'" he said in his best terrible Southern accent. Kit smiled.

"I'm going to go put some bread in the toaster and see what I can muster up for breakfast," I said, trying to relieve myself of the two of them. Kit gave me a look.

"No need. Your Scotsman is already whipping something up for all of us again. Seriously, Soph, where did you find that guy? Wandering around the Highlands?" Erik asked with a smirk on his face.

"Ha, ha. You know the story," I replied, trying to lead us further away from the realization Kit and I had just had. There was so much more we needed to discuss, and we had been cut horribly short.

"Hon, why don't you go help the Scotsman that you are now so enthralled with so we don't look like poor house guests," Kit encouraged. I started to object, but she shot me a look and I closed my mouth. Erik got up.

"Okay, I can take the hint. I interrupted something. You girls finish up though, I think I heard the kids rustling about and they will not be so forgiving," he said and sauntered back into the house.

Kit stared at her paper she had quickly folded into her lap. "What. Was. That." She said quietly.

"That was my new favorite exercise for when I am trying to get to the bottom of something I don't understand. Nine times out of ten it is immeasurably helpful."

"Ya think?" she mused, looking up at me, still clearly bewildered. "Where did you learn that?"

"Listen, we clearly have more to uncover for you, but we are out of time right now. Let's put a pin in this and try to come back to it tonight after everyone goes to sleep. Okay?" I encouraged as I could hear the kiddos making their presence known inside already. Kit looked up to the house and sighed.

"Alright. You're right. Damn, sometimes I wish we were back on our own traversing the countryside. It was so much easier...in a way," she added guiltily as she looked at her adoring family.

"I know. I get it. Holy Shit. This is huge," I said excitedly. Kit looked at me.

"And we didn't even get to your dream yet!" she replied.

"Who said it was a dream?" I raised one eyebrow.

Blue lotus tea.

Chapter 12 – Josephine, June 1911

I woke the next morning with a heaviness I could not identify. My head was cloudy and I tried desperately to wipe away the fog so I could remember why I felt this way.

There was a knock on the door which startled me. A flood of memories hit me then: leaving the ballroom, Oscar coming to check on me—which gave me a warm feeling—and then his mother coming to check on us, which quickly squashed the sensation. Then Oscar leaving to go back inside, leaving me outside with her. Her accusation that I was up to something, and then her self-satisfied demeanor the rest of the evening.

No wonder I fell asleep so quickly last night, for wont of forgetting the whole evening's events. I slowly swung out of bed so I could answer the door. There had been a second, more enthusiastic knock this time. As I passed by the chaise with my gorgeous gown draped over it, I smiled sadly. I had such hopes for the evening being dressed as I was. Of course she would have ruined them.

I answered the door to find Alice standing there with another silver tray. The smell of English Breakfast tea, fresh scones, and clotted cream wafted into my room... and I instantly lost my appetite. How could I possibly eat after last night's revelations? Oscar finally learned who I was, and yet not in any way I would have preferred. And had we almost touched hands? I rubbed the sleep from my eyes at the thought. I must be conflating my dreams with the waking world.

Alice breezed in past me, not waiting any longer for an invitation, closing the door behind with her foot. She walked over to the small table by the fireplace in between the two wing back chairs and set down the tray.

"Good mornin' miss" she said, much more chipper than usual. I reluctantly smiled in her direction as I walked over to grab my summer dressing gown and pulled it over my nightgown.

"Are you so tired that I don't get a 'allo?" she continued, busying herself with preparing the tea in the steaming pot and setting out the food.

"My apologies, Alice. Good morning" is all I could flatly manage, and I sat down on the chair to the left.

"I should think you would be brimming with excitement this morning, miss, after all the festivities last night and all," she said and set to straightening my room, taking my dress to the wardrobe and hanging it.

I followed her with my eyes and tried to determine if I could truly share my thoughts with her, or if it was safer for all that I kept them to myself. She was in fact under the employ of my "sworn enemy," and I would not want to put her in an awkward position. I absentmindedly poured some milk into the teacup followed by the tea, stirring in one sugar. When I looked up to take a sip, I found Alice studying me with her hands on her small hips.

I had yet, until this moment, truly regarded the young girl. She was petite in stature, had classic Celtic hair with strawberry-colored tendrils poking out from her cap, and soft brown eyes with flecks of gold, as if they held magic within. I decided she had a fairylike quality, and given her help the night before in transforming my hair, my "Fairy Godmother" assessment may not have been that off base.

"I apologize, Alice. Last evening..." I hesitated but decided to forge ahead. If not Alice, with whom could I speak in my increasingly prison-like surroundings? "Last night did not go as I had anticipated," I said with a sigh, and took a long sip of tea. The warmth seemed to cheer me up a bit and I began eyeing the scone.

"No, miss? Are you sure?" she asked, with a slight wink and an odd knowing expression crossed her face. I cocked my head to the side in confusion.

"Why do you ask me in that way, Alice? Of course I am sure," I responded, a bit defensively. I had not even told her of the night's events and she was already so bold as to question them?

She could tell I was getting flustered and quickly interjected. "I only mean to say, miss, perhaps not all is as it seems." And she turned away to finish placing the gown in the wardrobe, evaluating the rest of the room.

"Well, as you were not there, I can assure you, they are." And then before I could stop myself, I spilled everything that happened in great detail to her. She flitted about the room trying to make herself busy, though there was not much to do since I kept a tidy space. When I finally finished, I covered my mouth, realizing all

I had said to her without gauging her comfort level. "Oh Alice, I am so sorry. I should not have put all of that on you, especially about your Mistress." At this, she laughed.

"Oh miss, never mind all that. I could tell you stories would make your hair stand on end and your cheeks blush!" She covered her mouth, realizing what she had said. We both broke out into shared laughter.

I sighed and slouched in my chair. "I just...I had hoped that I would have been able to introduce myself to Oscar in my own way, and certainly without her involved. I do not know what it is about him, but he confounds me. Not that he is mine to figure out, but...there was something about him," I said dreamily.

"Well miss, if I may..." but she was interrupted by a knock. I looked over at the door and then back to her, confused, as she was the only one who had ever come to visit me. She had a worried look on her face. I signaled her to go hide in the back corner of the room while I answered the door.

As I made my way, I heard something scrape along the floor, and saw a tiny sheet of paper come scuttling under the door, followed by soft feet retreating. I reached for the paper, bending over to pick it up, then grasped the doorknob, opening it to see whoever could have left the paper. There was no one there. I peeked my head out, looking up and down the hallway, but it was quiet and empty. I noticed the house was still; everyone must be asleep given the lateness of our return from the Palace, now that all the festivities of the week now concluded. I pulled myself back into my room quietly shutting the door. Alice came forward from the corner with a questioning look on her face, and I held up the piece of paper shrugging my shoulders.

I peered down at it and realized my first initial on the outside. It was folded into its own envelope like closure and sealed with a wax imprint. The furrow in my brow deepened as Alice came alongside me to see what I was studying. A look of recognition dawned on her face and she smiled, quite satisfactorily if I was to read her expression correctly.

"What is it?" I asked her. She just continued to smile. "Alice?" I was getting nervous. What if this was a continuation of the Viscountess's chiding I received last night? Why would Alice be so pleased about that?

"Nothing, miss. Only, as I was about to share with you, last night may not have been as unfortunate as you may think...and if that note is what I think it may be, it is proof in the pudding, so to speak," she said and walked over to the vanity as if she was going to get me ready for the day. I had no intention of leaving my room, let alone have her doll me up again. I opened my mouth to tell her as much when she hushed me and said, "Come, sit. I can at least brush your hair out from last night while you read." For being a young girl, she certainly knew how to command an audience. I dutifully listened to her and walked over to the velvet stool to sit down.

As I began to break the seal and unfold the paper, she took a brush to my hair and started. I loved the sensation of the bristles gently scratching my scalp. It reminded me of home, safety, and warmth, and I started to relax a bit. I began reading and my eyes opened wide as I realized who the note was from.

"Dear Josephine,

I feel I must apologize for last night. I have a better sense of you now, and can only imagine that you had other ways in which you wanted to reveal to me our true connection, after so diligently navigating away from the topic in front of my friends. (Which I must add I will be forever in your debt for not outing me to them!)

That said, I know how abominable my mother can be and truly hope she did not ruin your evening after I left. One can only imagine how your stay as been under the same roof with her, and I...not having taken notice.

I understand that your brother has relatively free reign to do as he pleases, which does not surprise me in the least, however I am also to understand that you have not had much opportunity to see our fair city or even, perhaps, leave your room on the regular with my mother prowling about. I wish to reconcile that disparity. If, for no other reason, than to further apologize on my family's behalf for what you have endured, up until this week, to which I understand has truly been your first opportunity at collegial frivolity.

Join me tomorrow morning as I ride to the countryside with some friends for a garden party at one of their families' estates. Before you balk, it is entirely proper as some of their sisters will be accompanying, and I have already secured my father's permission as part of your chaperoning family. I wish to rectify your imprisoned solitude most expeditiously and set to rites what I should have noticed and compensated for all along.

If you are willing, meet me in the gardens today at two o'clock whilst the house takes its afternoon respite, and we can plan your 'escape'.

Yours,
Oscar

'Breathless we flung us on the wind hill,/ laughed in the sun, and kissed the lovely grass.'"

I looked up into the mirror's reflection at Alice, realizing my mouth was agape, and found her mindlessly brushing my hair, smiling and humming to herself.

"Alice?" I looked down at the note and began reading again, but looked up to her once more. "Alice, what do you know?" I playfully demanded.

"To what are you referring, miss?" she retorted with equal parts play and demure.

"Alice, I know you know something. You were about to say something earlier. And how does Oscar, the man who did not know I existed, suddenly 'have a better sense' of me now?" I asked, quoting from the note.

Alice continued to brush my hair as she clearly began weighing her words in her head. "Oh, alright, miss. It's just too delicious," she smiled, setting the brush down. "Last night, after everyone got home and went to their rooms, Mr. Oscar called for his sherry. He has always treated me like his baby sister and as I was still up and about, I was only too happy to take it to him. Usually, I bring him his glass and he takes it with thanks and closes his door. However last night, he invited me in."

I inhaled sharply, in shock. Alice raised her hands in defense. "Oh no, miss, nothing like that! We left the door open and I only stood in the threshold so as not to suggest any impropriety." I released my shoulders again.

"He was conversational enough, which is not abnormal, sharing the events of the evening with me as he knows I love his stories. And then the questions began," she added and I looked at her, confused.

"Questions?" I queried.

She grinned. "Questions," she responded, leaving no room for error.

"Questions about what?" I wondered where on earth this was going and if I really wanted to hear it. What kind of man asked a young girl under his parents employ to join him in his rooms? At night?

"Questions about a certain young lady who he had discovered lives under the same roof as he, and by whom he is completely confounded," she said with a wink and a smirk. She let the words hang there in the air to make sure I was fully grasping what she was saying.

All I could manage was a look of understanding and, "Oh." And I felt that warm surge swell in my sternum again. I sensed myself getting flustered and moved to stand and walk. I needed to think. Or at least, not sit still.

Alice nodded her head in agreement with whatever remained unspoken. "He was asking if I had the opportunity of meeting you. What did I know about you, what had your conditions been like since coming here...all innocent in nature I assure you, miss. If I am to read in between the lines, it seemed as if he was asking out of pure concern. If I may be so bold as to offer an opinion, miss," she finished.

I stopped pacing, sitting back down at the table to grab a scone. I broke off a piece and dipped it directly into the clotted cream. Alice giggled. I look up at her, not realizing what I'd done in the presence of another. I was so used to taking breakfast in my rooms without anyone around, perhaps my table manners were lacking.

"Alice," I started.

"Yes, miss?"

"Did you read the note as I was, since you were behind me?" I carefully asked, not wanting to accuse her of anything, but also desperately wanting to know her thoughts. Was such an invitation even possible? And if the Viscount gave his permission, did that mean the Viscountess knew about the adventure? Surely, she would never agree to such a thing. She nearly had a stroke seeing us outside the Palace together and concerned over impropriety, I could only imagine what she would think of this suggestion.

"No, miss, I did not" she answered. I looked into her eyes and could see the truth there.

"Alright then. Well Oscar, has written a most gracious note and is trying to atone for the sins of his mother these past few months, referring to what I have 'had to endure.' As that information is likely owed in no small part to you, I will confide in you, his offer."

Her eyes grew wide.

"He has asked that I accompany him to the countryside tomorrow for a gathering of his friends and that he has permission from the Viscount to do so," I divulged. Her eyes looked as though they were about to pop out of her head. "So, my question to you is, given your understanding of the family, and knowing what I shared about last night, do I have need to concern myself with whether the Viscountess is privy to this request? Because if she has, it may behoove all parties for me to decline, so as to keep everyone safe...though it would be most disappointing to have such an offer in hand and not take advantage of it," I rambled out loud.

"No, miss" she answered with authority.

"No?" I pushed.

"No, the Viscountess does not know of this. Knowing Oscar, I mean his lordship, the way I do, and having seen the family interaction, I am almost certain this is not something that would have been shared with the mistress." She bit her lip, considering her next words carefully. "I feel like we would already know if she was aware, or the ask would never have come at all," she finished and looked to me.

I considered her words. "Thank you for your honesty."

She nodded and asked, "Will that be all, miss?"

I nodded back. "Yes, but you can leave the tray. I find my appetite is returning and I should like to finish this remarkable vanilla scone." She curtsied and left me be as quietly as she came.

I sat with the note unfolded in my lap, savoring the perfectly crafted scone. Alice must have had a hand in baking them this morning. I had come to recognize her proficiency in making the delectable treats even before she was completely known to me.

What would I do? Of course, I wanted nothing more than to escape the house untethered to the Viscountess and her ever-watchful eye. To do so in the accompaniment of Oscar and other people my age seemed like a dream come true. Is this not what I had been hoping for, dreaming of, and otherwise trying to speak into existence over the past few weeks? It seemed improbable that the opportunity was presenting itself now. And yet...the Viscount gave his permission. However, that did not mean that the Viscountess was unaware. While a cruel and self-involved woman, she was not without the power of observation. Would it be obvious?

I quietly finished everything on the tray, having been hungrier than I anticipated, and stood, pacing. I always thought better when I was in motion. I decided I should at the very least dress for the day, regardless of whether I was to meet his lordship at the aforementioned time.

I found myself slipping into my best day dress. A white lace blouse with short sleeves and a high collar, though sheer at the neck, with a white and black pinstripe fabric for the remainder of the dress. It had a small cinch at the waist with a bow to the side, and shorter layers cascading over the long straight skirt. It did not require me to wear all the traditional accoutrement underneath and so I could get away relatively comfortably during the day.

I found myself reflecting on the poetic quote at the end of the note. It was by Rupert Brooke, if I was not mistaken, an entirely playful and jovial of a line, that I would not have mistook Oscar for having known, let alone added. It seemed dissonant with his overall persona I had come to observe, but then again, what did I know of him? Apart from the fact that he seemed to avoid being near his family at any opportunity he had.

Before I knew it, Alice was back at the door, knocking to remove my morning tray and inquire if I was to partake in lunch. With her there, it meant it must be about quarter past twelve, since everyone who would eat lunch did so around one o'clock, and then went for their rest around two...leading me to my window of time in which to make a decision. I told her I was not up for lunch today and she left. I found myself too concerned with who I would see at the table and what rouse I would have to play in hiding the possibility of an adventure. No, best to stay in. I sat down on the chaise to stretch out.

A day in the countryside. It seemed like a dream. We left our home in Bath so many months ago. The air was so crisp and clean. The sun seemed to shine brighter. As much as the city of London was breathtaking in its own right, I did find myself more and more homesick for a place that had a slower pace and seemingly more enjoyment of the simple pleasures in life. The constant grab for the next best luxury or title just did not appeal to me. I saw myself walking through the tall grasses along a hill, when I looked up to see a figure standing in front of me. He had ice blue eyes and was reaching his hand out towards mine to bring me along with him, as if he had something to show me. I began to follow and then tripped over something in the path, which made me jump. I realized I had fallen asleep!

I sat immediately upright. What time was it? How long ago was Alice here checking on lunch? Did I miss two o'clock? Suddenly, I was acutely aware of what I wanted to do and stood up. I found the closest shoes I could put on and quietly slipped out my door, heading down the hall to check the grandfather clock downstairs in the foyer. I managed to get to the railing to squint down at it, and saw the small hand was already on two and the large hand was leaning toward five past. Would I have missed him?

Before I went rushing downstairs, I had to take measure of what I could hear in the household. The last thing I would want to do is come across someone and have to lie about what I was doing; I was never very good at it. I took a deep breath to quiet my nerves and listened.

Nothing. It seemed everyone was about their business as usual at this time of day, which was to say, no one was around me.

I slowly navigated my way downstairs and towards the rear of the house to enter the small garden out back. I quickly realized that Oscar also could have meant the Belgrave gardens up the street, but sincerely hoped he would not have meant this to be so covert if it truly was all above board.

Upon entering the garden, I did not see anything. They were not that big, so there would not be many places for him to hide or disappear into. A huge rush of disappointment filled my chest. Here I was being handed a holy grail of sorts, to have a day unencumbered by my current situation, and I fell asleep. I started to quietly berate myself for something so foolish when I heard a 'swish' come from the far corner. I stopped in my tracks. Was that a swish of skirts? If so, that was not Oscar I was about to encounter...

I felt a gentle pressure on my arm from behind and nearly jumped out of my skin. I whirled around to see what touched me to find myself looking up into those eyes. They were grinning, completely lifted in amusement and I heard a soft chuckle. I exhaled a huge sigh of relief.

"Oh, it's you," I managed.

"Well, who else could it be?" he asked amused.

"I thought I heard...nevermind. I guess I have become a bit jumpy in my current environment."

That sobered his joy a bit and he looked down at his feet. "Yes, I feel that I am partially responsible for that. I am truly sorry," he said and then looked right into my eyes to show his sincerity. My breath hitched at him looking at me so directly, let alone in such close quarters.

"It is not your fault. It could be much worse. At least here, my brother has much to keep him entertained and he gets to have some adventures before school commences in the fall," I responded.

He seemed to think on this. "Well, I am glad you are here at least. It allows me the opportunity to rectify it. I was concerned you were not going to come," he admitted.

Could I tell him I fell asleep or would that make me appear foolish? What did it matter anyway if I did appear as such? He was not courting me, nor I him. This was purely a chaperoning opportunity and he was being incredibly courteous.

"Yes, well, I was not entirely sure I should take you up on your offer. I would not want to place you in an awkward position with...anyone," I retorted, surprising myself with my boldness.

He laughed. It was husky and melodic all at once. "While I appreciate your concern for my welfare, I assure you the offer is quite above board and we even have my father's approval, as I mentioned," he trailed off, then added with a wink: "And I can equally assure you that my mother knows nothing about it, nor will she."

I felt myself grow hot and cold all at once, as if I was both melting into my shoes and freezing from a cold shiver up my spine at the same time. *What on earth?* "Well then, I accept your most gracious offer. I have missed the countryside and could use a day of respite," I responded quite formally. He read the tone and half bowed, lowering his head.

"Then it shall be done! Meet me outside the front of the house at half past seven tomorrow morning. We will leave from there."

A look of horror came to my face. The front of the house? At that hour? The Viscountess's quarters were at the front of the house, surely, she would see us. The look seemed to register with him.

"I am assured that my mother will be well in hand at that hour and away from any windows where prying eyes may see what we wish them not to," he said with a devilish grin.

"If you say so," I managed, not completely convinced. "Half past seven tomorrow morning."

"Brilliant. I look forward to escorting you, Miss Findley, for a day in the countryside." And he walked away, back the direction from which he came, fading into the background.

Suddenly, I could not wait for tomorrow morning and was willing the hours of the day to move faster so I could get to sleep and not think about the excitement of being out of confinement. I twirled around and went back into the house. Alice met me on the steps near the kitchen before I could go anywhere. She looked at me and considered the flush in my face. She nodded her head and whispered, "I will be up this evening, miss, so we can lay out the proper attire for tomorrow. We will have you ready to go, have no doubt."

She turned and walked away and my mouth fell open. Her perception continued to amaze me. I went back to the front of the house and decided to spend the next few hours in the library. A good book would be the cure for both distraction and whiling away the hours so as not to drive myself crazy in excitement and anticipation for tomorrow.

Chapter 13 – Sophia, June – Present Day

The next few days passed by in a blur. We finished our sightseeing of Inverness with a visit to Culloden Battlefield. Kit and I took all the pictures of touching stones we found as an ode to our favorite TV series. We also managed to trek everyone around to Urquhart Castle near Loch Ness, Clava Cairns, and a shopping stop at the Victorian Market and Leakey's Bookshop for good measure.

At this point, Maddy and Ryan were supposed to have joined us. However, they called yesterday saying they were going to be late because Ryan ran over on a shoot in the south of France, and they would just meet us at our next stop. We were all bummed as we had hoped to share the magic of this spot with them, but Kit and I merely looked at each other knowing full-well this was par for the course with these two.

Summer Equinox was only two days away now. We were supposed to be meeting in the village of Falkland, about two and a half hours away. Kit and I were able to persuade our crew to make the side quest on our behalf by promising them some true ocean views, and not just the inland levy kind.

We packed up the house, said a quiet thank you, left a basket of local goodies for the owners in gratitude, and were on our way. Given that we were meant to have already had an additional car in our caravan with Maddy and Ryan, and the unexpected addition of Violet to our mix, I rented an additional vehicle with which to make the journey.

Much to my delight, I secured a Mini Cooper convertible, bright lime green. Perfect to fit two people and Violet in the back. While Bryce offered to drive with Erik and let Kit and I take the Peugeot, Erik laughed at the suggestion, clapped him on the shoulder and said, "it looks like it will be you, me, and the kids, mate. These girls are on their own wavelength."

Bryce looked momentarily confused and then realized his gaffe. "Right, my apologies ladies, I was not thinking," he said, holding his hands up and backing away slowly.

I was relieved to not have to be cooped up in the same vehicle as him with all the energy from everyone else. It was just a dream, and already a few days ago, but I couldn't shake this sense of guilt at the thought of Paul and everything that came rushing back.

Soon the vehicles were packed, and we were rolling out for a drive over to the East Coast. "There's Kent, and Keen, and there's Aberdeen!" we sang as we pulled away from the cottage.

I had loaded my Spotify playlist with some Scottish "bangers" so Kit and I could have some background music as we talked. I wanted to revisit her dream and the meditation analysis that we hadn't been able to complete from a few days ago. The eagle soaring and then on the ground kept plaguing my thoughts. But my friend had other plans.

Just as The Proclaimers started singing about how far they would walk, Kit turned to me, reaching her arm behind to the backseat to give Violet a pat and asked, "Alright, what's up, buttercup?"

Not sure if she was speaking to me or the dog, I drove on, referencing Waze to make sure we were actually headed in the right direction. The boys were in front of us, and I couldn't always trust they wouldn't get distracted—or get us lost. When I didn't answer, she stopped petting Violet and turned to face me. "Hey, you."

I realized she was talking to me and not Violet, and said as much. She laughed. "Spill."

I half glanced at her, half gave her side-eye. "What?" I asked innocently.

"Nope, not falling for it. You've been off since I found you the other morning. Clearly the blue lotus tea got to you too. Spill the tea," she added, smirking at her witty wordplay.

"Um, no. We need to use this time to finish your analysis there, chica. We do not need to spend any time on my neuroses...that was the beginning of this year, remember?" I pushed back.

She was silent. Her "mom stare" was on point, but as I was neither her child nor her patient, I could withstand it....I thought.

The silence stretched on and I felt her eyes boring a hole through me. I realized I wasn't going to win. "Ugh, alright. But only if you promise me that we can come back to your meditation exercise interpretation. We had only scratched the surface!"

She smiled. "Yes, of course. And besides, you wouldn't be able to do your analysis while driving anyway. This way you can talk and drive, and I will listen and review as needed."

I sat for a minute trying to figure out where to start. It's not that I didn't want to share it with her. She had become my person in all matters, and had only elevated as such after our shared three weeks traveling this amazing country. It's just that it was a part of my life before her, and one I had locked away very carefully, for reasons that I had yet to even uncover myself. It was probably time I revisited those ghosts, but was I ready?

"Soph. It can't be that bad. Remember, we've already discovered a whole life together where we were killed protecting each other and still managed to find each other in this one. I think I can handle it," she prodded.

Man, she knew how to get to the heart of it.

"I know, it's not that, or you, it's just...a part of my life I had locked away a while ago. Locked and threw away the key. Why it is resurfacing again now is beyond me, but I don't know how I feel about it or even what to do with it, and it is super awkward given I found Bryce, and he's honestly the best thing that has ever happened to me and I don't want to lose him and..." I was spiraling now and Kit was a little stunned. Clearly it was more than she had anticipated.

"Okay, I'm going to stop you right there. Normally, I'd tell you to 'say more,' but I think in this case we need to say less. And start from the beginning."

As if on cue, the song on the radio changed to Conor Maynard's cover of "Someone You Loved," and I half-laughed half-gasped. Kit looked at the screen to see what I was reacting to and said, "okay," knowing full well I had an odd connection to music and what plays when.

I took a deep breath and launched into the retelling of my dream-slash-memory. Kit listened intently as scenes of the Scottish Highlands went whizzing past us. I got to the end of the dream, and stopped.

"So, what happened?" she asked softly, when I had paused. I shook my head.

"He left," I said. I had nearly forgotten the playlist in the background and then the Indigo Girls' "Ghosts" started to play and I begin to sniffle. How this song came to play on this list I couldn't fathom. It was the song I used to listen to on replay after him. The music Gods were at it again it seemed.

Kit turned the volume down. "Soph, I know the dream was only a portion of the story, and you relived what I'm sure was a lifetime of memories in one evening, but I also know you, and there is more."

I kept my eyes on the road and tried to focus on directions, and not the barrage of questions, feelings, memories, smells, and everything else assaulting my brain all at once.

Sensing an energy shift, Violet looked up from the little ball she had curled herself into in the backseat and rested her chin on my shoulder. She always knew what I needed. I reached back and patted her head, grateful once more to be reunited with her.

"You're right. And honestly, since a few days ago and that dream, it's like I've been living in two parallel universes. I'm almost reliving every absolute moment from back then, including all the emotions; the love and wonderment, alongside the aches and pains, while also walking in my current world alongside Bryce. To say I'm confused is both an understatement and asinine. I love Bryce. I'm with Bryce. We were brought together, as if karmically through time, to resurrect something that had been lost, and yet..." I drifted off.

"He felt like home too, and you don't know why or how it could possibly be, given your previous assertion that there is only ever one person for us," Kit finished my thought for me. I nodded.

We were silent for a moment.

"I see why you've been off then," Kit added and turned to face forward, rubbing the back of her neck after twisting so long to face me.

"What do you mean 'off?'"

"The last few days, you've been off. At first, Erik and I thought maybe you and Bryce had had a row in private, but then I realized Bryce seemed confused too, he just wasn't saying anything," she explained.

"Oh, great, so now everyone knows something is up?"

"Yes. And no. It's not like you have a poker face, Soph," she said, elbowing me congenially. I started biting my lip. "Oh, stop that, you'll make yourself bleed."

"Yes, Mom," I said.

"Listen…" she began. "It's not as if Bryce expects you haven't dated, or even loved before him. I'm sure you guys have traded all the war stories about that already. To quote a stellar romantic movie from our generation, 'A woman's heart is as deep as an ocean.'"

I groaned. "*Titanic*? Really? Don't you think that is a touch dramatic in this case?"

"Not in the least," she said. "Besides, it's true. We are capable of such depth that even most of our friends are not fully aware of all of it."

"I guess you're right. But the ocean analogy freaks me out a bit," I admitted. She gave me a look. "I don't know, I've always just been creeped out by the ocean. It's dark, it's deep, one could sink for days, and humans have only been able to explore a small percentage of it compared to other terrain, so seriously, what else is down there?" I wondered out loud. Kit just laughed. "I'm serious! I have a healthy respect for the ocean. I don't mind looking at it or being on a boat, but in it? No, thanks."

"So why then are we literally driving to it now?" she asked.

"The irony is not lost on me, but just because it freaks me out doesn't mean I don't like seeing it, or the energy it provides. " I laughed, knowing full well I was coming across as a walking dichotomy. I looked at the

GPS and we had only a few more minutes until we arrived at our destination. Thankfully, Spotify had stopped messing around playing any more emotionally traumatic songs that conjured up old memories so I could begin to settle my mind.

"We aren't done with this, by the way," Kit pointed at me as she started gathering the few things she had gotten out of her purse during the drive.

"Done with what?" I innocently asked. She just stared at me. "Fine," I groaned. "We also need to circle back to your stuff. It is much more fascinating than mine!" Kit shook her head.

We pulled into the parking lot where we would stay for our little one-day jaunt, Marcliffe. The next VRBO we had reserved in Falkland technically started today, but since we were already pre-paid, there was no rush. It was fun trying to explain where Falkland was to everyone because they immediately thought of "the Falklands," as in the islands quite far away rather than a small village near Fife. Marcliffe looked like a pleasant hiatus nonetheless, and even included mini golf on site for the kids, and special amenities for dogs. It was the perfect fit for an impromptu visit.

Everyone jumped out and proceeded to do the road trip stretch before we grabbed our bags and went inside to check-in. Making good time, we still had an opportunity to enjoy the grounds and get to the beach. While checking in, the clerk told us about Newburgh Seal Beach where we could catch seals lying around, which the kids thought was a grand idea.

Going our separate ways at the elevator, we each went to our respective rooms to settle our bags, get freshened up, and take a moment to stretch out before we reconvened to head to the water.

Bryce carried our bags into the room while I guided Violet in, sniffing everything she could reach. She was pleased when the same check-in clerk had offered her a complimentary biscuit, seemingly deciding that she liked this place. She found the offered dog bed and curled up, sighing as if she hadn't just been taking a nap on the ride here.

I ran to the bathroom, realizing I drank far too much coffee before we left the house, followed by far too much water on the drive. When I was done and opened the door, I walked straight into burly arms and a bear hug.

"I missed you," he said, holding me tight and placing his chin on top of my head.

"I missed you too," I responded, and then caught myself comparing his bear hug to the hugs of old with someone else, I abruptly pulled back at the thought.

"You, okay?" he asked warily.

"I'm fine," I managed to choke out, and walked to inspect the room and see if there were any bottled water as my throat had gone suddenly dry. He watched me as I moved, assessing my true motives. I turned back. "I'm fine, truly."

This seemed to assuage any concern. "Did you have a good ride with yer' friend?"

I didn't know how to respond to this. Was it good? I certainly spilled my heart and soul out, and it wasn't even about him. Once again, I started to feel guilty, though over what I had no clue. My hesitation caused him to furrow his brow. "Sophia, it's not a hard question…"

"Sorry, no," I said, trying to gather my thoughts back to the here and now. He raised his eyebrow.

"No, it wasn't a good ride?" he asked.

I realized my gaff. "Oh no, sorry. No, it's not a hard question. Yes, we had a good ride. I guess I always get a little thrown off when we move sites, and having my friends here, Maddy changing plans, and Violet unexpectedly with me, I'm just off my game. Plus…"

"I know. Has he emailed you again then?" he asked.

"Not yet, but I know it's coming. And it will likely arrive in the form of an ultimatum," I said. I had hoped, with my time spent with Kit this past week that we would have been able to walk through my pending decision with the university and what I wanted to do with my life; not unearth old memories like an archeologist on a dig. I moaned to myself. "Hashtag adulting, I guess. The things they don't prepare you for when you can't wait to grow up."

He laughed. "You're right" he said and walked towards me with growing purpose, as if he were stalking his prey. "But there are some good things about adulting too." And he had decided he would remind me since we were finally in a space all to ourselves.

Thankfully, I had set an alarm for when we needed to be ready to meet downstairs in the lobby. I was afraid after all the driving I may doze off and didn't want to miss going to the ocean. While we hadn't dozed off exactly, I was still grateful for the reminder.

Realizing the hotel was a bit further away from the beach than we originally anticipated, we all piled into the larger vehicle and went off in search of sand.

Chapter 14 – Josephine, June 1911

For one who had become quite proficient at sleeping in, I was up and dressed two hours before meeting Oscar. While excruciating to wait, I had too much nervous energy bound up inside of me to simply lay in bed. I had fully anticipated Alice to knock on my door and check to see if I needed any help, but she never came.

About twenty-five minutes after seven, I quietly made my way downstairs to the front hall and managed to unlock the door, swinging it open without its old hinges giving me away. I breathed a sigh of relief as I descended the stairs and was out of the house unnoticed. Then I felt a tap on my shoulder and whirled around, completely caught off guard, sure I was about to spin into the face of the Viscountess. Instead, it was a footman. I recognized him as the one that had been driving the carriage my brother and I had been using. He gave me a shy smile.

"'Scuse me, miss. Robert, at your service," he said with a cockney accent as thick as Alice's, and he gave a slight bow of his head. I wondered if there was a relation there.

"Yes, Robert?" I acknowledged his greeting.

"If you will come with me, miss, I will be your driver today," he offered and turned on his heel indicating I should follow.

Suddenly my stomach dropped; would Oscar not be joining me on the ride? Was it all a ruse to simply let me get out of the house? An uneasy feeling washed over me and I hesitated. Robert turned, sensing I was not willingly following and read the look on my face.

"Mr. Oscar is waiting for you at the carriage, miss. He likes to see to the horses 'imself before a ride to the country." And Robert turned again.

Well, that explained it. Of course he does! Why was I not surprised that the son of a Viscount should want to tend to the horses himself? I smiled and followed Robert. As we turned the corner to the carriage house, I saw him.

He was dressed in an oatmeal-colored lightweight wool three-piece suit, coat flung over the side of the carriage, with a sky-blue shirt and white club collar, shirtsleeves were rolled up showing off his strong forearms. The vest was still buttoned however, even if his paisley printed tie was loosened. His straw gambler hat was on the seat of the carriage and his raven hair had been lightly slicked back, still accentuating his slight waves. He was so fully concentrated on brushing the horse and securing its tack that he had not noticed us approach, nor me staring, thankfully. The horse whinnied and he finally looked up.

"Thank you for dispatching her, Robert," he said with a grin to the footman. They seemed to have an understanding between each other, which made me wonder how many people he had enchanted under this roof, and if that was how he was able to stay out of sight of his otherwise omnipresent mother.

"Not a problem, sir, not a problem. Though I must insist that we be off if we are to make your arrival time to Mr. Tate's this afternoon," he said. I raised an eyebrow. This afternoon? How far were we going into the countryside? I had only anticipated a couple hour ride, but if we were not arriving there until this afternoon, would we be able to make it back before dark?

Reading the thoughts on my face, Oscar said, "There is somewhere I'd like to show you first before we head over to my friend's. His luncheon does not start until half past one, so we will have plenty of time."

I continued to look dubious of his intentions. He smirked.

"Do you not trust me, Miss Findley, Honourable Daughter of Baron Crowley?"

I stared at him as I walked over to the carriage steps and he offered his hand to help me up. "I am unsure as of yet, sir," I said, took his proffered hand, and stepped up into the carriage. He seemed pleased with this and grabbed his coat, swung it around himself and topped his head with his hat. Robert took the front seat and the reigns, and we were off.

The ride was silent at first. I was not sure what one should discuss on such an occasion and was still in awe of being out of the house without a specific royal decree or my brother in tow. It was shaping up to be a beautiful day in mid-June, and I was abundantly thankful that I chose the baby blue linen day dress with whitework embroidery at the hem and along the sleeve edges. The white lace blouse merely poked out from the square neckline to help bring some delicate accent to my decolletage. I had elected to bring my large, wide-brimmed straw hat with matching baby blue satin ribbon tacked around the center.

Placing my hand on top of my hat, I tilted my head toward the sky with my eyes closed, taking in a deep breath as I did so, and exhaling slowly. This seemed to please Oscar as I heard him muffle a laugh to my side. I opened my eyes a bit to look at him.

"Do I amuse you, sir?" I asked before closing my eyes again.

"You do, in fact. I have never met a girl quite like yourself," he said with satisfaction.

"Girl? I will have you know I am almost nineteen, sir," I said as I brought my hand down into my lap and my head level with his.

He held his hands up in surrender. "Yes of course, I meant nothing by it. I was trying to compliment you is all." He looked crestfallen.

"I only jest, your Lordship," I said with a smile. He smiled back and paused.

"Please, after all this time and all you have been through, I think you have earned the right to call me Oscar."

Now it was my turn to pause. I had certainly called him by his namesake in my dreams, but to say it to his face felt premature. He sensed my hesitation again and gave me one of his radiant smiles that reached up to those ice blue eyes. I sighed.

"As you wish, si-...I mean Oscar" I choked out. He nodded his head in approval. I considered.

"I seem to be at a disadvantage," I mused. He looked confused and tilted his head.

"A disadvantage about what, Miss Findley?" he asked.

I laughed. "Well, first off, if I am to call you by your namesake, then I suppose you should call me by mine, which is Josephine," I clarified, realizing that he probably did not know what my actual name was since his mother had stopped short of using it the other night.

"Fair enough. And second?" he prodded.

"I am at a disadvantage because I believe you to have found out information about me from a mutual source and yet that same source has divulged nothing about you, so..." I let my voice trail off. He smiled again, only this one was more rueful than radiant.

"Oh, you do, do you? Well, what is it you would like to know? I am an open book for you, Josephine," he said, flinging his arms open wide.

Hearing my name spoken from his lips made my heart flutter and my stomach do flips. Why must he have such an effect on me so, and yet what was that other sensation...familiarity? My mind wandered from the task and conversation at hand for a moment and suddenly he dropped his frivolity.

"Josephine, are you alright?" he asked with concern. It was his tone that brought me back.

"Yes, of course! My apologies, where were we? Oh yes, what would I like to know..." I tapped my pointer finger against my chin for added effect. In truth, I simply wanted to answer "everything," to which I realized that would be entirely improper, and yet before I knew it, the word passed from my brain to my lips and out into the open. My hand flew to my mouth.

"Forgive me my Lord, Oscar. I did not mean to answer so boldly." I chided myself inwardly. How could I be so foolish? I really must get a hold of myself or this day would flounder, and quickly.

Thankfully, he laughed, a loud, deep and throaty laugh that made my heart sing. "Alright, that can be arranged, though I think you will find yourself most disappointed."

"I highly doubt that," I whispered. He tilted his head again. "I only mean to say that you have been a relatively unknown variable to me this entire time. I was more likely to see a zebra or an elephant up close from the Royal Menagerie than you. So, I know nothing, have been told even less, and thus, I have no expectations and could not be disappointed in the least."

He smirked at my rambling explanation and then I could tell went inside himself, likely reproaching himself once again for not having noticed me or my brother.

"And please, stop chiding yourself for not knowing. Having lived under the same roof for months now and learning more about...your family dynamics...I understand acutely why you keep yourself scarce," I said. I saw his shoulders visibly relax.

"Thank you for that. I do not deserve it, but appreciate it nonetheless." He paused. "Where to start..." he said, putting his hand to his chin in thought.

"Well, how about you tell me where you go every day, who your friends were that I saw at the Hall, or the basics like hobbies and the like," I encouraged.

"Right, then. I go here, there, and everywhere every day. Anywhere that will take me away from the house and allow me to have my freedom while it is still mine to have. I understand I must settle down and do my duty eventually; however, I am trying to maximize my ability to learn, see, and understand the outside world to the fullest before I begin to curate my inside world." I marveled at his response and he kept going.

"My friends, as you call them, who were at the Hall are essentially all acquaintances of fellow peerage families. I would not refer to them as my true friends, as they merely are entertained by my antics and how I am the leader of the group for our activities. That said, I would say a good friend of mine is Frederick, whom you will meet later today." He paused and looked down at me.

"Mr. Tate?" I asked. He nodded.

"Indeed. And as far as my hobbies, I love reading, chess, and play a fair amount of cricket when I can find a place to indulge in the game."

I was stunned at the massive amounts of information he was so willing to share in only a short time of us speaking, but grateful all the same. His direct candor was refreshing and yet so wholly different than his family. It further confounded me how he was related to any of them.

"Do those answers suit?" he asked playfully.

"They do indeed. I was just thinking about how I had not anticipated such a candid and thorough answer for you only knowing me for such a short period of time," I admitted.

"Yes, it was rather brazen of me to share all of that with you," he said. "However, there is something about you that makes me feel like I could share anything."

He sat forward then, indicating that our conversation was at a brief standstill and allowing me to take it all in.

"Robert, about how much further?" he called up front.

"Only thirty minutes or so now, sir," Robert called back.

I looked at him, and then to the sky. "How long have we been riding?" I asked.

He consulted something on his wrist and said, "about three and one-half hours, if you can believe it."

I clearly did not.

"Time flies when one is having fun I suppose," he said and smiled.

"What is that on your wrist?" I asked, peeking over to get a better look.

"Oh this? It is called a wristwatch. Wonderful achievement, is it not? A version of them has existed for some time now, but this is one of the first launched by Louis Cartier, only this year. I have a fascination with them as they are so much more convenient than the traditional pocket watch. What do you think?" he asked holding it out for me to inspect.

What would they come up with next? I marveled at both the watch as well as how long we had been riding, and yet it had only felt like a few minutes. I wondered where he was taking me.

We sat in silence for the last bit, taking in the sights of the countryside and breathing the fresh air. It was not out of lack of things to discuss, and more about being completely comfortable and content in each other's company; something that was foreign to me and yet so incredibly familiar. I took a deep inhale and exhaled with satisfaction.

"I know. It is wonderful is it not?" he asked.

"What?" I replied.

"The fresh country air," he said matter-of-factly. I nodded in agreement.

"I love London and being in the city, but I have started to become homesick and miss this," I said, waving my gloved hands in front of me. "The fresh air, the lack of city noises, the open spaces...and even as silly as it seems, the Roman baths at village center. There is something so beautiful and intriguing about them to know that we can still be connected to something so ancient and even other-worldly."

He looked at me and smiled, but said nothing. The carriage stopped and I looked around. Over to the left, I saw a great massive field with cattle grazing, and right next to that some sort of ruins. They looked familiar as if I had seen them before, but could not place how or why.

Oscar got out of the carriage and stepped to the side, holding his hand out for me to take.

"You do not have too long, sir, before we have to go if you wish to make it to Mr. Tates' on time," Robert advised. Oscar nodded.

I walked forward, holding my hand up to shield my eyes from the bright late morning sun, surveying the scene in front of me. There were, what looked like freshly excavated ruins. Then I remembered something my father had read to me and Charles a few years ago about a Cisterian abbey that had been worked on in Surrey. Founded in 1128, Waverley Abbey was thought to be the first monastery in Britain by the Cisterians from France, making it a huge historic find. I continued my pace, being completely drawn in by the old stones.

"How on earth...what made you think of bringing me here?" I asked him in a hushed whisper, not wanting to disturb the ghosts of the land.

"Well, I knew it had been a while since you had been to the countryside, and being from such a historic town yourself, thought you might appreciate the old girl," he said, as he too surveyed the structures in front of us with pride. I was at a loss for words.

"I know they are not exactly Roman ruins like your baths, however, since we were going to be somewhat nearby, I thought perhaps it would be an appropriate adventure for your first one out of the city. Stretch your legs and all that," he said jokingly. "Besides, I felt I owed it to you for a full experience. I love them, and take any excuse to come and walk around these hallowed grounds if I am ever out this way. There's something about feeling connected to history, in a time and place that one cannot get from reading about it."

I marveled. The stones were beautifully worn with age, and yet I was in awe that almost 800 years later, the main structures still stood. I think I was most taken with the low rounded cloisters that still maintained their curve after all these centuries.

Oscar watched me walk around and he seemed pleased. "Good," he said aloud and I turned to look at him. "I am glad you like them."

"Like them? They are gorgeous!" I nearly shouted. "It just makes you wonder how they could have built something like this back then without the tools and education we have today. I marveled at Westminster Abbey in the same way just the other day at the coronation..." I trailed off as I kept walking.

We must have stayed for about forty-five minutes, walking and taking in the sight before we saw Robert head our way. Oscar waved his arm up and down to let him know we were coming and Robert stopped his progress. Oscar then held out his arm for me to hold.

"The ground is not entirely smooth. I would rather you not take a tumble on our way back before we get to the picnic," he said with sheer charisma. I smiled, and willingly linked my arm in his.

It was only just before noon, and already my first day of escape was more than I could have hoped for. This man was a kindred spirit.

My only regret was the vague recollection that he was seemingly betrothed to another.

Chapter 15 – Sophia, June - Present Day, 1 Day to Summer Solstice

The evening's activities had gone remarkably well. We were able to get to the beach, breathe in the fresh briny air, and let the kiddos and Violet run around. After the drive they all had steam to blow off, and it was fun watching them play without a care in the world. Kit and Erik walked along somewhat behind, keeping their distance but remaining watchful all the same. Bryce had come up behind me to watch the scene, wrapping his arms around my waist and setting his chin on my head once again.

I stared off into the horizon. It was peaceful here. I had not been to a real beach in quite some time. It's not that I didn't like them, but the same feelings about the ocean came back to me each time I was near one, great respect for it, soothing, but also a feeling of distrust I couldn't shake.

Bryce seemed to understand my contemplative mood and didn't interrupt my thoughts, though with how tight he was holding me, I could tell he wanted to.

"I've been waiting to tell you since there's so much on yer mind with your own work and things are...well...unknown for the immediate future beyond this trip..." he eventually started. I turned to face him.

"Yes?" I cautiously asked. Something about the tenor in his voice had changed and he seemed nervous about whatever was coming next. I looked off to see where everyone had gone when he hesitated. We were alone.

"Well...I..." he stumbled, brushing his hand over his hair trying to assemble his thoughts.

"Bryce? What is it? Is everything okay?" He was worrying me now. I grabbed him by his wrists and held his hands together in mine by his chest.

"It's just ... I received an email from the university, my uni, and they're to have an event in a few weeks..." he started. This didn't seem so bad. Yet. "And I'm to be honored for my work in the department's name." He finished and looked shyly off to my right.

"Well for heaven's sake, why are you being so bashful about that? This is amazing news! Congratulations!" I threw my arms around him and squeezed his neck. "I'm so proud of you!" He beamed, seeming to relax a little. "Why on earth would you be so reticent to tell me?"

"I don't know. It's just with your situation with your job, and me not knowing whether you're staying...and honestly, you've been so off these past few days..." he admitted, sounding every bit the Scot he was. "I would very much like for you to accompany me, but don't want to put any more pressure on you."

I stared at him. Had I really been so off as to make him question my intentions with him? I had to get a handle on all of this.

"Bryce. I appreciate that, and you, for your concern. But please, in the future, do not ever hesitate to tell me amazing news, especially when it concerns you being recognized for all of your hard work. My situation is something I must figure out, and soon, but that doesn't mean that we can't celebrate you!" I squeezed him.

"Thank you," he said, and hugged me back. Turning hand-in-hand, we started walking towards the group who had begun coming back to us. "Oh, and..." he started.

"Yes?"

"It's formal. Black tie. So, you will need to find a dress if you are going." He grinned something fierce at me. I could only imagine what vision he had in head. But mine was equally as smile-worthy thinking of him in a tux. Or would it be a formal kilt ensemble?! I suddenly got weak in the knees and he steadied my hand in his grip looking over at me questioningly.

We all gathered together again and went on to see the rest of the sights in the area, choosing to eat back at the hotel and let the kids take advantage of the mini-golf.

I smiled to myself now as Kit drove to the Falklands. She caught me.

"What are you grinning about over there?" she asked as she deftly swerved the narrow streets and drank her coffee.

"Oh, nothing. Just the thought of Bryce in a dress kilt." I smirked. Kit practically slammed on the brakes in shock but recovered.

"A what?" she squeaked.

"Ya heard me," I said, smiling broadly. She gave me side-eye, expecting an explanation. "He told me last night while we were on the beach that he is being honored at his school for his work in the field, and it is a black-tie affair. It's in a few weeks."

She looked quizzically at me. "And why is he just saying something now?"

"Well..." I guess now was as good of time as any, given that we still had a couple hours until we got to our destination. "He hadn't wanted to bring it up given my own professional situation, not knowing what I'm going to decide or where I will be in a few weeks. He didn't want it to seem like he was pressuring me to make a decision one way or another."

It was Kit's turn to be contemplative. "And what *are* you going to do about your situation?" she asked gently. "With 'all the things'" she started, waving her hands around as we always did when saying the phrase, "we haven't talked much about your plans beyond this trip. I have to say I had been wondering myself, but didn't want to pry if you weren't ready."

I shrugged my shoulders. "I honestly have no idea."

She looked at me and then back at the road.

I subconsciously reached for Violet in the back and started petting her out of pure habit, my thing when I was stressed or needed to make a decision. "It's just, I love it here. I love Bryce. And part of me doesn't want to leave. Ever." I continued, petting Violet while thinking.

"But..." Kit interjected.

"But...I came over here to find myself, or at least re-discover myself, and don't want to simply get lost or diminished in my own life again. I've felt so free here, but I do miss teaching, and having a purpose beyond wandering the countryside, tagging behind a hunky guy." I smiled.

"He is one hunky Highlander," Kit mused.

"Hey, watch it," I teased and we both laughed.

"So, what are you going to do?" she pushed. When I didn't answer right away, she decided to take a different tact. "Let's look at what you do want, as far as attributes, in your life. Not specifics, but things you are sure of, that you want as pieces and parts," she coached. I could see that Dr. Kit was coming out of vacation mode.

"Okay," I retorted, "I'll play along." I thought for a minute and sipped my own coffee. "I know...that I love Bryce." Kit shook her head. But then I caught myself thinking about Paul.

"Or do you?" she pushed.

"Yes. I do. Regardless of Paul coming back into my awareness, for whatever reason, I love what Bryce and I are building. I guess my hesitation would be that..." I paused to find the right words. "That I was under the impression I was building something with Paul back then too, and then, what happened...happened."

Kit allowed some space before she spoke and then said, "yes, and while I do want to revisit that because you have yet to tell me the details other than 'he left.' Let's put a pin in that for now, as you like to say." She smiled warmly at me to show she was not reprimanding, but trying to keep me on task.

"Yes, okay. So, what else do I know?" I asked myself. "I...love being here, but I miss my house. I love the time I've been given, but I also am starting to feel directionless. I know that I miss my students and being able to help mentor and coach them, but I don't miss the politics or the people at the school." I stopped, trying to think of more.

"So, what does that tell you?" Kit asked. I looked at her blankly. "I mean, what does that tell you about options you need to consider? Build a story arc about it, miss marketer." She smirked.

"Alright, sassafras," I responded. "I'm picking up what you're putting down. I know I want to teach. It fulfills me so much more than corporate life ever did. However, if I'm honest with myself, I think my time with that school may be done and I am meant to move on. Not from teaching itself, but perhaps in a new and different place, with maybe..."

"A new subject?" Kit asked, as if she was reading my mind. I stared open-mouthed at her. "I know you too well Sophia Aitken. You have gone too far down the rabbit-hole with the esoteric and exercises to not have an interest in shifting foci. You love it too much."

"Well, I feel seen," I admitted and placed my hands in my lap. She laughed and gave me a self-satisfied grin knowing she was right in her deduction. "Alright miss smarty-pants, if you have me all figured out, then where I am going to teach? And what?" I asked.

She paused for full dramatic effect. "It's too bad you don't know anyone over here that has connections with a university that also has some pull, that could possibly find you a place within the ranks..." she said, and looked at me briefly before turning her attention back to the road.

I gawked once again. The answer was so obvious I could hit myself for not having seen it myself. Could it really be that easy?

She continued, knowing she'd left me speechless. "And it's really too bad the same person doesn't have a formal event coming up with all of his colleagues with which he could make introductions to key people who could be instrumental in getting you placement."

"Alright, alright" I cut in, not being able to stand her mock-condescending cadence. "You're right. It is too bad." I said, and she playfully hit my arm. "I will talk with him about it. Do you think he'd go for it? I mean, it's implying a lot and I'm not sure if he's ready for that kind of commitment..." I faded out, old doubts and pain creeping in.

"Soph. Anyone who has been in the presence of you two knows the man is biding his time before he proposes so as not to scare you off. He adores you. The fact that you would come to him and ask if he could help you find a position here would only show him that you are committed and will make him breathe a huge sigh of relief." She patted my hand. "He's going to be thrilled. I promise."

I went silent. Could it really be that easy? Was I ready to move my life here? What about my house? I took a deep breath. One step at a time. I had to see if he even liked the idea, beyond just Kit saying so. And could I really just shift focus? I doubt that would be so easy, but at least I could get a foot in the door with my marketing and then maybe build some workshops on the side.

Kit seemed to sense my resolve and smiled. "Besides" she added, "we're here!"

I looked up and saw we were turning into a long driveway leading up to a large white country mansion. "Kit!" I shouted. "What did you *do*?"

She looked at me innocently. "What? We needed a place to stay."

"So, this is what happens when I let you pick a place? You decide we need to spread out? This looks like each person would have their own bedroom!" I said, amazed and super excited to go exploring.

"And bathroom," she added.

I laughed and remained in awe of what I was seeing. The grounds were resplendent as I noted what looked like a garden path leading to the back of the house, and trees and shrubs lining the way.

"It was the night shot on the listing that did it for me. You could see all manner of stars, and I thought it would be quite appropriate for us during solstice," she said, putting the car in park.

I didn't even notice there was already another car parked until there was a shadow at my side window. I jumped, and saw a familiar faerie-like silhouette, with the same dark hair I saw last time. But as the eyes came shining through, they looked wholly different.

"Maddy!" I squealed and quickly unbuckled my seatbelt to eject myself from the car. Violet stood up and barked, sensing excitement.

As soon as the kids were done hugging "Auntie Maddy," she took a step back and then came running at me, as always, for her famous jump hug. Violet wasn't sure what was going on and thought I was about to be attacked, but Bryce was able to catch her just in time.

"Hiya Soph!" she exclaimed.

"'allo gorgeous!" I responded in my mock English accent. "Hi, Ryan!" I called to him as the guys were all greeting each other like old friends, even though this was the first time they were meeting each other in the flesh, not over video chat.

"So, do we need to give him the old what for like you did to me?" Bryce asked, looking at Erik. Ryan looked between the Scot and the Viking and seemed ready to run. He was a tall, dark and handsome man, but every bit his sleek English heritage, and would not have lasted long in a fight with either of these two.

Erik considered. Just as Kit sighed and was about to tell them to knock it off, he said, "Nah, he's good" and they all laughed.

We all grabbed our bags and head to the bright blue front door, a stunning accent against the whitewashed exterior.

"This is quite the place you picked," Ryan said as he admired the structure. Being that he was an architectural photographer, I could almost see him salivating.

"Wait until you see the inside!" Kit gushed, quite pleased with herself and the find.

We entered to a light and bright hallway, painted a soft yellow, with a beautifully carved table and gilded mirror, complete with a historic looking wooden chair. The stairs leading up to the first floor were painted white and covered in a plaid runner.

"If this is just the entrance, what's the rest of the place look like, Kit?" Maddy asked, setting her bags down and practically bouncing up the stairs. I looked at Kit as Thora and Tate followed, happy to have another energetic being amongst them.

"It appears we have three children now," I said with a laugh.

"Let's explore!" Ryan said. He set his bags and gear down beside Maddy's to begin a thorough search of the mansion.

I shook my head and looked at Bryce, who was just smiling and seemingly happy to be amongst this group of friends.

"You were right," he said as he took my hand and we went up the stairs.

"About what?" I asked, admiring the artwork on the walls as we ascended.

"She's an effervescent type, yer Maddy," he said. I laughed.

"Yes, that is definitely a good word to describe her. Especially since she's been with Ryan and the last time you saw her. He seems to have opened her up in ways I never thought possible..." I contemplated.

"I'm glad you are amongst your own right now. I'm sure it has not been easy being away from your home all this time," he said cautiously, nervous to express his thoughts out loud.

"No, it hasn't, but there's this great Scottish guy who has been easing the burden," I said, and squeezed his hand.

Chapter 16 – Josephine, June 1911

The ride to Mr. Tate's property was a pleasant one. Oscar and I fell into a rhythm of conversation like we were old friends, completely comfortable in each other's presence, able to talk all manner of topics. I was fascinated to learn more about him as the mystery unraveled before me. There was something I could not quite put my finger on though, that felt as if I had truly known him all along.

Thankfully, the estate was on the way back to London, otherwise I was unsure how we would still be back before day's end without the Viscountess becoming suspicious at my absence. It was not until the carriage ambled up the gravel path to the house that I recalled Oscar having said this was to be an outing with his friends and their sister's. And yet, I had not seen one other soul outside of our little riding party. Had he lied?

Just as I was getting nervous about the implications, Robert parked alongside a few others in the curved-drive in front of the house. It seemed there were too many to leverage the porte-cochère to the side, and with the sun shining as brightly as it was, the cover was unnecessary today.

I looked around and still saw no one. Oscar must have sensed my unasked question and said, "everyone is already out back it seems," while offering his hand to me to help me down. I delighted in his helping me and the frisson that passed over my skin at his touch; even with a glove on, the sensation was similar to what I experienced when I listened to music.

"I think the gravel path to be somewhat treacherous as it was in the field, Miss Findley, and I think it wise for you to hold onto me once again." He deftly took my hand from his and hooked it around his arm.

He was challenging me, I could tell. So, I played into it without reacting and said, "a fine suggestion your Lordship, but please do call me Josephine."

He seemed pleased with my response and his eyes flashed. "As you wish," he said and we continued around back where we heard voices and laughter.

Turning the corner, I was fully prepared to drop the charade so as not to leave him with questions from his friends, but he seemed perfectly happy walking into the group still arm-in-arm. No one noticed or batted an eye, which made me wonder how many times he had arrived accompanied by another in this manner. My mouth fell from the smile at the thought. He immediately noticed but then we heard a jubilant, "finally!" from across the way.

A man of about the same age was walking over to greet us, with a glass in hand, presumably Oscar's friend Mr. Tate, host of this garden party, I took the opportunity to assess him as he approached.

Not quite as tall as Oscar, but seemingly just as dashing, his golden hair shone in the sunlight. He had a playful cherub-like face with deep set brown eyes, and a profound dimple in his chin. At first pass, I could see that he would likely be a favorite of the ladies at the Queen Charlotte's Ball during "debs" season. However, he did not carry the normal aloof air about him as others in his position typically did, making him an obvious kindred spirit for Oscar given his similar temperament. He wore a light tan suit like Oscar, and a salmon-colored shirt with paisley tie.

"Miss Findley, may I present Mr. Tate, son of his Lordship Brass, Earl of Cartwright. Mr. Tate, may I present to you, Miss Findley." Oscar released my arm so that I could curtsy, but he held onto my hand to help me balance, though I needed no such support.

Mr. Tate half bowed in response, while also noting Oscar's attachment and smirked in his direction. "A pleasure, Miss Findley. I am pleased you could accompany my friend here, though apologize it must be with one so boorish as he, and you are so obviously lovely," he said. To this Oscar batted him on the shoulder.

"Come on mate, I am on my best behavior, do not go spoiling it for me before she has a chance to believe the veneer," he joked. I could feel the warmth between these two friends and I could tell their relationship was different than the others I had seen him with during the past week at the coronation events.

"I only jest, Miss Findley. Oscar here is one of the good ones. I am only surprised he has not been betrothed to another yet." At that, Oscar's smile immediately dropped and Mr. Tate cocked his head. Oscar shook his head in a micro-movement, imploring him not to continue. Mr. Tate resumed his jovial tone and said, "let's get you some refreshment. If I am to understand your tardiness, it is because you have already been on a ride this morning and could use a cool drink."

Mr. Tate took my arm from Oscar's and escorted me over to the beverage table through the small groups of people who were gathered in conversation. At the table, there were ample pitchers of tea and lemonade set about. A lemonade did sound quite perfect at the moment, and I could see my host would not be dissuaded from his current course. Besides, it gave Oscar a moment to greet the others in the group, as they were so clearly wont to do, and it gave me a moment with Mr. Tate.

"Thank you kindly, Mr. Tate. I appreciate your allowing me at your personal gathering as Oscar's guest," I demurred as he poured me a glass.

"It is nothing, Miss Findley! Truly. And please, call me Freddy. All my good friends do," he offered, handing me the delicate crystal cup filled with the freshly made lemonade.

"But I hardly know you, sir! We've only just met," I insisted.

"That may be true, but as you are a friend of Oscar's, you are a friend of mine," he mused.

"To be truthful, I hardly know Oscar either. We have only just truly met in the past few days," I admitted, not wanting to give the wrong impression.

"That may also be true, however Oscar has never asked to bring a guest to one of these parties before, so I think you may be closer friends than you realize," he said with a wink. He began walking away as he was called to another corner of the garden. "Excuse me, it seems my sister has need of me for a moment."

"Of course," I said, and watched him leave.

I looked in Oscar's direction, shocked but also pleased at Freddy's revelation and him not usually bringing a guest. Seeing that he was otherwise engaged in conversation, I looked to my left to consider the food table. I could not tell if others had begun to eat and we had missed the invitation to start, or if we were still waiting to hear it. The food looked absolutely tantalizing. Not to say anything against cook's spreads at the Carlisle's, but this was more of what I was used to: small sandwiches of cucumber and egg, cold meats of roast chicken and ham, fresh fruit, and of course Victoria Sponge cakes and pastries. My mouth watered. I looked around again to see if anyone else had a plate in front of them when I found Oscar at my side.

"I apologize for that. I did not mean to leave you on your own," he said, grabbing a glass and pouring himself some tea while eyeing the Pimm's.

I laughed. "First, I do not mind, and you have nothing to apologize for. Second, if you would prefer the Pimm's, do not demure on my account."

He nodded. "I appreciate that, you are far too forgiving of me and my wayward tendencies; perhaps we save the Pimm's for after luncheon." Then he slowly led me away from the food table and towards the original group of people with whom he had been speaking, much to my chagrin. My stomach grumbled in protest.

"And when would that be exactly?" I whispered, so as not to be rude. He smiled.

"Soon, I should hope. I too am ready to devour that table!"

The rest of the afternoon passed delightfully. I met more of his true friends, as he referred to them, people who were more at home on the country estates away from the hustle of the city, and those who enjoyed the arts more than politics. We ate, drank, and listened to each of the group member's talents. Some were well versed in prose, and read from their favorite poet's latest verses, thus helping me understand where Oscar had been able to quote Rupert Brooke from. Others had brought their violins and started to play music while we all languished in the gorgeous summer afternoon sun. At one point, I found myself needing the facilities and Freddy's sister, Veronica, practically jumped at the chance to take me.

"I am happy to show you around, Miss Findley, come with me." She took my arm in hers as if we were old bosom friends. The familiarity with which she conducted herself did not shock me so much as put me at ease. I was glad for the company.

"Well, Oscar has certainly taken to you!" she gushed as we walked through the French doors to the rear of the house and through the hallway painted baby blue, with windows lining the outside.

"Whatever do you mean?" I asked, pausing in our progress. She patted me on the arm and kept us walking, lest there be servants around the corner who would hear.

She lowered her voice. "Well first, he has not once brought a guest with him to one of my brother's soirees, and second..." she trailed off as we approached the door leading to the water closet. "I have known Oscar my whole life and never seen him this afflicted by anyone."

She smiled. I blushed.

Afflicted? That made me sound like a disease.

"I think you have the situation..." I started, but she happily interjected.

"Oh, please do not think I judge, Miss Findley. I love Oscar like my own brother. I only mean to convey that I see a change in him, and I think you are the reason," she said matter-of-factly and then pointed to the door. "The loo is in there. I must see to the kitchens and request our food be refreshed. Will you be able to make your way back?" And she was off, almost floating as she left. For a girl of sixteen, she carried herself like the woman of the house.

Stunned, I went in to relieve myself. As I wandered back through the hall, I took a moment to take in the house. It was a gorgeous rustic mansion; still with tall ceilings and outside walls lined with windows as was the fashion, however much more inviting than the brownstones in the city. The hallways were painted in a light baby blue that reflected the summer afternoon sun, making them look like the sky. I caught sight of what appeared to be a formal ballroom across from the French doors leading out to the gardens, and felt called to search further. I softly padded across the black and white tiled floor to the heavy wooden door and pushed my way in.

It was gorgeous. Parque floors that glistened, walls adorned with beautifully painted murals of Victorian balls, showing guests whirling around the dancefloor, men in white ties and women in large ballgowns, dripping with jewels. There was an elegance to the room that elevated the rest of the country atmosphere, and yet it was not out of place. I looked up to see an elaborate chandelier hanging above me. I closed my eyes and could almost hear the waltz being played. I found myself swaying to the imaginary music, and, completely forgetting myself, began to dance around the room.

In my daydream, I was in Oscar's arms as he skillfully twirled me around the room in time with the music. I could almost feel his strong frame supporting mine, until I realized it was not only my imagination in the sensation. I opened my eyes to find his watching me, and taking the place of my imaginary partner. Part of me sensed that I should stop immediately, but the other part was so drawn into the daydream I could not. It was as if I was a marionette on top of a moving platform, and I could not stop moving.

Letting whatever music he heard in his head play out, he came to a slow stop, all the while staring into my eyes, evaluating my reaction. I kept the scene going and curtsied to him in thanks for the dance. He smirked and half-bowed in return, and then offered his arm.

I found myself whispering, "that was fun!" I felt like a little girl again, daydreaming, carefree, and dancing. When was the last time I had felt so free?

"You were positively radiant," he said, almost under his breath.

"I'm sorry?" I asked, not quite hearing or understanding him.

He stopped walking just at the threshold of the room and dropped my arm. "You were radiant, I said," as he looked into my eyes once more.

"Oh. Thank you. It was silly really. I just...I was just coming back from the WC, and I felt called to this room. I let myself in and I am afraid I got carried away in a daydream of balls and gowns and beautiful music," I explained.

"Well, you carried me right with you...Sephie."

I smiled. No one had ever called me a pet name before, and I quite liked the sound of it coming from his lips.

"Sephie?" I quietly asked.

"Is that alright?" he asked, taking a step closer and intertwining his fingers in mine. I pretended to think about it, when all I could focus on was the energy coming from his fingers, and the seeming familiarity of the sensation. He looked at me expectantly and I realized I needed to answer.

"Yes. Yes of course. I have just never had a special name before...or anyone to call me one," I admitted.

"That is a shame, though I am glad to learn there is no one of import you are already promised to," he said, stepping even closer. I looked down at our right hands, still intertwined and feeling like they always would be. He took his free hand and lifted my chin to look up at him.

Ice blue. The color brought both a chill of anticipation and warmth of knowing. Before I knew it, his lips were on mine, and I was falling. Falling into the depths of that blue, and I had an odd sensation I would never stop. .

That night, as I shared the happenings of the day with Alice, I kept that last part to myself. I was thrilled to have a co-conspirator with whom to converse, however there were some things that needed to be cherished on their own. Alice gave me a knowing look, as if she deduced there was more but she also knew well enough not to ask. She helped me into my dressing gown, hung my blue linen dress up in the wardrobe—now truly my favorite dress I owned—and brushed out my hair. The sensation of the bristles only heightened my already over-sensitized mood. After she left the room, I sipped my chamomile tea she had brought, and relaxed into my thoughts. I quietly moved from wingback chair to bed, snuggled in under the covers and reflected further on my day.

As I fell asleep, I saw twirling skirts, golden parties, and ice blue waters. The music quieted and I heard someone whisper "Sephie," and I fell asleep.

Chapter 17 – Maddy, June Present Day, 1 Day until Summer Solstice

"That was delicious, thank you!" Erik said happily while pushing back from the table.

"It was our pleasure. We had to make up for missing Inverness somehow," Maddy said and threw Ryan a playful look. She had decided to make her famous vegetable lasagna for everyone since they passed a beautiful grocer stand on the way into town. She also picked up a fresh loaf of bread from the bakery and whipped up some garlic bread. She was pleased with how it came out.

She sat amongst the group and regarded everyone. The guys had fallen into easy conversation, listening to Ryan share the tales from his latest shoot adventure, and the kids had gotten up to continue exploring the house. When she turned her attention to Sophia and Kit, she was actually surprised not to find them already in deep conversation.

"I think we need more wine!" she proclaimed and got up to open another bottle.

Kit and Sophia looked at each other and then in unison responded, "none for me, thanks."

Maddy cocked her head to consider questioningly and Kit spoke up: "How about some tea instead?" Maddy was a little disappointed but shrugged her shoulders and walked over to the coffee and tea station in the corner of the kitchen. She removed the kettle from its stand, filled it with water from the stylish farmhouse sink, and set it back on its base to begin the boiling. Tea? Since when did her friends opt for tea instead of wine? Or bourbon?

She turned around and saw that Kit had called the kids back down to help clear the table and the men-folk had moved outside to find chairs and continue their conversation. Good, she thought. We have too much to catch up on and it's better they're out of the way. She joined the cleanup crew and everything was packed away or washed and dried in no time.

"Can we go play a game in the library? Please?" Thora asked while Tate nodded enthusiastically, as if that was going to help persuade Kit to give a positive answer. Kit looked at us and back at them. She must have thought we would occupy the library instead, and suggested that they grab the game and take it up to their rooms. That seemed to satisfy them and they happily went skipping out of the kitchen.

Kit looked at Maddy and Sophia. "What? I thought the library would be better suited for us. There is so much to catch up on and I didn't want to be outside with the guys!" Maddy laughed and Sophia nodded in agreement. The kettle went off and Maddy watched as Sophia lifted mugs from their hanging spot on the wall, loading up a tray to take with them to the room of inquiry.

They each took a seat, Kit in the plaid wingback chair by the fireplace opposite Maddy, and Sophia on the matching couch. Sophia set the tea tray down on the brown distressed leather ottoman and began to pour.

"What kind did you make, Soph?" Kit questioned, somewhat hesitantly. Sophia laughed.

"Not that one! I found some chamomile in the drawer," she said. Maddy thought there must be a story there.

Seeing the expression on her face, Kit clarified. "You'll see. Sophia found a new 'special' tea that she happened to give me the other night, she says by accident..."

"It was, I swear!" Sophia interjected, crossing her heart and then her fingers, raising them in front of her. "Scout's honor."

"Uh huh," Kit said. "But anyway, let's just say it has some special properties to it that bring about some interesting dreams, and leave it at that." She blew on the tea in her cup.

Maddy cocked her head. What kind of tea could that be? Maybe some CBD?

"It's blue lotus tea, before you go too far down that line of thinking there, Mads," Sophia chimed in, looking at Maddy next to her on the couch and handed her a teacup. Maddy took it, smelling it for good measure just to be sure. "Oh, for goodness' sake you two!" Sophia said, and then started laughing. Violet walked in just then as if she had been searching the whole house, and looked up at Sophia.

"Sorry, girl, no dog beds here...or are there?" Sophia said and looked at Kit questioningly.

"So, when did Violet get added to the mix? I was stunned to see her!" Maddy said, and she pet Violet's head.

"That was meant to be a surprise for Sophie. We knew she missed her, so Erik used his connections to make it happen," Kit said smiling. Man, those two were in love. It was impressive to still note in her tone after all their years together. It gave her hope that there was an example of love everlasting out there. "And yes, there actually is a dog bed, I arranged for one to be left for us when I rented the house since I knew she was coming. I will go grab it," she said.

Kit left, and Maddy and Sophia sat in silence for a bit. Sophia had a weird edge to her that wasn't normally there, Maddy noted. She seemed to drift off to another place and Maddy saw her hands tightening around the cup as her knuckles started to whiten. It didn't seem like panic, but she was clearly thinking about something.

"So...how goes it?" Maddy asked, a little concerned. Maybe things weren't going as well with Bryce as she assumed? They seemed fine. Though now she realized Sophia chose to sit next to Maddy instead of him at dinner.

She didn't seem to hear her right away, and just as Maddy was about to ask again, she turned to her. "Just peachy. You?" She took a sip of tea.

Maddy evaluated Sophia for half a second, deciding if she was going to stick to that answer or not.

She determined that if there was more to it, Kit was likely getting to the bottom of it already and there was no reason for her to harp on it...just yet.

"Same!" Maddy said enthusiastically and started to pull out her phone from her pocket. Just then, they heard a "nah-ah-ah" from behind and turned to see Kit returning with the dog bed in tow.

"We're not going to start this conversation off with cell phones in hands!" Kit declared. "We are going to speak with each other like normal functioning adults that do not require the constant stimulation received from those things." Maddy smirked. That tracked. Kit watched her expectedly.

"I understand. I was just wanting to show some pictures from the latest shoot, but hey, if you don't want to, that's cool," Maddy said teasingly and started to put her phone back in her legging pocket.

"Oh, no! I think we can make an exception for that," Kit said and bounded over to squeeze in on the old couch while setting Violet's proffered bed down beside Sophia.

For the next half hour or so, they put their heads together and peered over Maddy's shoulders to watch her life pass before them. Milan, Gargnano, Verona. Then the latest with Nimes, Nice and some town she couldn't quite recall.

"Okay, I want her life!" Sophia said as she sat back in her seat and leaned into the couch while sipping her tea. Kit extricated herself from her side and meandered back to the wingback.

"Me too," Kit responded, and offered up a 'cheers' to the air with her teacup.

"Oh, come on guys, it's not all that glamorous" Maddy retorted and tried not to sputter into her own teacup as she kept from laughing. She couldn't help it. She was so incredibly happy. Happier than she'd ever been. Her friends noticed and just stared, waiting for an explanation.

"I'm sorry. I can't help it!" Maddy exclaimed, feeling a bit guilty for how happy she was when Sophia, at least, seemed to have other things on her mind.

"Do *not* apologize!" Kit interjected.

"One iota!" Sophia emphasized. "Seriously. Or I *will* have to pinch you."

"Okay, okay. I appreciate that. It's just, I haven't felt this happy in a really long time. Or ever. It feels like this huge weight has been lifted, one that had been on me for...I don't know how long, and I just feel..." Maddy stopped to find the right word.

"Relieved?" Kit guessed. She'd always had an uncanny ability to finish others sentences.

"Yes. That's it, relieved," Maddy agreed, and sat back sipping her tea. Kit and Sophia gave each other a knowing look and smirked into their teacups. "Alright, what is up with you two?" Maddy asked with an edge to her voice. "You've been giving each other looks all day. Did I do something? Have something on my face?"

"Oh, settle down" Kit said in her mom voice. "We've all been feeling that way since the Spring

Equinox, you know that. We just haven't been in the same room to celebrate that change since then, and..." she trailed off.

"And it's already been interesting around here since Friday the thirteenth, so we're vibin' off that too," Sophia jumped in. Maddy relaxed after all that.

"Okay. As long as that's all it is," Maddy said, hesitant.

"We promise," Kit assured her.

"Scout's honor" Sophia finished.

"Well, then tell me all the happenings! Don't keep me in the dark," Maddy insisted.

"Do you want to go first?" Sophia asked, looking at Kit.

Kit nodded. "I think I better. It might be a bit easier to wrap our heads around collectively before we dive into..." she circled a wide-open hand towards her as if she is warding something off "whatever it is you have going on." Sophia mock pouted and Kit laughed.

"You're not wrong" Sophia agreed.

"Will someone please just start? I'm having major FOMO and need to be read in," Maddy exclaimed, and they all laughed.

"You start, I'm going to go pee and get some more hot water," Sophia said and took the tray out of the room. Violet looked up and watched her leave, seemingly considering getting up to follow, but decided she was too comfortable and lay her head back down.

Kit dove into the dream she had directly after consuming the blue lotus tea. Just as she was getting to the investigative work around some of the pieces and parts, Sophia came back in, humming to herself, and set the tray down; she busied herself with making another round of tea. Maddy was sitting, staring at Kit, completely mystified by what she was hearing.

"So, then what?" Maddy asked.

Kit shrugged. "We still haven't finished breaking everything down yet. We got a little...sidetracked" Kit said, taking the teacup from Sophia once again and sitting back into her chair.

Maddy looked over to Sophia, willing her to start in on her story. "Oh, I think we should finish up this one before we go diving into my crazy. It's next level, and..." she trailed off.

"That had better wait until the boys can't come in and surprise us," Kit suggested. So, there *was* something wrong with Bryce, Maddy thought to herself.

"Alright, so we know that the Eagle represents freedom, power, vision and connection to the divine," Maddy recited. Kit nodded. "And you found that a shield represents divine protection, faith and defense against negativity." Kit nodded again. "What did the color mean again?" Maddy asked.

"Blue also meant divine protection, peace, truth and a heavenly connection," Kit said.

"Right. So why was the smell of smoke and fire significant?" Maddy asked. Kit shrugged again.

"We don't know. We had to stop..." she started.

"Because a Viking walked in!" Sophia interjected and giggled. Kit threw a pillow at her head.

"That whole thing does give oddly specific Old Norse vibes," Maddy said. "On top of your dream and, let's face it, who you're married to, do you guys think there is a connection?" Maddy mused and pulled out her phone to look up the relevance of smoke and fire.

"Honestly, we aren't sure." Kit admitted. Sophia was silent. Kit turned to her, questioningly. "Soph?"

Sophia was reticent, but decided to speak up. "It's just..." she started.

"Yes..." Kit encouraged.

"It's just...it's all just so familiar with what I experienced with my recurring dream. Perhaps you haven't had it to the same magnitude or length of time as I had. The first-person view, the hands that were yours but not, and then what you came up with in your 'vision quest,' shall we call it, it could all fit with a past life memory of sorts. Just coming to the surface now that..." Sophia stopped.

"Now that we've reconciled the other one," Kit finished.

The other one. It had been hard for Maddy to jump on board in that particular conversation, but since meeting Ryan and opening up to other possibilities, as well as recognizing too much of herself in the hatred of her dark dream, she had been willing to lend it credence. That, coupled with everything else Zabina had told her, made it hard to think otherwise. And there was the change in her eyes too...

"Okay," Maddy interjected, "so we're talking another past life potential. How many of them can we possibly have? I mean, for all intents and purposes based on what we did resolve from that one, and what we know now, wouldn't that have been...it?" she pondered out loud and looked down again at her phone to see what had come up in the search. "Jesus H Christ!" she exclaimed looking at her screen.

"What?" Kit and Sophie asked in unison.

"Get this. I wasn't being rude in getting my phone," Maddy continued and gave Kit the side-eye. "I was merely looking up the significance of smelling smoke in a spiritual context," she finished.

"And?" Kit asked with pure interest.

"The search overview says, 'smelling smoke spiritually often signifies a spiritual presence (like ancestors or guides), a transition or purification, prayers rising, or warnings—bridging the physical and spiritual realms—though it can also represent past struggles or unfinished business, with interpretations varying from messages of comfort to omens, and sometimes linked to the power of God, often connecting to fire's symbolism of transformation or destruction,'" she finished in awe. "That doesn't help answer my question about multiple past lives, but this certainly lends support to what you're saying Soph; something, or someone is trying to come through for Kit for some reason..." she trailed off while silently re-reading her screen.

The group was quiet, considering.

"Perhaps," Sophia began. "But, going back to your other question Mads, I also think that there could be several past lives our souls have experienced, and then when you consider the fractal conversation like what Tate could be to Kit's past life..." she trailed off.

"And now my head hurts," Maddy said and sipped her tea.

"Wow, I never even considered the fractals piece and adding that in.... that's wild, Soph. How did you come to that?" Kit asked.

Sophia shrugged her shoulders. "I don't know. It's just how my brain has been trying to understand all of it...and other things," she answered and stared off into the distance.

Just then, they all heard the pitter-patter of little feet running down the stairs from above, while they also heard big feet plodding in from outside. Kit checked her watch and they all realized it had long since gone dark.

"Momma, we know it's late, but we just finished playing Life for the fourth time!" Thora exclaimed excitedly.

"Yeah, I won three times. I had a stratergy," Tate announced proudly.

"And what was that, Sir Tate?" Bryce asked as the guys came through the door into the small space. Suddenly the room was getting tighter and tighter, and the cozy atmosphere from a few seconds ago had completely dissipated.

Tate looked up at him, "I stayed single! No marriage for me. Or kids. Did you know they're expensive?" he asked with such innocence it was hard not to smile. The group laughed, the guys all gave each other knowing looks, and Kit glanced at Erik with a grin.

"Why yes, dear, I think we kind of had an inkling..." letting her words trail off.

"Momma, can we stay up for a little longer? Please?" Thora begged, with a slight whine to her voice. Anyone who knew children could tell it was the sound of exhaustion creeping in. Erik looked at Kit, the group sitting around the tea tray, and back to the kids. Before Kit could even open her mouth to respond, he did for her.

"Not tonight, little love" he answered and caught her eye as she was about to protest. "We've had a long couple of days of travel and it would be good to get your rest. Plus, Mommy and her friends are still catching up, and we want to give them some privacy." Erik finished. Kit mouthed a 'thank you' to him and he bobbed his head.

"Can Uncle Bryce and Mr. Ryan help put us to bed then?" Thora suggested. The guys were all looking at each other somewhat surprised at the request. Erik shrugged.

"I guess so, as long as they're up to it," he said.

"Yeah! Party in my room! Let's go boys," Tate said with as much enthusiasm as if he was about to ride a rollercoaster. The group all chuckled following the kids out of the room.

"I think we will probably follow suit and head up ourselves afterwards," Bryce recommended loudly to the others while planting a kiss on Sophia's forehead. Ryan and Erik threw a hand up in the air as they were leaving to show they heard him and agreed.

"That was well managed by you," Sophia responded, grabbing his hand as he went to join.

"You girls clearly have a lot of catching up to do, and since each of our rooms is well equipped with a TV, the menfolk will be well in hand. Good night, ladies," he said and tipped an imaginary hat to them.

"Good night!" they all responded in unison.

After they'd gone and the footsteps on the stairs were silent, they all looked at each other. There was a notable shift in the air of the room, not only now that the larger group was gone again, but that the conversation would follow suit.

"While I know, for at least Kit and I, our drinking habits have changed a bit, I do believe we are going to need something a little stronger if we are shifting gears," Sophia announced, gathering the teacups onto the tray. Kit nodded. Maddy agreed.

"Yeah, and why is that exactly? I noticed that at dinner when I offered to open another bottle of wine," Maddy asked.

"I can't speak for Kit, but I noticed more and more that I didn't like the way I felt waking up in the morning, and it affects my meditations, and quality of thoughts that come through. Hashtag, this is almost forty, I guess," Soph said with a laugh. Kit just nodded her head in agreement again. "I'll be right back" and Sophie left the room.

"Don't tell me she has another past life story too!" Maddy joked, turning her attention to Kit. Kit just smirked.

"No, nothing as easy as all that," Kit answered in response.

"Easy? A past life remembrance is easy?" Maddy said in surprise.

Kit nodded. "I think in comparison, in this situation...possibly."

Maddy considered this as they sat in silence waiting for Sophie's return. She came back in the room a few moments later with three rocks glasses in her one hand, and a bottle of brown liquor in the other. Peerless, single barrel. Suddenly, they were all transported back to her family room, drinking on the floor just before Maddy was to leave for her English adventure and ultimately meet Ryan. Sometimes life could stun her with the full circle moments.

Sophia handed out the glasses, placed the bottle on the ottoman tray, and quietly turned behind her to close the door to the room. Even with the boys saying they were going to bed, it was anyone's guess how long it would be until they fell asleep.

"Gosh, Soph, this must be serious," Maddy joked, trying to bring some levity to the air.

Sophia gave her a half smile. She raised her glass in a silent 'cheers', they clinked, and she started.

"It was the same blue lotus tea night," she said. "I had a strange thought as I fell asleep on the couch, and then proceeded to have a very vivid dream all night, which has led into days of living in a parallel universe."

Maddy screwed her face up. "Um, what?"

Sophia gathered herself, took a deep breath, and dove in sharing the details about the dream that was more of a memory, and how she spent the last few days feeling like she was walking between two worlds. When she finished, she took a gulp of her now iced down drink and sat looking at the glass with utter guilt on her face.

"Soph. Are you saying that you still love this other guy from your past?" Maddy asked trying to reconcile everything she had just been told.

"No." Sophia looked at her. "Yes? I don't know. I'm so confused. It is so incredibly weird to be walking along in my waking life next to this guy, who is karmically tied to me, and then be re-living my own past in the same lifetime, feeling every nuance of what that relationship was. It was like we were two parts of the same whole, and it's hard to shake."

Maddy took a sip of her drink, one of her favorite when she was with the girls, and Soph had dropped a true maraschino cherry into each glass for a little added decadence.

Sensing Maddy was still processing, Kit spoke up. "Soph, you have nothing to feel guilty about. It's not like this guy is even in your life anymore."

Sophia looked up then. "But what if, after all this, I said that...I might want him to be?"   "But you said he left?" Maddy asked. Sophia nodded her head. "So why would you want him back in your life if he left?" Sophia brought her glass to her mouth and both Kit and Maddy noticed it was shaking a bit.

"Soph...you have only said he left, but not why" Kit coaxed. Sophia let out a huge breath.

"He left because..." she started, wrestling with herself. "He left, because I pushed him away." Maddy and Kit's mouths dropped open.

"But in January, when we were in Edinburgh, you said that you only believed there was ever one person for everyone. Are you saying you think..." and Maddy stopped, looked around and then lowered her voice as she realized she was getting a little exuberant, and even with the door closed didn't want the men to hear upstairs. "Are you saying that you think this Paul guy is your 'one,' and not Bryce?" Maddy finished, completely floored.

Sophia shrugged.

Maddy sat back in her seat, clearly confused by the whole thing, then immediately sat up and forward, grabbing the bottle in the middle of the tray. "Girl, you need a bit more of this, because this just got heavy," then she quoted a favorite line from *Just Go With It*, "we're goin' in deep, y'all!" which at least made everyone laugh.

"And what do you mean that you may want him to be back in your life?" Kit queried. Sophie thought for a moment, obviously confused herself.

"I realize now, especially reliving it through fresh eyes, that what we had was real, unlike what I had been told by others at the time, and that maybe we are meant to just be there for each other now in a different way. When I say that we felt like two halves of the same whole,

I meant it, on a cellular level, and now that I'm aware of it, I don't know...it's just different."

Maddy spoke up then. "What do you mean, 'unlike what you'd been told by others?'"

Soph thought again, as she was replaying those conversations in her head. "You know, the age-old response to saying you'd found the one at that age and others not completely understanding the degree to which you felt it. That 'you're too young' and 'that's cute', so you start to believe the narrative and not your own feelings or awareness."

"So, you push them away?" Kit finished. Soph nodded.

They sat in silence again, each contemplating what had been shared and the possible ramifications.

"Soph?" Maddy said.

"Yeah?" Sophie answered, as forlorn as ever.

"You keep referring to Bryce as a karmic tie, instead of a soulmate' like it's an intentional delineation...," Maddy said, surprising even herself with where this evaluation was going.

"And?" Sophia said turning her attention from her glass up to her.

"What if..." Maddy paused, trying to find the right words. "What if this Paul guy is, what did you guys call Tate, a fractal?" she continued, which made Kit sit up in her seat.

"Say more," Kit coaxed again.

"Well, I'm only following logic you guys have shared, but perhaps there is something there with him being a fractal of someone. Possibly even a fractal of Bryce's soul from the other past life," she said, but her brow was furrowed as even she considered the convolutedness of her statement, internally questioning whether a fractal of the same soul could co-exist when the soul did.

They watched Sophia, who was now deep in thought. It seemed like gears were turning and there was about to be a lightbulb moment.

"Soph?" Kit started, ever the mom-figure. "You good?" she asked. Sophia nodded slowly.

"It's just...there's this thing I read a couple months ago that I thought was an interesting concept, but I hadn't paid any mind to it. Just took note and put it away in the vault for future research or reference as needed," she said, still clearly pondering.

"And...are you going to share with the class?" Kit asked. Sophie shot her a look as if saying 'too soon.' Kit put her hands up in a small 'don't shoot' gesture in apology.

"I don't know if I can vocalize it yet. I can't recall the exact language. It's right there on the tip of my brain, but it aligns with something Maddy said about karmic tie versus fractal," she said, her head obviously swirling.

"Soul tie?" Maddy asked. Kit and Sophia stopped and looked at her.

"Where on earth did you come up with that phrase?" Kit asked, looking impressed.

"I don't know, it just popped in my head. Almost like I heard it but no one was speaking," she said matter-of-factly, and took the last sip of her drink.

"Huh. Soul tie…" Sophia considered. What on earth did that mean? She thought.

They each decided that their brains had had enough catching up for one evening and took the glasses and bottle back to the kitchen. They silently climbed the stairs and whispered their good nights to each other.

After Maddy had gotten ready for bed and snuggled into Ryan's side, she lay there, thinking: soul tie. I'm not sure what that is, but it sounds interesting. But where did I get that from?

As she fell asleep, she could see Zabina sitting in front of her at her small round table in her shop, pulling cards and seemingly hearing things from the beyond. Zabina, the kind lady who had read her tarot cards and helped her begin to lift a veil she hadn't known she wore, looked up and smiled at her, as if she saw her there in front of her, plain as day. Maddy had a thought enter her head, and Zabina simply started nodding to her.

Chapter 18 – Oscar, June 1911 – Summer Solstice/Saint John's Day

Oscar had never been one to give into the fanciful, or believe in much, but he had a growing appreciation for what had transpired this week, and the apparent magic it held. For how else could he explain Josephine?

It was a bold step to truncate her name to Sephie this afternoon, and yet it had felt so right. He had only just met the girl and figured out who she was, but there was an almost immediate connection that he could not explain. She had seemingly bewitched him, in a way that no other person or interest of his had done before.

Sephie was a true marvel. How anyone could have survived under the same roof with his mother for a straight week, let alone six months, was beyond him, and yet here she was. Still blooming as beautifully as the red roses in their back garden, and more intriguing than anyone his mother had tried to entangle him with thus far.

The rest of the summer solstice gathering had gone as planned. Freddy was never one for not celebrating the unconventional, and he had gathered quite the group of non-traditionalists. The music, the poetry, the food...it had been the perfect St. John's day to spend with Josephine, allowing her time away from the house. She had taken to the Abbey far better than he could have hoped. Even their carriage ride back was a balance of thoughtful conversation and silent appreciation. There was a kindred comradery that was hovering just at the surface he could not ignore.

He wanted more days like that. He needed more days like that. Suddenly, he couldn't imagine not having more days like that, and urgently needed to plan them out. He rang downstairs for his nightly sherry, hoping Alice would take the sign and be the one to deliver it to him. He required a co-conspirator in all of this if it was to work. He looked at the time, he really should try to speak with his father this evening about his mother's obvious plot, but he also needed to design his own. The conversation with his father would have to wait.

True to form, Alice was the one who knocked on his door, delivering his nightcap. They smiled at each other with Cheshire cat-like grins. Good, she must have already been to see Josephine, which meant she knew her perspective on how the day went. He asked Alice to come just inside the doorway as she had before, while he took his glass and proceeded to sit across the way by the fireplace in his favorite well-worn, forest green velvet wingback chair.

"Your lordship," Alice half-curtsied and remained where she was.

"Alice, you are a dear for delivering my drink. I appreciate you" he said. She really was like a little sister to him, more so than his own mousy one. Gertrude had been under his mother's thumb for so long that any hope he had of a shared sibling spirit had been crushed long ago, and he could not allow the same to happen to him.

"I assume you have already helped Jo…Miss Findley…prepare for bed this evening?" he cautiously inquired, and took a sip of the dark ruby liquid.

"I have, my Lord" she said with a small smile, but did not offer more.

Slightly vexed that he would have to pull information out of her, he prodded: "And?"

"What, my Lord?" she innocently asked, knowing she held all the cards. He just stayed quiet and looked at her. When it was clear she would be better at this repartee than he, he sighed.

"How did you find her mood, then?" he asked.

"Oh, that!" she exclaimed as if she had not known what he was asking. He laughed. She would be great fun for anyone who could match wits. She smiled. "I found her to be quite pleased with spending the day in the countryside and away from the city, my Lord. The fresh air did her good, both for her spirits and her coloring. I was afraid she was going to become translucent had she stayed inside for much longer, sir."

Now we were getting somewhere, though the more excited she spoke, the stronger her cockney accent became, and it took him a bit to completely decipher what she was saying.

"I'm glad to hear it" he said, nodding his head. "I'm very glad to hear it."

"It could also be the energy around Midsummer's Day and the summer solstice though," she said, under her breath and almost inaudibly.

"What did you say, Alice?" he asked, staring at her now.

"Oh, nothing, sir. It is only fancy I speak of. Nothing your lordship would prefer," she said, starting to blush.

"No, no," he said quickly, now wanting to know everything she had to say. What would Alice know about this day? "Continue. What were you saying about Midsummer?" he asked. Oh, how he wished he could offer her a seat across from him, but he knew it would be improper and did not wish to cause harm to her reputation.

She seemed to consider how much she should share, or if she should at all.

"It is alright, Alice. I promise. I was just contemplating the goings-on this week and how they feel...different" he mused out loud. This seemed to put her at ease.

"Well, it is just that I was having a similar conversation with Miss Findley. She was quite familiar with Midsummer given she grew up toward Stonehenge. She was excited to have someone with which to speak about it." She paused.

"Go on," Oscar encouraged and sipped his drink again.

"Well, all I know is what me mum has shared. Midsummer, also known as Saint John's Day for some and Summer Solstice for others, carries a special energy around it for the year. It is a time when one can celebrate their 'inner sun,' and often times experience growth in personal power and transformation with understanding truth, renewal, and connection. Me mum always said it was a good time to stop and enjoy life in a way that was different from other times of year, because the turn to summer came with such joy and warmth, sir."

Remarkable. In all of his reading about different religious and spiritual beliefs relating to many different topics, he had never heard a topic distilled down to something so perfect and consumable, and from his own family's kitchen girl.

Oscar watched her for a moment as she stood there, unsure if she had said too much, considering to himself that sometimes wisdom came from the most unlikely of sources.

"Alice. You are not all that you seem, are you?" and flashed her a smile to put her at ease.

This made her visibly relax again as she dropped her shoulders. "I suppose not, sir. Though it is me mum who has always instilled in me the different ways and understandings of the world. I just made sure to listen."

"Indeed. Well, you perfectly summed up exactly what I could not vocalize, and further convinced me there is a sort of magic at work this week," he said and finished his sherry.

Alice beamed, clearly appreciative of his compliment. He placed the glass down on the small side table. "Now, whatever will we do about Miss Findley?" he asked, looking towards the empty fireplace.

"Sir?" Alice asked, confused.

"Well, if she had such a lovely day out of the house, I presume I should plot more outings for her so she can continue to get some...fresh air. As you say, it seemed to do her well and bring some color back to her. We would not want her to be unhealthy on our account if we can help it, would we?" he said and peered over at her conspiratorially.

She smiled again. "No sir, we definitely do not!" Alice enthused. She was quiet for a moment and then asked, "how can I help, my Lord?"

Oscar pondered. He knew that Josephine enjoyed, and had an affinity for, ties to ancient times. She also had made mention of her wonder at architecture. She also liked to dance and appreciated beautiful things...

"If I may, sir" Alice's tiny voice pierced his thoughts.

"Yes?" he answered.

"While I know you will want to make everything 'just so,' perhaps it is the act of having something to do, away from here, that will impress her most. Of being seen, sir. And perhaps less about the where," she offered.

"Alice, you are a true force of nature, and wise beyond your years. You are going to make some man very lucky one day, to receive your advice and counsel," Oscar said, with as much warmth as an older brother would have. She blushed.

"You are too kind, your Lordship," was all she could manage.

"I believe you are right, though I do have some specific thoughts brewing." He slapped his knee and rose, walking over to his writing desk. "What say you that we plot out a plethora of activities over the next several days. Most of which will have to be tied to the city so that 'me mum'" he intoned as Alice had about her own mother to show kinship, "does not become supremely suspicious at the uptick in activity. However, perhaps towards the end of it, we can swing another countryside visit." He felt satisfied with that. Now to the details.

"Alice, I am going to write a letter each day, with a hint as to where we are going, but not telling Seph...Miss Findley...exactly where," he added, catching himself calling her by her new nickname in front of Alice. She either did not notice, or was not about to let on. She nodded her head, smiling.

"This will be some fun, sir. Though I should mention, you will want to be quite creative in your hints. Miss Findley may surprise you with her ability to deduce information," she said slyly.

"I have no doubt, and I look forward to the challenge" he said, and he set to writing the first note.

Dear Miss Findley, Sephie,

I have reason to believe that today's adventure has done wonders for your health. I am told you once again have color in your cheeks, though I never found them wanting...

I should think that in order to keep improving upon your current state, we should rally again. What say you to meeting me by the back garden at half past nine tomorrow morning for our next adventure.

Where, you ask? I leave you with this to ponder...

Where the language of time stills so all may encounter her beauty; where a key made of stone transports one to other worlds yet truly explored, and ancient sculptures from a temple of the Gods comes to life.

Yours truly,
Oscar

"Afoot and light-hearted I take to the open road | Healthy, free, the world before me, | The long brown path before me leading wherever I choose."

He finished with an unnatural flourish to his signature that he had never done before, but chalked it up to excitement over the growing plan. He presumed with how well-informed she was about the Cisterian abbey from earlier today that she would easily deduce where they were going tomorrow. He hoped she had never been there and that he would be able to introduce her to the wonder that was the British Museum, but on the other hand, she had mentioned having come into the city often with her family. The thought at not being able to lead her wide-eyed into the amazing building made him stall for a moment, though he was not sure why. He was also unsure if it was wise to use his nickname for her in the letter, and so quickly, but he could not help feeling the sense of warmth and familiarity it allowed. He relished in it. The poetic quote was meant to be a charming extra since she mentioned how surprised she was at his first one.

Deciding he was being foolish, and obviously confusing Alice at his hesitation, he folded the letter in on itself, melted and poured the wax onto the paper, and sealed it with his crest. Handing the letter to Alice, he felt a jolt of excitement course through him and he hoped he was making the right decision. He knew the more he engaged with her, the more he would pull attention toward him in the house. There were only so many people he could count on not to tell his secrets, but he also no longer cared.

He would face entire troves of people and inquisitions from his mother if it meant he could spend another day in her presence. She was smart, witty, and just audacious enough so as to not blink at his own boldness, to make him think he had found a true partner. Not one with which he could simply co-exist, as his mother was so keen for him to settle on, but one with which he could experience life side-by-side, arm-in-arm, hand-in-hand, as they had today. He loved how he felt when he was with her, as if life was effortless. He did not have to work so hard at keeping that internal voice, one that sounded an awful lot like the screech of his mother, at bay.

If his plans for the next week held, it would certainly put his assertion to the test, and he would know…though some part of him, a very loud part, already sensed he was correct. He had never felt like this with anyone, and had always laughed at his few friends who had described this feeling, though he was not ready to name it out loud. There was something wonderfully familiar, as if they had known each other all along, or in another lifetime.

He handed the note to Alice, who was only too eager to receive it. "Miss Findley has likely fallen asleep by now, my Lord. She was quite tired when I left her and she was readying for bed. Should I wait until tomorrow morning to deliver this?" she asked, looking at the small folded paper in her hand.

He did not want to take the risk of someone finding it in Alice's possession, nor that anyone else should enter Josephine's room should she be asleep. He contemplated.

"I can keep it on my person while I sleep tonight sir, and bring it to her in the morning with her breakfast. She never goes down to join the rest of the house in the mornings and always dines privately in her room, around seven," she offered.

"Guard it with your life, Alice," he concluded.

She nodded. "I will," she said, and spun on her heels to leave the room, quickly turning back around to retrieve the sherry glass and bring it back to the kitchen.

"Thank you," he responded and walked to shut the door behind her after she'd gone.

Excited at the prospect of another adventure, he set to getting ready for bed. He began to doubt his plan for a moment, wondering if she would accept another bold invitation after having just made one. Perhaps she did not feel the same spark he had? Perhaps she was too kind of a person to have pushed back when he kissed her that afternoon, not wanting to make a scene or embarrass him in front of Freddy and the group. She had been the one to keep from mentioning their acquaintance at the ball and other occasions...

As the doubt continued to creep in, so did his mother's voice. "You should be down on your knees thanking me for such a match!" His blood began to boil. How could she be so insolent to think that what she had planned was anything close to what he wanted; and yet he knew he had to obedient on *some* level, though he abhorred the thought. Then he remembered his father. He really did need to speak with him, and soon, so as to cut off whatever diabolical plot his mother had conceived. Katerina. As if she could hold a candle to half the woman he had come to know Josephine as.

Josephine. Sephie. He had no idea where the name came from when he spoke it to her what seemed like only a few hours ago, but it felt...right. And that kiss. Sure, he had kissed a few other girls in his time, audacious as that was to admit, but he was a boy and he had been curious. His charm had brought only willing partners with whom to experience the sensation of lips pressing on each other, though he had not truly understood the hype until this afternoon. The doubt started receding.

There was no way she could have kissed him back the way she had if she did not feel something, anything, for him. He smiled to himself as he crawled into bed and settled in.

"Focus on that kiss, Oscar. And the way she felt in your arms while you danced," he whispered to himself to strengthen his conviction. She had felt perfect being held in his frame. Light, but not wispy, purposeful but not combatant to him leading. Like two puzzle pieces finding each other; a perfect fit.

The thought lingered for a moment until he too fell asleep dreaming of grand balls, dancing with Sephie in his arms, and all the warmth of the sun emanating from her...though he had a vague sense of a storm coming from behind in the wake of her gown. Like an ocean, coming to swallow them whole.

Chapter 19 – Sophia, June Present Day – Solstice

It had been a tumultuous night of sleep, to say the least. I was afraid I had kept Bryce awake with my tossing and turning, and almost went down to the library so as not to bother him, but he just kept still and softly breathing as if undisturbed.

The few times I had dozed off were fretful. I saw swimming faces of Bryce, then Paul, then ocean water, then other faces I didn't recognize. Then words were swirling around my head as if on an invisible chalkboard: 'karmic tie', 'fractal', 'soul tie.' I was going to have a headache before the day even started. I needed to get up and get my head on straight.

I slowly swung my feet out from under the covers; not entirely sure I would be placing them on terra firma. Violet looked up at me from beside Bryce, having cozied up to him in the middle of the night again. I wasn't about to fight her on it, as I knew the warmth he exuded while he slept. I patted her on the head, quietly got out of bed, throwing my trusty grey shirt on, and went downstairs.

Once again, I was the first one awake in the house, so I started the pot of coffee. The aroma quickly wafted through the kitchen and I found myself perking up. Thankfully, I left my travel backpack in the kitchen last night, so I could easily grab my journal and head outside to the back verandah.

I couldn't bring myself to calling it a porch, given the view. This mansion Kit found had sprawling gardens out back that the "porch" overlooked. Set with wireframe furniture, the dining set did not look all that inviting, so I set my things down at the overly stuffed outdoor armchair, set at a 45-degree angle to the rest, clearly looking like a throne. I imagined the guys chatting out here last night and wondered which was the one holding court.

I slowly lowered myself onto the cushion, being careful not to knock my coffee cup over that was now gingerly sitting on the ledge of the arm rest. Picking the mug up, I stared at the expanse over the rim, while breathing in the glorious steam rising in front of me. Closing my eyes, I took a deep breath in and slowly released it. Life, was interesting.

To think I would have been sitting in the back of a Scottish mansion in the Falklands a year ago, or heck, even six months ago, I would have laughed in your face. The idea of Scotland had only been a lovely dream to Kit and I, as we discovered more about spirituality and the increasingly important role it was playing in our lives. Being here, having found Bryce, after a few months of undeterminable chaos, was still stunning.

I was brought back to Kit's question on our drive. What did I want? Truly. I hadn't been wrong in my assertion about teaching, or not missing the politics either. However, upon further reflection, I think it was less about changing subjects. I still had a lot to give in the way of teaching marketing. It was more about what else I wanted out of life beyond just the job. Yes, I was incredibly fulfilled teaching young minds and helping them pave the way for their future, leveraging my own hard-won lessons, but I also was coming to recognize I needed more facets to my life. Perhaps it was about completely diving into life for myself, head first, and in an outward way, instead of keeping it so close to my vest. I was clearly fascinated by all it had to offer and all there was to learn. What was I afraid of? People thinking I was weird? That had been a common theme my entire life and I wasn't about to change now. Bryce clearly wasn't deterred by it, and had even been touched by all the possibilities himself, and that is who truly mattered.

Bryce.

We had been brought together by seemingly impossible fate, and here I was questioning whether I was actually supposed to be with him. It had all happened to fast. Was it too fast? And what did I mean by continually referring to him as my karmic tie? I had been very intentional and consistent in my language around that, even if I did not understand why. Did I not think of him as a soulmate? What even was a soulmate? And Maddy bringing in the fractal and new phrase: soul tie.

The sound of fluttering wings caught my attention and I looked out in front of me to find a crow...or was it a raven? The bird had landed on the partial stone wall, and was staring at me. Its feathers were almost iridescent in the morning light and I found myself enraptured, staring back. "Soul tie" resonated in my mind.

Suddenly remembering I wanted to know more about that word, I placed my mug down and started researching. The concept was distantly familiar, as if I had read and possibly saved something about it before, probably doom-scrolling through Instagram. I typed "what is a soul tie in spirituality" into my search engine. What appeared as a definition, or explanation, wasn't surprising, but it didn't necessarily feel aligned either...

"A soul tie is a deep, intense spiritual and emotional bond between two people, forming in any close relationship and feeling like an unbreakable connection that goes beyond the physical, often leaving lingering effects even after the relationship ends...these connections are believed to link souls, creating magnetic pulls, shared feelings, and profound impacts on well-being, with roots in religious/spiritual traditions."

I considered this. Then a new thought popped in my head so I typed, "soul tie vs. karmic tie," and read...

"Soul ties are deep, often intense emotional and spiritual bonds formed in this life through intimacy or trauma, ranging from healthy to toxic. Karmic ties are intense connections rooted in past-life, unresolved, and often chaotic lessons aimed at breaking cycles. Soul ties provide connection/support, while karmic ties are for karmic lessons, and stem from past-life, unresolved issues (karma) and reincarnation."

Huh. There was something niggling just at the edge of my awareness, but once again I couldn't quite grasp it. And where on earth would Maddy have come up with the concept? I kept reading.

"In short, a soul tie is a powerful bond with another soul that can be positive or negative, while a karmic tie is a 'lesson-based' relationship designed to help you evolve, often by breaking negative patterns."

That still didn't quite hit what I was feeling about the term soul tie. I looked back at the raven, who almost seemed to be egging me on. Soul tie...multiple past lives...soul...origin? I typed: "What is a soul tie in relation to a soul's origin?"

"A soul tie is a profound spiritual or emotional bond between two individuals, often described as an unseen 'energetic cord' that links them beyond normal relational boundaries. In relation to a soul's origin, soul ties are typically seen not as pre-destined connections, but as bonds formed after incarnation through intense experiences, intimacy, or deep connection, allowing portions of one person's essence to become entangled with another's."

That resonated, but in what context I was unsure.

So, which was Bryce? If he was either...I could see where he absolutely fell into the karmic tie camp given the past life connection, but was I ready to believe that's all he was. Was he a "lesson-based relationship"? That felt debasing even on a level I couldn't admit.

Something caught my eye in the corner of the screen, an article referencing karmic ties, soulmates and something called a twin flame. A what?

I opened my journal and started recording everything I could, up until the new phrase, "twin flame," and stopped. I wanted to dive into my three visuals exercise, but wasn't sure it could handle this. My thoughts were interrupted by the back door opening and the sound of dog feet on the stones of the patio. Next thing I knew, there was a cold nose at my arm and a tail wagging happily behind it.

"Morning, love," Bryce said as he brought the coffee pot over to me and refreshed my cup. I slowly closed my journal, though by now I was not worried he would ever pry. He was a rare breed, and I smiled at the thought.

"Morning," I replied and brought the mug to my lips with renewed interest in the strong smell and steam.

"What's the plan for everyone today?" he asked, sitting down on one of the white wireframe chairs. Watching him, I wasn't sure if the chair could support his mass, but it somehow did not fail.

"Well, with everyone having traveled over the past few days, we were thinking it could be a low-key day on the grounds, so we could prep and enjoy the evening festivities," I said, wiggling my eyebrows. He looked over at me, skeptical. "It's solstice! We have to have a bonfire and do all the 'woo-woo' things!" I said, too gleefully. Even though I hated how it sounded since others used it as a derogatory term, it still fit the situation. He looked around the expanse of the gardens and grounds.

"And where might you propose to do such a thing?" he queried. I wanted to laugh. So, it wasn't that we were going to be engaging in the energy of the solstice, but the mechanics of where to do it that most concerned him.

"Kit already thought of that. She asked the owner if it would be okay and if there was somewhere specific they would prefer us to do it." I offered checking off the list on my fingers.

"And…" he said, not quite believing we had permission, given the property. Just then, Kit walked out, wrapped in her linen robe and coffee mug in hand.

"They said we were most welcome to have a fire," she said with a smirk and Bryce raised an eyebrow. "In the firepit down by the canal, and we should have pails of water nearby just in case." We both laughed.

"Bonfire, indeed" Bryce muttered under his breath, amused.

"Well, it may not be a traditional bonfire, but we will raise the power of Ra nonetheless!" I said with dramatic emphasis. He smiled at me as he got up.

"Well, I am going to raise the power of the stove and get some brekkie going for the lot before the rest wake up and descend upon us, deciding they need a sacrifice to the Gods instead," he quipped and walked into the house. Kit chuckled.

"He's a funny one" she said, taking a sip of her coffee and looked over at me. "How'd you sleep?"

"With my eyes wide open. I didn't sleep a wink. Well, maybe one or two winks, but truly, I tossed and turned most of the night. I'm surprised Bryce got any sleep at all," I admitted.

"I figured," she said knowingly and took the seat Bryce had just occupied. My turn to glare. "What? We got pretty deep into it with Maddy last night, without many answers, and then she throws that curveball at the end. Of course you didn't sleep!" she concluded.

I nodded. Curveball indeed. "What was with that? That she 'heard it but no one spoke?' That was a new one," I said.

"Yeah, maybe she's starting to hear spirit," Kit said with a laugh, and then we stopped and looked at each other.

"No," I began. "You think?"

"It couldn't be, could it?" she asked.

"Maddy?" I finished. We just stared, seemingly sharing the same thought: Could she?

A few minutes passed and we decided that it was a question for another time. By then, we heard more rumblings coming from inside, signaling that the rest of the house was slowly getting up to start their day.

"I suppose we should go in," I waffled. Kit nodded.

"Are we still planning—" Kit started.

"Yup. Relaxing. low-key day followed by fire shenanigans tonight," I answered.

"Wonderful!" she said and we went inside.

The day was the restorative balm we all knew we needed. Galivanting around the country had certainly been fun, but also draining. The kids were perfectly happy running around, playing hide and seek over the grounds with Violet tagging along. The adults all went into their own separate corners at one point or another to nap, or read, while others were happy to congregate outside on the back verandah or in the library. At one point, while Kit was upstairs napping and Maddy was deep into fashion house research for an upcoming project with Mary, I walked into the library to find Ryan and Bryce playing chess. I didn't know why it struck me out of the ordinary, or that it was surprising he should know the game, but I guess I had yet to see him play it these past few months. It also made Paul come flooding back into my awareness, something I did not want today, so I did an about-face and walked out so as to keep those thoughts from taking hold.

Soon our "feast" of roasted chicken and fresh vegetables was done, and we were gathering our supplies to take down to the firepit for our little ritual to honor the longest day of the year. We had our floral crowns that Thora and Tate made during the day, bundles of rosemary, mint and calendula, and I had pre-brewed our infamous blue lotus flower tea for my girls, while the guys carried down a bottle of Macallister's to share. Thankfully, as was with Inverness, we had escaped the parts of Scotland known for their midges during this time of year, but I was hoping the smoke thrown off by the herb bundles would still keep any other bugs at bay.

We gathered around the small firepit perfectly placed next to the small canal, more like a creek, running through the property. As the sun set, we lit the fire, enjoying the beauty of the landscape and relaxing vibe of the day. The kids ran around jumping and playing, swinging their crowns in the air, and throwing them up and catching them. The guys each stood behind us with their arms wrapped around our shoulders watching the flames leap and lick at the wood. We all seemed to be mesmerized by the dancing fire.

I looked over at Kit, who had gone almost stark white. I couldn't tell if it was the lighting playing tricks on me or if she was actually experiencing something. My looking at her broke her eye contact with the fire and she glanced towards me, but it seemed almost through me for a moment, as if she was somewhere else in a different time. Finally, her eyes focused and when I thought she was actually seeing me, I mouthed, "Are you okay?" She slowly nodded her head, not even convincing herself, and then looked back at the fire, but closed her eyes, almost as if she couldn't bear the sight of it.

The kids started to slow down and when they were laying on the outstretched blanket about to fall asleep, I took my chance. "Hey guys, why don't we get you up to bed now. The Aunties want a turn."

"We do?" Maddy mouthed in my direction.

"We do," I answered and jutted my head in Kit's direction. Maddy hadn't noticed the obvious panic in our friend and being near the fire. While I would have preferred for us to have stayed there to continue our discussions, Kit was reacting to or seeing something that none of the rest of us were and I did not want to unnecessarily prolong her stay. Besides, the guys did us a solid and put the kids to bed last night. We could do the same tonight and let them enjoy the fire while we cozied up in the library again.

The kids did not put up any resistance, and I grabbed Kit's hand gently leading her away from the fire so she could keep her eyes closed against whatever she saw. About halfway back to the house, she finally re-opened them and whispered, "thanks."

"No sweat!" I said, keeping it upbeat in case the kids heard.

We all went inside and up the stairs to their respective rooms. Thora wanted Aunt Maddy to braid her hair before bed, and Tate just wanted his mom to tuck him in so he could read. Since I was not requested, I ran downstairs to the kitchen to make a second pot of tea and prep the tray to bring into the library. We all silently congregated in there once our roles were dispatched, and sat in silence, sipping the azure-colored liquid.

Maddy looked at me and then Kit, still not quite understanding what had transpired.

"Kit?" I called to her gently. "You, ok?" She didn't respond. "You looked like you saw a ghost out there, and given that all of us are together, I'm not ruling that out just yet," I continued with a half-smile trying to lighten the mood. Maddy stifled a giggle.

"I'm not sure," Kit began.

"Did something happen?" Maddy jumped in, trying to help coax whatever it was to the forefront.

"I'm not sure," Kit said again, almost as if in a trance. She finally looked up. "It's just the fire. When I was staring into it, and then smelled the smoke..." she paused, collecting her thoughts. "It was as if I was transported back in time, to my dream. I can't quite explain it, but I was at another bonfire of sorts, and I felt terrified. People were panicked all around me, and I was just frozen in place."

I wasn't sure if this was an appropriate time to pull our 'say more' phrase, so I just let her talk as she was ready. She was clearly processing something, and even though she had looked up in our direction, I once again felt like she was looking through us, not at us.

Maddy looked over at me on the other side of the couch, and I could see her take a micro-movement closer to me, obviously creeped out by what we were witnessing. A cold breeze blew through the room then, colder than what we should be experiencing in a closed space. That seemed to bring Kit out of her reverie and focus her eyes.

"Hi," I said, recognizing she was back. She took a sip of her tea, considered it and then set it down.

"Perhaps I shouldn't have any more of that tonight," she said, looking at it with concern.

"Okay," I said and sat still, afraid if I moved too quickly, I would set off whatever that was again.

"Who's Astrid?" Maddy asked.

"What?" I asked, turning my attention to her. Kit turned white again and nearly knocked over her teacup as she was setting it down.

"Astrid," Maddy repeated. I shook my head; I had no clue. I'd never heard that name before, but it obviously meant something to Kit.

"Where...did you get that from?" Kit hesitated, her voice shaking now.

Maddy shrugged her shoulders in true Maddy-fashion. "I dunno," she said and sipped her tea. "Why? What's it mean?"

I had never seen Kit this shaken. "It's just that..." she started, cleared her throat, and tried to regain some of her famous composure. "That's the name I heard being called in my dream, and then again by the fire."

I stared from Maddy to Kit and back to Maddy again. Maddy didn't seem to know what was happening. I replayed the stilted conversation Kit and I had that morning about Maddy in which we were half-joking about Maddy having come into an ability.

What on earth was going on? Friday the thirteenth seemed like a warning shot now with what the Summer Solstice had brought. I had been pulled into living a parallel universe of two lifetimes in the same timeline Kit was experiencing...something. And now Maddy, of all people, was beginning to experience what one could only describe as hearing spirit?

"Okay. Fun time is over. We need to find a shaman. There are too many unexplained things going on, and we need some answers." I said, rather more emphatically than I meant to say it.

"What do you mean?" Maddy asked, still confused.

"I agree. But where and how are we going to find someone out here? It's not like we are in the middle of a city center," Kit said.

"Guys, what are you talking about?" Maddy interjected. I continued, unable to stop the train of thought.

"I don't know, but Scotland must be full of magical spiritual types. I mean, it led us here and..." I was cut short.

"Guys!" Maddy shouted. I stopped and looked at her.

"I'm not sure what you two are going on about, but if it's spiritual guidance we need, perhaps we can contact an old friend of mine," she said and smiled.

Maddy? Have an old friend to contact about this stuff?

"Maddy, dear, I love you for saying that, but I don't think…" Kit offered up.

"No, you don't understand. Zabina," she clarified. Both Kit and I mouthed, *oh!*

"Exactly" Maddy continued. "And besides, now I know why she showed up in my thoughts as I fell asleep the other night."

Kit and I looked at each other. Well, alright. From what I recalled, Zabina wasn't a shaman, but at least she was a place to start.

"I will write her in the morning," Maddy said, satisfied that she had been the one to offer a solution when we had been in a tailspin.

"Great. You will write her in the morning. And then we will decide what to do," Kit replied, somewhat focused, but also partially gone into her own reverie again.

Here goes nothin,' I thought to myself, and sat back in the couch sipping my tea, wondering what was ahead.

Chapter 20 – Josephine, June 1911

I was stunned. Another outing request, and so soon? I could not imagine my luck.

Alice had uncharacteristically woken me up by entering my room around seven o'clock. She knew I preferred to sleep in during the week, so as to strategically miss the morning breakfast with the family. When she practically throttled me awake, I did not know what to say, and before I knew it, she had shoved the note in front of my face. Seeing the seal, I sat straight up in bed and cracked it open to read. She walked over to the wardrobe and searched through what I had.

Of course, I would be meeting him in the garden to go on another adventure, as if I could resist! I sprang out of bed and practically skipped over to see what Alice had chosen.

"How 'bout this, miss?" withdrawing the white pinstriped number from a couple days ago, the last time I was in the garden.

"No, not yet. I only just wore that one," I mused as I looked into the space. "Let's do…" and I pointed at another striped gown, wholly different in structure and weight. "This one."

She grasped its hanger and brought it over to the chaise, laying it out while I undressed. I slipped on the white and violet striped short-sleeve linen dress, with lace overlayed at the shoulders, and she tied the thin indigo velvet sash at empire-waist level into a tidy bow at the back.

I dutifully walked over to sit at the vanity so she could work her magic on my hair; it had become my favourite part of our morning ritual. It would only be a simple knot so as to accommodate the medium-brimmed hat with flowers around it. The way Alice could make it look was nothing short of a miracle.

"Now, miss, I recommend you finish your breakfast and tea, as I suspect you will not be eating again any time soon," she said as I walked over to the tray at my seat.

"Alice, do you know where we are going? Has he told you?" I wondered. His cryptic riddle was one I thought I had already worked out, but it would be nice to validate.

"No, miss. He has told me no such thing..." she stopped to consider. "Nor would I tell you if I did know, miss, given he wanted it to be a surprise of sorts."

"Alright then," I said, and smiled to myself. This was all just too delicious.

"Will that be all, miss?" Alice asked as she eyed me up and down to be sure she had helped with everything she could.

"Yes, Alice. That will be all. We would not want you to be found helping me in my room," I whispered.

She looked as if she would take the bait and comment, but instead said, "do not forget to put on your long string of pearls and those short gauze gloves. I think they should look nice with that dress." Then she turned and walked out, leaving the tray to pick up later once I had finished.

It was only quarter to eight. What was I to do for an hour and fifteen minutes?

In the end, it did not matter. I was so consumed in my own thoughts with replaying scenes from the day before and wondering what would unfold in the immediate future that the time flew, and soon I was grabbing my reticule, slipping on my violet shoes, and quietly walking out the door. Once again, he had chosen the perfect time for me to escape as everyone was about their daily duties in their respective parts of the house. I looked down the hall towards the music room where I heard Gertrude practicing the piano. A small pang of guilt rushed through me. Should she not be enjoying some adventure in the city with her brother as well? Perhaps all in due time they could bring her along too.

Guilt subsided, I walked to the back door and out into the sunlight. It was a bit cloudier today than the past few days, but warm all the same. I heard a familiar rustle and walked toward it.

"Good day, Miss Findley," he said taking my hand. "Josephine…" he said a little quieter and brought my hand to his lips. "Sephie," he said even quieter still after he had kissed my glove. I just stared for a moment.

"Good day to you too, Oscar," I replied, not wanting to play the same game. He smiled.

"Robert is ready for us, let us be off," he declared as we walked to the carriage house. "Have you figured out where we are going yet?" he asked once we were situated.

I thought about the clue again: *...where the language of time stills so all may encounter her beauty; where a key made of stone transports one to other worlds yet truly explored, and ancient sculptures from a temple of the Gods comes to life.*

"I believe so," I mused. "I think it to be quite obvious with what you gave me," I added confidently.

Impressed, he asked, "Well then?" fully expecting me to tell him my guess.

"Oh, I'm not going to tell you what it is!" I clarified. This astonished him.

"Why Josephine, you surprise me. How am I to know if you got it right unless you tell me your prediction?" he asked with eyebrows raised.

"I suppose you will just have to trust that I will be telling the truth," I said, and smiled my most toothy grin to match his audaciously charming one. He laughed.

"Alright then, one cannot argue with that face. I fear I have been bested for the first time," he said jovially, seeming pleased with where the day was starting.

It took about thirty minutes in the morning traffic for us to arrive at the front entrance. Much to my delight, I had been correct in my suspicion, the British Museum. I practically squealed as we came to a stop. "I was right!"

My joy was so genuine, there was no way he could have mistaken my guess for anything other than my true answer. "You are pleased then?" he asked, helping me down.

"Oh, most absolutely," I gushed. "It has been a dream of mine to see this place. My father and I have talked about it many times, but always he has too many obligations when we come to the city, and my brother would only be interested for five minutes before he would want to leave."

Oscar smiled at her exuberance. "Wonderful. I had hoped this would be amenable," he said, and they started up the stairs of the Greek revival building. "However did you guess it?" he asked.

"Well, it really was quite obvious once I took each clue at face value," I said, looking over at him. He seemed dubious. I stopped on the second stair from the top to explain. "'The language of time standing still' seemed to point to museums since they preserve moments in time for people to witness," I began to count off on my fingers. "A key made of stone transporting one to other worlds felt to me like it could be the Rosetta Stone that helped translate ancient Egyptian," I continued. "The last clue about temples and Gods took me a bit, but I eventually remembered that the Elgin Marbles are here, directly from the Parthenon," I finished.

At this point, his mouth was practically hanging open. "Miss Findley, you amaze me," he said, though as a compliment or accusation I could not quite tell.

"Is that a good thing?" I asked, dropping my eyes to fiddle with my hands. He reached down to grasp one in his and waited until I looked up at him again.

"It is a unique thing. I am unaccustomed to speaking with a female so heartily educated in the classics as yourself. Usually all they want to talk of is parties, and peerage, and..." he trailed off, not wanting to continue that line of thinking. I squeezed his hand to bring him back.

"I understand. It is why I usually keep to myself because I have found most men do not want to engage in conversation with me about learned subjects as it is considered improper," I encouraged.

He held my gaze for a long moment, considering. "Do we not make an odd pair?" He smirked at his own question. Something flashed in his eyes making them icier for just a moment, then it was gone. How odd.

We proceeded into the museum and spent the rest of the morning, as well as the early afternoon, wandering its halls. It was everything I could have hoped for, and what my father and I had discussed. Greek and Roman antiquities, Egyptian marvels including real mummies, Medieval relics, artifacts from the Americas and Africa, manuscripts of gospels and novels...it was all spectacular. We engaged in conversation in each hall, testing what the other knew. It was interesting to note that if one of us lacked in a certain subject, the other balanced it. We truly were a complementary pair.

At the conclusion, when we felt we could not possibly absorb anymore, I started walking slowly. While I was ready to be done with the museum, at least for today, I was not ready to go back to the house. Oscar must have sensed my hesitation.

"Care to join me for an afternoon tea?" he asked and offered his arm as we descended the stairs. I lit up.

"Tea would be splendid, thank you," I told him, and we walked towards Robert who had sensed his master approaching. I tried to think of where we could go. I believe I had heard of the Hotel Russell, but then panic struck as I thought about who might be there and see us out together. Once again seemingly reading my every thought, Oscar jumped in.

"Let's go to Bloomsbury, Robert. Kardomah tea rooms or something of the like, I should think would suit our needs," he instructed. I looked at him a bit confused.

"As you wish, sir," Robert replied and took off into the throng of traffic around the square. Oscar turned to me.

"I presume your stricken look was realizing that if we went to the nearby Hotel Russell, we would not only be seen, but questioned, and it would sooner or later get back to my omnipresent mother that we were out and about?" he asked. I nodded my head. "I felt going to Bloomsbury into a more regular tea room may provide us some cover and be less conspicuous to my mother's friends. Should we be seen there, it would only be as happenstance as 'the Viscountess's son would never be seen in a chain establishment such as *that*'" he said in a mock snobbish tone, finished with nose in the air for added effect. I laughed, and marveled at how well he could predict his mother's actions, almost as if they shared an equally calculating mind. I shook the alarming thought from my head.

"You really do think of everything. Thank you," I said with pure gratitude.

"Not to worry!" he responded.

"No, I mean it. You have truly thought of everything and been so incredibly gracious over the past couple of days. These adventures have renewed my spirit and I appreciate the lengths to which you probably have to go to conceal them. It does not go unnoticed," I said and looked down at my hands fidgeting in my lap. When had I become such a fidgeter? Then a hand came into view and settled over mine. I looked up.

"It is my honor," he said, so genuinely it almost hurt my heart. I blushed at his kindness.

The afternoon spread was delectable, and just what the doctor ordered after a long morning spent walking the museum. It took everything in me not to shove the small tea sandwiches in my face for how ravenous I was. Oscar delighted in watching me restrain myself and even called me out on an extra petit fours, or two, that I snuck.

As we made our way back through the streets to Belgravia, a feeling washed over me that I could not quite name. Contentment? Is this what it felt like to be in a relationship with someone who was your equal? I looked over at Oscar, who was watching the streets pass us by. To think just last week, I would not have known him from the neighbor, and yet here we were, having gone on two adventures together, comrades-in-arms, escaping his mother's watchful and critical presence. Could I, I wondered…

"Yes?" he asked, eyes staying focused on the streets.

"What?"

"You were going to ask me something, I think," he said, still not breaking his gaze outward.

How in the world did he do that?

"It's only…I wondered," I started, but could not quite bring myself to the question. He turned to me, watching my face intently now. "I just wondered…why?"

"Why what?" he asked, head cocked to the side.

I sighed. For one who was so intuitive about what I was thinking, he could also be oblivious. "Why me? Why help me out of the house? I mean, we barely know each other, your family obviously has plans for you, and after the other night with your mother at the dinner…" I stopped myself from saying too much.

He was thoughtful in his consideration.

"Because", was all he answered. I frowned. "Is that not a satisfactory answer?" he joked. I shook my head. He stilled.

"Because even in all of the chaos, you saw me. It may have been as a whirlwind, but you saw me. You considered my feelings and position above your own in every situation. Because of truly understanding what it is like to live under the same roof with my mother. We are kindred spirits you and I, and we should stick together," he finished with a smile.

"Oh," I said, somewhat disheartened.

"Did I say something wrong?" he asked looking confused again.

"No. You spoke from your heart, only…" I trailed off. I could not believe I was being so brazen.

"Only…" he coaxed.

I decided there was nothing to lose. "Only I thought that perhaps there was more there, but what you describe is more brotherly pity for a long-term houseguest. I understand. My thoughts were misplaced and I grow too bold, I apologize your Lordship," I admitted and once again looked down at my hands, but decided it better to keep head held high and looked out the window instead.

There was a short, but unimaginable moment where he was not going to correct me. Then he leaned forward and took my hand.

"Sephie. Why on earth…" he stuttered, something I had not heard him do once before. "How on earth could you think that after what I just said. There is anything in me but pity. Sympathy? Yes. Empathy, absolutely. Brotherly instinct…I should hope not," to which he winked at me breaking the tension.

"But. Your parents. Katerina. The Earl…" I protested.

"Are but things to be of my past and nothing for you to concern yourself with," he reassured me, leaning forward even more, taking my chin in his fingers. "I promise."

I stared into those eyes once more and found myself swimming. No, drowning. I wanted to believe him. I could feel his own conviction in his words, but I was also not so naïve as to think that one such as he could so easily escape his familial duties. There was too much on the line, and his mother was not one to be willingly made a spectacle.

"You will see," he said in response to my thoughts once again, and sat back in his seat.

We arrived back at the house and Robert parked. "Miss, allow me to walk you through the gardens to the door," he offered and took my hand. I looked over at Oscar.

"What about you?" I whispered. He winked.

"I have a different path to take, in a different direction to throw them off our scent!" he answered with an amused smile.

"I thought this was sanctioned by your father," I practically hissed in his direction as I alighted from the carriage. He put his finger to his mouth to signal that I should quiet down.

"It is, he just may not know the frequency with which I have these little adventures planned," he admitted and then jumped out of the other side of the carriage as softly as if he were a cat. I tried not to giggle.

Kindred spirits indeed. It was starting to feel more like espionage among fellow spies.

I reluctantly took Robert's arm and he graciously walked me up the stone path through the garden to the back door. Alice was there waiting to help me sneak upstairs, should I meet any resistance. As I was ascending the main staircase, I heard the front door open and sensed a presence breeze through the house.

"Oscar, my dear boy, where have you been?" I heard the Viscount call from his study. I turned to look down and caught a glimpse of him as he walked toward the open door. He must have sensed my attention and cast his gaze upwards. He smiled as he answered.

"Oh, you know me, father, here there and everywhere," he said, vanishing into the room to carry on the conversation. I continued on my current trajectory toward my room and tried not to trip over my skirts in the process.

The rest of the week went on in the same way. Alice would bring me a note with a riddle to solve on where we were going next, and I would prepare to meet him in different locations around the perimeter of the house for us to go off to the next place. Acting as tourists in his own city gave me a thrill. While I had been to a few of the locations before with my family, I found I experienced them through a new lens with Oscar.

The Natural History Museum, where we both determined it was a "nice to have" visit but nothing that required a ton of attention. We found ourselves walking into the room with dinosaur bones and proclaiming, "and there are the dinosaurs!", and promptly walking out to go find another tea room in the corner of the city where we would not be recognized. We also went to The Tower of

London, my personal favorite. I had always felt a strong connection to that place, and a profound sadness when looking at Traitor's Gate or considering Ann Boelyn's story.

I loved the ravens and the story of why they were there. While staring at them strutting around the grounds, I further validated the assertion that Oscar's hair had the same warm vibrancy as their wings. There was also some familiarity in their eyes. With the effortless brilliance and knowing that emanated from them both, I thought they must be kindred spirits in some way. A likeness I suspected I would connect to him in my mind forever, making me love the bird even more.

One of the more interesting jaunts was the forty-five minute ride we took out to Hendon to see the Aerodome. An acquaintance of Oscar's named Claude Grahame-White was considering buying acreage out that way to start an aviation school. Oscar was completely taken with the idea that one could quite literally "fly" through the sky and wanted to witness it himself. We ran into several aviators out there, including some women whom Mr. Grahame-White had trained in his Women's Aerial League. They were most impressive, and of course all taken with Oscar, though he had not noticed. Whether because he was in complete awe of the aircraft he saw in front of him, or because he increasingly only had eyes towards me, I was not going to speculate.

By the time the week was concluding, there was one last surprise. Oscar refused to even give me a hint for this one, and instead opted for complete silence. Alice had me up and dressed just after six in the morning, in one of my best travel dresses. I could not imagine where we would be going at that hour, or why I would need to wear such a thing, but I had already learned not to ask too many questions if I did not want to ruin the plans.

At that that time of day, the only part of the household who would be awake would be the staff. They all loved Oscar, so we did not have to steal away into the carriage as we had the rest of the week. Alice made sure we had a basket packed with bread, meats and cheese, a bottle of ginger beer, and some glasses. She also snuck some of my favorite scones in, should we need an additional snack later, though I doubted they would last that long if I had my way.

Oscar pulled the curtains on the windows as we set off so that I could not see where we were going. Soon enough though, I heard the unmistakable sound of train whistles and my eyes grew wide.

"This is one of those times where you just trust me and go along with it," he said. "It will be worth it, I promise." And he smiled one of his dazzling smiles.

In that week, I *had* come to trust him. More than I had anyone in my whole life. We had become two peas in a pod, and had begun relying on each other's thoughts and opinions in a way that felt intimate for two people who only just met earlier in the same month.

"I do." I smiled, and tried not to burst out of the carriage into the chaos of the station.

I loved train travel, and Oscar knew it. We had talked about it as we discussed the merits of aviation and the future of mass travel. He believed that aviation would overtake trains. While I thought it a bold concept, I disagreed. There was nothing like being on a train. The sound of the tracks, the cushion of the seat…it was much better than any carriage one could claim to have been in, plus there was the efficiency of getting from point A to point B. Which brought me out of my reverie and back to the present moment. What was point B today, I wondered?

Oscar checked his watch and let out an inaudible word under his breath. He grabbed the basket, and my hand, and next thing I knew, we were quickly making our way through a large crowd as he called out to Robert, "Six o'clock, Robert! We will see you back here at six o'clock!"

Robert waved, and we were gone. Oscar looked around and quickly located the platform he knew we needed, and we raced forward. The train was just starting to pull away from the station. "We will have to make a jump for it!" I heard him breathe into my ear.

"Jump for it? You are joking, right?" I panted back. I was not accustomed to walking briskly in my travel clothes, let alone running. The skirts were constricting enough to make it seem an Olympic sport. He looked back at me and smiled.

Thankfully, one of the conductors had spotted us approaching and rushed to the closest stairs to help. Oscar placed my hand onto the railing and the conductor reached for my other hand to hoist me up. In one quick motion I was aboard, and I watched Oscar try to manage the same, while also carrying the basket. I doubled over laughing while also trying to catch my breath at the spectacle in front of me. After a few attempts, he made it.

The conductor patted him on the back as he was catching his breath. "Good man. I will come back for your tickets once you are settled," he said, and he moseyed on by.

Oscar, still panting a bit, pointed to the opposite car and said, "let's try in here." It took everything in me to stifle the giggle erupting from my core. He eyed me suspiciously, which did not help. I took a deep breath and led the way into the first car. We found two seats opposite each other near a window and sat down, Oscar placing the basket underneath his seat and allowing me to face forward.

"Okay, now can you tell me where we are going?" I asked. He shook his head. Disgruntled, but amused, I turned to look out the window. Before I knew it, I was asleep. Trains had that effect on me typically, the lulling motion alone could make anyone drowsy, but combined with the early hour and our race through the station, I didn't stand a chance.

Eventually, I felt a light tap at my elbow. I fluttered my eyes open, not quite sure where I was, and saw Oscar watching me. He had come forward to touch my arm, but sat back now and readied himself to disembark. "We are almost to our station," he said softly as I gained my bearings.

"How long was I asleep? How long have we been riding?" I asked

"You have been asleep for about five minutes less than we have been riding," he smirked. Clearly, he was still holding this surprise close to the vest.

I looked outside. The landmarks seemed familiar, but I could not quite place them in my sleepy stupor, and then it dawned on me. I nearly jumped out of my seat with anticipation. "You didn't!" I exclaimed, straightening my hat and pinching color to my cheeks. He just looked at me and smiled, clearly satisfied he had done so well.

Sure enough, as we rolled up to the station I saw in big bold black letters: BATH. I could not believe it. He had brought me home.

As we got off the train and started toward the queue for a carriage, I squeezed his arm in amazement. "We have spent so much time in my city showing you the sights that I thought it was high time you do the same for me", he said, looking down at my awe. I just continued smiling and holding onto this arm. "Are you pleased?" he whispered into my ear. There were no words. I simply nodded my head for fear of bursting into tears if I opened my mouth.

Home. It had been almost seven months since we had left for the city, and yet it felt like years. I missed every sight, sound, and smell that were barraging my senses. I had a grin plastered to my face everywhere I looked, and yet I knew I needed to stop, but could not.

"Good," he said, and led me to the open waiting carriage in front of us.

Chapter 21 – Kit, June Present Day

Kit was having trouble wrapping her mind around it. It was one thing to have listened to Sophia when she spoke about her recurring dream a few months ago, or even Tate as he described the same thing from the same viewpoint. But experiencing it for herself? Was she going mad?

One moment, they were laughing and enjoying the fire, Erik's arms around her, just swaying and listening to nature. The next, she was having a full-blown vision, having stared into the flames and come out the other side to a completely different world. She was once again wrapped in furs, only this time smelling smoke and seeing fire all around her, as if her village was completely ablaze. There were screams everywhere, and yet she stood frozen to the ground, not knowing what to do. It was not a familiar sensation. Thankfully, Sophia pulled her back to reality; otherwise, she could have very well gone catatonic in front of everyone.

Now nestled back in their room against Erik, she felt safe. She always felt safe when she was with him. For all the joking of his build, strength, and background, there was something about his masculinity that was unbreakable, but also soft. He was a tender husband, loving father, and fierce friend. She noticed her heartrate slow as she thought about him and started to breathe normally again, aligning with his soft cadence while he slept.

Enough, she thought to herself. Maddy will write to her friend in the morning and perhaps there are ways to find answers. If it is truly another past life, then there is obviously a lesson to be learned in it, and the only way to the other side was through. She had not backed down from any previous threats in her life and she wasn't about to start now. This seemed to provide additional peace of mind, and she was able to finally drift off.

This time, she didn't dream of herself, but she saw all the symbols from her meditation visions and then some. It was beautiful, shifting in and out of focus like a kaleidoscope. She could have floated there forever.

In the morning when she woke, she rolled over to place her hand on Erik's chest, but found he had already gone. What time was it? She knew Sophie had a full day planned and didn't want to be the reason they would be late. She swung her legs out of bed and walked into the bathroom. She could hear the sounds of plates clinking and food being prepared downstairs, so she thought a quick shower couldn't hurt. It would at least reset her from last night and hopefully straighten out her head.

She stood in the warm shower, letting the water cascade over her body and closed her eyes. She found herself speaking, whispering words into the water from another time...

> *"Freya, Great Goddess of the Vanir*
> *I call upon you for protection,*
> *Your shield and strength,*

As I navigate these unknown waters and seek a world beyond..."

She stopped. It didn't scare her so much as startle her, how easily these words flowed. She had heard of Freya in passing once or twice, but had not studied her, or read about her at any great length as she would have the Greek or Roman gods and goddesses. Yet somehow, the words flowed and brought comfort.

She finished her shower, got dressed and went downstairs, being carried by the smells of bacon, toast, and some savory dish; a quiche, no doubt, knowing her husband. It was his turn to lead the breakfast meal and he would want to surprise her with her favorite. She smiled.

As she entered the room Tate was the first to spot her. "Mommy!" he beamed. His enthusiasm never ceased to warm her heart.

"Good morning, little love," she said, looking back at him and then over to Thora. "Little loves," she corrected herself upon seeing that small, pouty face. "How'd you sleep?" she asked as she tucked in between them and pulled up to the table. Everyone else was seated, so she assumed they had saved the spot for her.

"Good!" Tate responded, then realizing his volume might be a too much, he repeated himself in a more hushed tone.

"Okay, I guess," Thora said, playing with the tag on her napkin. Ever since she was a baby, she had a thing for playing with tags, no matter where she found them.

"Why just 'I guess?'" Kit asked, patting some stray hairs down on the back of her head.

"'Cause Tate was talking in his sleep again. He never shuts up during the day. You would think he might when he's sleeping, but *no*..." she said.

It was going to be a long day if she was already this cranky.

"Nah-uh, no I didn't!" Tate shot back. "Besides, how would you know, we aren't even in the same room!" He looked pleased with his defense.

"Well, if it wasn't you, then there is some other annoying little boy in this house at night that is talking up a storm..." she said, not super convinced herself.

Knowing exactly when to step in, Kit said, "Well I'm sure it's nothing that Daddy's breakfast can't fix, right, my darling?" She gave Thora a sympathetic look. This softened her immediately and she nodded her head.

"Here, here!" added Ryan, who seemed to be eager to fight the kids for the first morsels. "It smells divine, old chap!" Everyone laughed and settled in.

Erik walked the fresh quiche over to set a slice in front of Kit first and gave her a small kiss on the tip of her nose.

"Awwww," Sophie and Maddy trilled in unison.

"Oy, you're making us look bad, mate," said Bryce. "Cut it out!"

"I have to get my brownie points same as you gents," Erik said, and moved on to the kids to serve them next. Everyone else dug in to grab strips of bacon and toast for their plate, and Sophie started to pass the orange juice.

"Fresh squeezed," Maddy said with a smirk. "Found that at the grocer stand on the way in, too!"

"Right now, I just need caffeine. Stat." Kit said, looking around for the pot. Sophie got up to retrieve it from behind her. "No, Soph, I can manage!" but before she could finish her sentence, it was passed over to her and her mug was filled.

"So, what's on the docket for today?" Ryan asked in between bites.

Everyone looked at Sophie who was trying to finish the bite of bacon and toast she had just shoved in her mouth. She held up her finger to indicate that they should give her a moment. She swallowed. "Well, there is a great hike we can do that takes us on a loop around one of the Lomond Hills and behind a waterfall!" she said, excitedly trying to amp up the kids for a hike versus all the castles they'd been seeing. "There may even be a deep dark tunnel option if we're lucky."

Sophie did know how to rivet children's attention. No wonder she was such a beloved Professor. Poor Soph, Kit thought.

"And then?" Tate asked with a mouth full of food. Erik shot him a look.

"And then I figured we could wander the 'wee village' of Falkland. It was one of the filming sites for a show your mom and I like to watch, and it also has some small shops and some of the other historical buildings around town," she continued.

"I may know a pub or two where we can get a wee dram to whet our whistle, should the need arise," Bryce added with a smirk to the guys.

"Yes, I'm sure you do," Sophie said, with a bit of an edge that bordered on concerning. She quickly looked down at her plate, catching herself.

"Great!" said Maddy. "What time will we be leaving?"

Sophia considered the clock on the wall. "Nine-thirty-ish?"

"Works for me! I'm just going to pop upstairs and shoot off a quick email," Maddy replied, winking at Kit. Both Sophia and Kit nodded their heads.

Catching the kids trying to sneak away from the table, Kit said, "and you two can help Daddy and the guys clean up from breakfast." She could tell they were about to lodge a complaint, but she gave them her side-eye and they complied.

"I'm going to get a bag ready with a few extra essentials. I'll be back," Kit indicated to Erik, and he waved her off, already in the middle of clean-up duty.

She left the kitchen and a thought occurred to her. She walked into the library to have a look at the books on the shelves. She was sure she wouldn't come across anything about Old Norse Gods, but it couldn't hurt to try. She surveyed all the shelves, but didn't readily see anything that stood out, so she walked towards the stairs.

As she was climbing, she heard Maddy ask, "Kit, is that you?"

"Yeah," she called back.

"Can you come 'ere for a sec?" she asked.

"Yeah," Kit answered, "be right there." She walked down the hall to Maddy's room. It was equally as bright and light as her own, but instead of a white wire-frame bed, Maddy and Ryan had a four-poster bed with a canopy. Another princess bed, Kit muses to herself. At least she will have stayed in one room with a bed like that this trip. "What's up?" she asked as she entered the room.

"I have my email to Zabina ready, but was hoping maybe you could check it over? The more I read, the crazier I sound to myself and want to make sure I am representing the...situation...correctly," she admitted, clearly unsure of herself.

"Sure thing," Kit said. Maddy got up to let Kit read on her laptop.

Dear Zabina,

It has been a little bit since we last connected in December. Life has been a wild ride ever since, but I think you knew that was coming. To say my perspective has shifted would be a vast understatement, and I have you to thank for that. In the best way possible. My life has never been so fulfilling as it has in these past few months.

Anyhow, I write to you today with purpose. I am once again with my friends, the ones I mentioned the last time we spoke, and we are having some...experiences. We were hoping that you might be able to provide some insight for us. Would you be available to connect virtually through a meeting app or video chat or something? We really could use your help.

I know you are not a fan of technology, so if it isn't possible, I understand, but I just didn't know who else I could ask. We are in the middle of seemingly nowhere in Scotland (Fife/Falkland), and I had to take a chance.

I hope to hear from you soon. Thank you again for all you have done for me. I don't know if I will ever be able to repay you.

Hugs,
Maddy

Kit smiled. It was so Maddy that it was hard to edit any of it. There was a sincere urgency in the undertone too that wasn't overt, but if Zabina was all Maddy said she was, something she would definitely pick up on, and she wasn't sure she wanted that altered either.

Maddy was watching her for a reaction, biting her lip.

"It's perfect," Kit said, turning back to her.

"Really? You're sure?" she asked.

"Absolutely. I wouldn't change a thing" she said reassuringly. Maddy let out a sigh of relief and Kit watched as her shoulders relaxed. "Now send it on its way so we can get on ours!" Kit instructed, and got up to prep her bag for the day.

They all assembled downstairs in a matter of minutes. The kitchen was put to rights, the kids had their shoes on, and Violet was tucked away in the library for the day. It was a miracle given the number of humans that had to be ready, but the group seemed to be itching to get out of the house.

It was a tight squeeze, but the eight of them tucked into the seven-person van and went off to the East Lomond Hill entrance. The ride was a quick twenty-five minutes, and relatively silent as everyone was still content from breakfast. Kit looked back at Maddy to find her on her phone.

"Mads, what are you doing? I thought we agreed…" she started.

"Oh hush, I was just checking my email to see if I had anything yet," Maddy responded before Kit could finish.

"You said last time it took a couple days for her to respond."

"I know, you're right, but I had to check!" Maddy said, putting her phone back in her pocket, slightly dejected being reprimanded by Kit.

They parked and unloaded out of the vehicle like it was a clown car. Thankfully, they were still early for the day and no one was around to see them. It didn't keep a few of them from laughing at the spectacle themselves. Everyone grabbed the bags and waters they had brought from the house, checked their shoes, and set off for the trail.

What a glorious morning! Kit took a deep breath as they walked. It really was gorgeous countryside, and it brought her back to the earlier part of the year when it was just her and Sophia traipsing about. The weather was arguably nicer now. Windbreaker tied around her waist, she was in the middle of the train of people as they made their way up the hill.

Sensing a presence approaching from behind, she assumed it was Erik coming to walk beside her and she fully expected him to grab her hand. When she turned her head, she gasped.

"Sorry, doll! I didn't mean to startle you," Maddy said, laughing. Kit groaned.

"It's fine, just not who I was expecting," she admitted.

"Sorry. Anyways, look!" she whispered excitedly and handed her phone over. Kit took it begrudgingly, not sure what would have her so excited when they had only just begun the hike. Then she saw it.

My Dearest Girl,

Such a pleasure it was to receive your note this morning. I must admit though, Zabina has been waiting patiently for you to reach out. You saw me the other day in your mind, did you not? I think you did.

Anyhow, with regard to your question, Zabina is honored you would think of her, and trust her with your friends as well. However, as you already point out, she is not so good with the technology. I think instead, I'll send you to a friend of mine. She lives close to St. Andrews, and perhaps not too far of a drive for you to see her. She is...more of what Zabina thinks you and your friends need at this time, rather than old Zabina.

Her name is Mary. Mary Rose Fife. She is a fiosaiche, Scottish for "visionary" and more of what you seek. She comes from a long line of Ban-eolascach and cailleachs. She lives along the edge of River Eden, outside of Kincaple just before you get into St. Andrews proper. Her house has a stone fence and thatched roof. Her door is purple, but radiates as amethyst in the light to anyone with the gift. Zabina is sure you will recognize it at once. She is already expecting you and your friends.

I am proud of you, my girl. When you come to me those few months ago you wear such a dark veil over your beautiful face. Now, Zabina can tell, even through this technology, how radiantly you glow. Brava my strong one. You keep going. I see great things for you.

Hugs (as you say),
Zabina

Kit looked over at Maddy amazed.

"She knew you'd be writing so she was waiting for your email?" Kit asked quietly. Maddy nodded, grinning. "And what does she mean that you saw her the other day in your head?" she asked, but Maddy held her finger up to her lips to shush her, shaking her head.

Not now, she mouthed. Kit nodded.

They both looked up at the front where Sophia was leading the group.

"Should I go up and tell her?" Maddy asked excitedly. Kit considered.

"No, I think you need to wait on this one. She seems to be in her element right now, walking among nature. After the past few days, let's let her be for the moment." Kit finished

Kit couldn't believe they got an answer so quickly, and that there may be a solution in their own backyard. She wasn't 100 percent sure, but she seemed to recall from the VRBO listing that the house was about the same distance away from St. Andrews as they were to today's adventure. How serendipitous! Though should she be that surprised, given all the turns of events the three of them had experienced?

She couldn't wait to share with Sophia and see what she thought...and to see when they could squeeze it in over the next few days before they left for Edinburgh.

Chapter 22 – Josephine, July 1911

It was obvious to me as we rode from the train station to city centre that Oscar had clearly envisioned a quaint little English village, and not the broad expanse that Bath truly held. I decided that we had to start from the namesake and move our way out and back to the station later in the day.

The Roman Baths. I had been fascinated with them since I was a little girl. They felt like home. While not relatable to some, my father was just happy to have someone with whom to share the history. It was a common bond and ultimately what led to our discussions of history as I grew older.

While The Great Bath was the largest part of the complex, I think it was the Temple of Sulis Minerva that truly held my interest. There was something about bearing witness to the ruins of a temple once dedicated to both a local goddess, Sulis, and the Roman goddess, Minerva. The room seemed to hum with forgotten energy, and I swear when I was a child, I once saw the Gorgon's head come to life.

Of course, when I told Oscar these stories and my recollections of touring the Sacred Spring, Bathing Suites, and the rest of the museum, I became self-conscious that it was making me sound like a child, rather than the woman I wanted to be in front of him. However, my fears were assuaged as soon as he mindlessly took my hand and we walked, grinning at me after I finished.

From the baths, we strolled across the street to Bath Abbey. While it was relatively similar to other abbeys built across England in its time, Oscar was impressed to learn that it was known for being the last medieval church built in England. He was also most impressed with the sixteenth century fan vaulted ceiling. While staring up, he said, "I understand now," almost to himself, but catching it, I asked, "What do you understand?"

"Why you are always staring up at the architecture," he responded matter-of-factly. "How could you not, if this is the example with which you grew up?" he finished and glanced at me to find my face somewhat aghast. "What? Do I offend?" he asked, concerned.

"No, I just..." I looked at him completely flustered. "I am not..." I cleared my throat. "I am just not used to being seen, or understood, outside of my own family, that is." I blushed.

He considered me again. "Well, that, my dear Sephie, is a damn shame" and he walked further into the abbey to inspect some of the stained glass. I was left in utter shock at his brazen phrasing, but also with a warm tingly feeling in my stomach.

We went to one more museum, and soon, Oscar was finding us a carriage. "Royal Victoria Park, if you please, sir," he heralded. The driver simply nodded his head and we were off. I looked at him skeptically. "Yes, I know my dear, we could have walked it after the other strolling we have done today, but lest you forget, this basket is getting rather heavy and I just wanted a moment's rest for my arm before we got there."

I cocked my eyebrow. "How is it, you always seem to know what I am thinking?" I tried to brush aside how effortlessly he had just referred to me as "my dear" and not shoot straight out of my seat with sheer excitement.

"Sephie, it is not as if you have a poker face," he laughed, but paused to consider. "I suppose I have not been able to do that with others before, now that I think about it...perhaps it is because of our kindred spirits that I can read your mind as easily as I can hear my own," he concluded.

Every time he uttered my full name, let alone his version of it, the frisson came back. Now he had quite possibly read my thoughts as if we were one. Oh, how I never wanted this day to end. It was just too exquisite.

"Here you are, sir. That will be one shilling sixpence for you and the missus," the driver announced. Oscar handed him three shillings and we disembarked. "Kind of ya, Govna," the driver yelled and pulled away.

We walked into the fifty-seven-acre expanse and it was absolutely breathtaking. There were still tulips blooming everywhere. Even though Oscar had never been here, he led me through the spaces, over a bridge and to a large tree overhanging the small canal, finding a shady spot for us to sit. He spread out a blanket from atop the basket, and set out our meal. He'd managed to find the perfect hiding spot from any passers-by, and yet not so hidden to appear improper. As soon as I spotted Alice's scones, I could not help myself and I tore into one. Oscar laughed.

"You know those were supposed to be for the train ride home should we need them," he reprimanded, grinning.

"I know, I am sorry, but she truly makes the best and I cannot resist! Besides, I could not wait. I did not realize how hungry I was until you started bringing everything out," I admitted, though not sheepishly as I continued to tear at the scone. He laughed again.

"It's ok," he said and he leaned in to whisper. "They are my favorite, too!"

We proceeded to enjoy every last morsel that had been packed and washed it down with the ginger beer. While it is not my favorite refreshment, it was quite perfect for today. I leaned back on my hands and looked out to the canal, watching the ducks as they grouped together and then floated apart. I sighed contentedly and lifted my face to the sky. Closing my eyes, I tried to soak in every delicious moment. Of freedom. Of home. Of summer. Of him.

I brought my eyes back, level to the canal. The ducks had continued their dance a little further down; I wondered if that was what their entire day consisted of. I stared back at the water. A feather floated seemingly from nowhere and gently sat on the surface. I watched as it barely made any ripples, and yet did not submerge either. I wondered what it was like to feel that weightless and free all the time.

"Wouldn't it…" I said, just as he was about to break the silence as well. I turned and looked at him. "You first."

He shook his head. "No, no, ladies first," he allowed. I considered the look in his eyes.

"Well, I was just considering the duck feather, and how beautiful this day is, and…" I caught him grimacing. "No" I laughed, realizing I had started off by commenting on a duck feather. "What I mean to say is, would it not be wonderful if every day could be this effortless? This free?" I asked, and I looked out to the water again.

He was silent for a moment. Reflective. When he made no move to speak, I said, "your turn." He directed those ice blue eyes at me and I saw such intensity in them I was almost alarmed.

"What if it could be?" he asked, gaze boring into my very soul. I was caught in it, like the feather in the current, carrying me away.

"What if it could what?" I responded, almost absent-mindedly.

"What if it could be…this effortless? Every day? Just you and me?" he asked. I was stunned. I could not believe my own ears. I wanted to pinch myself to be sure I was not dreaming, but I was also too scared to move and break the mirage I was convinced I must be in.

How could this man, my enigma, be saying such a thing…to me? And yet, if I allowed myself to consider, there was almost a note of desperation behind his words.

In spite of the shock on my face, he continued, undeterred.

"What if, Sephie? I mean it. This past week has meant more to me than..." he stopped to try to find the right words. "What I mean to say is, I love you. I am in love with you. I want this to be my life, with you. You have made me believe that there is a match for us out there and it does not have to be with someone who is picked for you, but one who is truly meant for you. One that lights your soul on fire, and keeps you guessing. One with whom you can share all your thoughts and secrets. One..." he was inching ever closer to me as he spoke and I was frozen, caught in his current and not wanting to move, even if I was to drown.

"One who you can read their thoughts as easily as you can read their face," he continued. "You want to protect from the world's cruelties, and yet you cannot imagine traveling the world without them, to see all the wonders it holds. One with whom to escape..." he stopped himself there. Oscar reached out to brush away a small wave of hair that had somehow fallen out of place and then rested his hand on my cheek. He went to move it away from my face, but I found my own hand shooting up from my side and holding it there.

"I love you, Josephine Findley, Honourable Daughter of Baron Crowley. My Sephie. My only hope is that you might possibly feel even remotely the same way too." There was concern in his eyes now because I had not uttered a word in return, of affirmation or rejection. All I could do was stare, drowning. He began to look crestfallen and I finally took a breath.

"I do," I said, almost in a whisper, barely audible. He raised an eyebrow as a quiet request for me to repeat myself.

"I do love you, too, Oscar Carlisle, Honourable son of Viscount Carlisle. I do not know by which fates I have come to be in your favor, but yes. This week has been more than I could have ever expected, and I have come to care for you in ways I knew not possible. Only…" and at this, I started to tear.

"What is it my love?" he asked softly, causing my eyes to begin to overflow.

"Only you are betrothed to another, and your mother has already told me that if I should make a ruin of her plans…" I managed to choke out before he interrupted.

"You need not worry about my mother. I am a man. A son of a Viscount. For whatever her plans may be or were, they are over now. I choose to whom I marry, and I most certainly choose the woman I love. *She* cannot change that, nor will my father let her." He said it with a veracity that I had not yet seen in him, which made me wonder who was he trying to convince?

"I am not worth going to war with your family, Oscar," I said, looking in my reticule for a handkerchief. Finding none, I patted my eyes with the edge of my gloved palm. He was shaking his head.

"Yes, yes, you are my dear. This week has only proven to me how much. We are two parts of one whole, you and I. I can feel it in my soul, as if it has always known you, from the beginning of time."

I could not argue with him anymore and relented. This man. This beautiful, confounding man had just professed his love to me. Me. The daughter of a baron, who had been locked away in his mother's house. It was almost like a fairytale, complete with a Fairy Godmother in my Alice.

I simply nodded my head. He understood its meaning and drew me into his chest, holding me close. My tears had subsided, and I pulled my head back to look up at him. He looked down at me, and the next thing I knew, our lips were as one. I felt a rushing sound in my head, as if we were being enveloped by water. Everything around us dissolved, and it was just he and I, floating through the universe, forever entwined. The kiss was breathtaking.

He pulled away, looked into my eyes, and seemed to make a decision in that moment.

"Come, we will pack up and head back to the station. We will announce our intentions this very evening!" he said excitedly as he gathered the remains of our picnic.

"Tonight?! Oscar, shouldn't we..."

"Tonight," he cut me off. "I want my life to start with you as soon as possible, which means we have no time to waste," he proclaimed, offering his hand to me, helping me to my feet. Once standing, he looked around. Seeing no one, he took me in his arms and kissed me again. Once again, I was there, floating through the ether, with him, forevermore. As if our souls had joined from centuries past and present into one moment.

I pulled away this time. "Alright, tonight then." He smiled, and we rushed off towards the station.

This time, I sat next to him on the ride home. There was no way I would be falling asleep on this journey and we had too much to discuss.

While he had been intent on starting University in a couple of months, we decided we should take some time and explore the world together, starting with a voyage to America. It was still unknown how long my parents would be over there, and we felt that we could go visit them while also escaping the clutches of his family for the immediate future. He seemed almost restless at the thought. Regardless of him wanting to choose his own path, there would still likely be fallout and we thought it best to remove ourselves from all that. My final concern was my brother, but Oscar assured me he would not be in harm's way.

"I will find the first ship I can crossing to America tomorrow!" he declared as we pulled into Paddington, back in London once again. I smiled. I could not believe this was happening.

We had arrived back in the city earlier than we had told Robert, and thus were surprised to find him waiting there for us nonetheless. He had a look of concern on his face that made us both falter.

"Robert?" Oscar asked with a sternness in his voice. "Is everything alright?" Robert seemed to hesitate to say anything in front of me as he looked between us. "It is alright Robert, whatever it is you have to say to me you can say in front of Miss Findley," he assured the footman.

"It is the Viscountess, sir," he stumbled. Oscar's face froze. "She had called on Miss Findley to come downstairs to attend to Gertrude while she practiced piano, and as she was nowhere to be found..." he trailed off. Oscar muttered something under his breath. I raised my hand to my mouth. Oscar looked at me.

"Do not worry, I will speak to my father as soon as we return," he said, grasping my wrists together and then helping me up into the carriage. The whole ride back was silent as we contemplated what we were about to walk into, and what we would do.

Looking back on it, it was as if time stood still the moment we entered the house. No longer needing to keep up pretenses, the carriage pulled up to the front door and we walked in together. As if on cue, his mother was standing on the landing looking down from her perch and his father appeared out of his office. Trying to make a united front, we both walked towards his father, only for the Viscountess to hiss down to me as she descended the stairs that I was to go up to my room since it was a "family matter" that needed to be discussed. I looked up at Oscar to see what he wanted me to do, but his face was stone. The next thing I knew, he was being pulled away from me by his free arm as his mother moved towards the door of his father's study. Alice came from around the corner, read-faced and one side of her cheek quite swollen, likely from a lashing she had taken from the mistress of the house. She led me upstairs so I could be out of the way and safe, for the moment.

I strained to hear anything coming from downstairs, but it was silent. Eerily so. As if the rest of the house had been swallowed up. Alice left me in my room in dire straits, but I also could not stand to be around anyone at the moment. Not until I could see Oscar again and know of what occurred. I suppose I fell asleep when the waiting got to be too much because it was now morning. Sunlight was streaming in the crack in the curtains. I sat up, realizing I was still in my dress from the day before, confused until it all came rushing back.

I ran to the door to find Oscar. Bleary-eyed and only half awake, I almost tripped over the figure in my threshold. "Charles?" I asked, not recognizing my own voice, for how scratchy it was after all my crying the night before. He did not respond. "Charles, move. I have to find Oscar at once. I..." but he cut me off.

"He's gone."

Chapter 23 – Sophia, June Present Day

The rest of the hike on the East loop of the hill and through the Maspie Den was quite idyllic. The kids were champs and didn't complain too much, even if it wasn't their cup of tea. Thankfully, Kit had brought enough snacks with her that even if there was a remote inkling they were about to go off the rails, she would shove a beef jerky stick or piece of fruit at them and they would settle down.

Now that we were in the town, it was quite remarkable. There was the Palace, the House of Falkland, the Town Hall, the Moncrief House and the Brunton House, all considered "Category A" listings for historic buildings in the area; something Bryce had taught me meant "buildings of special architectural or historic interest that are outstanding examples of a particular period, style, or type."

Of course, my favorite and Kit's, was the Bruce Fountain. Made popular by our favorite show, I couldn't help but stare at it and have the scene replay in my head; the spirit of a past love stares at the image of his love in the future, before she knew they'd ever met; just waiting. The moment and convolutedness of the storyline were not lost on me given my current musings and situation. Recognizing I needed a moment, Kit ushered the group to go look at a shopfront across the way. I pretended I was taking my time photographing all the details, when I was really just trying to stay in the moment...and to see if the Bruce had any wisdom to share. Another raven landed in front of me, atop the fountain. I smiled. Ravens were quickly becoming my favorite bird, they felt familiar and akin to a kindred spirit, though in what way I couldn't vocalize; perhaps it was something about the warmth of their dark feathers, or their seemingly all-knowing eyes.

Then I heard a song floating on the breeze, I looked around to see from where it emanated, but couldn't decide if it was the apartment window above the shop, a car that had just started with its windows open, or some other origin. It was one that I had heard in Scotland before and I truly loved, the upbeat versions I had experienced always brought a smile to my face: "The bonnie, bonnie banks o' loch Lomond."

Kit caught my eye as she waved me over. Clearly if I stayed apart from the group any longer, it would become conspicuous, and yet there was a look in her eyes that also beckoned me. I approached her with my head cocked as I found her staring in a shop window.

There in front of us were tools of the esoteric trade, a deck of tarot cards here, some oracle cards there, and spread out on a beautiful wooden bench were a set of obsidian stones, each with different markings etched into the shiny ebony rock —runes. I looked at her and both our eyes were wide.

"The guys would like to find some place for a 'wee dram,'" Maddy said as she approached us, invoking a Scottish accent on the 'wee dram' part.

Pulling her eyes away from the shop window and quickly searching on her phone, "well, it seems we have our choice of the lot," Kit said. "But I say we go here," she pointed at the screen with a wicked grin on her face. Upon seeing what she was looking at, Maddy and I nodded our heads in agreement. Another stop on the TV show set tour we didn't know we were on.

"Alright boys, let's go to The Covenanter Hotel!" Kit proclaimed as we left the shop and walked up behind the rest of the group.

"The what?" Erik asked and recognized the grin on his wife's face. "It's not a pub is it," he mused.

"No, it is!" Kit defended. "It has drinks, but it also has cake and coffee for those of us who don't fancy ourselves a dram just yet," she said innocently.

He hesitated, but also knew there wouldn't be another option. The kids were already spun up at hearing the word "cake," and so it was already signed, sealed, and delivered.

The hotel was everything one could ask for built in the late 19th century, in a small Scottish village. The guys were able to find something to "warm their joints" after the hike, the kids were happy with the crumb cake, and the girls were able to get some fresh coffee as an afternoon pick me up.

As the guys were all comparing tasting notes and the kids were happy stuffing their faces, Maddy leaned over to me with her phone. "Soph, look!" she said. I glanced at Kit to see if she could indicate what would be so exciting that Maddy had to share with me on her. That was when I saw it. Maddy shook her head.

"You emailed her this morning and she already got back to you?!" I asked under my breath as I read through both emails quickly, scanning for anything I could discern.

"Uh huh," she said, seemingly happy at my reaction.

"Wow, and she knows someone nearby? That's remarkable, what are the odds?" I asked both of them as they watched me hand Maddy's phone back.

"With normal people, a million to one, but with our group..." Kit mused.

"You're right," I said. "You're always right."

"It's my curse," Kit said and took a sip of her coffee.

"Alright, alright. So, when do we think we can see her?" Maddy asked, trying not to squeal out loud and disrupt the boys prematurely. The kids seemed to have gained some steam back and were playing tic-tac-toe on the back of the paper placemat.

I considered the request, and our timing over the next few days. "Well..." I thought out loud. "Tomorrow was a day that I had down for rest, and then the following day was going to be a surprise visit to St. Andrews arranged by Bryce..."

Kit's mouth fell open. "Seriously? Erik is going to lose it. Nice work!"

"What's St. Andrews?" Maddy asked.

"Only the birthplace of golf, Maddy!" Kit enthused.

"Oh. Ew. Okay…" Maddy worked that information through in her head. Clearly golf was not something that interested her.

"Oh, come on, Maddy, like you wouldn't at least want to see the origin of sport that is now played by the likes of some hotties?" Kit said winking at her.

"Hotties? Golf? Try me," Maddy said.

Kit started pulling up pictures of golfers from our generation and younger to prove her point. I watched with amusement as Maddy's features went from composed, trying to not to react, to full blown wow factor.

"Alright you two, that's enough," I said, sounding like the mom role Kit usually took on. "If we don't care about going there ourselves, we could always drive separately and let the kids and guys go for an adventure on their own while we go visit Mary. Or, we could try and go tomorrow while everyone else is resting," I offered.

They considered and then Maddy said, "could we combine those two and have the St. Andrews Day moved up to tomorrow, *and* we don't have to go?"

Kit laughed. "Geez Mads, greedy much?" She looked at me as if she too agreed with that plan but didn't want to say so.

"Um…I'm not sure. Bryce made the plans at the course because of some work he had done a while ago, but I can ask him once we get going again. Explain the situation," I said, not sure how he would react to a change like that.

"Great!" Maddy exclaimed and set to finishing her coffee in one gulp. "Let's go then" she said and then promptly stood up.

Kit and I looked at each other and shrugged. When Maddy got something in her head, we knew all too well there wasn't much to do until it was followed through on.

"Ladies?" the gents called out, though we couldn't tell which one since all three accents were now starting to blend after having spent time together.

"Yes?" we called out in unison.

"We were thinking..." Ryan started, but took one look at all three of us staring at him and backed off. looking at his two mates for support.

"We were thinking," said Erik coming to his defense, "that we were done with the sightseeing for the day and would like to head back to the house."

We each looked at each other in turn to consider, then over at the kids. They too seemed to be ready.

"Alright," I answered for all of us, and we all finished our respective drinks and left.

Back to the car, we piled in, making the short drive back to the mansion. It was still breathtaking to drive up and think this was where we were staying. Kit really had outdone herself. I just wished we knew a bit more about the history of the place since everywhere in this country had a story to tell.

We each went inside to change and get into our comfy clothes that were more suitable to lounging around the backyard than hiking up the countryside. As Bryce and I went into our room, Violet perked up from the bed to say hello. She must not have heard us come in downstairs and had clearly moved levels since we left. She had been snuggled up to Bryce's side of the bed.

"Awww...baby girl. You like Mr. Bryce's scent, do you?" I said, cupping her head in my hands and massaging her ears. She let out her signature little groan. Bryce just smiled, but stayed rather quiet as he found more comfortable shorts and shirt to throw on.

"So, the ladies were talking..." I started and he looked up, clearly catching him mid thought.

"Yes?" he asked.

"Sorry, did I interrupt something for you?" I asked with concern, sensing he was deep in thought.

"No, not at all. Go on," he encouraged. I was a bit doubtful, but went on.

"We have something that the three of us would like to do, but it would cause a slight change in plans. There are a few ways we could go about it, but one of them involved asking if it would be possible for you to change the St. Andrews day to tomorrow, and with not as many of us going..." I asked, biting my lip.

He considered. "Actually, that wouldn't be a problem at all. It may be preferred. Part of the challenge was getting such a large group in, but if we are reduced by three, and a day earlier, I think they might agree. Let me just get changed, and I will go call," he said, and went into the bathroom.

Well, that was easier than expected. But something still felt off with him. Perhaps I was just conflating my own feelings of apprehension and guilt and projecting them onto him. Oy. Okay, now I couldn't wait for our visit to Mary, I needed answers. Or at the very least, clarification.

I went downstairs and updated Kit and Maddy. They were ecstatic, and each crossed their fingers, hoping Bryce could make it happen. When he came downstairs, he sought us out and let us know everything had been sorted.

"Thanks, babe," I said and gave him a peck on the cheek. This seemed to brighten his spirits a little, but then they waned again. His brow furrowed and he obviously remembered something. I put a pin in it and figured I would ask him later. In all the crazy of the arrival here and seeing Maddy and Ryan, I hadn't had the opportunity to speak with him about what Kit and I had discussed in the car. She seemed to be certain that he would take the request well, but with how he was acting right now, I wasn't so sure. I guess I could try bringing it up tonight when we went to bed.

The rest of the day was perfection of a different kind. The hiking had worn all of us out. The kids actually self-prescribed a rest in their rooms after changing. They didn't sleep so much as read and reset, but it was still great that they were learning how to discern that for themselves. The guys seemingly did the same thing, lounging outside on the verandah. Ryan felt like introducing the guys to a truly English custom and brought out a bottle of Pimm's to share. Kit, ever the homemaker, had taken some of the remaining lemons in the kitchen and whipped up some fresh lemonade. We decided to take it down by the water near the firepit to enjoy so we could still be outside but away from prying ears.

Conversations ranged from trip critiques, to recent books, until Kit turned and asked me, "Have you talked to Bryce about your strategy for the ball?"

Maddy practically spat out the sip she had just taken. "Wait, what? Strategy? Forget that, did you say ball?" and she stared at me.

I hesitated. "Uh yeah, she said ball." Not quite sure what the expression on her face was.

"Sophia Mary, Elizabeth, whatever your middle name is, Aitken! How have we been together for three days and you have not mentioned a *ball*! Spill. Immediately." She sipped on her drink for added affect.

Kit laughed. "I'm sorry, I thought she knew," she added sheepishly.

"Well, if I haven't had time to talk to Bryce about what we discussed, when would I have mentioned to this one that I have to find a gown in the midst of all of this?" I asked, completely baiting the fashion house queen now. Maddy's mouth dropped open.

"Okay, I've heard enough, when are we going shopping?" she was practically crawling out of her skin now.

"Probably not until Edinburgh. And even then, I might be limited, but I'm sure I can find something," I retorted, looking at Kit for reassurance.

"Um, excuse me. Do you recall what it is I do for a living?! I can find anyone, anything, related to fashion. Just leave it to me." And with that, we lost Maddy to her phone and researching.

The next morning came and I realized that while I had gone up to bed with the intention of staying up to talk with Bryce, I was either more exhausted than I realized, or he had stayed up way later than I expected, and I was asleep by the time he came to bed. Either way, it was going to be a day of us going opposite directions, which had been rare the past few months. I felt a little prang of guilt and longing. The guys didn't have to get up early for their adventure, so I got up, got dressed, kissed him on the cheek, and left the room as quietly as I could.

As if on cue, the three of us were all leaving our rooms at the same time, trying to close the doors without making a noise. When we all saw each other and realized this, it took everything in us not to burst out howling, which surely would have echoed down the halls.

We loaded up in the lime green Mini Cooper, put the top down, more so for Maddy's comfort in the back than the weather, and went off to the east. None of us knowing what this visit would bring, but each of us hoping for something.

Chapter 24 – Josephine, July 1911

He's gone.

The words still echoed in my head and my heart nearly two weeks later. I recalled the morning like it was yesterday...

A wave of emotions flooded my being. Anger, hurt, despair, concern, doubt, denial, confusion, anguish, betrayal. The last one cut the deepest. By whose hand was he gone? And why?

I had backed into my room and my brother came in, closing the door behind him. I sat down in my favorite chair, stunned. Charles looked at me with some concern. I looked up at him.

"Why?" I asked him, though how he would know the answer was beyond me, it was the only word I could mutter.

"I do not know, I only..." he hesitated, deciding what to say. "I passed by his rooms this morning and there was all manner of chaos as things were being packed up."

I thought for a moment. If his room was still being packed, he must still be in the house somewhere. I had to find him. I made a move to stand, but Charles came over and placed his hand on my shoulder, shaking his head.

"I know what you are thinking, dear sister, but he is not still here. I heard the maids talking that he had left in a carriage very early this morning and that the Viscount was to send his things after him once he was settled," he finished, all the while keeping those mossy green eyes on me, evaluating my every micro expression.

"I do not understand," I whispered to myself, shaking my head. The past week had been so wonderful, and yesterday? Positively sublime. I brought my fingers to my lips and gently brushed over them where I had last felt his kiss. How could this be?

Just then, there was a knock at the door. We both turned our heads to the sound. My legs would not propel me up, so Charles walked over and took charge. He opened it slightly to see who was there. Then he opened the door wider and stood aside to let them pass, quickly shutting it again once they did.

Alice was by my side in an instant. The side of her face was still a bit red and puffy, and I wondered what happened to her.

"Oh miss, I had feared you had already been told before I could get to you," she said, and sank down on the floor in front of me.

"Whatever do you mean, Alice?" I asked, still feeling like I was floating through a dream. Or a nightmare.

"Mr. Oscar. He is gone, and I fear I may have played a role in it, miss." At this, she started crying. I looked down at her.

"I do not understand, Alice. How could you have..." I started, but she cut me off.

"It was while you were gone the other day, miss. The Viscountess had inquired as to your whereabouts, and no one could tell her where you were. I made up a story that I had heard you were feeling unwell and had taken to your rooms," she said sheepishly. I nodded at her in approval, which made her straighten herself a bit.

"Anyway, she seemed suspicious, so the next day she asked around again. Once again, no one had seen you. She came to me to ask if I had been up to your rooms to check on you. I had said, 'No, your Ladyship, I was not aware that you would want me to do so.' I thought I was most convincing, and she told me in this case it was fine, and to go see if you needed anything. The Viscount had come into the kitchen at that time confused, so I replied to the Viscountess that I would go check on you as soon as my duties in the kitchen were dispatched, and would take some tea just in case."

I just stared at her as I listened and tried to comprehend all she was telling me, and why that would lead to Oscar being gone.

"Anyway, I did as I told her and took some tea up to your room. I left the tray in here for a bit and went back for it later, for good measure. She called me into the library to see how you were fairing and I told her you were on the mend, but needed more rest. She only nodded, so I thought all was well." Then Alice looked down at her hands.

"Then yesterday, she called for you to come and listen to Gertrude practice piano, something I know she has never done, but she clearly knew something was going on and was testing you. When one of the other maids went to check your room and found it empty, she was furious. She came to find me and I offered that perhaps you were feeling better and out for a walk in the sunlight for some fresh air." She paused. "It was then that she slapped me across my face. I did not know such small hands could do such pain, but like a whip they were." She gently touched her cheek.

I gasped. "Oh, Alice. I am so sorry. You should not have been put in a position to lie for me like that. I wonder why the Viscount did not step in..."

Alice merely shook her head. She clearly would not know something like that. I was still bewildered. How did it go from me not being in my rooms to Oscar being gone? Presumably sent away? Was it all planned? Had he already known he was going away and so this was a last week hurrah for him, playing chaperone and having fun at my expense? He was an enigma for sure, but I could not imagine him being so cruel as all that.

"I am still confounded though, Alice," I said, finally narrating the thoughts in my head out loud. "I do not understand how it went from my being absent to Oscar being gone?"

"All I know, miss, is that one thing led to another and it was found out that not only had you not been sick in your rooms, but that you had been with Mr. Oscar the entire week. The Viscount brought Robert in and asked where the last place was he had driven you. They were confused how it could have been a day trip when the carriage was back at the house. Poor Robert did not know what to do, but ultimately, he told the Viscount everything."

My heart hurt for Robert. I was glad that it was the Viscount with whom he spoke, but still. He was such a loyal fellow, that couldn't have been easy for him.

"The next thing I knew, miss, Robert was going to fetch you from the station, but also to try to warn you. After you arrived home and sent me away, well, cook kept me busy in the kitchen so I could not hear what happened. There were a lot of slamming doors after a short while, and then silence. I had intended to take Mr. Oscar his traditional glass of sherry for his nightcap, but none was ever called for, and cook would not allow me to just take it up to him, given everything going on. She did not want me to lose my position, should her Ladyship find me wandering around upstairs without invitation or cause." She bit her lip. "I tried, miss." I saw a tear fall down her cheek.

"Alice, none of this is your fault. I am sorry you got mixed up in any of it. You are a good friend. Please do not chide yourself, you did nothing wrong." I took her chin in my hand so I could look her in the eyes and she would know my true feelings. Then I stood. Resolute, I added, "I will just have to seek an audience with the Viscount himself. Surely, he cannot deny me that."

Charles helped Alice to her feet and they watched as I paced back and forth, talking to myself as if I was alone in the room.

"Sister, he may not be able to deny you the request, but are you sure you want to walk straight into the lion's den, and so soon?" asked Charles. "He may have been friendly to us while we have been here, and surely more welcoming than *her*, but the fact is, he has now had to send his eldest son away, and likely you played some role in that." He looked at me with some concern.

For being a boy of thirteen, almost fourteen, Charles was wise beyond his years. Though I suspected it was more about his powers of observation in the household over the past seven months that truly gave him such perspective.

"I appreciate that, brother. But if I am but part of the cause, I have even more reason to understand what is going on." And I marched naively downstairs to the Viscount's study.

Two weeks later, the conversation still stung. Oscar had in fact been sent away, because of me. The Viscountess was furious that we had been spending time together. Not only was my absence suspicious, but one of the Earl's friends had seen us out at one of the museums, and reported it through the chain. Defending his daughter's honor, almost called off the pending betrothal. The only way he would let it stand was if Oscar was distanced from me, and since I was under their family's watch, and they were unable to send me away, the only option was to send Oscar away. Of course, the Viscountess made it sound as if he did not acquiesce to the "request", noting that my virtue would be called into question within the peerage and my name besmudged before I could find a proper husband.

I was shocked. I asked where Oscar had been sent to and when he would return, but no answers were given. Then I was sent to my quarters and told I was not permitted to come down unless it was for meal times, or a short walk in the garden out back for daily fresh air. I had declined both on the account of not wanting to be seen by anyone in the house, nor having to make false conversation.

Two weeks locked away in my rooms before would have been a dream come true. Now, it was a prison. Alice did her best to bring me extra scones, and keep me company when she had a moment, but even she had to be careful. Where the Viscount had wanted her to help me before, it was clear that no help was warranted now. I could not tell if he was mad at me. In some way, he may have even been glad about the two of us courting, if it was not for *her*. However, his hands were clearly tied and he was apparently choosing his battles.

Today was dragging on like any other when a soft knock came at the door. I sighed and placed my book down on the end table. It was the only respite I had, reading and dreaming of other lands, and this interruption was most unagreeable. I padded over to the door unenthusiastically and opened it slightly. It was those moss green eyes, no longer staring up at me, but at me. Had I not realized how much he had grown over the past few months?

"Josie, I have something for you!" my brother practically squealed. It had been a long time since he had referred to me as such, he had only called me that when he could not yet say my full name.

"It had better not be a bug…" I said, pondering what would have him so excited.

"Well, if you are going to be rude about it, I will not share what it is…" he said and made to turn around. Whatever it was, had to be better than what I would be doing for the rest of the afternoon so, I let him in.

He strode in like a man with purpose, and something behind his back.

"Well then, let's have it." I said, holding out my hand with one eye closed, just in case.

Charles was beaming from ear to ear as he produced a small cream item from behind his jacket and softly landed it in my open palm. I looked down in awe. Could it be?

I turned it over in my hand and sure enough, the red seal was affixed to the back.

"Where did you get this?!" I whispered in disbelief.

"Well…I was out in the main gardens, when a man approached me. He asked if I was the 'green-eyed monster what belonged to a Josephine.' I knew that was your nickname for me, so I listened to him instead of ignoring him. I shook my head and he handed me that note. He said, 'Make sure your sister gets that, you hear?' And he was off." Already bored with his mission dispatched, he started for the door.

"And you did not recognize the man that approached you?" I asked, wondering if it could have been Oscar in disguise.

"No, it was not him..." he said reading my thoughts. "But someone like him. He dressed the same, but had blonde hair and a round face." And with that, he left me to my reading.

Freddy, I thought. It had to be. I had shared my nickname for my brother with Oscar during our week together. He also must have been aware where Charles liked to frequent to people-watch during the day and sent Freddy with the note. Maybe I should reach out to him to see if he knew where Oscar was...

I cracked the seal and unfolded the paper, anxious for answers.

My Dearest Sephie,

I am so sorry I am not there. This was not as I expected or intended. When we returned that glorious day, for it was glorious indeed and my only beacon of hope lately, well, we had obviously been found out. My mother had grown incredulous to your absence, and began circling through the servants in the house to see what they knew. I fear poor Alice took the brunt of it. I tried speaking with my father immediately about the situation and explaining that we were in love and I planned to ask for your hand officially, but my mother erupted. She shared all that had transpired with the Earl, Katerina's father, and their plans. I cared not, save that you would have gotten caught in all of this and been disgraced. I had to leave, or at least let them think I was gone, as penance, and to give breathing room to the situation, so that I could have time to strategize.

I have a plan, my dearest. We had talked of going overseas to the Americas once we announced our intentions. I say we stick to that plan. I am currently searching for the best vessel on which we may depart. I promise to send word once I do; and I hope it sooner rather than later, my love.

For now, I will leave you with one of my most favorite Scottish folk songs. It is one of the very few good things of my Scottish heritage from my mother.

By yon bonnie banks and by yon bonnie braes,
Where the sun shines bright on Loch Lomond,
Where me and my true love were ever wont to gae,
On the bonnie, bonnie banks o' Loch Lomond.

Until I can get word to you again, have hope, and keep the faith. And if you happen to hear this song, know that I am nearby.

With greatest admiration and longing,
Oscar

Hope. Faith. While those two had been dwindling over the past two weeks, this letter renewed both quickly. He had a plan, or at least was formulating one, and all was not lost. Of course he left to keep my honor, and of course it was superficial to appease his mother. I had certainly seen him give in to her in small ways since meeting him during coronation week, but hoped against hope that with me, it was different. It had to be. I held the letter to my heart and breathed a sigh of relief. Something

I had not been able to do since I heard the words, "He's gone".

I heard a knock at the door again, and this time went to answer it more quickly, except, the letter was still in my hand. I could not let anyone else in the house know of its existence, even Alice. I would have to find a better hiding place for now, but shoved it under my pillow as I walked over to the door.

I opened it and found Alice with my mid-day tray. For once, I actually felt as if I could eat. "Oh, thank you, Alice, I am positively famished," I uttered as we walked over to my small table.

She eyed me closely. "You seem to have a bit of color back in your cheeks miss, are you feeling better then?"

"I am, indeed, Alice, thank you." But I offered no other words as to why.

"I am glad, miss. You were beginning to look a bit peaked…if I may say so," she offered, trying to coax out the mystery behind my uptick in mood. I would not be so easily swayed.

"That is kind of you to say, Alice." I looked around the room for an excuse. "I happen to have stumbled on a fascinating book that is taking my attentions elsewhere. Perhaps it is that to which I owe my elevated mood," I offered.

She looked dubious, but nodded anyhow. "If that will be all, miss." I nodded in return and she left back to the kitchen.

"Alice?" I called after her with a thought. She turned. "Would you be so kind as to let her Ladyship know that I would like to take my offered walk in the garden this afternoon. I am beginning to get a bit stuffy in here, and, well, I would like to play by her rules," I said and winked in her direction. Alice cocked her head, trying to understand what game I was playing, but I merely smiled back at her. While I missed her as my confidant, I was not about to get her embroiled in all of this if I was to truly escape and run away with Oscar. The notion sent shivers up and down my spine at the thought.

"Yes, of course, miss." And with that, she turned and walked out of the room, closing the door behind her.

Chapter 25 – Sophia, June Present Day

"Ladies, are you seeing what I'm seeing?" Maddy cried out from the backseat. Kit and I had been too enthralled in talking about the countryside and reminiscing of our earlier trip that we weren't sure to what she was drawing our attention. I squinted to the horizon.

"What are you talking about, Mads?" I asked, not seeing anything that should have caused her voice to quiver like it had.

"The glowing door?" She pointed directly in between Kit and I. We followed where her finger was pointing.

"Oh, you mean the purple door ahead? Isn't that what we were supposed to be looking for?" Kit asked.

"No, I mean, yes, we need a purple door, but don't you guys see it glowing? Like an amethyst like Zabina described?" Maddy added. We shook our heads. Maybe it was a trick of the sunlight on the door, but I wasn't seeing it glowing.

"Weird." Maddy said to herself.

"Stone fence. Thatched roof. Purple door. I guess we're here!" Kit said, and gathered her things from her seat so we could go in. We all got out of the car, stretched and looked at the house, deciding on whether we should actually approach it. It felt odd just showing up to a house like this, in the middle of nowhere, completely unannounced. But, Zabina had assured us her friend Mary was already expecting us so, here goes nothing, I thought.

We took our first steps toward the door and suddenly it swung wide open. A small woman stood in the threshold, waving us towards her. She was not what any of us was probably thinking we'd find.

Petite, with grey white hair cut short, and a colorful scarf tied around her head, dressed in what looked like a silk jumpsuit from the sixties for all the color and flow. The pattern of the suit competed with that of the scarf in her hair, but also somehow complemented it. She looked like a walking commercial for everything the decade represented.

"Well, isn't she zesty," Kit said under her breath as we started walking again, having stopped at the shock of the door opening. I tried not to guffaw.

"I *love* it!" Maddy enthused. "This is going to be fun" and she smiled with a wide grin like she was a kid and about to get into some terrible mischief.

"Come on in, doves! I've been waiting for you. I wasn't sure if you would be here today or tomorrow, but I've been ready," she said in a huskier voice than I had expected for her size. What was that accent? It wasn't Scottish, but it wasn't quite English either. It almost felt "old world," whatever that meant...

We all went through her door one-by-one and stopped just inside the entrance, unsure if we were supposed to slip our shoes off or not. For all the mystic elements we saw on the outside of the home, thatched roof and witch bells hanging by the door included, the inside was completely modern farmhouse. This woman was turning out to be a walking dichotomy.

"Welcome, welcome! I'm so thrilled you could make it. All of your people have been coming in in droves since I got the message from my friend, and I just couldn't wait to meet you," she said, closing the door and turning her sparkling emerald eyes on all of us. I peeked over at Kit with a knowing smile hearing 'all of your people have been coming in' as a flashback to the last time she and I went to do something like this.

"We are grateful you were available and willing to help us out," Maddy said. "There's been some...interesting things going on, and we just could use some extra guidance." She stared at her feet.

Mary looked at her and considered. "I'm sure you could," she answered. Glancing back at Kit and I, she motioned with her hands: "Come, take your shoes off if you wish, and let's go into the parlor. I have some tea waiting for us and I'd like to get to know you a bit better before we dive in." And with that, she wandered off into the main room ahead, opposite the two-sided fireplace.

We openly gawked as we removed our shoes and walked in to follow her. For all the color Mary was wearing, the décor of her house was devoid of it, as if she had sucked it out from the environment itself and decided to wear it instead of decorate with it. Considering how we were looking around appraising her place she simply said, "I don't like my environment to distract from my work." And left it at that.

We all nodded our heads and took a seat around the center coffee table where the tea set was steaming. I tried to ascertain what it could be, but there was no distinct aroma emanating from the pot. Then I noticed there was more than one pot...three to be exact. I cocked my head to consider.

Mary noticed my querying look and smiled. "Now, it seems the three of you have some stories to tell. I'd like to hear them each and in their own time, and then we can figure out the best path forward from there. Okay?" she asked. We were all a bit breathless and found we could only nod our heads. She nodded her chin forward in the direction of the tea. "As it happens, you each sat down at your designated pot, so feel free to indulge whenever you are ready."

"Thank you," I finally managed to say as I picked up my pot and sniffed. Mary smiled an enigmatic smile again.

"Special blends for each of you. You will love it, I promise!" she enthused. "Now, who wants to go first?" She looked around at each of us.

"I guess I can start," said Kit, reaching for her teapot and pouring herself a cup. Well, if Kit had no reservations about walking into a stranger's home in the middle of nowhere and diving into specially concocted tea brewed for us, then I guess I shouldn't either. I was feeling a little Hansel and Gretel about all of it, but why not? Kit took a sip of her tea and relaxed back into her spot on the couch she had chosen. The white damask material seemed to glean in the sunlight, and I wasn't sure I had seen fabric like that before. Kit dove into the dreams and visions she had been having, the animals and shields she had seen in the meditation exercise, and the research we had done trying to discern what it all meant.

Mary listened and nodded. "Those are called totems, my dear" she said, finally sipping whatever was sitting in front of her. It looked a bit like lemonade, but in this house, nothing was as it seemed.

Kit cocked her head. "Like a totem pole?" she asked. Mary finished her sip and nodded.

"A bit, yes. What you were being given tells a story with each piece, just as a totem pole does," she finished. We all nodded. That made sense.

"Ok, me next!" Maddy said, giddily sitting at the edge of the chair she had chosen. She had practically downed the entire pot of her tea already, and I wasn't sure if it was nervous energy, caffeine, or that she just had to go pee. Not waiting for a response, she launched into how things had been going for her since she met with Zabina. How her spiritual world had opened up and she had started noticing different patterns and things when she was studying other religions and artifacts as they traveled. Mary seemed impressed, as if she knew how heavily shrouded Maddy had been her entire life.

"And then you've been hearing the voice?" Mary interjected just as Maddy was finishing up. She stopped short in setting her cup down on the table.

"Voices?" Maddy echoed back, unsure.

"Yes. Almost like you have a thought, but it wasn't your own, and it felt placed there like you heard it, but no one was speaking," she said frankly.

Maddy considered this, stunned. "Yes, but how did you…" she began, staring at her. Mary just smiled and patted her knee.

"It's okay. You're not crazy. We'll get there," she said, as reassuringly as she could. Then Mary turned her emerald gaze on me.

"And you, my dear?" she said, anticipating my story as if she already knew it. I shrugged my shoulders.

"I guess mine seems less and less esoteric and more like just a relationship come back to haunt me," I admitted, especially after listening to Kit and Maddy tell their stories. Mary nodded as if having an unseen discussion.

"I see," she said. She paused, letting the moment fill with silence.

I knew how effective that tactic was on my students. I thought I was completely immune to it by now, but apparently not. "It's just that, by comparison, me having a flashback dream to a past relationship doesn't seem all that out there…" I started and took a breath. Kit cut in.

"But it's not just the dream, doll," she said, urging me to say more without saying it.

I sighed. "I know." Then I dove into how I had felt like I was living in two parallel universes, or timelines. I felt like I had one foot in the present and one foot in the past, my immediate past, not like last time of being someone else.

"It's been messing with my head and I'm not sure why he would be coming back to the forefront, given…" I flailed my hands around, "all of it." At this I picked up my teacup again, took a long sip, and sat back.

"Well. We have our work cut out for us today, don't we?" Mary mused, and there was a sparkle in her eye that was undeniable. One could tell she loved days like today and we were going to provide her a lot of fun, it seemed. "Since this isn't technically a group session, and each of you has very different things going on, I'm going to take you each back to my room one-by-one for your sessions," she said. We just sat and stared at her.

"I will work with each of you using some reiki and other energy techniques to see if we can't sift through the clouds that are covering each of your experiences and remove some of the layers causing confusion. Then, we will come back out here and you can sit, relax, and reflect while the next of you goes. Sound good?" she asked, and slapped her knees as she stood. "Who wants to go first?" Then she turned and walked off.

Maddy jumped up, dropped her purse to the chair beside her, and scrambled to follow Mary down the hallway she just left. "Have fun!" Kit called after her, and then turned to face me.

"Now what was that all about?" she asked, eyeing me suspiciously.

"What was *what* all about?" I asked.

"Why were you diminishing your experience in comparison to us? Don't do that," she said and slapped my shoulder.

"Ugh, I know. I'm just…" I considered, "out of sorts. Bryce has been weird lately, and I haven't been able to talk with him about our idea yet, so…" I squirmed in my seat next to her on the pristine white couch and looked around. "How do you think she keeps this place so immaculate? I can't imagine having to keep it clean!" I tried, changing topics.

Kit knew exactly what I was doing but decided to go along with it. "You're telling me! With kids, I wouldn't dream of ever having a place like this. But she obviously has a reason for it. Maybe it helps keep her own personal noise down…like living in selenite, always cleansing everything," she considered out loud. We continued to make small talk for about an hour until we heard a door open down the hall. Maddy came shuffling back and sat down, looking completely drained.

"You good?" I asked her, catching her eye for contact. She nodded her head quietly and took a sip of water from a glass she must have been given in the back room. She smelled of something too…white sage? No. Frankincense? Maybe…

"If my Freya would come to me now," we heard Mary call from the backroom. Kit stiffened, and then must have remembered what she had told her during her story about the prayer that flowed so easily in the shower, and nervous laughed a little. She took the last sip of tea and stood up.

"Coming!" she called out. "Guess it's my turn, ladies. See you on the flip," she said, and she marched down the hallway with purpose only Kit could muster in that gait.

I turned my attention to Maddy, who was still sitting in her chair quietly and contemplative. Two words I wouldn't normally associate with my friend.

"You good?" I asked her again, this time she raised her eyes to mine.

"Yup. Just…" she paused to consider her words carefully, "just…absorbing," she finished, satisfied with the word on which she landed.

"Fair enough. You ready to talk about it or…" I started.

"Nope, not yet," she said, and paused again. "I have a feeling this is going to have to be a group debrief later, after we're back at the house and in our respective spots in the library."

"Ok, good deal," I answered, and we sat in silence for the next hour until we heard the door open and Kit wandered back, much more slowly than she had when she walked down the hall. Gracefully, though almost unseeingly, she sat down on the couch and settled in. I was going to ask her if she was okay, but she just closed her eyes and put her head back as if she too were completely drained. That is some energy work, I thought to myself. These two looked like the plug had been pulled from them. I wondered what had happened when I heard Mary call.

"Okay, Dreamweaver, your turn," she said. Suddenly I had lyrics from Gary Wright's "Dreamweaver" in my head and I smiled to myself.

"Be right there!" I called back. I stood and assessed my friends, just to make sure they were actually okay. Maddy seemed to be perking back up again, sipping on her water. She was also seemingly taking notes in her phone about something, which I took as a positive sign.

Walking back to the room where I saw my friends emerge, the atmosphere changed. It was almost crackling with something I hadn't felt before, not unlike static electricity. The smell shifted too. She must have been burning more than sage back here, but I couldn't quite put my finger on what it was. I turned to the doorway on the left where I heard some soft Gaelic music. The room had almost an orange tint to it, thanks to the gauzy curtains over the windows. Looking around, I saw all manner of elemental pieces on shelves in the room. She had sticks and jars of dirt for earth, seashells and dried seaweed with some river rock for water, feathers and bells for air, and of course a candle burning for fire. Her collection of "trinkets" was expansive. Most I couldn't readily recognize, but it was impressive none the less. I thought back to the word that Zabina had used to describe her, a "callieach," and it made me smile. She seemed to sense my train of thought.

"Yes, these pieces represent each of the known elements, and some otherwise unknown elements. They have been passed down in my family for centuries, and always help with my work," she clarified, proudly surveying the room.

"I can see that, how incredible!" I mused, taking it all in. I doubted it could be *centuries* of pieces, though. Mary was moving the chair from the center of the room and instead unfolded what looked like a massage table, complete with a hole for your face if you were to lay belly down. I looked at it skeptically.

"I have a feeling, while you think your work is superficial, it goes a bit deeper, and I can't have you falling out of a chair while we discover it," she explained, patting the table.

"Okay, whatever you say!" I said, with reservation, but also respect. Of course I had to defer to her, I needed to figure out what was going on. I jumped up, swung my legs forward and laid down on my back. She set a pillow under my head and proceeded to stand at that end.

"Now, close your eyes and breathe in the smoke," she directed. I did as she asked, taking in a deep inhale. Sage, palo santo, frankincense...but there was also sandalwood, and... something floral I couldn't quite put my finger on. Jasmine? "Breathe in and out please," she said, obviously aware I had not yet exhaled. "Now quiet your mind and listen to the music. Just listen..." she was saying, but her voice was suddenly quite far off.

I knew enough about my own meditative states to recognize I had fallen into this one rather quickly. I sensed she was still at my head, hovering her hands over my face, or more accurately my third eye. I just tried to focus on being still.

I saw blues clouding my internal vision. Hazy at first, and then multiple hues blending and bending together. I saw Paul then, just standing there, then he started to blend and bend like the colors and he shifted into Bryce. I started to get cold. A bone-deep chill that was radiating from my center, and then I saw dark water. It was somewhat still, and I could tell it was nighttime. It was silent, and should have been serene, however, I felt anything but. Panic rose in my throat, and before I knew it, I wanted to grasp at my neck, like something was around it, or in it.

Was I drowning? It was an odd liquid sensation to be having on dry land. I fought the urge to reach up and protect my neck. I realized I wouldn't have been able to raise my arms if I wanted to. They felt stone heavy, like I was sinking further and further into the mattress of the table, and yet all I felt was cold around me. My body started convulsing and just as I heard Mary's voice come back to me, counting backwards and she snapped, I saw a face before me...no, above me, looking down at me, but I couldn't tell whose face it was.

I sat bolt upright, almost smacking Mary in the head on my way up in the process. While I wouldn't say she looked shaken, she definitely looked concerned.

"What...was that?" I asked, almost out of breath.

"Well, my dear, I'm not sure." She walked over to her incense bowl, grabbed it and the large white feather, and started going around to each of the corners of the room, waving smoke up into them.

"Goddess of the North, bless and cleanse this space, so that your wisdom may guide us.

*Goddess of the East, bless and cleanse this space
so that we may use our best intellect to discern
what it is you will have us know.*

*Goddess of the South, bless and cleanse this space
so that your child may embark on the
transformation you deem fit with which to bestow
her this day.*

*Goddess of the West, bless and cleanse this space
with water that soothes emotion and brings the
introspection required for the path of this being.*

Said times three, blessed be."

Mary finished her clockwise walk around the room, which I knew was intended to bring energy in rather than force it out. She set the bowl and feather down, and then walked to a water pitcher by the window I had not noticed, to pour me a glass. I reached out to her before I knew what I was doing and took the glass. As I brought it to my lips to drink, I remembered the feeling of water in and around my throat from before and abruptly stopped. I was desperately thirsty, but also terrified.

"It's okay, drink," she urged. She watched me take a tentative sip and set the glass back down on my lap.

"What..." I started, but couldn't bring myself to ask the full question.

"We had to remove some things...from around your neck" she said gently, appraising me and deciding what I was ready to hear. "I am not sure if you saw the same exact things I did, but there was water, you were in it. You were drowning. And you had invisible rope around your neck that was keeping you from speaking your truth. I removed it." She was speaking with measured words. I took another sip of water.

I had seen everything she said, except for the rope. I had felt that. She hadn't said anything about the men's faces.

"Did you see..." I started, but she shook her head.

"I know you had visions of males, but as I have not experienced them, I cannot tell you any interpretation beyond this: One is your mirror, and one is your lesson. Both represent pieces of you and are part of your soul contract in this lifetime, in one way or another. Whether they are two sides of the same soul, or fractals therein, I cannot tell you. I also cannot tell you from what they belong."

I considered. Part of that tracked. She was probably sensing Bryce's and my past life attachment. But the rest was not helping. "What about at the end, the face from above?" I asked, curious, even though she was already speaking in riddles. She only mentioned two men from description, not three.

She paused for what seemed like forever. "I need you to hear me, Sophia," she urged, making direct eye contact to be sure I was listening. I looked into her emerald eyes and nodded. "I believe we just discovered a past life for you, but it has not been cleared. A life in which..." she hesitated. "A life in which you died at the hands of your significant other, in the water." I stared at her as she continued. "It was a life where you were not allowed to speak up for yourself, and you carried that wound in your throat chakra into this life, likely as a karmic lesson for yourself. It is why I had so many things to clear from your throat," she said. I took a sip of water.

"Okay," I managed.

"You may find in the coming days that whatever reservations you have had in the past for speaking up for yourself, or vocalizing your truth, will no longer be hampered. It will be a heady and liberating feeling, but it will also be like building a new muscle. You will want to go slowly so as not to injure it, or anyone else in the process," she said, placing her hand on top of my own.

I wasn't sure if I could ask what was on my mind. It would require further background and conversation and I wasn't sure how long we had already been in the room; my head was in a watery time warp.

"Ask," she said.

I launched into my shortest version of the past months that I could, and ended with the culmination of Bryce and who I believed him to be from that past life.

"So, if we are who I think we are, and are able to karmically find and heal each other in this life, then there is no question who my mirror is now...is there?" I asked, not quite believing my own words. And yet...that past life with Bryce had nothing to do with water.

Mary lifted her hand from mine and walked over to the window contemplating. "I'm not sure. Souls and their contracts are very convoluted and multi-faceted in each lifetime, let alone dragging in the past life dynamic. It is true that you could have been meant or contracted to karmically heal each other from that past life in this one, but it is equally as possible that other versions of your soul through time, i.e. past lives, or even fractals of your souls, could have had other contracts," she answered. Now my head was spinning.

"So, what about Paul? How does he fit into all of this?" I asked, running my fingers through my hair, trying to stymy a headache before it started.

She shrugged. "Nothing. Everything. He could be coming into the forefront to remind you of a simpler time and a different version of yourself that was lost, or he could be a warning," she said and I sighed. "Or he could be nothing," she added. "Not everything is something. That is for you to discern."

I finished the water in my glass and went to stand.

"Steady now, love, while it was only a short session, we uncovered a lot...but as we were unable to clear it, you still have some work to do, and only you can do it." She held her hand out to me so I could steady myself on her if I needed.

I slowly walked out of the room and felt the air shift again. Walking towards the front of the house, I tried to recall everything I had just experienced, but already it was becoming hazy. I hoped it was just the immediate after-effects and not how I would remember everything. I came upon Kit and Maddy whispering to each other, but somewhat back to the land of the energized compared to how I had left them. They looked up at me and I realized what I must look like to them given what I had witnessed on their own faces.

"I'm fine. No worse than you guys when you emerged, I'm sure." I laughed. They were still staring. "What? Do I have something on my face?"

Maddy shook her head and bit her lip. "Not quite."

"What?" I asked again, concern growing in my chest.

"It's just...it looks like you have rope marks around your neck," Kit said quietly. I looked around to find a mirror, but realized a woman like Mary would not have any in her home. She was likely to believe they were portals, and that would add complexity to her daily life. I grasped at my neck instead to see if I could feel anything. It felt fine.

"Huh," was all I managed before Mary emerged. She must have had to do her own clearing ritual after an afternoon like that. When she approached us, she looked completely refreshed.

"Well, how do you girls feel?" she asked as if we had just emerged from a spa treatment, looking from one to the other. We looked at each other too, trying to find the right words.

"I'm not sure," Maddy admitted for all of us.

"That's fair," Mary said with a smile. Each of you is at a great precipice. It will take some time to integrate the work we did today and for you to truly extract all you were meant to from the experience. I'm afraid energy work is not exact and it is completely dependent on the individual to be sure the full integration of intentions is met," she said, but kept her eyes on me. A chill came over me and traveled down my spine. My legs felt heavy.

"What do we owe you?" Kit asked, opening up her purse.

Mary smiled. "Absolutely nothing, my darlings!" and she bent to start clearing the tea things.

"But surely…" I started and she interrupted.

"I would be more offended if you even thought of paying me," she chided.

"But how can that be? You spent so much time with us, and expended your own energy, not to mention shared your own experience and wisdom, we can't possibly accept," Kit urged.

"Absolutely not. I did this as a favor to Zabina. She is one of my oldest and dearest friends. When she says that there are fellow wit-, women in need, I am only too happy to help," she practically sang.

We didn't know what to do. None of us felt right about not paying this woman and walking away, but we didn't want to offend her either. Perhaps we could go back to the fruit stand that Maddy found and put together a thank you basket to drive over on our way out of town, I thought. The girls must have been thinking the same thing because they were shaking their heads, and Maddy winked.

"Alright, if you insist, but we don't feel right about it," Kit tried one last time.

"I do. Now, why don't you get out into that sunshine and back with your families. They will be anxious to share their day with you, even if you cannot with them," she said with a wink.

We gathered our things, put on our shoes, and thanked her one last time. We walked back and silently got in the car. Kit said she would drive since I was still looking a little pale.

"Everyone have everything?" she asked as she adjusted the mirrors. Maddy and I shook our heads. "Good, let's get out of here," she said, not in a harsh way, but also not super-disappointed to be leaving.

"Anyone else feel..." she started.

"Yes," Maddy and I both said at the same time.

"Good, me too," she responded, and turned onto the main road.

We drove back to the mansion in silence, not because each of us didn't have something to share, but because none of us felt ready.

Chapter 26 – Josephine, December 1911

Dearest daughter,

We hope this letter finds you well and enjoying the holiday season. Your father and I wanted to let you know we will set sail for home after the new year. While we will be unable to come directly to retrieve you and your brother, we anticipate being able to send word for you towards the end of February, once we are settled back at the estate.

I wish we could be with you and Charles for Christmas. America has been a wonderfully exciting trip, but I am ready to return to our house with both of you at my side.

We are sending a couple of small gifts your way, and will hold off on the big surprises for when we are home. Please be sure to keep an eye out for any small parcels.

Love you and see you in the new year,
Mother

The letter still lay open on the side table. I had gotten it a few days ago and while it warmed my heart to finally hear from my mother, it was also cruel. I would not be spending the holidays at home with them, and yet

I was also afraid of leaving here in case Oscar should try to send word to me.

It had been almost five months since his last letter in which he stated he would be finding a vessel for us to depart to America. I did not know by which fate I had been cast in a Greek tragedy, but this was starting to feel like I was Clytemnestra being left alone by Agamemnon while he fought the Trojan War.

Only this was an internal war with his own family. I feared the worst: that he had forgotten me after so many months, or that the distance was beginning to wear him down. Either way, I would be left alone and without him. I cried myself to sleep once we had reached the fall and there still was no word. Now, I was too numb to even do that. Charles tried to help keep my spirits up by coming back at day's end and regaling me with the latest stories from the gardens and all of his people-watching, but it was to no avail. Since he could not start boarding school with my parents yet to return as planned, the Viscountess had started him with a tutor, much to his chagrin, to keep him from wandering around so much on his own. It was done under the guise of it being a request from my parents, but I highly suspected that she was concerned with her son sending secret messages through him. She had become even more paranoid since she sent Oscar away, and if possible, overbearing. The whole house felt it, and for them, I truly felt sorry.

"Alright for me to come in, miss?" Alice asked quietly through the cracked door. We had dispensed with her even bothering to knock any more since I was most likely not going to answer anyway.

"Yes, of course, Alice," I said. She walked in holding my dinner tray. I could smell the pine and cinnamon that adorned the halls and banister, the scent wafting through the open door.

"Shepherd's pie," she announced as she set the tray down. Eyeing the letter from my mother still in its place, I heard her softly tutt to herself.

I know she did not approve of my wallowing, even if she could understand it on some level. I still had not told her of our plans from that last meeting, but with her intuition I was sure she sensed there was something bigger at play.

I bee-lined for the small glass of port sitting at the corner of the tray and sipped that first. The look on her face said it all.

"Now, miss, I know it has been months, and your parents will not be home for another few more, but really, it cannot be as bad as all..." she stopped herself short and considered. "No, on second thought, I will bring you another glass after you finish." This caused me to sputter and giggle. "There now, that's better. I missed that sound," she said with a mischievous grin.

"Alice! You knew exactly what you were saying now, didn't you!" I said with as much enthusiasm as I could muster. She may not know everything, but she did still know how to get me to smile.

"I know not of what you speak," she said and winked back at me. I set the glass back on the tray and considered the steaming pie. My appetite had all but evaded me and my clothes no longer fit as they once did.

Had it not been for Alice's scones, I surely would have wasted away to nothing. They were also the last tie I had to *him*, and so I relished whenever they were available.

"Any packages today, Alice?" I asked. The few parcels my mother had spoken of were at least some small bit of light in an otherwise dim world. Under normal circumstances, I know Charles would have been waiting for them from his perch, but the tutor that the Viscount had found per his wife's instruction was truly brutal and kept him as busy as possible for what seemed like all hours of the day.

"Not today, miss" she said, absentmindedly tidying around the room as she waited for me to take a bite. She no longer trusted that I would actually eat unless she saw me start. "Though..." she started, and then stopped herself, weighing whatever it was she had to say.

I sat down quietly, placed the napkin on my lap and picked up the fork and knife to make an attempt at the pie. It was not a personal favorite, but it did smell divine.

"Well, miss, there were no packages as it were, however I may have overheard some news," she said hesitantly.

Her idea of news and mine were further and further apart these days, so I only half paid attention as she walked back over to me and I took my first bites. The gravy was not half bad, and the pastry was flakier than usual. I may actually enjoy this food tonight.

"His Lordship is coming home for Christmas, miss," she said and bit her lip, waiting to see how I would react. It took me a moment to process what I was hearing. I set my fork down and wiped at my mouth with the napkin.

"What did you say, Alice?" I asked, still unsure that I had heard her correctly.

She just looked at me and shook her head up and down.

My heart skipped and my breath caught. He was coming home? Was it truly possible? What had shifted that this would be allowed? Then I paused my racing thoughts. How could this be that *she* would not let him come back to the house if I was still here, and yet I knew I would be here because my parents had said so in their letter. There must have been a different reason, the one I feared most.

"We must not get our hopes up, dear Alice. I cannot imagine they would have kept him away all this time only to bring him back when nothing has significantly changed," I said, still puzzling this change of events in my mind.

Alice continued to bite her lip as if there was more.

"Yes?" I asked, quickly losing my patience. I know we had not been the confidants we once were, but surely, she had not gotten so peevish as to not share everything.

"It's just, well, there is to be a party, and…" she was stalling now, but a party did not seem like something one would quibble over.

"And?" I said coaxing her along.

"And, the Earl and his family will be in attendance." This she said while letting her voice drop at the end, as if she too was unhappy with the turn of events.

Well, there you have it. The other shoe has dropped. Of course, they would not invite him home unless there was proper motivation. "I see," I managed, before sitting back in my chair. What little appetite I had mustered was now gone again. I wiped my mouth once more and placed the napkin on top of the tray. Alice's shoulders dropped, knowing this would be my response.

"I am sorry, miss. I should not have said anything, or at least not until you had finished a proper meal."

"It's alright, Alice. I was not even that hungry," I lied, so she would not feel bad.

"Miss, I know these past few months have not been easy. I can only imagine what had transpired between you and his Lordship that would cause you such turmoil in his absence, but I do see this as an opportunity, Earl or no Earl. But, if I may miss, we must do something about your color!" she sputtered.

I must have looked shocked at her outburst, but I stayed silent to let her continue.

"I am sorry miss, but, with you not getting fresh air and not eating, you have lost some of your vim and vigor, and if you are to win him back, or at the very least, turn his head, I must insist you eat something. And we must consider what is in your closet to wear for the party and get you ready," she said with as much confidence as she could muster.

I could not knock her for what she said. I had let myself go. The more I thought about it, the angrier I became. Why? How had I let one person affect me so? If he could so easily forget about me and leave me to my own devices, then I suppose it was time I did the same. Now, I was not going to gather my strength so much as to "win" him, but to impress in spite of him. I suddenly did not want him to be aware of my supreme longing for him, or how bad the situation had gotten. I stood up, almost knocking the tray over, which startled Alice.

"What do you suggest?" I asked her, staring straight into her eyes. She must have recognized the fire coming back to me and smiled.

"Well, miss..." she said, and she wandered over to the tray, lifting my napkin off of the top, being careful not to get any residue anywhere. "I would start by finishing your meal." And she winked.

One week later, and the house was abuzz. I could even feel it locked away in my room. However, I, like the house, was preparing for the arrival of its long-lost young master. We were both doing the best we could with a bit of spit and polish to be sure we were ready to impress. Only I did not have paper decorations, evergreens, and candles adorning me. No, this night had called for something special.

After deciding to come back from the land of the lost, I wrote to my mother, asking if it would be possible to secure a dress for the party. With mutual peerage coming, I knew I had to represent my family accordingly.

She was only too pleased and allowed me to make my own arrangements. And I did.

This dress was to be my revenge. For all the months of wallowing in self-pity, I decided it was time to hold my head high and not continue to be a pawn in someone else's game. If he was going to play me as his parents were him, he thought wrong. I could not believe it had taken me so long to see it.

Let him try to engage with me, I, will not fall for it', thoroughly convinced that his mother had won out over him, I thought to myself as I looked at my reflection, feeling emboldened by what looked back.

Thanks to Alice's insistence, my color had come back to my cheeks and I had begun filling out again, though in different places than before. My true womanly form seemed to be shining through and I no longer had a straight profile, but more of an hourglass figure.

The dress, was a deep scarlet red, made with rich velvet that rouched and cascaded in all the right places from the bodice, across my hips and down to the floor in a short train. The sheer silk material at my shoulders and arms looked like it had been spun by the angels themselves, and matched the burgundy hue. There were small crystal embellishments along the wide square neckline and a matching crystal brooch at the center of the low v-back just above where the column skirt and train started. I had a long string of pearls that added beautiful depth, and Alice had once again worked her magic with my hair, this time in a low and curled chignon at the nape of my neck. I elected to wear my simple pearl stud earrings, and matching three-string pearl cuff.

I did not know what the rest of the household was wearing this evening, but I did not care. My dress felt like the exact armor I needed to go into this particular battle, once again reminding me of my Greek tragedy, and gave me strength. I was still bewildered as to the circumstances that allowed me to come down and be a part of the festivities after so many months of being imprisoned. The Viscountess must have had some assurances from someone that all would be well and I was no longer a threat, but by whom I could not say, nor did I dare dwell... Other than my new found resolve fueled by anger, but I also did not want to give her the satisfaction at having "given him up."

There was a knock at my door, and I assumed it would be Charles come to escort me downstairs. I padded swiftly over and opened it. Charles stood there, staring back at me. Once again, I found my shy younger brother looking at me with such wonderment that I almost lost my bearings.

"Too much?" I asked him, though if he knew to what I was referring I had no idea.

He seemed unsure of how to respond, and merely shook his head side-to-side. That was good enough for me, so I picked up my train loop, placed it around my wrist, and walked out the door, closing it behind me. I linked my arm with his and we started for the head of the stairs. Feeling rather confident, I was actually excited where this night would take me.

Then, just as we got to the edge of the banister, I heard the front door open and voices come inside. It must be the Earl's family. I looked over at Charles and when I saw shock on his face, I thought perhaps I'd been wrong in whom I had heard. I looked back and that is when I saw it. I was not wrong that it had been the Earl's family arriving, but *he* was with them. Gasping, I put my ivory satin opera-gloved hand to my mouth. The small action or sound was enough to catch his attention and he looked up. I quickly dropped my hand to my side and did my best to school my face into nonchalance. I could not let my armor crack this early in the evening and at the mere sight of him.

Charles must have sensed my hesitation, but started us down the stairs anyway. He was eager to attend the dinner so that he could just as quickly excuse himself from the remainder of the festivities and climb back to his room.

I dropped my eyes walking down the stairs so as not to trip, and we deftly came around the corner. As we did, I noticed Oscar's attention was back with the Earl's family, and Katerina was standing just at his side. Dressed in a pretty pink satin gown, she looked positively glowing amongst the candles in the hallway. Oscar kept his back to us and did his best to ignore our presence until we were all ushered into the dining room for our aperitifs. I managed to shuffle into a corner so I could be present, but out of the way of the mainstream conversations. I needed to keep myself steady and aloof, resistant to his charms—something I thought I was fully capable of until I had seen him again. The flash in his eyes as he had looked up at me and then not again the rest of the evening had been more disarming than I had prepared for.

No wonder no one would tell me where he was. Had they truly sent him off to live with the Earl and his family? It would make sense if they were trying to keep him and Katerina in close proximity, and yet under watchful eye. I am sure the Earl had plenty of rooms, or even a separate apartment in which Oscar could live, and even be taken under the Earl's wing.

But that also meant, unless he was off on their country estate, that he had been in the city all this time. My anger boiled up inside me again as I worked all this out over the gazpacho, roasted duck with cherry compote, glazed carrots, and other courses being rotated in front of my golden charger. I could barely keep up with the amount of food coming from the kitchen and only managed to sip the claret, which the footmen kept full. By the time dessert was served, my head was swimming, with my own confused and angry thoughts as well as the wine, and I found I was ready for bed.

Seeming pleased with herself, the Viscountess was only too happy to allow my request to be dismissed from the table. A victory indeed. I did not know what I had expected from the evening, but it was certainly not this.

Everyone moved from the table into their respective after-dinner rooms. The men went into the library for cigars and brandy, the ladies moved into the parlor, and I took my permitted leave and climbed the stairs. My feet felt heavy as I ascended, making my way back to my room.

Alice had clearly been there since the fireplace was already lit, and my dressing gown laid out on the bed. My head was still fuzzy from the amount of claret I had consumed, and I could not fathom changing out of my gown on my own at the moment, so I shuffled off my slippers and sat down by the fire. Staring into the flames, I was mesmerized, and felt like I was in a trance. I did not know how long I stayed like that, but I heard muffled sounds below go from a dull roar to a mere whisper. I assumed that the household had retired and everyone else not living there had departed.

What an evening. I suppose it was my worst fear come true. Oscar had not only been sent off and away because of me, but he was also being indoctrinated into a family and class for which he claimed he had previously no ambition or desire. Yet now he was at the mercy of them, and their absolutely characterless daughter. Perhaps I would have felt a bit better about it if she showed even a sliver of personality, but she had none. I had not directly spoken with her, but I had observed her, and she truly was a dullard.

Just as I was coming out of my flame-entranced meditation, I heard what sounded like a soft knock at the door. It must be Alice coming to help me undress. Finally, I thought, and said, "come in." No one answered. There was only a slightly familiar sound of paper scuttling across the floor. I sat up and looked in the direction of the door and saw it. A cream piece of paper folded on itself, with a red seal.

I looked back at the fire, then back to the spot on the floor, thinking perhaps I was dreaming and this was not real. I even pinched my arm for good measure, and when it hurt, I winced and stood. I approached it as if I was cornering a cat about to slip away, because I was sure it would disappear before of my eyes. I bent over, picked it up, and gingerly brought it back over by the fire, as it was now the only source of light in the room.

Dearest Sephie,

I hope I may still call you that after these many months. I have nothing to say except that I miss you, desperately, and am so very sorry for whatever pain I may have caused you. I was beginning to think that perhaps my parents were right when they sent me away, that my frenzy for you was mere childish whimsy and that once I was secure in my standing with Katerina, I would understand. While I longed for you, I also realized I would have to let you go, so that you could live your life and not be held back by me or my family.

But time apparently makes one blind. Seeing you again this evening. Being in your presence. I realize now, they are the ones who are wrong. We may be young, but what we have is true.

My darling, you are a vision. And for all your reserve and restraint you showed this evening, I know you had a million and one thoughts circulating in that intelligent head of yours. My only fear is that the reserve and restraint that I witnessed may have been born from your no longer loving or needing me in the way that I love and need you. Am I too late? Has the damage been done?

I pray that we have not lost our magic. That under it all, you will understand. I had to do what I did to save you. And I would do it again, even if it meant a thousand more moments of having to look up to you standing at the head of those stairs, looking every bit the vision of Helen of Troy.

We are still not safe. While tonight was performative in this game of chess in which we find ourselves with her, I am afraid this is a long game in the art of war. I have a plan, where we may still be together, but I am afraid it will take a little more time. Will you wait for me? Or have you forsaken me after all this time? I would not blame you if you have, though I must admit, especially after having seen you again tonight, it may be the end of me as we know it.

Please try to get word to me if you can. Though I do not want to say exactly how, should this somehow get into the wrong hands, I believe you and I have a mutual 'cherub' who would be willing to assist.

I love you, my darling. I disappoint myself at times for being too easily influenced by her, no matter how much I fight it. Please forgive my having to ignore you this evening, and all the time leading up to tonight, I fear had I not, this charade would have all fallen apart.

I hope to hear from you in the very near future. And I hope, it will be in the affirmative.

With all my heart,
Oscar

"And I will love thee still, my dear,| Till a' the seas gang dry."

And just like that, my icy armor melted before the fire, never to return.

He did love me. He had been fighting for us, even if not the entire time, even if unknown to me. He did have a plan. I had let my imagination and isolation get the better of me. I knew that his mother would be pushing all sorts of things into this head, and had despaired that it had worked. Perhaps it had in a way. He admitted as much in the letter. But also, apparently, I was wrong—time had made him blind and yet I had been the salve he needed.

I grasped that letter to my heart and nearly burst. I knew just what I had to do, and thankfully through whom to do it. But first, I needed to sleep. Perhaps truly for the first time in months.

Chapter 27 – Sophia, June Present Day

"Good morning, beautiful," I heard as I started to stretch awake. It startled me a bit, which shook the bed and Violet emitted a little annoyed moan. Bryce laughed.

"Sorry. Good morning, I wasn't expecting you to be awake and I was just stretching…" I admitted, not sure if I wanted to be awake yet or not. He took that as an invitation and pulled me into him.

I realized it had been a minute since he'd done so. We had been going, going, going so much on this trip, separated into our little groups, that we hadn't yet had a morning to just relax. Violet seemed to be happy with the vibe, but not with the space encroachment. As we tried to snuggle into each other as the puzzle pieces we were, she stood, arched her back and stared at us disapprovingly.

"Alright girl, you have a bed over there if your highness is so bothered," I quipped. She seemed to understand, and then defiantly curled up into a ball at the corner, out of the way, but still very much on our bed.

Bryce started kissing my ear, which I didn't think I was ready for, given how he had been the past few days. I turned my head and he pouted.

"What? I can't love on my love?" he asked, half-jokingly, but I could see something in his eyes.

"No, I didn't say that, it's just..." I stalled. He cocked his head to look at me more directly.

"It's just, what?" he asked, concern rising in his voice. I felt his arms tense around my waist.

"It's just...you've been...I don't know. Weird lately?" I tried. He looked confused. "Off. Like, you've been here physically, but your head has been somewhere else." He still looked at me dubiously. "Or maybe you're just mad at me about something?" I tried again.

He made a show of thinking. "Nacht, I'm fine my Bonnie Lass. Just not used to sharing you with so many people. Maybe I miss having you all to myself on our adventures," he said and gave me a wry smile.

So, he wasn't in the mood to talk about the last couple of days. Or perhaps it truly had nothing to do with me. Or...and this was the more likely, he was just feeling 'frisky' after so many days and was letting the testosterone override anything else that was bothering him.

"Okay, if you say so," I said, somewhat disappointed I didn't have an answer.

"I do," he said and pulled me in tighter. "Now, why don't we take advantage of the quiet morning and..." as if right on cue, we heard the pitter-patter of little feet running down the hall. I laughed. He tried not to groan.

"I get it, but obviously there are other plans. I did have something I wanted to discuss with you if you truly are okay..." I started, but then hesitated with the look in his eye. Was that annoyance? Concern?

"Oh-kay" he said, drawing out the two-letter response.

"Well, I don't have to!" I said, getting up from the bed and starting to feel somewhat annoyed myself.

"No!" he said, and he pulled me in again. I was trapped in his embrace from behind, which was not an advantageous position. "If it means we can lay here a bit longer, we can read the entire encyclopedia," he mused. My shoulders relaxed. "What did you want to talk about?"

"It's just. It's kind of awkward, and now that I think of it, maybe too forward, so perhaps I shouldn't..." I started talking myself out of saying anything before I had even begun. So much for throat chakra clearing, Mary.

"Soph, whatever it is, it cannot be that bad" he said, trying to reassure me.

I thought about how to approach it. Direct was best. "Okay, so you know how we've been circling, talking about what I should do and decisions that need to be made with the University?" I asked. He nodded, not wanting to interject and cause me to stop my train of thought.

"Well, I've been giving some thought to what it is I want out of my next move. If I could craft anything, what would the parameters or non-negotiables be?" I looked at him to make sure he was with me.

"And those are..." he ventured.

"I love teaching. I miss my students. I miss our discussions, the 'ah-ha' lightbulb moments, the sharing of my story for them to learn from, but also how much I learned from them in turn. I miss the relationships I built, and I even miss all the relationships I would have built to come," I admitted. His face was darkening. He obviously thought my talk track was going in a specific direction, and away from him. I flipped over to face him and put my hand on his chest.

"But I also love you. I love spending time with you. Exploring the countryside. And I certainly don't miss the people I taught with, save for maybe a couple." I winked. His face was brightening again. "I do, however, need a purpose. Traversing Scotland with you over these past few months has been an amazing bonus to my forced sabbatical, but I can't keep doing that for the rest of my life. I've been in a space before where I allowed myself to be diminished, and part of this trip's purpose was to make sure I didn't let that happen again. Exploring what it is I want, and almost more importantly what I don't." His face was falling again. I could tell I wasn't making myself clear and I was botching this all up.

"So, what are you saying, Soph?" he cautiously asked. I put my hands over my face and rubbed it to wake myself up a bit more. Maybe I was still half asleep and that's why the words weren't coming out.

"I'm saying..." I thought for a moment. Maybe I would try Kit's language. "I'm saying, wouldn't it be nice if I knew someone who had connections at another University where I might pitch my experiences and services so that I could have a purpose, do what I feel I'm called to do, and also be near my hunky Scots Guard?" I said in one fell swoop. Maybe my throat chakra was starting to open after all.

He looked bewildered for a fraction of a second and then it hit him. "Really?" Other words tumbled out. I smiled. He pulled me in close, tucked my head under his chin and kissed the top of my head. Then he pulled back to look me in the eye again to confirm his realization of my meaning. "You mean it?" he asked softly. I nodded. "I will call my Dean today!" he exclaimed, and released me so he could lay on his back and think.

"Well," I said and he pivoted his head to look at me again. "You could do that...or, we could use the ball as a platform of introduction..." I felt a little odd offering it up since it was to honor him and I didn't want him to think I was trying to usurp his evening.

He considered that for a moment. "I think it is a brilliant idea, Bonnie Lass, and we absolutely shall use it as an opportunity for intros, but I think I want to give my Dean a head's up and maybe even line up some super-warm intros on your behalf," he said, thinking out loud. I loved watching his brain work. "Yes, I think that's the approach. Then you can be the belle of the ball!" he added.

"No, I don't want to be the belle of *your* ball. I just wanted to start softening the path to make it easier when I try to connect with them afterward. We don't even know yet if they have a spot for what I do, or if they'd accept a professor like me. Remember, I don't have my Ph.D., just my MBA. I don't qualify for tenure-track, and yet I would be looking for something that was more than an adjunct. It's a 'golden goose' type of position," I confessed.

"I understand love, just leave it to me" he said with confidence. We snuggled for a moment longer before he kissed me on my forehead and added, "Now I think I hear more feet, which means breakfast must get underway. Remind me again what it is we have planned for the day?"

"Nothing. We planned it as a low-key relaxing day since we will be heading back to Edinburgh tomorrow or the next. The girls and I just want to run on errand, but otherwise, there is nothing," I said, remembering the idea we had of taking Mary a 'thank you basket' of sorts. We had intended to do so on the way out of town, but it would be just as easy to leverage the time we had today…

"Right. Alright then, it gives me time to think. And cook." And with that, he swung out of bed, changed into shorts and a t-shirt, hit the bathroom, and went downstairs, with a pep in his step I hadn't seen for a bit.

God, it was supremely sexy when he took charge, I thought. And, I hated to admit it to myself, it was kind of nice to have someone who took care of me instead of me always having to be the caretaker of myself and others. It was exhausting, and refreshing to have found someone who could, and would. It had been a while, I mused, but stopped that train of thought before it left the station and muddled my mind for the day.

I laid there for another minute or two, enjoying a stretch, spread eagle on the bed, and then got up. Violet took that as her cue to get going as well. With it being a relaxing day, I merely changed into comfortable shorts and t-shirt myself, bushed my teeth, and went downstairs. The smell of Highlander Grogg coffee meandered up the stairwell and made me smile as I descended.

Everyone was seated around the table except Ryan. I looked to Maddy who smirked. "Let's just say Mr. Big Shot Photographer man is more accustomed to shooting vistas of courses, and not playing on them. He's a little sore."

I laughed.

"Hey, yeah, we never got to ask when we got back yesterday, how was St. Andrews?" Kit inquired as she started passing the toast that had just been brought to the table.

Erik laughed. "You didn't ask because y'all were walking zombies when you came back! What the heck happened to you?"

We looked at each other and shrugged our shoulders. We had yet to speak of it, so there was no way we could tell them.

Kit took the lead. "We, were perfectly fine. And, we're not telling you muggles what transpired! Now, don't switch the topic."

Tate and Thora giggled at their mom using the word "muggle" to describe the group, and then grew concerned that maybe she meant them too. She read the look on their faces and interjected before Erik could… "don't worry darlings, I didn't mean you."

Erik mock-scowled at the insult and carried on. "Well, us *muggles*," placing extra emphasis on the word, "had an amazing time!" He beamed. He clearly couldn't help himself. Bryce laughed in the background as he finished the next omelet.

"Oh, did you now," Kit bantered back, not missing a beat.

"Yes. Seriously. What an amazing surprise and opportunity," he said, then he turned to me. "Soph, you are not allowed to ever leave this man, and if you do, can I have him?" He was all smiles.

I winced a bit, given the conversation Bryce and I just had so fresh, with me basically asking him to put his reputation on the line and get me hired at his school. But I understood his sentiment. Only Kit noticed my reaction, but didn't say anything, and clearly catalogued it away for later.

"Well, I'm not sure you're his type, but I will take it under advisement," I responded, looking Bryce's way. His back was turned to me focusing on the stove, so I couldn't read any expressions. Weird.

"Best. Day. Ever." Erik enthused. Then looking at Kit, he turned and blew her a kiss. "Except the day I married you dear, of course." She groaned.

"If I had something to throw at you I would!" I said.

"Get a room, you two," we heard from the stairwell as Ryan slowly made his way down.

The rest of the morning carried on with similar topics of conversation, the guys and kids weighing in on their time spent at the course, and finished with everyone pitching in to clean up breakfast.

"Right. Well, with us having a slow day, I'm going to go up to the market and grab a few things for that basket," I said out loud to the room.

"Ooo, I think I'll come with. I want to grab a couple things to take with us tomorrow, or whenever we leave," Maddy added. We both looked over at Kit.

"Okay, I will come too, but I don't want to be too long. I promised the kiddos we'd go hike the grounds today and look for fairy gardens," she responded. Tate and Thora nodded their heads enthusiastically at the idea while their mouths were full.

"No worries. We can grab whatever we need from the market, run it over to Mary, and be back before lunch!" I said confidently.

We all went to change into public-facing attire, jumped back into the Mini Cooper and drove off. At the market, we found a ton of goodies; fresh produce, dried herbs, warm bread...all things we thought our sixties-loving energy woman would appreciate. I left it to Kit and Maddy to assemble it into a respectful package while we drove back to Mary's cottage.

It didn't take us long to get back to the area when I slowed down a bit, surveying the land. "Guys, did I miss a turn? Or maybe I'm blind...I don't see it?"

Kit and Maddy looked up from their project and glanced around, too. "Huh," Kit managed.

"Are you sure you went the same way?" Maddy asked.

"I mean...I think so. It's not like we could use GPS for the place yesterday. I followed the same directions Zabina had given us. But I see no stone fence, thatched roof or purple door..." I said still scanning the horizon.

"Pull over," Kit suggested. I shrugged and found a safe spot to pull over on the narrow road amongst the tall fescue. We all got out of the car and wandered around.

"I must've gotten turned around guys, I'm sorr—" I stopped short. Something colorful caught the corner of my eye to the right. I walked forward to pick it up; it was a colorful silk scarf, blowing in the breeze. I raised it through my fingers, turning to show the girls. They both stopped in their tracks and raised their hands to their mouths in astonishment.

I glanced back down at the scarf, and then out to the water. The house was gone. One could easily say that we were in the wrong spot except, how was her scarf here?

After a minute, I began walking back to the car, scarf in hand. Maddy ran over and pulled it from me to study. "Well, this is unlike any piece I've seen...I wonder who makes it?" she muttered to herself, turning it this way and that trying to find a tag or a logo or something. "It's incredibly well made..."

I looked at Kit.

"It's all incredibly Brigadoon if you ask me..." she mused and we got back into the car.

I put it in drive and we pulled away from the spot. I noticed an odd energy shift, and buzzing in the air, similar to what I had experienced when I walked down

Mary's hallway. I thought of the word Zabina used to describe her again. Cailleach, indeed.

That night, after a day of lounging and enjoying the mansion in the countryside one last time, I settled in for sleep. Still mystified, but completely content in the overall happenings that transpired. And then, it started...

As I came to, I felt like I was drifting in something cold and liquid. When I finally opened my eyes and looked up, I realized I was not drifting...I was sinking. The inky blue water was becoming darker all around me as what little bursts of light from above grew dimmer.

In sudden horror, it struck. He had let go of me.

Why? He was supposed to be my protector. We were in this together. We had just been through hell and made it to relative safety, for the time being, but now? I was sinking away from the water's surface, and watching him, watch me, fall...further and further below.

I clutched myself in pure fear and wanted to scream out, but I did not want the water to invade my lungs. I tried to reach up to bring myself above the surface again, but my already heavy wool clothes were water-logged and weighing me down, while the water around me was ice-cold and restricting my ability to move.

I continued to sink, looking up to him, getting smaller and smaller...

I bolted up in bed, gasping for air. Neither Bryce nor Violet were bothered by my sudden movement or choking sounds.

What was that? A dream? A flashback? Oh, not again...

With horror I realized that the silhouette I saw at the end of my session the day before with Mary. I was drowning in my dream, and I heard Mary's words: "One, is your mirror, and one is your lesson..."

Chapter 28 – Josephine, February 1912

It had taken some doing, but my oh-so-observant brother had been able to use his powers to deduce where Freddy lived in the city. The next task had been talking Robert into taking the message to him. While he had been reluctant, he also still harboured guilt in being the one to tell the Viscount about our week, and he said he would find a way to ferry the letter over to him in the course of his day.

I had not been too terribly loquacious in my writing to Oscar, as I was afraid someone was going to intuit what I was doing as I wrote, so kept it brief.

My Dearest Oscar,

Your note has given me such a sense of relief, you cannot imagine. I had truly lost all hope and gotten so angry at you thinking you had forsaken me. I am sorry my love, I should have known better.

Yes, of course, I still love you. Yes, of course, I will wait for you. I do not know for how long you think we must wait, but you should know that my parents travel back from America in the new year and will send for my brother and I to join them back in Bath. My mother anticipates the end of February, so it shall be important that you not try to find me under your parents charge then. I hope that this is welcome news and only further supports your plan.

I will patiently wait for your word, and will not lose hope again.

I am yours,
Sephie

Thankfully with all the frivolity of the holidays, Robert had found an excuse to dispatch himself on errands during the day and delivered the letter to Freddy. While I had no idea when or if Freddy would be able to deliver it to Oscar, I had hoped it would be sooner rather than later and there would be a response.

Unfortunately, that had been five weeks ago, and now Charles and I had packed up our belongings and were currently making our way back home.

I sat on the train looking out the window at the world speeding by, remembering how the last time I had done so, I was on the train...next to him. Charles had gone to wander through the cars as he could not sit still, even for the relatively short ride. He was also worried about our trunks remaining secure and said he wanted to watch out the caboose to ensure nothing was falling off on our way.

I found myself humming a tune, and realized I was humming it because someone nearby was singing it, quietly, but there.

By yon bonnie banks and by yon bonnie braes,
Where the sun shines bright on Loch Lomond,

I smiled. And then I started cautiously looking around, my heart beginning to race. Hadn't Oscar said in one of his previous letters that if I ever heard the song, it would mean he was nearby? Of course, he probably meant metaphorically, as in it would mean he was thinking of me, or I was in his thoughts, but perhaps...

I caught a flash of dark hair under a bowler hat in the row opposite me. The gentleman had his head turned; it could not possibly be? I stared. Willing him to look at me, growing more and more confident that the song had created a shock wave that would produce Oscar directly in front of me. Then the man did turn his head, probably sensing someone staring at him. My breath caught, but it was not him. I tried quickly looking the other way so as not to be noticed. I was not sure if I had been successful, but was too upset to care. I do not know why I got my hopes up so quickly, other than I wanted it to be true.

Instead, I closed my eyes and rested my head against the window. It may be early afternoon, but the stress from packing and leaving, was finally catching up with me. I could feel my body start to relax as soon as we stepped on the train and we were that much closer to being home and out of the clutches of...her.

I once again was being lulled to sleep by the movement and soft hum of the tracks. Then I was dreaming.

I realized as I came to that I felt like I was drifting, in something cold and liquid. When I finally opened my eyes and looked up, I was not drifting...I was sinking.

I clutched myself in pure fear and wanted to scream out, but I did not want the water to invade my lungs. I tried to reach up and out to bring myself above the surface again, but I continued to sink. Looking up, I saw a figure above me. They could save me!

Someone grabbed my shoulder just then and I startled awake. I must have caused a bit of a scene because everyone was staring at me when I became fully aware and present as to where I was and what was going on around me. Charles only looked at me confused.

"Josie, our stop is next. I thought you should know." And then he sat down opposite me, evaluating me with those eyes. I tried straightening up in my seat and putting my hat to rights on top my head. "Are you alright?" he asked, not convinced with my charade.

"Yes," I blurted out, too quickly.

He considered me. "If you say so..." and turned to look out the window.

Grateful he was not going to continue to interrogate me, I did the same. 'What was that about?' I asked myself. Had I been dreaming of drowning? What did that mean? Drowning in my affections? Surely, I could not be so sappy. And who was above me watching it happen? Were they friend or foe? Were they helping me? It did not seem as if they were, but I also felt sure they would...

The train came to a stop while I was in my reverie and it took Charles knocking my knee for me to notice we were there. I stood, looked out the window for any sight of our parents, and then grabbed my reticule and filed outside. Looking for the baggage tickets, I gave them to our driver to claim our trunks. Numbers 23, 44, 86 and 105. I looked around, shielding my eyes from the midday sun, to find anyone from our household. Then I saw him. My parents may not have been able to meet us there, but one could not mistake Rupert. He was my father's Butler and Valet, and oldest confidante. I was somewhat surprised to see him there and not one of the footmen, but it was also a comfort.

"Rupert!" I heard Charles cry. He barreled at the old man as if he wasn't growing in size and strength, and was still very much the little boy that Rupert would fly over his head when no one was looking. For all of his English formality, he had a soft spot for children, especially my brother. Having none of his own and a life-long bachelor, I imagined it was his opportunity to envision what it would have been like, had he a family of his own.

"Master Charles," he said, looking him in the eye at first and then taking him into a warm embrace. It had been the longest any of us had ever been away from each other, and it was good to see him.

I quietly walked up to them and cleared my throat. "Miss Josephine, a pleasure it is to see you. You are looking particularly well, which pleases me to no end," he said and bowed his balding head in my direction. "While I could have also done with an embrace such as Charles received, we knew it improper in public." I gave him my warmest smile, gently grasped his forearm and patted it. This made him smile and place his hand on top of mine.

"Now, where are those baggage tickets?" he said, getting back to all business. "We must get you home, your parents are waiting with baited breath to see you."

Before we knew it, our trunks had been collected, stacked into the carriages, and we were on our way home. Home. It had been a while since I could think of the word and not have a knot in my stomach. The last time I had felt that way was the day Oscar and I had spent together. The carriages passed by the park where we had our picnic and I practically swooned, but knew I had to keep up pretenses. No recent letter or not, I was not about to give away the game now.

Our homecoming was all you would expect from our parents. For everything that Oscar's parents were, Charles' and mine were the exact opposite. Warm, inviting, loved their children and took pride in any manner of accomplishments. It had been a long year not being together.

After a round of solid hugs (my father truly gave the best of them), I took a moment and looked around the house. When I caught myself looking up at the ceiling, I stifled a laugh. I really did do that often, considering Oscar's acute observation. My heart ached a little every time I thought of him, but at least I had hope. Perhaps we may even be able to arrange a time to discretely see each other now that I was out from under his mother's roof and omnipresent eye. I shook my head. Thoughts for another time. My parents had spared no expense in cooking up a true family reunion dinner.

It was wonderful being back home and walking the halls, seeing our staff who were, for all intents and purposes, family to us. Even cook came out from the kitchen to say hello, and presumably evaluate how well we had been nourished while we were away.

"Looking a bit thin there, miss. Did they not feed you adequately?" she said, eyeing me up and down.

"They fed me well enough Ms. Hangendorfer, however nowhere near the likes of you," I said, which caused her to puff up her chest and smile a bit.

"Well then, you will be in for a treat tonight I should fink" she said, and turned on her heel to go back to the kitchen.

Feeling the exhaustion creep back in, I told my mother I wanted to go lie down a bit before the meal. She looked at me with her soft brown eyes and brushed a wayward hair from my forehead. "Alright, my sweet girl. It seems this year has been harder on you than we anticipated. For that, I am sorry," she said, sensing my weariness was not just travel-related.

"I am alright, mother, truly. There is no need to apologize. Besides, all will be right again in the world. We are home!" I tried to sound somewhat enthused. But the immediate future was still in such turmoil and unknown chaos, I did not know how to feel about it all. Was I home now only to have to pick up and run away soon? Oscar said it would take time for him to figure something out, but how long? Should I tell my parents anything? Would they support the relationship and our plan?

I climbed the stairs up to my room, second door on the left. It creaked open as I entered and I surveyed what lay before me.

My trunks had already been brought upstairs, and one of the maids had begun unpacking some of my dresses to keep them from wrinkling. I went to sit by the vanity, if only to rest my feet and set down my reticule. Looking into the mirror, I was reminded of all the time I had sat in front of one with Alice behind me, brushing my hair and sharing her unexpected wisdom. I suddenly missed my friend with a fervor. Would I ever see her again? She had been a bright spot, my one constant through it all. I was not sure I had properly conveyed that to her and wanted to write to be sure she understood. But would that be proper?

Suddenly, the dinner bell was rung. So much for a lie down. I shook my head to rid myself of the melancholy that was threatening to consume me. I quickly changed out of my travel clothes and into a cream lace top with dark brown wool skirt. I affixed a cameo brooch I had all forgotten about, at the center of my high collar. I touched at my hair, still tied in a high psyche knot, and pinched my cheeks. Giving myself an approving nod, I turned and went down to dinner to hear the tales from my parents' travels abroad and how their year had gone without us.

Chapter 29 – Maddy/Kit/Sophia – June, Present Day

Maddy packed up the last of her things lying around the room and zipped up her suitcase. Ryan eyed her skeptically from the door. "Are you sure you have everything?" he asked with the patience of a saint.

"Yes." She glared at him. His eyebrow raise was well earned. She had a history of forgetting things everywhere they stayed, but she counted it as part of her charm.

She watched Ryan heave the bag over head to carry it downstairs and then looked around the room. Patting the wall as she exited, she thanked the room for a fabulous stay and tried to show gratitude to this rather sentient space.

She had learned over the past few months that each place could be more alive than one thought, and homes were at the crux of that. She was amazed she hadn't come to realize it before, but as she has been told now, by multiple soothsayers, and even her own experience, she had been under a dark veil for so long.

She jogged down the stairs to get to the car. Everyone else had seemingly packed up the night before, or at least was up earlier than she was getting ready, so she was the last one out. Kit approached the front door to make sure it was locked behind her. "Bye, house!" she sang, and patted the doorframe. Kit gave her a side-eye and then walked back to the Mini.

The guys had graciously offered to take the kiddos in the Peugeot so the girls could have one last debrief on the way to Edinburgh, the end of the trip. They would not be staying in a VRBO in the city, but rather revisiting a familiar (and favorite) old haunt at 100 Princes Street. Their last venture there had been so extraordinary, they couldn't not have chosen it.

Maddy climbed into the back, realizing that she would be sharing it with Violet as well. They looked at each other, and Violet seemed to determine it wouldn't be all bad to have a human in the back to pet her, and lay her head down again. Maddy laughed. "Well, thanks for your overwhelming approval."

They were all tucked in and ready to go. The guys drove away first and wound down the drive away from the white mansion, with the mini following. Just as they were settling into the drive, Sophie spoke up.

"So," she said. Both Kit and Maddy looked at her expectantly. When she didn't continue, Kit circled her hand in front of her indicating she should continue her talk track. "Well, I thought it would be obvious!" she intoned. When neither of them spoke again and just stared, she sighed. "I thought we could use this time to debrief from Mary's! We haven't had the opportunity and I am dying to know what you guys experienced."

"Oh! That," Maddy practically ppp-shawed in her ear. "I mean, I guess I can go first if you want." She knew each of them was anxious to discuss what they learned.

It'd been a few days, and it had all gotten a bit fuzzy, so she pulled out the notes she'd taken.

"Well, she had me come in and sit down on this chair. Then she surrounded me with blue apatite, lepidolite, selenite, and fulgurite" Maddy said, looking at her notes. The girls looked astonished she would know those words. "Don't worry, she told me what all of them were, I haven't gone *that* crazy!"

"What I found interesting, or weird, was that she wasn't playing any music," Maddy continued. "Didn't you two say the last time you did something like this there was some chanting going on or something?" The other two nodded, but clearly didn't want to interrupt her train of thought. "Well, even Zabina had some instrumental stuff going on in the background when I went to see her, but Mary left it silent."

"Huh, I wonder why. She played music for me," Kit mused.

"And me," Sophia added.

"Well, there was a reason," Maddy teased suspiciously, carrying on. "She told me to close my eyes. Then she lit some incense and said it was a combination of mugwort, sandalwood, frankincense, and patchouli. Whatever it was, it was unlike anything I had smelled before, and it was divine!" she said.

"Oh, that's what I smelled when you walked out!" Sophia said, wrinkling her nose.

Maddy chuckled. "I closed my eyes and started breathing in the smoke. As I did that, I started to see wind chimes blowing in the breeze, then what I thought was a figure eight, drawing itself in midair in a purplish-blue color, but then I had a flashback to tenth grade biology and realized it was the inner ear. It was weird that it was all about hearing and yet she wasn't playing anything in the background," Maddy mused. "And that's when I heard it."

"Heard what?" Kit asked, positively transfixed at this point, and also seemingly impressed that Maddy would remember anything from tenth grade biology so readily.

Maddy smiled, happy to be reeling her into the story. "A voice," she said, and let the statement hang in the air.

"What do you mean, a voice?" Sophia asked from the driver seat.

"I mean, a voice. Just like I have been describing it to you guys," Maddy said.

"Yes, but what did you hear? What does it mean?" Kit asked, ever the clinician.

"Well, I couldn't understand it then, but when Mary was done making circles around me, shifting the smoke into the circle she created with a feather, and balanced the room, she said this." Maddy looked down at her notes again and then read aloud:

> *"I call forth the ancient power,*
> *In this time and space,*

There was silence in the car for a moment, and something shifted. "Okay, but what does that mean?" Kit asked, breathier this time as if she, too, was under a spell.

"Mary said that the work I had done with Zabina, uncovering the connection of my past life with you two, knocked something loose for me. I had been too heavily 'veiled,' before" she said with air quotes, "to have noticed it or even let myself believe it. But apparently...I'm clairaudient."

"Clair what now?" Sophie said, looking in the rearview mirror so she could see Maddy's eyes.

"Clairaudient. I can hear spirit!" Maddy said excitedly.

"So, when you were coming up with the random names and suggestions the other night by the creek," Kit started, "you're saying that was spirit talking to you?" Maddy shook her head. "And also explains why I 'saw' Zabina in my dream the other night, she was kind of a spoiler alert; but also, why Mary's door was glowing for me and not you guys?"

"I've only ever heard about people seeing spirit, not necessarily hearing them," Sophie added, clearly confounded by what she was hearing.

"Common misconception actually," Maddy explained. "There are actually five clairs," and she counted them off on her fingers. "Clairvoyance is seeing, clairaudience is hearing, clairsentience is feeling, claircognizance is knowing, and clairalience is smelling," she finished proudly, obviously having done her research.

"Interesting," Kit pondered and shot Sophie a look.

"Oh, it is!" Maddy enthused.

Sophia laughed. "So, you're telling me that our originally almost orthodox catholic friend has not only renounced her old and resolute ways, but now possesses a gift, or ability, of communing with the dead?"

Maddy couldn't tell if she was being obtuse or impressed and began to get defensive. Sophia looked in the rearview mirror when Maddy didn't respond and Kit was clearly unsure of how to take it either.

"No! Maddy, don't give me that look. I only mean to say, in the words of the great prognosticator from our generation: Isn't it ironic?" And she smiled in the mirror.

Kit couldn't help herself: "don'tcha think?"

Like Pavlov's dog, Maddy couldn't not contribute and soon they were singing the entire song at the top of their lungs. They all laughed as they finished.

"Alright, so who's next?" Maddy asked. "I told you mine, now you tell me yours..." and she brazenly raised and lowered her eyebrows at the two in the front.

Kit looked at Sophia, who took her hand off the wheel for a moment to present it to Kit palm up as if to say, "after you."

"Well..."

Kit was still somewhat flummoxed at what Maddy had just shared, and that what her and Sophia had been only joking about was actually true, but the ride was not slowing down and they still needed to get through Sophia's story too before they got to the city. She knew there would be little breakout time once they got there, so this was it.

"Well, do you want all the ritualistic details, or should I dive right in with the results?" Kit asked.

Maddy tried to make eye contact with Sophia in the rearview mirror again to confer, but as they were twisting and turning on some narrow winding streets, Sophia's attention was unavailable. Maddy realized this and spoke up for the both of them. "Was the ritualistic much different than what I described?" Kit shook her head. "Then yes, we need the full blow-by-blow please."

"Okay. I walked in and sat on the same chair you had, Mads. But she played music for me. What, I wouldn't be able to tell you. It had deep drums to it, and an ethereal female singing in a language I've never heard, but somehow recognized. It was beautiful, but quite melancholy." She seemed to be traveling back to that moment hearing it.

"Anyway, she placed some crystals around me as well, also a few that I recalled from our time with the Shaman, but a few that were different...kyanite, snowflake obsidian and ancestralite," she said.

"Ancestralite...like ancestor?" Sophia asked. She was the resident crystal whisperer, having started quite the collection. "Interesting," she said, "carry on," and waved Kit on to continue.

Kit laughed. "Yes, mistress!"

"I only mean—" Sophie tried to explain.

"I know, I know. I'm just teasing. Yes, like ancestors. So, you can tell where I'm going with this. Anyhow, I started seeing the same images we had told her about that she said formed a totem: the eagle, a blue shield, and the smell of smoke. It was the smell of smoke that ultimately created a tipping point and I was suddenly in my dream. There was a snowy landscape among longhouses. I have what we now know are runes in my hands, only now when I raise my head, I see a village on fire. The male presence by my side, urging me to hide the stones, is also forcing me to run," she paused. "And was calling me Astrid." Kit was now looking at Maddy, tears streaming down her cheeks, but her voice remained steady.

Maddy was stunned but reached forward to put her hand on Kit's shoulder. "Are you okay? You don't need to continue if you don't want to."

"No, I'm okay, really. It's just heavy. Anyways, so the vision finishes with me having run away with this male presence on a Viking ship and we were out to sea," she finished.

Everyone was quiet for a moment. Then Sophie asked, "so what does that mean? I get that it was a replay of your dream, but did Mary have an interpretation or draw some sort of conclusion?"

Kit nodded. "Apparently, it was another past life. The male presence was Erik." Sophie's mouth dropped. "We were the leaders of our village, but it came under siege from a rival clan over territory, and they destroyed us. We tried to fight, but ultimately, we had to abandon our home with the few survivors left and leave." She was looking down at her hands now, as if seeing different ones in front of her. "The runes were the way in which I had focused my energy in that life. Being able to work with spirit in that way, and my abilities and predictions were known far and wide." She turned back to face Maddy. "You said something about 'just knowing' as one of the clairs? I think that's what she was trying to help me see or understand."

"Claircognizance, yes. That would certainly explain a few things," Maddy trailed off.

Kit chuckled. "Yes. Because of the care we had for our people, and the fact that we couldn't save them in that life, is why we each went into service of others in this life. It's our soul's penance for abandoning our clan then and not being able to keep them safe." She hung her head.

There was a quiet in the air that asked not to be disturbed for a moment. Almost like an unspoken moment of silence for that life and those people, now that they have been brought to awareness.

"Can we just..." Sophie broke the reverence. Kit glanced up. "Can we just go back to the fact that I have always called Erik a Viking and you have just confirmed not only that he was one in a past life, a real one, but you guys are together again in this life?! How amazing is that?!" she squealed.

Kit laughed a hearty belly laugh now. "I know, I know. The irony was not lost on me."

"And I knew your name then before you did!" Maddy exclaimed and began to sing again. I'm sensing a theme here," Maddy continued, and they both turned to Sophie. When she didn't start speaking immediately, they only stared harder. Realizing she had two sets of eyes on her she turned to see what the problem was, taking her eyes off the road for a moment.

"No, no, not yet. I want to know if Mary said anything about Kit and Erik being together again! Is it a soul mate thing? A karmic thing? What?" she asked.

Kit shrugged. "We didn't get that far. I think she felt like that was enough exploration and revelation for one day since, ya know, an entire village died," Kit said, with an edge to her voice.

Sophia looked at her and placed her right hand on her leg. "I didn't mean that what you just shared was insignificant, doll. I was only curious about how your two souls are entangled and what that means," she explained softly.

Kit placed her hand on top of Sophie's. "I know, I'm sorry. It's just a lot to take in and I'm not sure how, or if, I can share this with Erik. So many pieces of it make sense, but just as with everything we've found in this space, where there are answers come even more questions."

Jumping on the obvious bookend, Maddy said, "So…" while staring once again in Sophia's direction.

I was flabbergasted over what my two friends had just shared. The least obvious one of the bunch had learned that she had a supernatural ability in the world of spirituality and could hear spirit. If you had told me that six months ago, I would have laughed in your face. The other had now confirmed my previous, though impossibly accurate suspicion that her husband was in fact a Viking in a past life. And more interestingly, that their souls were together in that life too, at the helm, leading together, much like they were in lockstep in this lifetime. I found myself wondering about the...what had Mary called it? Soul contract. It was truly fascinating. I had only pushed on that tie because I was hoping maybe Mary had shared something with Kit that would be helpful for me in discerning all the men in my life at the moment. Or at least in my head. And the fact she ended up on the sea in that life, while I was dreaming of my own water, well, there was another parallel for us.

I apparently had gotten too lost in my thoughts before answering Maddy because before long, she was pinching me on my shoulder.

"Ow!" I shouted. "What was that for?"

"Spill. Now. We don't have much more time," she said, and sat back. Violet raised her head to evaluate if she needed to retaliate on my behalf, but must have decided I deserved it and put her head back down.

I let out a sigh. "Alright, fine. It's just...I don't know that I have as much clarity as the two of you, and feel like I only have more questions."

"Okay, so let's start with the obvious. What the heck was with the rope marks?!" Kit asked. Just like her to get down to brass tacks.

"Those. Yeah. So, I have to go back to go forward on that one. Mary walked me into the room and instead of sitting in the chair that the two of you sat on, she pulled out a massage table and had me lay down," I started. The two of them gave the side-eye to each other and smirked. "Oh, stop it, not like that!" They laughed.

"Anyways, she said she needed me to lay down because my story was not as 'superficial as I thought,' and she didn't want me falling off the chair as she worked. She had some Gaelic meditation music on and I almost immediately went into a trance after smelling whatever incense combination she had. I started seeing water, then Paul's face, which then transformed into Bryce's face. Then, I was sinking and choking as if I was drowning, and I could feel her pulling something away from my neck. When she called me back, I sat up really quickly and just before I opened my eyes, there was a face hovering above me, almost like they were looking at me from above the surface of water."

Now they were looking at me aghast.

"The weird part is," I started.

"There's another weird part?" Maddy interjected. I glared at her in the mirror.

"The weird part is, that night, I had a dream about drowning in dark water. There was someone at the surface who I was feeling like should be helping, but they were literally just watching me go down." I admitted, and took a breath.

"So, who is it?" Maddy quietly asked. "Paul or Bryce?"

"Who is what?" I responded.

"The face you see hovering above you letting you drown?" she clarified.

I shrugged my shoulders. "I don't honestly know. It could be either of them, or neither. There was nothing distinctive about the silhouette above the water. But what Mary did say about them is that 'one is a mirror, and the other is a lesson,' whatever that means. She was speaking in riddles more than she was helping me discern what was going on like she obviously did for you two."

Kit had remained relatively quiet. "And the rope?"

"Ah yes, the rope. She said that the rope was an invisible one. That what I experienced from the water was a past life in which I drowned at the hands of my significant other, and the rope was symbolically what kept me from speaking my truth in that lifetime, and I carried it forth into this lifetime and 'soul contract,'" I finished with air quotes.

Kit seemed to ponder this. "So...it's not that she didn't give you answers, it's that you haven't had time to properly interpret what she has given you yet."

"Say more," I encouraged.

"You said that she didn't help you understand anything, and yet she did. A lot actually. You, too, have another past life that needs resolution. She was able to remove the ropes that had kept you from speaking in this life, because it was time for them to be removed. You don't think that's ironic timing given the decision you have to make with the university and quite literally speaking up for yourself? While also being at crossroads with Bryce and having to also speak up for yourself and what you want for your life…or in other words, speaking your truth…" she trailed off.

I sat, contemplating what she was putting together. She had always had the uncanny ability to help me see the forest through the trees.

"Ok…you're not wrong. But what about Paul? Where does he fit into all of this? and she said 'nothing, everything, not everything is something'" I finished. Kit laughed at this finding it supremely amusing. "What?!"

"One is your mirror and one is your lesson," Kit repeated as if was obvious. I gave her a dubious look and she sighed. "Soph, weren't you the one looking into soul ties vs. karmic ties, and then stumbled on twin flames? What did you find about them all?"

I thought back for a moment, the last few days swimming together in my head. What did my notes say? A soul tie was an intense bond while a karmic tie was past-life related and lesson based. I tried to recall what I had read about the twin flame thing, but realized Bryce had interrupted my deep dive and I never got to it. I communicated all of that as such.

"Well then, I think you need to do some more research, because you haven't parsed it all out yet. But the pieces are certainly there," Kit responded with finality.

"But what does that all mean for Bryce? Am I making the right decision about staying here? Should I be going home? Was he the one in my dream that let me die in that lifetime?" I was stream of consciousness babbling now.

"Whoa there, let's take one thing at a time. And right now, we are pulling into town and you need to get a grip," Maddy chimed in from the backseat. "But I also want to know: What the heck is a soul contract?" We all shrugged our shoulders.

While I had been driving and paying attention to the roads, apparently, I hadn't synthesized exactly where we were, or the fact that we had indeed gotten into city centre and were almost at the hotel. I took a deep breath.

"You're right. It's just...awkward. To have all of these pieces and not be able to put them together when you're also trying to make life-altering decisions," I moaned.

"Hashtag adulting my friend. Add in the spiritual layer and awareness and it takes it to a whole new level. You're welcome," Kit said with a laugh.

We all turned our attention to the matter of arrival. The hotel had graciously offered to return both rental cars for us, so we were making sure we didn't leave anything behind. We pulled up in front of the familiar black flag and parked. We all got out and stretched our legs. We'd covered a lot of ground in those eighty minutes.

Bryce and the guys were all busy pulling the bags out of the trunk from the Peugeot and Ryan's car. I found myself staring at him with Mary's words, and my dream, echoing in my head.

Are you a mirror...or a lesson?

Chapter 30 – Oscar, March 1912

It had been months since Oscar had seen his good friend, Freddy. Partially because of his self-imposed servitude, and partially because Freddy painfully reminded him of that day with Josephine. But Oscar had been given a reprieve from his duties for the day from the Earl and helping with his estate, and had managed to get Freddy a telegram to meet him on Regent Street, at a little book store where they could have a private and inconspicuous conversation. He would have preferred somewhere in the West End, but it had more recently been taken over by the suffragettes conducting protests.

Freddy had been a good and loyal friend through all of this, never complaining at the errands he asked him to run and constantly checking on Josephine, even though she was not to know. It killed him to have to stay away from her when he was still so close, especially after seeing her at Christmas and reigniting his passion for her. Up until then, he had almost been convinced that he had been wrong in his affections toward her, listening to his mother that she would be forgotten. Almost.

Now, with her out from under his parent's roof, there may be an easier chance to communicate his plan with her. He knew it would be too conspicuous for him to go see her, but Freddy...

"'Allo, mate!" he heard him call. They were both approaching the Regent Park bookshop at the same time from opposite directions. It would look like a random meeting to any passers-by. Oscar laughed at the greeting as it sounded nothing like the refined English with which Freddy usually spoke. Perhaps he took his assignment to be covert a little too seriously.

"Good morning, Freddy. How are you today, old chap?" Oscar asked and clapped him on the back.

"Just fine, my friend. Though I wish you would not refer to me as 'old chap' when you are significantly older than I!" he answered.

Oscar scoffed. "I do not think three months qualifies as significantly older," he said, and he opened the door for them to go inside.

While it was no library, it seemed the few patrons within were still using hushed tones. Oscar walked towards the back corner where they could be alone to discuss his plan. And his request.

"So, what can I do for you now?" Freddy asked, diving right in. Oscar could not tell if he was miffed at being asked to do so much, or just in a hurry.

"I apologize, Freddy, if this is getting too much to bear, I can change tactics. I just need to know and I will plan accordingly..." he trailed off, thinking to himself. He was not sure what those other options would be, but he also did not want to belabor his friend and take advantage of his kindness.

"Not at all! I just know your time is short and we have to be careful, don't want to raise suspicion and all that, Freddy whispered with his hand raised to the side of his mouth. That made Oscar smile and relax a bit.

"Thank you, I do not ask this of you lightly. Please know how truly grateful—"

"Yes, yes, you have said all this before," Freddy interjected. "Let's get to the part with my covert mission," he said and rubbed his hands together as if he was a silent movie villain.

"Alright then! Well, as you know, Seph, er, Josephine is now back at home in Bath. I was wondering if you wouldn't call on her at her family's home. You can bring your sister if you like, for propriety's sake. I know the two of them enjoyed meeting last summer," Oscar started. Freddy nodded his head.

"Yes, and what am I to call on her for?" he mused.

"I do not know, you can make something up. Use your sister as an excuse if you must, but only be sure and give her this letter," he said, and slipped something into Freddy's side coat pocket.

"What is it?" Freddy asked without missing a beat.

"Instructions," Oscar said simply.

Freddy looked at him, confused. "Instructions for what?"

Oscar truly was happy that his friend had been willing to help him these many months, and he partially felt he owed it to him to give him the full picture, but he had come this far and did not know if he wanted to further involve him in his plans, should it come back to haunt him. He considered for a long moment before he said, "best you not know."

Freddy's face fell a bit, but he also seemed to understand. It was not just about Josephine, but also the goings-on at the Earl's household, and Katerina. These past few months had been absolutely excruciating, pretending to fall for the girl and want to get to know her better. It was all a rouse for certain, and he played his part well. He almost felt bad for her, and how much she had fallen for it. He would feel sorry for her in the end, and for the life they would not lead. He could admit to himself on some level that he had grown to find merit in it, but that was no matter now. First things first. He needed his plan to be in motion and *look* like it could succeed before he worried about the fallout.

Freddy was watching his friend's face as he worked through all of those internal musings; he reached out a steadying hand and placed it on Oscar's forearm. "I understand, old chap. You needn't say more."

"You are a wonderful friend, Freddy. Truly." Oscar enthused.

"Yes, yes, none other like me, I know. Just do us both a favor, and once you get the girl, never let her go. I fear you will live to regret it." And with that he smiled, turned on his heel, and walked away. Oscar thought he heard him humming a tune as he went and tried to place it, then smiled to himself as the lyric came into his head.

"Come Josephine in my flying machine..."

How completely appropriate, and antithetical to his plan.

As he wandered back to Mayfair, and the massive home of the Earl, used for an abundant amount of political and social engagements, he whistled the tune. He was flying high himself, from creating the inertia that would be his plan. It was too good, and he was quite proud for all of the details he was able to foresee.

He walked up the stairs of the tan façade and into the foyer to hang his coat and hat. One of the many rotating footmen ran over to receive him and help him with his things. He did not enjoy all the fuss that occurred in the household, but reminded himself it would only be a few more weeks, if he had his way.

"Thank you, Nigel," he said to the young lad.

"Yes, sir. You are most welcome, sir," he said back, eager to be of service.

Oscar started making his way to his room when Nigel cleared his throat to get his attention. He stopped and looked back. The boy was red in the face.

"Yes, Nigel?" he asked, as uninterested as possible.

"It's um, your father, sir" he started. Oscar looked around, concerned his father was lurking around the corner.

"What, here?" he asked.

"No, sir. What I mean to say is that, your father, has sent word for you, sir. He would like you at their home by eight o'clock sharp this evening, sir," he added in one last 'sir' for good measure. Oscar's shoulders relaxed.

"Ah, yes. Thank you, Nigel" and he continued going up the stairs to his room.

Thankfully, his quarters were at the back of the house, a long way away from Katerina's room, which was located directly next to the Earl's. It seemed he was to be the best steward of her future and would have no one questioning her honor with Oscar in the house. It was a bit awkward living there, and he had offered to stay above the carriage house. But at the thought of his future son-in-law doing so, the Earl balked. Instead, he gave him the entire rear wing. It had a rear entrance, which he was told was preferable for his use than the main stairs, but since everyone was out for the afternoon, did not think anyone would notice or mind.

"Very good, sir," he heard Nigel call after him.

Once he got to his room, he sat down in the chair by the fireside and considered starting one. Spring was still brisk in these early days of the season, and while he had managed to miss any rain during his venture, there was a slight chill he could not shake. Just as he was about to get up and arrange the wood, there was a knock at his door. "Come in," he called.

George, the house steward walked in. "I am sorry to disturb you my Lord," he said and stood just inside the threshold.

"It's quite alright, George. How can I be of service?"

"I wanted to let you know that someone stopped by today with an invitation for you," George said.

"Yes, yes. Nigel has already dispatched the message. I am to be at my parent's house by eight o'clock this evening" Oscar finished.

"Very good, sir. Is there anything else I can do for you? Send someone up to light the fire perhaps?" George offered.

"No, thank you, George. I can manage" Oscar said.

"Thank you, sir. I will let myself out and leave you to your peace," George replied, and with that, he was gone.

Oscar decided that while he was chilled, he also did not want to go through the effort of starting a fire. For some reason, this house and his fireplace always took a grand effort to manage to get going, and he suddenly found himself completely drained at the prospect of having to engage with his parents, especially his mother. After Josephine had shared what she said to her at the Coronation Dinner, and her general treatment of his love, as well as he continued efforts to disparage Sephie and his feelings. all because of her own selfish ambitions, it took everything in him not to seethe at her. And his father. Though his father had been mildly supportive of them spending time together originally, when push came to shove, he was, in fact, no better than his mother, as he succumbed to her will instead of listening to what his son wanted. It was an eye-opening and disappointing experience realizing that his father, the one with whom he had a special understanding regarding his mother, choose peace in the household over his first-born's wishes.

Thankfully, the visits with them since the end of summer when they ushered him out of the house, had been few and far between, but no less daunting. His mother continued to extol the virtues of marrying up and that all this "love" nonsense was the whim of a young boy and not the man he was supposed to be. He had actually started to feel the seed of doubt plant itself into his thoughts. He hated to admit it, but she had made a point, and while he would not relish in relenting, all the time away had been hard.

The hardest time had been at Christmas when he saw Josephine again for the first time in months. He thought it would be easy to be in her presence and plant himself in this new life, but the moment she appeared from above, he fell for her all over again. She was worth all of it. She had to be. He knew then he truly had to put on a show and completely ignore Josephine the entire evening, otherwise his mother may intuit something was amiss again. It crushed him to not even look at her for fear she would see through his rouse.

Not for much longer, he thought to himself. Feeling somewhat energized by that, he walked over to his wardrobe and opened it. He pushed aside coats and shirts to reach into the back where there was a somewhat hidden compartment. Reaching inside, he pulled out a black walnut box. When he tipped the top back, it revealed a gentleman's case, lined with red velvet, good for storing expensive trinkets. Anyone looking at it would find it mundane, at least in this household. It was what was underneath that counted. He flicked a small button at the hinge and the inside released to reveal that the top could come out, and there was a hidden layer under the trinkets. This was where he had been storing his hopes and dreams for the last seven months. This was where the secrets of his heart were kept, locked away in the bottom of a trinket box, designed to hide all manner of things.

He fingered the slips of paper, looked at the headlines of the news clippings, and saw all the sailing listings he had accumulated. They were all adding up to one thing: freedom.

He tucked everything back in, pleased to see nothing had been unduly disturbed, and placed it at the back of the wardrobe again. He shuffled the clothing back into place covering the gaping hole, and closed the large doors. He checked his wristwatch. Four o'clock. He had a few hours to kill before his supper tray came and then he would have to depart for his parents' requested meeting. He might as well take the opportunity for a bit of a rest. He would need all the strength he could get for this evening's performance.

He laid down on the bed, just to close his eyes. In what felt like a few moments, he heard a knock at the door. He begrudgingly opened his eyes again, realizing it had gone quite dark in the room. He tried to check his watch, but could not find enough light to see the face. "Come in," he said, somewhat confused.

Nigel entered carrying his dinner tray. He looked around, also confused by the dark. "Shall I light a fire for you, sir?"

"No, thank you, Nigel, I will be leaving shortly for that meeting you told me about."

"Very good, sir. Perhaps I could turn on the main lights for you then, sir?" he offered.

"Yes, thank you, that would be splendid. I also would not want you tripping with the tray of my food. I'm famished!" Oscar tried to joke. He thought he heard the boy try to stifle a laugh, but was not entirely sure.

The lightbulbs buzzed to life, first with a slow dim and then gradually getting brighter as they energized and the filament grew warmer. Nigel set the tray down on the small table near his chair and backed out of the room as quietly as possible.

Oscar had taken to dinner in his rooms whenever appropriate. He only felt it proper to both minimize his engagement with the family and Katerina, as well as to understand what it may have been like for Josephine, holed up in her rooms all day as Freddy had discerned.

The cook of this household was not quite to the standard of his own with which he had grown up, and nowhere near what Katerina had implied that first dinner at the palace, but it was sustenance nonetheless. He let out a sigh and tucked into the food.

By the time he was done, he realized he should change and ready himself for his departure. While definitely colder than this afternoon, he still fancied himself walking the forty-five minutes it would take, if for no other reason than to have more time to himself.

He dressed in a wool suit, tied his paisley tie, and went downstairs to retrieve his coat and hat. As he walked into the brisk evening, he was glad to find he had left gloves in his pockets. He walked through Hyde Park and along the streets, daydreaming. What would life be like with Josephine in America? How thrilling was their adventure on which they were to embark? Then a dark thought crept in: Was he crazy to think they could make this work? Looking around the beautiful neighborhood, was he truly ready to give all this up? He was not a fan of the peerage and duty, but he also knew the rage in his mother and after he left, his father would take the brunt of it…

He shook his head and saw Josephine in his mind's eye. The thought of her face alone made him smile, what had he called her in that note, his Helen of Troy. He did feel as if they were living in some Greek tragedy. Then he let his mind wander to their stolen kisses, and he was warmed from the inside out. Her lips were where he wanted to spend the rest of his days.

Soon enough, he was climbing the stairs to his parents' house and knocking on the door. It was an odd sensation, presenting oneself to the household in which you grew up, but he was wont for what else to do now that he had not lived there for so long.

Robert was the one who answered the door. Oscar smiled. It was good to see him after all this time. He missed Robert and his cheery dialogue when they would ride. Robert smothered a smile at seeing him, not wanting to show inappropriate emotion. Oscar clapped him on the shoulder and merely said, "Good evening, sir," which at least elicited a small smirk.

Oscar removed his coat and hat, handing it to him. He did not really like the thought of Robert waiting on him in this way, but also understood he had been given a role to play and did not want him to get in trouble for not playing his part.

"Thank you, Robert" Oscar said, and turned, walking into the foyer. He took a deep breath. Well, the old place certainly smelled the same. He felt eyes peering down at him and he looked up to see his mother standing at the top of the landing where he had last made eye contact with Josephine. A chill ran down his spine.

He nodded his head in her direction, but said nothing, and proceeded to his father's study. He rapped on the door once and waited for his father to acknowledge him. "Come in," he heard, muffled by the heavy wooden door. He pried it open and walked through.

"Oscar, my boy!" his father said and immediately stood. "Well, this is a nice surprise. How are you?"

At this, Oscar paused. Surprise?

"I'm sorry, father, am I not here by your request?" he asked. "I was told that you had sent word," but he was cut off by another presence in the room.

"That...was me" the voice said, and he heard the door close behind it. There was no mistaking the tone, so he did not feel the need to turn around only to verify that it was his mother speaking.

"Lucille, whatever do you mean?" his father inquired, now looking just as confounded.

His mother seemed pleased to have hoodwinked both the men in her life and grinned like a cheshire cat. "We have a family matter to discuss, and I wanted to see my son. Is that a crime?" she asked all innocence and roses. Oscar smelled trouble.

She took a seat opposite his father's desk, while he stayed standing.

"Sit, both of you," she commanded. The men looked at each other and decided to follow orders.

"I called us together today because I am worried about you, Oscar. I fear you may be making a mistake...and a wrong choice," she said, looking sincerely concerned, though for whom he was uncertain.

Oscar straightened a bit, not knowing where she was going with this talk track. She could not possibly know about his plans; he had been too careful. But then again, she seemingly had spies everywhere. She had already proven that when she came at him the last time about Josephine.

Best not say anything just yet...see what else she has to say before you react, he thought to himself.

"Good heavens, Lucille. What is all this about?" his father blustered, clearly not wanting to put up with her games. Maybe he was finally losing patience with her? It would be too much to hope.

She looked at Oscar again. "I mean that Oscar has not made a formal declaration or asked for Katerina's hand in marriage yet."

He exhaled a quiet sigh of relief. So, she did not know, or at least, not yet.

"Oh, that," his father said, as if it was as important as him minding what was on the menu for tomorrow.

"Yes, *that*, Victor," she seethed, placing extra emphasis on his name. He winced at her tone.

"You know, if you two just want to continue the conversation without me, I needn't have come all this way to watch you bicker," Oscar interjected, rather bitterly. "You could have saved me the trouble and the time." This, he thought to himself, is exactly what comes of arranged marriages.

His mother stared at him then, as if she was trying to see through to the center of his being and read the thoughts of his soul. This made him laugh to himself since he was not sure she had a soul herself.

"Oscar, I am hurt. Of course we wanted to also see you, my darling," she oozed with a preternatural charm. She reminded him of a tiger trying to reel in its prey for the kill. Even his father had to keep from scoffing at that, and as he sputtered, he quickly turned it into a cough, clearing his throat.

"I thought that when you had me evicted from my own home, it would mean my decisions were my own. I did as you asked. I stayed away. What more do you want?" Oscar asked, trying not to provide too many double entendre statements that his cunning mother may read between the lines and pick up on what he was planning.

"Now Oscar, that is not fair. We only had you leave for your own good. You know that. You see that now, do you not? Katerina is the best choice for you, and this family, for our collective futures," she said, with stardust in her eyes, envisioning the elevation of having the daughter of an Earl as her daughter-in-law.

Oscar shook his head.

"Now, son…" his father tried, but Oscar cut him off.

"No, father, this should be my decision. A man should be able to decide if and when he proposes to a woman, not his mother. Did you not have that option when you proposed?" he demanded. His father cowered slightly. Clearly, he had not. Thinking about it, he could almost see his mother proposing to him to seal the deal for herself.

"If? If you propose? Oh, Oscar, please do not tell me after all this time that you have led this poor girl on and you do not plan on marrying her," his mother said, dangerously close to losing her composure. She sounded like a snake, hissing her words now. She stared at him.

He was losing ground fast and if he did not turn this around, would be drawing unnecessary attention on himself and motives over the past several months. He took a deep breath.

"I only mean to say, mother, that I would like to be the owner of my destiny and the one to decide when the proposal will happen," he managed. This seemed to quiet her tidal wave to a dull roar.

"Excellent. Well then, when do you plan on speaking with the Earl? A formal commitment should really be made in the next few weeks if you want to hit the summer season for a wedding." She was strategizing out loud. He tried not to burst. He had just asked her, no, told her, that it would be his decision on timing. And here she was, already steamrolling him and pushing her own agenda and timeline.

"Fine. I mean, to have the discussion by the end of the month, and propose at the start of April," he decided. He would be long gone by the end of the month, and on his way, before he would have to breathe a word to the Earl.

This seemed to please her, and quiet her misgivings. His father too looked relieved, if for no other reason than he would not have to tame his wife and her temper tonight.

"Well, this calls for a toast. Victor, dear. Ring your bell so Alice can bring some sherry." She rocked back and forth in her seat, clearly trying to contain herself.

"Indeed," his father said. He rang the bell and a few moments later, Robert answered the door. "Robert, please have Alice bring three glasses of sherry," he said. Robert quickly nodded his head and withdrew.

"Oh, I am pleased my boy. You are doing the right thing," his father said. Suddenly his mother stood, not able to contain her excited energy any more.

"I must excuse myself for a moment," she announced, retreating from the room. Oscar looked down at his shoes.

"As I was saying, I am pleased. I know it may not have been what you originally wished, but with this choice, you will be able to receive your full inheritance, and the Earl has grand plans for you and a country estate," he continued. Oscar looked up. Inheritance? Did they really think that that was a motivator? He just nodded.

"I know, Oscar. That may not be entirely important to you, however, had you chosen...differently, your future situation would have been far worse and you would not have lived a comfortable life. I understand you do not take the peerage seriously, but I also know you respect it. Going against your mother now that the Earl is involved would have caused problems for everyone," he finished. Oscar's heart sank at the notion. The way his father emphasized *everyone* made him wonder if Gertrude could get mixed up in all of this.

Was he being selfish? Going after his heart's desire? Was it his heart's desire? Doubt niggled at the periphery of his mind again, and he pushed it away. He had to hold strong.

Just then, the door opened and the Viscountess returned. She was carrying a small velvet box in her hands. Sitting down, she placed it in her lap. Oscar tried not to groan. This must be the family ring she intended him to use in the proposal.

There was a small rap at the door and his father said, "come in!" knowing it would be Alice with the requested glasses. At the sight of him, Alice nearly dropped the tray. He smiled half-heartedly at her and then looked back at his hands in his lap. She brought the tray around to each of them and then turned to walk away.

"A toast!" his mother started. "To good decisions, and new beginnings...for all of us!" she declared.

Oscar could swear he heard Alice's feet stop shuffling for a small moment, as she took in the words she was hearing. How he wished he could scream at the top of his lungs that it was not true. He wanted Alice to know he had not forsaken her friend. Instead, he raised his glass and sipped the blood-red liquid. Appropriate. He felt like he was taking a blood oath as he sat in this room.

The only solace was the countdown he had going on in his head.

Chapter 31 – Sophia, June Present Day

After getting the bags up to our respective rooms, we decided everyone needed a bit of respite before we hit the town and wandered.

Bryce decided he was going to take a nap, while I needed time to parse out all of the discussions we just had, so I took myself to the Wallace Bar, sitting down to a wonderful afternoon tea.

For the first few moments while their signature blend steeped, I just sat. Sat on the forest green velvet couch looking out the main windows to the streets below and castle above, off in the distance. I sighed; it was wonderful to be back where it all started. Even when Bryce and I had come back this way over the past few months, we stayed in his apartment outside of the city, so I hadn't the chance to return.

I sipped the tea, held the cup and saucer in my hand, and closed my eyes. Perhaps a nap would have been a better idea. I let the warmth of the tea run through me. There was something so relaxing about the ritual, it was hard not to love it. After a few moments, I remembered that I had research to do. I set my teacup and saucer down and picked up my phone. 'What is a twin flame?' I entered into my search bar.

"A twin flame is a deeply intense 'mirror' soul connection, believed to be one soul split into two bodies, designed to trigger profound spiritual growth, self-awareness, and healing...acting as a mirror to reflect both strengths and weaknesses."

Well, there was the mirror Mary was referring to. Curious, I typed in "soulmate vs. karmic vs. twin flame" to see if there was an overview comparison. Fantastically, there was.

"Twin flames are believed to be one soul split into two bodies, acting as an intense mirror to your deepest self, while soulmates are complementary, supportive partners with whom you share a deep, harmonious bond. Karmic relationships are intense, temporary connections centered on learning difficult lessons, and clearing past-life karma."

Ok. So, a Twin Flame equaled Mirror Soul, a Soulmate equaled Complementary Spirit, and a Karmic Relationship equaled Lesson-Bringer.

Mirror and lesson were both baked into the definitions of the nomenclature, and yet, nothing quite fit. Bryce, was definitely the past life connection, but I wouldn't categorize him as a "lesson," per se. Unless he was the one from the dream, no, other past life, who just watched me drown. But what lesson would there be? And us finding each other again? So, would he then fall under the "soulmate" category? We definitely fit the deep bond part, but was that only because of the past-life thing and not any true bond we shared now? Maybe that was what he had been brooding on this last week and why he had been acting so odd...

Then I remembered "soul contract" and entered that into the search.

"A soul contract is a pre-birth spiritual agreement or 'game plan' made by an individual's soul to experience specific life lessons, relationships, and challenges for growth. These agreements, often involving karmic lessons or ancestral healing, are designed to evolve the soul, covering aspects like family ties, purpose, and key interactions."

Oy, my head was swirling and the tea was no longer helping. Perhaps a bite of the shortbread would. I smiled to myself. The smooth, buttery crunch did do wonders for the soul, but I wasn't convinced it would help me sort all this out. Paul fit the "one soul split into two bodies" piece because I had always thought of our relationship as us being two parts of one whole, but I couldn't say that I experienced finding my 'deepest self' with him. Or maybe that's why I had pushed him away, ultimately because it was so intense and would have made me do work I wasn't ready for, I contemplated.

Just then, the hostess, in a gorgeous royal blue satin dress, walked over to see if I wanted more hot water. I was about to decline when Kit came through the door. Instead, I ordered another pot and asked for a second cup...and more cookies.

Kit sat opposite me on the dark plaid wingback chair. She stared at the tea set on the glass and brass table and looked over to the bar with interest. "Don't worry" I said, interjecting into her thoughts, "I already ordered another pot."

"Oh, good! I do love their tea here. Perhaps I can just signal her to bring some..."

"Cookies? Yeah, I asked for those too." I finished her sentence and winked.

"Brilliant!" she exclaimed and we laughed softly. She eyed me to see what condition I was in after the drive.

"I'm fine. I just couldn't take a nap. I'm tired, but not sleep tired," I admitted.

"Yes, and you also gave a weird reaction at breakfast to Erik saying you couldn't leave Bryce. You winced. What was that about?" she asked, not missing a beat.

The hostess brought over the new pot of hot water, already steeping with the tea, an additional cup and saucer, and more than a few more cookies, with a wink. She placed them down on the table in front of us quietly, and withdrew. Kit set to making her perfect "cuppa." adding the milk and sugar.

"No, I know. It was just odd timing is all. We had just had a conversation about him possibly reaching out to some folks at his uni on my behalf, and I felt somewhat awkward about it all once I realized I was basically crashing the night he will be honored," I said, and poured myself a cup.

"Is that what he said?" Kit asked.

"No, of course not. He was thrilled with the idea and said I could be 'the belle of the ball.' It was a me thing. He's just so nice and accommodating sometimes, I just…" I trailed off.

"Yes, pesky when those men are actually kind, thoughtful, and follow through on what they say isn't it? Damn him," she joked, taking a bite of cookie. She savored it as I had, with a satisfactory grin on her face. I wished I could reach across and slap her knee, or throw something at her, but this was not the establishment in which to behave such a way…nor could I reach her knee from where I sat.

I rolled my eyes instead. "Yes, I know. It's just…there's a lot going on in my head." I left it at that. She nodded, likely considering everything I had shared on the ride here.

"Yes, yes, you do. And it doesn't seem like you quite have all the puzzle pieces yet. However, you are accumulating them and a picture is starting to form," she cajoled. She glanced at my phone sitting next to me and nodded her chin in its direction. "Find anything interesting?"

I shook my head in frustration. "Yes and no. It's as you say, there are a lot of pieces but they haven't quite formed into anything yet." Then I launched into what I had just found on twin flames, and the comparison to the other categories, as well as soul contracts. She listened and nodded along.

"I see," she said. "So, you're still in limbo."

"That's a perfect word. You always find the most perfect words to describe…" and I waved my hands up and down my sides and all over to indicate "me."

She finished my sentence: "Your chaos?" I laughed.

"Well, I say the best thing for you right now to clear your head is for all of us to mount up and take the crew through the cobblestone streets," she offered.

I couldn't agree more, it sounded both delightful and therapeutic. "Why I believe I do concur, doctor!"

We finished our tea, closed out the tab, and went back to our rooms to collect everyone. Thankfully, we were all on the same floor, so it was easy to wrangle the group. Bryce had just woken up and looked a bit groggy, but incredibly cute with his hair all mussed up. I ran my fingers through it and kissed the tip of his nose. "Time to play tour guide!" I said, more exuberantly than he likely felt at the moment. "Or I can."

"Is that a threat?" he asked. "I do not think this city is ready for that just yet, my bonnie lass." He quickly freshened up in the bathroom, threw on his shoes, and we walked out the door to go explore the city, the one I considered my second home town, with our gang.

As we had been out walking, Maddy was noting different shops along the way, but also making a lot of faces.

"What's wrong, Mads?" Kit asked.

"I am just not seeing any formal wear shops...we might have to venture out a bit further," she groaned.

Kit and I laughed. "It's okay, Maddy. You guys don't have to do that part with—" I started, but she cut me off.

"Sophia, don't make me use your middle name, Aitken! If you think for one moment that you are getting off the hook of going dress shopping with me, I will be incredibly offended. It ain't happenin'!"

I held my hands up in surrender. "Alright, alright! But I don't think it will be as easy to sneak away and leave the kids with the guys again. They've been doing a lot of babysitting this trip."

"It's not babysitting when one of them is the father," Kit retorted.

"True," I agreed, "but all the same. I would feel incredibly guilty to swipe you guys away again for dress shopping when we wanted them all to be here with us for some group fun!"

Kit looked at me defiantly as we walked, and without taking her eyes off of me asked, "Erik?"

"Yes, dear?" he called back in a jovial tone.

"If we take the kids this evening and let you boys have a night out on the town, would you mind watching them for a few hours tomorrow? We need to find a dress for Soph to wear to Bryce's ball."

I watched Erik's face light up as he looked back and forth at Ryan and Bryce. None of them seemed to be bothered by the request.

"I mean, I would have watched them without the bonus bribe, but absolutely babe, sounds good to us!" Erik answered.

Incredibly satisfied with herself, Kit gave a high-five to Maddy and continued to stare me down with her motherly 'I told you so' look.

"Well, alright then, I guess we're going dress shopping tomorrow," I said, and Maddy squealed. I looked to her. "Since I do have a fashion whiz-kid at my fingertips, I'm going to leave all the searching of shops and determining which is the best for our venture up to you. My head can't take much more today." Maddy nodded and immediately took out her phone to start searching.

Kit reached in front of her phone and pushed it down. "Ah ah, you won't want to miss this, Auntie Mads," she said, and pointed at the kiddos as we turned the corner.

And there it was, Edinburgh Castle. Everyone seemed to say "wow" all at once.

"Indeed," Bryce responded to the children's awe, and then launched into full tour guide mode, regaling the group with all the history he could unleash; and it was only the front parking area.

The next morning, the kids were perfectly happy to relax in their beds with a couple books, and a movie on the tv for background noise, letting their Dad sleep off the late night with the guys. We had sent them in the direction of the Devil's Advocate and they seemed to enjoy themselves. We elected to have coffee and breakfast on the go, so we could both walk and see more of the city, but also arrive to the shop as soon as it opened. Leaving all our men to their own devices, we were off.

The store Maddy had chosen was a well-known Scottish Couture shop over on London St. It was about a twenty-minute walk from the hotel, so we would be able to take a leisurely stroll.

"It has amazing reviews online," Maddy said. "And I couldn't help myself when I saw it described as Scottish Couture. I mean, who could?" She was beside herself with excitement.

Maddy had texted us the website last night and I had taken a look at what I was getting myself into. They had everything from gorgeously intricate wedding gowns to a wide selection of formal dresses. I figured if Maddy liked it, and we couldn't find anything there, I was going to be out of luck for anything local and would have to resort to finding something online. Less than ideal, but at least I knew I would have a plan B.

When we approached the shop, Maddy's professional persona took over. She walked in and immediately made friends with the shop assistant, dropping lines about who she had worked with in fashion, and getting into all sorts of industry talk. Kit and I glanced at each other; it was fun watching our friend in her element, and we wanted to take it all in as we likely wouldn't have such a unique opportunity again.

They shuffled us into a dressing room and started bringing dress after dress for me to try on. It was a little overwhelming with all the attention I was getting. After a while, when I was losing hope that we would be successful, they brought in one final piece. My breath hitched.

It was a stunner...as all the others had been, truly, just not on me. Scarlet red satin, ball gown skirt, fitted one-shouldered bodice complete with handsewn crystal embellishments, all strategically placed. I held my breath as I stepped into it and we zipped it up.

All of the other dresses I had tried on would have needed some adjustments, but not this one. It fit like a glove, like it had been specifically made for me. I stepped up on the pedestal in front of the three-way mirror and just stared. I didn't even look like myself. Maddy and Kit were speechless.

Kit jumped up on the pedestal with me and started gathering my hair in her hands and arranging it up and off my shoulders so we could get the full effect. As she did so, and I watched my reflection in the mirror, I was staring so intensely that it was almost as if I saw both of us shift into a different time and place entirely: me getting ready in a gown, and her helping me with my hair. Then I blinked, and it was gone.

"What do you think?" Kit asked, seemingly not having experienced what I just witnessed. I continued to stare in the mirror.

"Well, if you don't get this one Soph, there is just no hope for you," Maddy chimed in. "Seriously stunning. And that color on you! And the fit!"

"Alright, alright," I interjected, otherwise I feared she would not have stopped. "I hear you. This is quite spectacular." I was still stunned by my elegant reflection. "And look," I said, shoving my hands at my sides and twirling side-to-side like a little girl. "Pockets!" We all laughed.

"Spectacular. Good word," Maddy mused. "Now: shoes."

Chapter 32 – Josephine, March 1912

"Freddy!" I practically launched myself at him when I saw him entering the front door. If Freddy was here, there most certainly was an update. I could barely contain myself, and then another figure appeared through the door. "Veronica?" I embraced her as if we were the oldest bosom friends.

Rupert was not quite sure what to make of the scene, but led us to the parlor where we could have some afternoon tea. I was somewhat mystified, but played along as if it had been part of a plan. As soon as we were seated and Rupert left the room to let cook know about our visitors, I sat on the edge of my seat.

"Freddy, what on earth are you doing here?" I whispered anxiously.

"It is lovely to see you too, Miss Findley. It has been far too long," he answered mischievously.

"Well, I, for one, think it has been! I told you I would have loved to visit her before in the city, did I not?" Veronica added in.

Freddy shook his head. "Yes, dearest sister, you did. However, as I explained, she was essentially under house arrest and there was no way—"

She waved him off. "Yes, yes, yes. Well, get on with it then." Then she looked around, evaluating the room.

Our home in Bath was beautiful, but not quite as resplendent as their country home I had witnessed last summer at the St. John's Day celebration. The parlor was warm and inviting, with oxblood walls, floral prints in brass frames, and cozy chesterfield furniture. It was my favorite room in the house, even if other rooms had a bit more flourish.

"I told you, now that she was back in the country, I fancied myself a stopover," then he turned to look me in the eye. "We happened to be in the area. Our uncle lives not too far from here and we thought we would say hello."

"Well, it would have been rude for you not to. I am thrilled!" I said, watching Freddy's every movement. I was assuming by his nonchalance that Veronica had no idea of the goings-on over the past few months, or that Freddy had been passing me messages, albeit very few. But they were messages nonetheless, so I played along. We would have to find a way to have her otherwise entertained.

Just then, Charles burst into the room, no doubt having heard we had unexpected guests, he was curious. Bless him.

"Charles! Mr. Tate, Miss Tate, allow me to introduce my brother," I said, all charm and warmth. He cocked his head a bit at me, but bowed all the same. "Charles, these are friends of Mr. Carlisle. I met them last summer. Perhaps you would be so kind as to show Veronica around." I looked to Freddy to help me find something that she liked so there would be reason for him to take her.

"Have you a library? Veronica adores reading," he declared. She gave him a side-eye, curious why she was getting the brush-off. But I caught a glint of admiration in her eyes, watching my brother. He may have only been fourteen to her sixteen, but he had completely sprouted in the couple of weeks we had been back home. The country air and cook's meals were doing him good, and he was filling out to be quite the handsome chap.

"We do!" Charles said, only too happy to be helpful. "Right this way, Miss Tate." He even offered his elbow to her. I smiled. That should buy us at least a little time.

As soon as they left, Charles being sure to leave the door open, as my father would want since I was now alone in a room with a man, Freddy turned to me.

"We probably haven't much time. Veronica likes books, she doesn't love them, so she will recognize the rouse and play a long for only a bit," he said. I nodded. "I have a letter for you." He pulled out the now entirely familiar cream paper. I swooned and reached for it, holding it to my chest for a moment. I started to crack the seal when Freddy placed his hands over mine to stall me. "Best you do so in private, yes?"

I stuffed it into my pocket and bit my lip. "Freddy, you have been so good to me in helping to deliver his messages. I hate to ask anything more of you…" He smiled and I relaxed. "Would you be willing to take a letter to Alice at the Carlisle's? I am unsure how you would be able to get it to her surreptitiously, but I feel I must get her a message.”

He looked confused. “Of course I can, but…”

“She is the kitchen girl,” I explained. “She was of great help to me while I was there.”

“It would be my honor. Do you have it on your person?” he asked.

“No, I will need but a moment to retrieve it,” I lied. I had only thought about writing to her recently, but had not expected this opportunity to fall into my lap. He nodded.

“Perhaps when your brother and my sister return, he can regale me with some stories over the tea and cakes.” He winked.

“You are too wonderful.” I leaned over and kissed him on the cheek, which caused him to blush.

Just then, Ms. Hangendorfer herself brought the tea and cakes to the parlor. I looked at her with an odd expression, confused, and then realized that she must think Freddy a suitor and she wanted to have her own look. I smiled; she really was too dear. Veronica and Charles followed shortly. While Charles would not normally partake in tea, where cook’s cakes were concerned was a different manner entirely. I knew it was now or never.

“Charles, why don’t you entertain our guests for a moment while I excuse myself,” I said in my sweetest voice. Charles was only too happy as I could tell he was completely besotted with Veronica, and it would mean I could not scold him for how many sweets he stuffed into his face. I walked briskly up to my room and sat at the writing desk. I knew I did not have much time, but still needed to express my thoughts.

Alice,

Being home has been a wonderful marvel and good for the soul. However, there are times when I sit at my vanity and brush my hair, I can almost feel your presence behind me, sharing wisdom and a few laughs. It makes me both happy and melancholy.

I am unsure if our paths will cross again, but I wanted you to know how much you truly meant to me during my time there. You were one of the few bright spots that kept me going, even during the darkest of times.

It's funny how in those times, one can still find the light. You are one of those lights Alice, and I will carry you forever and always, in my heart. (Nor will I ever be able to have my hair done in front of mirror in a beautiful dress without thinking of you!)

Thank you for your friendship. Thank you for your unexpected wisdom. Thank you for being you.

Always,
Josephine

I hoped she would be able to infer everything I was saying. It may be too subtle, but would she somehow know, or at least figure out, that once Oscar disappeared, that I was alright, and with him? Even now, a letter felt inadequate for all she had done for and given me, but it was the best I could do given the circumstances.

I wanted nothing more than to break open the letter from Oscar too, but knew I had been gone too long to not warrant some questions, so it would have to wait. I took it out of my pocket and hid it in the center drawer of my desk for the time being, just to be certain it did fall out of my pocket.

I joined the others downstairs again and managed to have some cake before my brother finished the rest. He must have found some interesting stories with which to keep them enthralled because they barely noticed when I re-entered the room, let alone how long I had been.

The afternoon visit continued on beautifully. It was as if we were lifelong friends who did this often. They were so easy to talk to. However, all good things must end and Freddy looked at his wristwatch, remarkably similar to Oscar's.

"Well, dear sister, I fear we have overstayed our welcome and must take our leave," he said.

"Nonsense. I do not believe that for a minute. Have we dear friend?" Veronica asked and looked at me.

"Not in the least," I gushed, and Charles enthusiastically nodded his head.

"Be that as it may," Freddy said, "we are now quite late in getting to Uncle's, and you know how he is about meal times." He gave her a frank look.

Veronica groaned. "Oh, alright. It is just...it has been such a delightful little side trip and I do not want it to end!"

"I am glad to hear it," I said, standing up. We all walked out of the room escorting them to the front door. Rupert emerged from somewhere and helped them with their coats and hats.

"Please, may we stop by again soon?" Veronica asked expectedly. I looked to Freddy to see if he would have any idea if that was possible knowing the contents of my letter. He did not seem to, so I promised we would figure something out. We kissed each other on the cheeks and they walked out to their waiting carriage.

"Well, they were nice," Charles said, almost dreamily. I smirked at him and nudged his elbow.

"Indeed," I said. Coming out of his trance, he saw my face and nudged my arm back. I had a quick vision of Veronica being of future solace to Charles after I left. It warmed my heart that he could possibly have found a companion so close to my own.

"Oh, stop it!" and he walked away to see what he could get himself into before dinner.

Since our parents were not yet back from their own afternoon visit with our neighbors, I took myself back up to my room to discover what Oscar had to say.

I pulled the letter from its hiding spot and sat in the chair by the fireplace. It felt thick, as if there was a lot written, so I wanted to be comfortable.

Dearest Sephie,

I hope this letter finds you well. Once again, I must apologize for the length of time in between my writing. Things have gotten...complex here, and I have had to forestall certain conversations and commence others. All to say, nothing has kept me from my determining our plan, I have just had to become even more wary.

I think I have the solution. Dear Freddy is such a wonderful chap for getting this to you, I just hope you receive it with enough time to ready yourself. It will take a fair bit of travel, but I do think it is the best way.

I have found us a ship! It leaves in April. While there are several ports by which we could embark even sooner, I think it best that we meet up at its last one in Ireland before it departs for America. Due to reasons out of my control, I will be leaving at the end of March to begin the journey. My departure will likely raise suspicion, so I hope it still gives you time to make arrangements. Ultimately, we need to be on board April 11. Can you find your way to Queenstown by then? Ideally, you would be able to join me there one or two days earlier so we can be sure our luggage and things are sorted together, and I will need to get you your ticket.

The ship itself sounds quite grand. While I would normally have booked us in First Class, I fear there may be too many people that could recognize us, or at the least me, and we would be found out. So I have booked us adjoining second class berths. I hope they will be to your liking. We will have to go under assumed names as well. I have provided you with that documentation in this letter so you may begin your journey as such, and become accustomed to the persona you will play.

While I am sure you are clever enough to find your own way, might I suggest you take the train from Bath to Liverpool, and then gain passage on a steamer from Liverpool to Queenstown. I have included some money to ease your way. Yes, I know you have your own, but it makes me feel better to provide for you since this will not be easily accomplished.

Plan to meet me at the BellaVista House. I will be taking a room there. Ask for a Mr. Patterson.

I hope this plan is satisfactory, my love. I cannot wait to have you in my arms again.

Impatiently yours,
Oscar

"May the road rise up to meet you.| May the wind be always at your back.| May the sun shine warm upon your face;| The rains fall soft upon your fields.| And until we meet again,| May god hold you in the palm of His hand."

I turned the pages over in my hands. He had truly thought of everything. No wonder he needed such time for planning! I searched through the bank notes and letter pages to find what my travel identity would be. Jane Patterson, 21, from Southampton, England.

Wait. Patterson. I checked back in his letter where he told me what name to give at the hotel front desk. Mr. Patterson. My cheeks blushed. So, we were to be a married couple crossing the Atlantic, were we? Or were we siblings? My heart dropped at the thought. He mentioned adjoining rooms, so there was still some propriety...then something dropped from in between the pages and settled on the floor. I bent to pick it up and could not believe my eyes.

A circular piece of metal that glinted in the light. A simple gold band. I brought my hand to my mouth. While it was not a true proposal, nor was it how I imagined receiving a ring, it was also one of the most thoughtful and romantic gestures he could have made, given the situation. I was positive it was also logistical, as a married woman traveling alone would not raise nearly as many suspicions as a single on. Still, it brought a tear to my eye.

So, Mr. Patterson, it is to be a joint adventure as we set off together, into the American sunset, I mused to myself.

Chapter 33 – Sophia, July – Present Day

It had only been a couple of weeks, but I missed my friends. I hadn't realized what a buffer that had become for us and all of our 'moods' that had been on-going. After our shopping excursion, we spent the rest of the time taking the kids around to all the tourist traps, and took photos of our food for Instagram. Unfortunately, we could not partake in the Christmas-themed restaurant, as it would not be decorated until October. But we saw and ate everything everywhere else. Hot chocolate, mashed potato bars, dessert sushi...you name it, we ate it.

Normally, Bryce was all in on showing off his great city. I wasn't sure if he was just tour-guided out, or if the weight of my ask was beginning to get to him. Whatever it was, he had been off for the remainder of the time with my friends, and had continued as such. My other fear, that he felt everything had happened to quickly and was regretting it all, kept taking stronger root. I had mentioned it as such to Kit, which she assured me was absurd, but I just couldn't shake it.

The date for the ball was tomorrow. I thought perhaps a venture outside of the city would be helpful, so I suggested we take the bus out to Rosalyn Chapel. I had yet to visit the venerated place, and it was still on my list. Bryce shrugged. "Sure."

Regardless of his unenthusiastic response, I grabbed my purse and his apartment keys and pulled him out the door. Perhaps going to a sacred space such as this one would lift his mood. I was wrong. Instead of putting him squarely to rights, the old place only seemed to set him off even more. Every question I asked seemed to annoy him, so I decided to casually walk away and go on my own tour. I left him standing near the front corner, at the start of the story devised by the architect. Meanwhile, I bee-lined it for the stairs to the basement, disappointed to see that the opposing triangle symbol Robert Langdon had described in The Davinci Code was not in fact there. I still walked down the steeply graded stairs.

I was surprised to find myself in a relatively empty space. One could tell it was old, just by looking at the mason markings on the walls and seeing the well-worn floor, but there was something missing. I walked around, evaluating the tiny space, and patiently waited for a couple to leave the even tinier back room where they kept relics from the build that had been found. I marveled at the carved stone from mid-fifteenth century and how they could have accomplished all of this with tools from the time. I walked back out into the main space and placed my hand against one of the walls. I expected to feel something, but there was no sense of the building's energy or vibrancy. It was dull. No...sterile. It was an odd sensation for something that was filled with so much symbolism and history. I was confused.

It was normally something I would bring to Bryce and speak about, but as he was not being his normal charming self, I decided to keep it to myself. For now.

He was just descending the stairs as I started to ascend. He looked at me as I brushed past and kept going on my way. I was not about to engage with him in a sacred crypt. I mulled around upstairs, taking in all the breathtaking work and varied artistry. The place really was amazing.

When he reappeared above ground, I led us outside and back to the bus stop. Normally, we would have mulled around in the gift shop so I could find some little trinket. Their shop looked amazing, but I knew it was not the time.

The ride back was a quiet one and I kept to myself. It gave me time to think anyway. I had finally gotten the long-awaited email from Dean Smith, and my head was wrapping itself around how I was to respond. I opened my email to read through it again.

Dear Ms. Aitken,

I hope this email finds you well on your sabbatical. While I am happy you have been able to make the most of your break, I am afraid it is time that decisions need to be made. I would very much like to speak with you in person about options. Can you please let me know when you will be back Stateside so we may discuss?

Sincerely,
Dean Smith

Short and somewhat sweet, I guess. I sighed. Usually, my thinking sigh elicited a reaction from the warm body next to me, but not even a glance. What the heck was going on with him? Then my phone vibrated. I looked down, a new message from Kit.

Kit: All quiet on the Western front? 😊

Me: Arctic-ly. He's taking cold shoulder to a whole new continent... :-/

Kit: Weird.

Me: I heard from the Dean.

Kit: Oh, do tell! What did Smithy have to say?

Me: Oh, just exactly what we expected...but he wants to talk in person.

Kit: Interesting. And? What are you going to do?

Me: <shrug emoji>

Kit: Well...you can't hide in Scotland forever, doll.

Me: Even if I wanted to, I'm starting to think someone else wouldn't...

Kit: Give him a break. He's probably just as nervous about your decision-making as you are. Go easy on him. He did just spend weeks on end with your friends...we may have completely wiped him out! :-D

Me: I know, I've just never seen or experienced him like this before.

Kit:...

Me: What?

Kit: Nothing. It was just a fleeting thought. No matter.

Me: WHAT?!

Kit: Nope.

Me: Ugh. Alright, well we are almost back to the apartment. Must make final preparations for the event tomorrow.

Kit: XOXOXO

Me: Ditto

As the bus came to a stop, I jumped up and ran down the stairs to be sure we got off on time. I had learned the hard way a few times. Bryce just nonchalantly followed and walked behind me with his hands in his pockets.

"I'm going to go grab a coffee, you want?" I tried.

"Nacht," he responded, still obviously in his own head.

"Alright," I said. I was really getting irritated. I started walking even faster to get away from him. Clearly, he had something on his mind and needed space. I was just beginning to worry how much.

I found my favorite little café on the corner that made the best French croissants. I deserve a little treat, given everything, I thought to myself. I found a table in the corner and sat down to people-watch. Lost in thought, I jumped when my phone vibrated.

Bryce: Hey, I'm knackered. I'm going to head to bed early to try and rest up for tomorrow.

I looked at my watch. It was only quarter after seven, still light out. Maybe some rest was exactly what he needed.

Me: Ok. XO

I waited for something, anything in response, but there was nothing, which only perpetuated the sinking feeling in my gut. I knew well enough how to keep myself occupied for the evening. I waited a little while to let him fall asleep, then returned for a good binge of an old movie, *Titanic*. The impending heartbreak felt about right after the last few days, and with everything else in my head, I knew it would be just the ticket. Besides, I couldn't get Kit's quote about a woman's heart being as deep as an ocean out of my head, and needed to watch it be said.

At some point between the grandeur of the dinner party and the inevitable fate of the ship, I fell asleep. The same watery visions came to my head and I once again bolted upright, only this time realizing I was on the couch, and Celine Dion's "My Heart Will Go On" was playing with the credits. I wasn't sure if that was a sign of things to come, or things that had been...

The day was upon us. All my angst and second guessing if I had gotten the right dress for the occasion kept boiling to the surface, Bryce's mood had not much improved and his energy was still all over the place. I was about to ask him if he wanted to abort the whole mission when he turned to me and acknowledged my existence for the first time in what felt like forever.

"Are ye ready?" he asked, as nonchalantly as if we hadn't just been silent with each other for a few days. I did a double-take. He was already dressed in his kilt and formal garb, looking quite handsome as I had originally imagined. Damn it. It was hard to remain desolate when he looked like that.

"I'm sorry?" I asked, confused and looking down at what I was wearing. Clearly, I was nowhere near ready to go. "Did I mix up the time when we had to go?" I asked, alarmed that perhaps I had somehow lapsed on when I needed to be where. He laughed at my expression. "Oh sure, I'm glad my utter confusion can provide you some entertainment after you practicing to be a mime these past few days."

Now it was his turn to look confused. "Aye? What do you mean?" he asked.

"Do you really not know?" Now I was getting mad. "You have been a walking zombie. Barely saying two words to me, and when you do, the only emotion you seem to be capable of is annoyance. Have I done something? Do you not want me to be here?" I carried on and his eyes got wider and wider. "'Cause if you don't want me here, or don't want to ask the other professors at the event tonight about opportunities, say the word. I do *not* need to go and keep you from your evening," I finished. I must have been bottling up a lot more than I realized.

He stared at me for a moment. "Have I really been so bad that you would think I no longer want to be with you?" he asked as he approached me and took me by the wrists.

I nodded, tears forming in my eyes. "Shit, I can't mess up this makeup. Maddy just got off the video chat with me and my tutorial." I wiped at my eyes gingerly.

He grinned, then he stared again, seemingly gathering his thoughts. "It's only, I haven't known what to say. We seem to be at a precipice, and I am afraid..." he trailed off. I just kept looking at him, willing him to finish. I needed answers. I needed answers to a lot of things, but I wanted him to be the one constant.

"I'm afraid that if there are no positions available, with that email from your Dean and all, that you will hightail it back to the States and that will be that," he admitted.

"Bryce McCollum. Do you mean to tell me you have been giving me the cold shoulder and basically pushing me away because you are afraid I am going to leave and never come back?" I huffed.

He slowly nodded, with little boy expression that nearly melted my heart.

"Well, that's the biggest load of bollocks I've ever heard," I said, and crossed my arms. This caused him to laugh heartily. "I'm glad I amuse you when I'm actually so incredibly pissed at you."

"Come here, my bonnie lass," he said and pulled me into his arms, even with mine still crossed. He bear-hugged me, but I wasn't ready to forgive him just yet. Handsome Highlander in a kilt or not.

I looked up at him when he wasn't letting me go. "I'm gonna need a minute there, *sir*." I said curtly. He let go of me with a smile, nodding, and I walked into the bedroom to finish getting ready, now completely confident in my dress and makeup choices. He could eat his heart out for all I cared tonight. Had he literally just put me through hell and back because he was nervous I would just leave? I didn't know what that said about me, but I didn't have time to contemplate it. We needed to sprint to finish getting ready and get to the venue on time.

When I emerged from the room, red dress, black strappy open-toed platform sandals, black cat-eyeliner and matching red lipstick, he just stared. Eat your heart out, I thought to myself, completely satisfied with his reaction.

The evening went about as one would expect. Bryce was lauded by his department and peers, the champagne was flowing, the food was spectacular, though I avoided the ever-popular haggis balls, and the conversations were nonstop. Every chance Bryce got, he was introducing me to this person who was head of this department and that person who just published in this journal. My head was swimming with the names and faces of all his colleagues.

He had taken a few opportunities to whisk me away to the dance floor. I didn't recognize most of the music, but just as it switched into more of a ballad and he slowed his lead, I recognized one. It was a slower version than what I was used to, but caused me to truly listen to the lyrics in a way I hadn't before.

By yon bonnie banks and by bonnie braes,
Where the sun shines bright on Loch Lomond,
Where me and my true love were ever wont to gae,
On the bonnie, bonnie banks o' Loch Lomond.

O ye'll tak' the high road, and I'll tak' the low road,
And I'll be in Scotland afore ye,
But me and my true love will never meet again,
On the bonnie, bonnie banks o' Loch Lomond.

'Twas there that we parted, in yon shady glen,
On the steep, steep side o' Ben Lomond,
Where in soft purple hue, the highland hills we view,
And the moon coming out in the gloaming.

O ye'll tak' the high road, and I'll tak' the low road,
And I'll be in Scotland afore ye,
But me and my true love will never meet again,
On the bonnie, bonnie banks o' Loch Lomond.

The wee birdies sing and the wildflowers spring,
And in sunshine the waters are sleeping.
But the broken heart it kens nae second spring again,
Though the waeful may cease frae their grieving.

It was such a sad and forlorn arrangement, but also, I had had no idea the heartbreak in the verses before this; the melody had been otherwise so celebratory. I found tears were streaming down my face, for absolutely no good reason. It was as if something was tugging at my heart, a long-ago forgotten memory or tie to the song, but I couldn't place it.

Bryce noticed me wiping at my eyes over his shoulder and pulled me back from his dance embrace. "Are you okay?" he asked quietly.

"Yes, fine," I breathed. "Just the song. I've never quite listened to the verses before, I suppose."

"Ah, yes. You'll 'ave heard the spritely version of the song, but not the whole thing then." He went off on an unnecessary soliloquy about the origins of the song, dating back to the Jacobite rebellion and a soldier dying in the battlefield, thus unable to return home to his true love.

I barely heard his explanation. I was not in the mood for a history lesson. For some reason my heart had just broken; the song carried such hope only to then be shattered. It felt...personal. I suddenly remembered the watery dream and silhouette looking down on me, then Mary's voice.

"One is a mirror, and the other lesson."

We had already walked off the dance floor at this point, and he was re-engaged with some friends in deep conversation. I watched. I looked at him then, not realizing how much I really did not know about him beyond the few months of historical travel and the whirlwind romance that had fallen into my lap thanks to a past-life tie.

I loved him, for sure. I had no doubts about that. But the more I watched him, and accounted for the past few days—as well as this new knowledge of another past life where I died at the hands of my significant other—the more a thought bloomed in my head.

Could I trust him?

Mirror or lesson, I suddenly had an overwhelming feeling, it was time for some space. I needed to go back and get my affairs in order with the school, whether I had answers from his colleagues or not. I also had a house that likely needed some TLC, and I think Violet was over the apartment living in a big city. It didn't mean that we wouldn't be back, but I suddenly realized: Me and my girl needed to go home.

Chapter 34 – Josephine, April 1912

The trip from Bath to Queenstown had not been an easy one. However, the act of leaving my family home, with little to no explanation and under the cover of night, had been the hardest part. I adored my family. It hurt me to no end that I could not share my plans or my feelings with anyone. I knew my parents would be supportive of my decision, but that did not mean they could know before we were safely away from his family. That, they would never understand. I could not bring myself to tell them the full treatment and experience of our time, well at least my time, there this past year. First, it was my father's friend. Second, my mother would never have forgiven herself.

Only Rupert could know. He had always been a trusted confidant my entire life. He would know what to do and say once it was revealed I had left. I thought back to that conversation as I loaded my bag onto the carriage to take me to the train station.

"Rupert, you are the only one I can trust with this. When the time is right, and you will know when it is, please give this letter to my parents. It explains everything," I said, folding an envelope into his hand at his side. He looked at me, bewildered.

I knew he would not necessarily agree, but he would support my decision. He weighed his words carefully, with a touch of fatherly concern. "Are you sure, Miss Findley?" he asked.

I nodded as tears filled my eyes. "I must," I said simply.

"Alright then," he said, and he embraced me.

It took everything in me not to crack.

That had been five days ago. While the journey itself did not warrant taking that long, I wanted to be mindful of moving too quickly and drawing unnecessary attention to myself. Oscar had provided me with enough money to take my time, stay at nice hotels along the way, and take carriages in between everywhere so I was not walking alone on any street. I received a few odd looks from some passersby, but they may have wrongly confused me for a suffragette and left me alone.

By the time I arrived at the BellaVista House and asked at the front desk for Mr. Patterson, I must have looked like a weary traveler.

"Is Mr. Patterson expecting you?" the clerk asked over his small round glasses and upturned nose.

I began removing my gloves and subtly flashed my new favorite accessory in front of his gaze. "Well, I should hope so, I am his wife!" I said jovially, not allowing his demeanor to deter me.

It had been three and a half months since Christmas when I had held him in my gaze last. I was not going to let this man at the desk keep me here any longer than necessary.

As he was checking the log book for hotel guests and their assigned room numbers, that is when I heard it.

"Jane?" said a husky voice. I turned, searching the room from where it may have come.

"Finally! My darling!" and a tall man with a moustache and raven black hair in a bowler hat approached me. He had on round spectacles, similar to the clerk, and I had to do a double-take. "Why Jane, has it been that long that you no longer recognize me?" he said, staring into my eyes. The clerk was watching from his perch and beginning to look wary.

Suddenly I realized that he was wearing a disguise to further throw anyone off our scent. Why had I not thought of that?

I threw my arms around his neck. "Oh darling, it has been such a long journey! Forgive me, I am weary," I said. And I was not lying, but thought I would say as such for dramatic effect. We were drawing an audience and I suddenly wanted nothing more than to lie down and rest, to get out from under the scrutiny.

"It's alright, Barrold, I have my key as I have only just left the room. I will take my wife up and get her settled in," he said, and grabbed my suitcase from where it sat on the floor and managed to hook my arm through his.

I could feel my body instantly relax at finally being in his presence. I did not realize how pinched I had been holding my shoulders until now. While I was sure that both of us wanted to walk a lot faster, we steadied ourselves so as not to draw any more attention.

As soon as we got inside the room, he placed my bag on a nearby table, removed his bowler hat and glasses, and stepped back. "Let me take a look at you! Are you real?" he asked.

I could not take my eyes off the giant moustache that was now on his face. My lack of reaction in return confused him, until he realized what I was staring at. "Oh, this?" he asked, pointing at his face. "How do you like it?" he said turning his head side-to-side. I shook my head. He laughed. "It's alright. I am not a fan either, which is why…" and he tore it off his face. I gasped.

"Oh, Bravo!" I finally said. He smiled and I flew into his arms. "Oscar," I sighed heavily.

"I know my darling. I asked a lot of you to make this journey. I am so grateful you are here," he said holding me close. Once he felt my tension melt from my shoulders, he released me from the embrace only to bring his lips to mine and kiss me so passionately I felt lost in time and space. This was why all of it had been worth it.

He soon pulled back and released me again. "Now, about the room," he said, looking around. It was a nice enough space, with a very large bed off to one side, a small sitting area, and a couch on the other side. My cheeks reddened at seeing the bed, but I remained silent. He smirked a bit. "I think, though we are married on paper, we shall save those formalities for when we are truly betrothed," he assured me, clearly not missing a beat in reading my mind. I nodded my thanks. "For now, you will take the bed and I will sleep on the couch tonight," he finished.

I protested. "No! You have already established yourself there, and I am smaller. I can more easily sleep on the couch."

This was met with a stern head shaking. "Absolutely not. You will take the bed, I must insist." There was no room for argument in his voice.

"If you insist, then I must, but what will we do for arrangements on the ship? You cannot possibly sleep on a couch the entire voyage," I said.

He smiled again. "I do have everything figured out."

I was more than happy to have the opportunity for an adventure on my own, but I was relieved to be back under his protection and I could relax. "Now what do we do?" I asked, looking around.

"Well, we can embark on the ship tomorrow morning after 11:30 a.m. It will make port by then, and they will take on the last passengers who are sailing across on her. Until then, I suggest we get you a hot meal, and we can come back and relax in the room for the evening. I don't know about you, but I am a bit anxious to get going and not sure if I will sleep all that much this evening," he admitted, matter-of-factly.

"Excellent. A warm meal and an evening accompanied by another human being will do wonders for me," I said.

He cocked his head. "So that is what I am worth? A 'human-being' for accompaniment?" he scoffed. I shook my head.

"No, absolutely not. Forgive me. I am tired, overwhelmed at seeing you again, and anxious for our journey. I am not entirely myself" I responded, shaking my head and gently placing my hand on his forearm.

"It's alright, I understand. Let us go get you dinner," he said and took my hand in his.

The next morning, I woke with the sun creeping through the drapes. I suddenly remembered I was not alone in the room and looked over to the couch. There he was, his six-foot frame sprawled out on the small piece of furniture. His dark hair tousled over his forehead, and his face, for once, not cleanly shaven. Looking at this man, who had taken my heart all those months ago so completely, I was in awe. My chest swelled and I was on the verge of tears spilling over once again. We were about to depart on an adventure together, and all because one soul had found another. No, I thought, not one soul finding another. Half of a soul finding its other half. It was the only explanation. I had always been tied to this man, somehow. How else would he have intrigued me so, or had the ability to finish my sentences as if he was reading my thoughts. That was it, we were two halves of the same soul, which is why this felt so effortless and gratifying.

I practically jumped out of bed, went into the adjoining bathroom, and began getting ready for the day. As I was undressing from my nightgown and into my travel dress, I smiled at the thought of him averting his eyes last night and practically putting a pillowcase over his head so as not to see anything he should not...yet. As I finished setting my hair, I heard him stir. I managed to walk out into the main room looking completely fresh and ready to take on the day. I wore a heavy cotton sky blue dress with a cinched waist, column skirt, and two-tone embroidered patterns along the mid skirt and bodice area. Coupled with a matching sky blue and white hat, I felt like royalty and ready to commence our overseas voyage.

I watched as Oscar stared at me from across the room, shook his head to make sure he was not dreaming, then smiled. I laughed, "Oh, come on, you, time is wasting. We have a ship to catch!" I exclaimed, trying not to squeal. He checked his wristwatch and jumped up.

"You, madame, are correct" and he raced into the bathroom.

I tidied up the place while I waited. I knew housekeeping would be in here the moment we checked out, but I wanted to be sure it hadn't looked like a married couple slept apart. There would be talk. Even if we would never see these people again, I would not have that on my conscience after all of his detailed plotting.

As soon as he was ready, we gathered our bags, went downstairs, ate breakfast, and were on our way. Neither of us could eat much with the anticipation of finally getting aboard. We both commented on a priest who had just come to check-in. He was carrying what looked like a camera and we overheard him telling the clerk about how he had just alighted from one of the grandest ships he had ever seen. I wondered if that was the same one Oscar had chosen for us.

Thankfully, he had arranged for our bags to be taken from the hotel to the port where the ship was docked so we did not have to trudge through the streets with them. As we walked, I looked out at all the ships that were there, and realized I did not know which one we were going to.

"Which is ours?" I asked as we sauntered arm-in-arm, very naturally. He looked around and then pointed.

"That one," he said with pride. I looked to the direction he was pointing and saw it. She was beautiful and quite something to behold. Larger than most of the others in port, she had four smoke stacks. I squinted to find the name and read it out loud.

"Titanic," I said. "Well, the ship-maker seems a bit proud of himself on that one, don't he," I said, mimicking Alice's voice, trying out an accent. He looked at me. I shrugged. "Just trying it out. I did not know if 'Jane' would have a different sound." He shook his head. "No? Alright," and I squeezed his arm.

Soon enough the clock indicated it was 11:30 a.m. and we knew it was time. Time to climb aboard and begin our journey to a new life. To say I was giddy would have been an understatement. Oscar had an electricity about him too, and yet for one small moment before we stepped aboard, I swear I sensed...hesitation?

For four days, we luxuriated in our situation. Our second-class accommodations would be first-class accommodations on other ships, or so I was told from my fellow passengers: mahogany furniture, white-paneled walls, a library with green upholstered chairs and beautiful writing desks, a smoking room for the men, and covered promenade decks. We ate countless amazing meals, met wonderful people from all over Europe, all traveling for different reasons to America, but all with a similar resounding note in their voice—hope.

I will never forget that first evening. Remembering my love of music, Oscar escorted me to the dining saloon after a robust dinner of lamb and vegetables, followed by a delightful plum pudding. There was a piano there as well as a string quintet, playing the most beautiful music. The group ran through wonderful pieces like Valse Septembre, Poet and Peasant Overture, Meditation, and On the Beautiful Blue Danube, among others. We quietly listened, intertwining our hands and letting the all too familiar frisson dance over our skin. Whether it was from the music or his touch, I could no longer tell the difference. More than once, I looked up and caught him seemingly in deep thought. It took everything in me not to raise my lips to his cheek and place a delicate kiss there with how blissful I was. It felt like I was waking from a long nightmare, to not only be away from my prison and out from her ever-watchful eye, but with him.

As the music concluded that evening, I felt exhaustion wash over me. I knew that my body was finally relaxing after all of the months of living in the unknown and I decided I needed to lie down. Disappointed, Oscar asked if I wanted him to escort me back.

"No, my love. I can find my way," I cooed at him, the wine, dim lighting, and music having entranced me. "You go enjoy the smoking room and keep up pretenses of us being good second-class passengers," I smiled. He smirked at me. I knew he was trying to keep a low profile as we had heard about all the gentry on board in first-class, which only bolstered his decision of us not traveling in that class. Still, I think he could also discern from my insistence that I may not trust myself alone with him in our berths, given the opportunity. His smirk turned into a wicked grin that made me weak in my knees. Soon enough, we would be in America and married, and I could let those thoughts, and longings, become reality. I blushed and turned away from him so he would not catch me.

"If you so say. I will let you get a head start for preparing for bed and then I will be in after my first cigar is complete, not a moment later," he assured me, grazing his finger across my cheek. I nuzzled my head into his hand a bit longer and then regretfully took my leave.

As I walked along the Promenade Deck, I breathed in the fresh sea air. It was a cool evening, and I was glad of my wrap around me. If I stayed out here any longer, the salt breeze may have awaken me completely. Not wanting to lose this deliciously content feeling before bed, I looked out to the water one more time and just marveled at the expanse. So dark. So endless.

It was on that fourth day, April 14, that I dared begin to dream of our new life out loud. "What do you think we will do? Where will we go?" I asked, as we walked along the decks that afternoon.

He seemed lost in thought for a moment, so I squeezed his arm. He smiled, and holding my left hand up he whispered, "well I should think we will get married first…" and winked. I giggled.

"Will we indeed? Then are we not married now, Mr. Patterson?" I said playfully, looking around to make sure no one was listening.

"In my heart? Always," he said and he kissed me on the cheek, though it seemed like he was trying to convince himself of something more than me.

Just then, one of the younger sailors came running up to us with a piece of paper in his hand. "Mr. Patterson, sir?" he asked.

"Yes, that is I," Oscar replied in a jovial tone. The sailor handed the paper to him. "Thank you, lad" he said, though he may not have been all that much younger than him. He turned it over in his hand. "It's a telegram," he said curiously.

"That is odd, is it not?" I asked, watching worry lines cross his forehead. He unfolded it apprehensively. I watched his face harden, and felt his arm go tense. He dropped my hand from his. "What is it?" I asked, concerned we had been found out. Could it have been my parents? Or Freddy? I could only hope it had not been his. His demeanor had certainly been more confident being further and further away from his family, but every once in a while, whether from my own guilt or projection, I did wonder if he missed his delicate lifestyle at the Earl's, and if I was worth it, even amidst his protestations.

He seemed to consider his response and then decided. "Nothing. Nothing to worry about," he said, brushing off whatever this message was. I was still confused and said as much.

Patterson was not our real name, no one knew under what name we were traveling, or was supposed to know that we were traveling, so how could he have received a message?

"Truly," he said. Noting I was unconvinced he added, "I must have built our personas too well as it was a message for a Mr. Patterson," he said, shrugged and shoved the telegram into his coat pocket. He reached down and took my arm into his, and we began walking again, though with a different pace. He may have wanted me to believe it was nothing, but something was bothering him now that had not been before...unless it was related to why I had caught him in a few pensive moments. I had brushed them off as him also taking relief in his plan being successful and us finally on our way, but was there more?

We went to dinner that evening and even though we were sitting and conversing amongst our newfound friends, Oscar was more contemplative than usual. He caught me looking at him a few times and would try to relax his facial features to give me a warm smile, but it never lasted long. After dinner we stayed up listening to music as we had the first night, but it was not the same. He did not seem to be enjoying the festivities as much as he usually did, so I suggested we head back to our cabin.

It was about ten o'clock at night when we each crawled into our respective beds in adjoining berths. I laid down and tried to settle my mind, but I could feel his rising tension and racing thoughts only adjacent to me. I got up and softly padded to the door. Gently pushing it open, I caught him sitting over what looked to be the telegram at the small writing desk in the corner of the room. He had his head in his hands and looked incredibly forlorn for someone who was supposedly on his way to a new life with his love. It created a confounding image and all of my original observations about him and his mysterious ways came tumbling forward in my thoughts.

"Oscar?" I asked quietly, not wanting to startle him. It took him a moment to answer.

"Yes?" he said, with a hint of something I could not quite discern.

"Are you alright?" I ventured. Another pause.

"I will be," he said frankly. I waited a moment.

"Oscar...what was in the telegram?" I tried one more time, and started walking forward into his room. I could feel him grumbling now and stopped my advance.

Taking a deep breath, he seemed to surrender. "We will discuss it in the morning" he finally offered.

Not once had he looked up to acknowledge my presence in the room. It took everything in me not to march over to his desk and rip the telegram from beneath his gaze, but as he already seemed upset, I did not want to be the cause of further creating strain.

I tried calming myself and my racing concerns. It was not a great response, but it could have been worse. I was trying to imagine what would have been in there that would have caused such a remarkable shift in his demeanor. I had hoped he would at least look up and give me a smile, but none came, and I slowly walked back to my bed. I did not like this sinking feeling that was developing in the pit of my stomach. Thankfully, the lulling of the ship did not let me stew on it for long, and before I knew it, I was asleep.

What seemed like a little while later, I thought I felt a shudder. Assuming I was dreaming, I rolled over. Just as I was falling back to sleep, there was a knock on the door and I heard voices outside. I heard Oscar get up to answer. It was an attendant.

"I am sorry to bother you, sir," he apologized. "There has been a small situation with the ship and everyone is asked to put a life vest on and be ready to come upstairs." He quickly left down the hall.

I got up and walked over to our adjoining door again. "What did he just say?" I asked, squinting at the light coming from the hallway, and not quite believing my ears. Oscar looked dumbfounded and did not answer right away. "Oscar?" I asked, getting increasingly nervous.

He snapped out of whatever his thoughts had just been. "I am sure it is nothing love, let's just do as he says."

I put on one of my warmest tops and brown wool skirt, along with my warmest boots. I wrapped my coat around me, and then donned the life vest. "Well, this is not comfortable," I said and turned to look at him. He only half-smiled. "I'm taking it off, if I need it, I will put it on above deck, but this is not something I want to walk around in for no reason," I said, and proceeded to untie and remove it. Oscar stayed silent, and seemed to be holding onto something in his coat pocket. The telegram?

As soon as he was ready, we left our room and went towards the stairs at the aft of the boat up to the promenade decks we had just been on only that afternoon. There was a steady stream of people all doing the same thing. As we climbed the stairs, I thought it felt like there was a slight tilt to the ship, but decided I must still be half asleep. I reached out for Oscar's hand as we ascended, if for no other reason than not to lose him. He absent-mindedly took it and kept progressing forward, though there was none of his typical warmth in his touch. The look on his face told me he was deep in thought, and I assumed it was in trying to figure out what situation we were in.

Soon enough, we realized it was chaos. This was no ordinary ship experience. We heard words like "iceberg," "sinking," and other terms that were far less familiar to me. I looked at Oscar with mounting fear in my eyes. He took me in his arms, and held me close. "We will get through this, I promise" he whispered, and then almost as an after-thought, "Sephie."

Looking around him, panic continued to rise on decks. I knew he was formulating a plan, which calmed me for the moment. I had already seen how effective his planning could be, so I was confident whatever it was he was thinking, would absolutely get us out of this mess too. I saw him watching the far-right side of the ship, where we noticed that it was lilting and closer to the water.

"I have an idea," he said and grabbed my hand. He raced through groups of people going the opposite way of the water and to the back of the ship from where we had just come. He got us to the side railings and said, "I think we should make a jump of it." I stared back at him. When I did not respond, he repeated himself.

"Are you joking?!" I cried. This was his plan? He shook his head. "Why on earth do you think that is a good idea—" he cut me off.

"Because. Everyone is rushing for lifeboats; they are getting overwhelmed. I had been speaking with John just a day ago and he had heard how the ship builder did not put enough life boats on here for wont of it being 'too crowded'. Soon the ship will start to truly sink forward and who knows how quickly. If we make a jump for it now, we can find some debris that is already floating in the water, and at least get away from this to relative safety, while we wait for the rescue ships to come to our aide," he urged.

I thought about this logic. I suppose in some way it made sense, but another part of my brain was going off with a big "DANGER" sign. I looked down at the life vest in my hands. Before I could make up my mind which to listen to there was a loud splintering sound, the ship shuddered as if it was being torn in two, and something exploded. I was being thrown through the air and collided with something at great force.

As I came to, I thought I felt a hand on my wrist, pulling me towards them and onto something hard. Then there was a momentary hesitation as if whoever it was, was deciding if they would continue helping. I felt the hand release, and thought I heard them say something. It was then I realized I was drifting. When I finally opened my eyes and looked up, I was not drifting…I was sinking. The inky blue water was becoming darker all around me as what little light from above grew dimmer.

What had happened? Where was Oscar? I had to get to him. And who had just had a hold of me, and why had they let go? I needed to get out of the cold water and onto something that would help keep me afloat.

I quickly realized then what the sound was I heard just before blacking out. The ship exploded somehow and came apart, throwing us overboard. And now, I was in the ocean; the deep, dark, cold water. But where was Oscar? Was he safe? I tried looking around.

In sudden horror, it struck, and I had no doubt. He had been the one to have hold of me. He had let go of me. The words I heard whispered dawned on me as they replayed in my head.

"I'm sorry Sephie, I must."

Why? He was supposed to be my protector. We were in this together. We had just been through hell and made it to relative safety for the time-being, but now? He must? He must what? I was sinking away from the water's surface, and as I looked up, I saw him, with one hand in his pocket, seemingly grasping something. The telegram. He was watching me, watching him, watch me fall…further and further below.

I clutched myself in pure fear and wanted to scream out, but I did not want the water to invade my lungs. I tried to reach up to bring myself above the surface again, but my already heavy wool clothes were water-logged and weighing me down, while the water around me ice-cold and restricting my ability to move. If only I had put on the life vest, perhaps I could have stayed afloat to talk some sense into him.

I continued sinking, looking up to him, getting smaller and smaller, wondering: How had it come to this?

Chapter 35 – Sophia – July, Present Day

It was obvious the ball had not turned out how either of us had expected. After our dance to the old Scottish folk song, I excused myself to the ladies to compose my emotions. It would not do to meet potential colleagues with tear stains and mascara running down my face.

When I returned, Bryce had seemingly reverted to his brooding self of the past couple of weeks, though he was affable with his fellow historians and their departments. Thankfully, he had not wanted to stay much longer either, and once he made the round of required goodbyes, we were able to take our leave.

Back at the apartment, I quietly changed out of my gorgeous scarlet frock, that seemed to have dulled with the night's energy, and into some wide-leg yoga pants and a t-shirt. I snuggled up with Violet on the couch under a blanket and laid my head back.

That was so *not* how I anticipated the evening to go. It's not that introductions and connections weren't made, and there were even some hints at moving conversations forward into a more formal space. Which was exhilarating, or at least, it would have been, had it not been for Mr. Shadyside. I knew something was bothering him, and for whatever reason he was not speaking to me about it. I was no longer buying his explanation before we left, which only further seeded doubt in my mind. I thought after the first few months of our relationship with everything we had shared, that communication would have been our strongest suit. Guess not, I thought to myself. It was really shining a spotlight on all I did not know about him and how much we had gotten caught up in the story, rather than ourselves. Or had we...

I realized it had been a bit since he had gone into the bedroom and had yet to emerge. Not that I was anxious to speak with him, but it was odd. I reluctantly got up and shuffled over to the door, which was closed. Weird. I knocked lightly, but when I didn't hear anything, I opened the door a crack, to find the room completely dark. Not only that, there was a large mound in the bed, softly breathing and already asleep.

I turned on my heel and went back out into the main living room of his apartment. It wasn't much, since it had been intended for a bachelor who wasn't there often. He keeps going down this path and he will be able to claim the bachelor thing again right quick, I thought to myself. I found my laptop and whipped it open. As I was looking for flights from EDI home, my phone vibrated. I knew it would be one or both of the girls checking in on how my night went, but I just couldn't bring myself to looking. Not yet.

I found a couple of options for flights in a few days that would get me back stateside with just the right timing to meet up with the Dean. Before I selected anything though, I thought I better check with Erik about

Violet. I knew it was not easy to travel with a dog, which is why I had never done it.

I picked up my phone to text Kit, momentarily forgetting about needing to report in for the dance and typed; completely dismissing the text she had just sent me requesting pictures and lots of question marks. Just as I saw the dancing ellipses, she must have given up trying to formulate a sentence and immediately called. My phone lit up and I answered as quickly as I could so as not to create too much disturbance for Sleeping Beauty in the other room.

"Um…I ask you about how tonight went and not only do you not respond, but you are asking me about flights home and bringing Violet back. WTF?" Kit asked. The last three letters were an unexpected touch from her.

I heaved a deep breath. "I know. The evening was fine. It just…let's just say it didn't go as planned, I wasn't the belle of the ball. Instead, I felt like I was with the beast, and I really need to get back to check on the house and speak with the Dean so…two plus two equals four," I finished.

She sat on that for a moment. "Alright…" she said hesitantly. "I will get Erik working on the dog info, so give me the flights you are interested in," she said and I could tell she was getting a pen and paper. I recited what I had pulled up in front of me and she took everything down. I could hear her speaking to Erik. "Okay, he's going to go get the ball rolling on that," she reported back. Woah, that was too easy, she didn't even force me to… "now spill" she demanded. There it was.

I shook my head, even though she couldn't see me. "I don't know. Ever since you guys left, and even before while you were here, it's just been…weird. Like we're out of step. We lost our flow. He's been broody, which is not like him; at least the him I've known for seven months. And I don't know where I stand. Now, we're at this thing to honor him, which it did, while he's making half-hearted introductions for me, I wind up crying in the bathroom."

"Wait, what?! Why?" Kit went into full protective friend mode.

"Oh, it was a silly song. It was a different version than I'm used to hearing and I could understand the lyrics, and they got to me, I don't know. That part wasn't him. It's just the past couple of weeks have not been great, and I'm afraid the bloom is off the rose. I could be making grand plans to be here, when in fact, he doesn't want me here. I just can't tell anymore," I finished, and hung my head in my free hand. Violet nuzzled into my leg.

There was silence on the other end. I wasn't sure if I had lost her or if she was contemplating everything I had just shared, and was going to pull a zinger out of nowhere to be able to explain everything to me in a way only Kit could.

"Kit?" I prompted.

"Yeah, I'm here. Just thinking about how to put this," she responded. I sighed. "So, what I'm hearing you say is that he has basically shut down and been acting weird towards you, and you don't know where you stand when, in fact, the couple of weeks prior to that, you had just been doing the same to him. And now you don't know where his mood and withdrawal are coming from?" I could practically hear her smirking on the other end of the line.

"Ouch!" I complained.

"What?" she asked.

"Don't sugarcoat it, girl, just lay it on me," I said, a little harsher than I had intended. It was her turn to sigh now.

"I know, I'm sorry. It's just, don't you think it might be a little suspect given where your head has been to get all defensive on him? Imagine what the few weeks before were like for him, while entertaining your friends and their loved ones. That would be a lot on a good day. Then you add in all of our collective stuff unfolding, on top of you being in a weird headspace not only with another dream, but another two dreams, one past and one past-present, or...present-past? Anyway, it's a lot," she said. I was shaking my head in agreement.

"I know, and you're right. However, that doesn't excuse him from not speaking with me about it. And before you say anything, I have given him plenty of opportunity. I have asked multiple times what was up, in different ways, giving him an entrée into a conversation, and he has not said anything. He's ghosted or come close to gaslighting me each time. I'm a big girl, I can have the conversations. And at this point, I don't want to entrench myself anymore with him if he's already having second thoughts," I admitted, then felt that pang in my gut.

Kit seemed to be mulling something over. "I get it. I do. You have to remember that not every moment is sunshine and daises, though. There will have to be tough conversations. I'm proud of you for trying to engage, but they are also not always going to happen on your terms," she was saying.

"Yes, but..." I tried interjecting.

"No buts. It sounds like you guys are at a major tipping point or cross-roads in decision-making, but each of you has a lot going on in your heads that is going to cloud judgement and block you from having those conversations until you get your own personal clarity. Perhaps coming home now is the right move. But Soph..." she was checking to make sure I was still listening.

"Yes?" I answered.

"You can't just leave. You will break that man's heart. Weird vibes or not, all of us could see that he loves and adores you. Whatever is going on, might be some past ghosts of his own he has to deal with, just as yours have come back to haunt you as well. Even if you have to parallel path it for a while, don't just give up on him" she urged.

"I'm not! I'm just..." I paused to think. What was I feeling?

"Hurt. Sad. Angry. Confused as hell?" She listed off.

"To name a few, yeah, Doc. Those and then some" I responded. We both laughed, which released some of the heavy.

"I get it. Love is not easy. Nor is it for the faint of heart. But neither is singledom either. You have to choose your hard." And with that, I could tell she'd exhausted her guidance.

"You're right. I know. I guess that is what I'm feeling. Before either of us goes any further down the road, we have some things to sort out as individuals so that we can truly come together. It's just...I'm worried with this other side I've seen that perhaps I'm only now seeing his true colors and he isn't who I thought he was..." I bit my lip. The image of that silhouette watching me from above popped in my head and I felt cold all over.

"Could be," she said, "or it could be all of the things dancing around in your head at the moment. I'm not saying they aren't doozies, or that you don't have a few things to figure out, but you also have to determine if you are going to let the past dictate your future. Learn from it, absolutely, but completely and utterly lead you down a primrose path that may not exist?" She let that thought hang there.

I sighed again. "Okay. But first things first, I need to get home to tie up some of those outstanding loose ends. Then I can do some soul-searching in my own space, hopefully re-focusing everything," I thought out loud. That picture, being alone in my cozy little house and around my own things, brought me a peace I hadn't realized I missed.

"I can feel you relaxing as you say that, so yes, do that. Start there. But don't be mean about telling him, even if tonight was a disappointment. You'll regret it," she warned.

How did she always know just what to say?

"Yes, Mom" I teased.

"Hey, be nice..." she said.

"Or what, you won't let Erik help get Violet home?" I offered.

"Oh no, never that. That pumpkin needs to come back so we can all see her. The kids are going through severe doggo withdrawals, and they need some fur-apy" she said.

"Fair enough. Let me know when Erik finds out what he can, I appreciate the assist," I said. I started yawning.

"Of course. Love you, get some sleep," she said.

"Will do, love you." And we hung up.

There wasn't anything else I could do that evening, so I curled up under the blanket on the couch and fell asleep there. Violet didn't seem to mind not having to move and she stayed by my side all night, my little furry protector.

The next few days were a bit of a whirlwind. Once I had my flights and paperwork, I needed to be sure Violet could fly in the cabin with me and not cargo, I had to pack everything up. Bryce, thankfully, got called on a job just out of town over in Glasgow, which made the packing a little easier. At least I wouldn't have to be prepping to leave under his watchful eye.

He still hadn't alluded to whatever was bothering him, and at this point, I had resigned myself to not knowing. Kit was right, it could have easily been borne from my own odd energy shift, or something completely unrelated to me. Until he said otherwise, I couldn't push, even if it bothered me to no end.

By the time I needed to leave for the airport, he had only just made it back in time from his trip to see me off. I was actually getting worried that he was going to miss me, and then concerned it would have been on purpose. I was in the middle of leaving him a note on the kitchen table when he burst through the door.

"I'm so sorry, traffic was hell, I just..." he said, panting, out of breath.

I had to smile at that. "It's okay. You didn't miss us; we were just about to go."

He looked at me with my laptop bag slung over my shoulder and my trusty suitcases by the door. He could tell Violet had taken a part of her recommended sedative dosage already as she was a little glassy-eyed looking up at him. He walked over to stand in front of me. I looked up into his eyes and tried to see that spark from before. I don't know how long we stared at each other like that, but I could feel the atmosphere shift around us. Eventually he took me into his arms and just held me close to this chest, resting his head on the top of mine. I sighed. Part of me wanted to cry. The other part wanted to hit him for taking so bloody long to do this. We could each feel tension release from the other in that embrace.

I had to let go first; we needed to get going. Part of the arrangement with Erik was him insisting on getting us a ride to the airport so Violet would be comfortable, and I wasn't going to say no.

"You be good, you hear?" he said, a bit awkwardly.

I gave him a strange look. It was an odd thing to say.

"I mean, travel safe. And...get your affairs in order, so," but he let the sentence die off. Whether he was too afraid to ask or announce what he wanted, he let it go. I nodded my head in silence.

"I will. And, you too. You know, as you put it, get your affairs in order," I quipped and he smirked.

I turned and started towards the door with Vi dragging a bit behind. He knelt down to rub her ears and put his forehead to hers for a farewell. She licked his face. He ruffled the top of her head as he stood.

I leaned down to grab my suitcase, but he caught my arm and brought me in for a kiss. One of his usual envelop-me-into-his-being kisses where the world fell away and we were floating in the ether. We had certainly kissed over the past few weeks, but it had been missing its usual passion. This. This was different. This had something behind it. Urgency? Desperation? He let me go. I had a tear forming just at the edge of my eye that I did not want to let fall.

"I love you, my bonnie lass. Dinnae forget about me" he said, and then helped me to the waiting car.

Once settled on the plane, I contemplated what movie to watch. Violet was secure at my side with a seat of her own and she had curled up into a ball, the drugs working their magic so she would rest easy.

I saw *Titanic* as I flipped through the options and laughingly thought about turning that on again, but since I had watched it so recently, wasn't sure that was the right choice. Instead, I went for another classic, *Gladiator*. Perfect, I thought to myself. I knew I could easily fall asleep to this, though what that said about me sleeping through such violence, I chose to ignore.

It was somewhere over the Atlantic that I drifted off. I experienced the deep dark waters and the drowning again, mystified at the silhouette from above watching me go down. Just as I was about to choke myself awake from dreading the water, the visual changed. The silhouette remained, but the background and scene were wholly different.

I was once again on dry land, in a large, Roman-looking city. I was standing at the top of a white marble staircase, dressed in colorful robes draped all around me. I felt the weight of something on my head and when I raised my hands up, could tell it was an ornate headpiece, or crown. I looked to my left, and that same silhouette was there, still faceless, but there was no way I would ever mistake that outline for anyone else. Just as I was about to reach out and touch it, it transformed into a raven and then fell away, as did where I was standing. It dissolved into sand, then turned into stardust, and I found myself floating.

I was floating into the ether and towards what looked like another large building, only made of an ethereal light. I was given immediate passage through the doors and then I was standing in a room. I no longer had a corporeal body, but still held form. In front of me was a large book. Enormous. It had locks on the side, and I was afraid I wouldn't be able to open it, but as soon as I brushed my hand near it, the locks fell open as if I myself had been the key. I looked at the pages, but I couldn't discern any actual words. The pages seemed to be made of light, and the harder I tried to turn them, they slipped through my fingers.

There were other beings passing by. I tried to get their attention to ask them what this place was, or how I was to read the book before me, but it was as if no one thing could see the other. I held my hands out in front of me to evaluate them again. Was I a ghost? As I continued to struggle and grow increasingly frustrated, I heard a voice resonate in my head, or was it just a thought? It was only a word, but not one I recognized. I tried asking "it" to repeat itself and once again heard one word, whispered, on the tails of constellations.

"Akash."

Epilogue

April 4, 1912

Dearest Mother and Papa,

I know this letter will find you in relative shock. I am sorry for the deception. You see, I fell in love with the most wonderful man while you were in America. We had plans to make our way to you before you returned, to notify you of our intentions and gain your blessing. Unfortunately, however, this man's mother was discontent in our love. She had plans most high for her son, and nothing was going to stop her. He had to leave his own home to save my grace.

He left, and in the time he was gone, concocted the best plan he could for us to run away. That is the journey I am on now, and one I hope you will support. As soon as we have settled at our destination, I will send word to let you know we have arrived safe, and provide you more details. I cannot give you any more information before that, if for no other reason than his own sake. While I trust you most implicitly, there are too many others that do his mother's bidding and we cannot take any chances. We are already fearful that she may know of our plans in some way, and I shudder to think what she would do, or say, to keep him from leaving, and us apart for her own gains.

I love you both so very much. It hurt my heart to be reunited with you so happily, only to have to leave again so surreptitiously. I cannot wait to share the entire story with you, in due time. I hope, like me, you will relish in it and come to know that your daughter has not only found true love, but the other half of her soul, her match in every way possible.

More soon, my sweet parents.

All my love,
Josephine

April 19, 1912

Dear Father,

I have only just made it to New York City as of last evening. Me, and several hundred others arrived at Pier 54 around 9:30 p.m. I am grateful to be alive after this whole ordeal and this was the first word I could send.

I received your telegram on board. As it happens, it was hours before...everything. What I am sure you have read in the papers is true, however I am also sure it does not come close to the horror that was experienced.

Your plea in the telegram to leave Josephine in America and return home was effective, though it does little now. I am ashamed to say, I considered it. I considered it most strongly. If for no other reason than to put you through no further pain or damage to your reputation given what mother was posturing to do alongside the Earl. I loved Josephine with all my heart, and recognized her as the counterpoint to my own. I also would have tried to find a way to make it work for all parties, if only you had given me the chance, and trusted me.

But none of that matters now. Josephine is gone, forever. I fear, though try as I have to rid myself of it, Mother's influence can still affect me and my decisions, and I do not know if I will ever forgive myself for what transpired that night amongst the chaos. I admit now in the harsh light of day that mother had in fact planted seeds of doubt, as much as I resisted. Your further request to return for the sake of Gertrude only further sowed those seeds as we carried on our journey and I was further away from what I had come to know. In the mayhem, I suppose I felt a solution had presented itself, and, not being the strong man I thought I was, I took it. Now, I fear my soul will never know peace, for what I have done to its other half.

You may tell Mother what you wish, only know that I will not be returning. I cannot, in good conscience appear back into a life I no longer identify with, nor deserve.

I will miss you father, and hope that for all the acquiescing and peace you constantly chase, you can turn your time and attention on Gertrude to find a suitable partner, so she may get out from under mother's rule. She does not do her justice, nor has she ever loved her properly. She deserves to be loved. Everyone does.

~O

About the Author

Sarah Heximer is the author of The Triquetra Chronicles, a dual-timeline series exploring past lives, forgotten histories, and the bonds between women that refuse to be broken by time.

A strategist and storyteller by profession, Sarah returned to fiction after years of filing away experiences she couldn't explain – until she stopped dismissing them and started listening. The Triquetra Chronicles draws on her own continuing journey through meditation, energy work, and the quiet accumulation of knowings she's stopped trying to explain away.

She writes for the woman who has always felt the pull of something she couldn't name.

Sarah lives in Ohio and can be found at sarahheximer.com and @sarah.heximer on Instagram.

Photo credit: Water&Moon Photo Co.

Also by Sarah:

- Stay tuned for the next in the series!
- The Harbinger, A Triquetra Chronicle (Book 1)
- Finding Your True Colors & Manifesting Your Dreams: One Journey to Self-Actualization

Thank you for reading.

If this story moved you, inspired you, or kept you up late turning pages, ***please consider leaving a review on Amazon or Goodreads***. Your feedback helps other readers discover the book – and means the world to independent authors such as myself. Just a few words can make a big different in helping others find it!